Once Upon A Predator

Dark Amusements Book #1

Alex Loch

First paperback edition July 2022

Print Edition ISBN: 978-1-7782373-1-7
Digital Edition ISBN: 978-1-7782373-0-0

Cover Design by Dark Predator Press
Cover Images © iStock

Dark Predator Press
P.O. Box 97, Komoka, ON, N0L 1R0, Canada

AlexLoch.com

Chapter 1

Jess Gets Lost In The Dark

Ten years ago...

The hand sailed through the air; the smack like a crack of thunder, but the impact was worse. It sent the girl stumbling backwards, the wall at her back the only thing keeping her upright.

"I saw that smile—", the woman growled, "—and while you're living under my roof, you'll show me respect. You stuck up little BITCH!" she spat, propelling a gob of saliva onto her lower lip. It rolled down and pooled in the cleft of her worn out chin. Her once porcelain white skin had turned a grayish yellow, and deep wrinkles etched the corners of her eyes and creased the skin around her mouth. She looked decades older than her forty-two years.

More colorful expletives flew from her lips, but the girl didn't react. Red faced, the woman glared at her for another moment before turning to stagger down the hall, bumping along the wall as she went. Midway, she swung back. The girl, having raised a hand to her still stinging cheek, tensed as she watched from beneath dark lashes.

"Cheek smarting just a little... bit?" *Just a little bit* was

1

Barbara's favorite phrase, the last word spat out as if she'd eaten something rotten. "You're lucky I put up with your shit. You'd be in some foster home right now if it weren't for me. Then we'd see who's laughing," Barbara sneered. Leaning heavily against the wall, she rolled around and weaved the rest of the way down the corridor before disappearing to the right.

Alone now, the girl slumped back, allowing the curtain of dirty blond locks to close over her face. Jess rubbed her sore cheek.

Tonight's rage had everything to do with Barbara's current boyfriend, Cal. Like her, Cal liked to party. Unlike her, more often than not he'd rather do the partying with someone else. Barbara just found out he'd been out with his ex. Jess didn't understand their relationship, but then she didn't understand Barbara. On nights like this, she kept reminding herself that all she had to do was make it until her eighteenth birthday. After that, she'd start fresh somewhere far away from her mother, who was *just a little bit* crazy.

Jess retreated to her room. Barbara rarely struck out more than once, but there was always the exception. Her stomach rumbled in hunger. She glanced around, but already knew there was nothing edible here. It held a single bed, a beat-up dresser, a banker's desk lamp on a bedside table, and stacks of books scattered around the room in various-sized piles. The best piece of furniture Jess owned was her grandfather's old desk lamp. It spilled a soft yellow glow across her blue comforter, part of the dingy cream-colored rug, the photo frame on her side table and the lower half of a poster featuring the luscious Josh Duhamel. Right now, even Josh couldn't bring a smile to her face.

Jess lifted the photo frame off the bedside table. On one

side, her friends Sam and Toby, and she grinned goofily at the camera. On the other, her grandparents smiled back. Her gaze paused on them, recalling happier times. Almost four years since they died, and she still missed them so much it hurt. Before their accident, she'd lived in the city with them. Although she remembered very little about the time before that, she suspected the long, jagged scar running from knee to upper thigh had something to do with why she ended up with her grandparents for most of her childhood. Her fingers found the raised ridge of skin under her light cotton pants.

Barbara's lashing out had just been the icing on the cake. Earlier during gym class, a group of girls shoved Sam over the bleachers and she twisted her ankle. It swelled to twice its normal size and was turning an array of green, purple, and black by the time she helped Sam to the nurse's office. Jess went back to grab their bags from the locker room when Barry, the poster boy for jocks, cornered her. When she threatened to yak on his new Nikes, he'd backed away, giving her enough space to dash back into the gym where she interrupted a Junior Ed class. Still, Jess preferred the gym teacher's reprimand to whatever Barry had in mind.

It had been a shitty day. It made her wonder if there wasn't a full moon on the rise.

The only silver lining she had were her friends and fellow outcasts, Toby and Sam. Toby moved to Murphy over seven years ago, and the locals still considered him a newcomer. To top it off, Toby was more artsy than jock, preferring to hang out with Jess and Sam over the guys. In a town like Murphy, that could get you beat. As for Sam, she was a local, but didn't toe the local line of bullshit. Having a different opinion didn't jive well with the natives and was likely why she seemed to be their favorite target.

Jess's stomach growled again. Sighing, she replaced the frame, grabbed her wallet and jacket, crept down the hall and out the back door. She didn't breathe until after she heard the click of the screen door swing shut behind her. Barbara often sat in the front room watching television and downing rye and cokes. The telltale blue light dancing through the sheer curtains of the front window as she passed by confirmed it.

Leaves danced around her legs and crunched underfoot with every step she took. There was a chill in the air that hadn't been there earlier. Jess tugged her unbuttoned jacket closed and headed south towards downtown Murphy. She debated on stopping by Sam's but thought better of it. The last time she'd shown up with a noticeable bruise they'd ended up in a fight and she just couldn't handle that right now.

Lost in thought, the distinctive snap of a branch nearby brought her back to the present. Whoever it was was approaching at a quick clip. With two blocks to go, she picked up her pace and crossed the street. Jess strained to listen for the other's footsteps, but heard only her own over the wind and the sound of branches thrashing. It wasn't long before she was opening the door to the pizzeria. Inside, Jess forced her tense muscles to relax as she approached the counter. After ordering a slice and a diet coke from a kid in a yellow polyester uniform with the name tag DANNY, she headed for a booth to wait.

She'd just sat down when the swish of the door opening drew her attention. The newcomer, dressed completely in black, stared at the menu board as he gave his order before turning to face the dining room.

Jess knew her manners. She knew to chew with her mouth closed, never put her elbows on the table, always remember someone's name, and never stare. But she couldn't seem to pull her gaze away from the dark stranger. Like a deer trapped in headlights, she stared as the dark man approached and couldn't help but wonder if this guy had been the one following her a few minutes earlier.

Once at the table, he just stood there, still and silent, as if allowing her time to adjust to his presence. In contrast to her first impression, the man wasn't dark at all. His skin tone was so light it was almost white, and the hair sticking out from beneath his tuque was platinum. His eyes, which at first glance looked black, were the oddest shade of blue she'd ever seen. It was almost as if God had tried his hand at chiaroscuro and created a human interpretation of the famous Italian light and dark technique. Even looking at him was unsettling.

"Do you mind if I join you? I hate eating alone." Without waiting for a reply, the chiaroscuro man settled in the seat across from her. Jess opened her mouth, but shut it again when she realized she had nothing to say that wouldn't be interpreted as rude or outright hostile. For the first time in a long time, she was speechless and all she could seem to do was stare at the brazen stranger.

The man's eyes widened. "Oh jeez, you think I followed you in here or something, don't you?" The question hung in the air, now thick with tension. It was only made worse when he added, "Well, you're right. I did."

Jess narrowed her eyes at her unwelcome guest as she muttered, "Excuse me?"

The man laughed, holding up his hands in mock surrender as he shook his head. "I saw you drop something on the road and thought you might want it back." Still chuckling at his own humor, he stuck out a pale hand and slowly unfolded his fingers. Initially, Jess stared at the offered hand as if it was a dead fish. It wasn't until the glint of silver caught her attention that some of the tension eased from her. In his palm lay a small silver cross, just like the one she wore.

Eyes widening, Jess dropped her gaze to her wrist. Her leather bracelet was present, but her grandmother's fine silver cross that always hung from it wasn't. She must have been twisting it again, a nervous habit she couldn't seem to quit. The small pendant was the one piece of jewelry her mother hadn't sold off after her grandparents died, and that was only because she'd begged her not to. Jess always wore it, in part because it made her feel closer to her grandmother, but also because she didn't trust her mother not to change her mind and sell it while Jess was out of the house.

She forced herself to relax, pasted on a polite smile, and met his gaze. After what felt like minutes, Jess finally dragged her gaze away from the visitor's odd blue irises down to his open hand again.

"Thank you," she said as she reached out to take the cross from his hand. When her fingers curled around the fine silver pendant, the coolness of the stranger's palm surprised her. A second or two later, she jerked her hand away when a nasty jolt stung the tips of her fingers. Luckily, her fingers hadn't let go of the cross.

"Sorry about that. I get my electric personality from my mother." The man chuckled and continued talking as Jess flexed her still tingling hand and then stuffed the cross into her pocket. He went into extensive detail about how his mother's watches always stopped working. That it didn't matter the make or quality of the timepiece, if she wore it, it would die sooner rather than later. "My mother literally and figuratively killed time!" He laughed.

The more he talked, the more creeped out she got. She

glanced around, hoping her slice might be ready to go, but Danny was nowhere in sight. Jess opened her mouth to excuse herself when she noticed her unwelcome companion had stopped talking. The unexpected silence drew her gaze back to him. He was watching her. The change in his expression was unsettling.

"So Jess, had a shitty life have you?" The stranger watched as she struggled to come to terms with what he'd said. He'd stated her name. It implied familiarity. Only she didn't know him from Adam.

"How do you know my name?" Jess asked, clenching her hands in her lap.

"You introduced yourself when I sat down," He stated, the corners of his mouth curving up.

Jess forced herself to remain calm. What was this guy playing at? He'd stated the blatant lie as if daring her to challenge him. They were in a public place with people less than twenty feet away. It would be stupid for him to try anything here. If she wanted to find out what this guy thought he knew about her, now was the time.

"Fine. And what exactly do you think you know about my life?" Jess said, keeping her voice as neutral as he had.

The stranger's hint of amusement bloomed into a full-blown Cheshire grin, and Jess realized she'd made a mistake. It was his eyes. His odd blue eyes darkened to black. Cool hands grabbed a hold of hers under the table and dragged her close, the table the only barrier between them now. The edge of the linoleum dug into her upper arms. She tried to yank her hands free, but his grip didn't waver. He had pulled her in so close onlookers would assume they were a couple enjoying each other's company. Almost nose-to-nose with him now, Jess shuddered. Aesthetically, he was an attractive man, yet everything about him revolted her. She dropped her gaze. When she wasn't looking into his eyes, she could think more clearly.

She opened her mouth to yell for help, but a sharp, searing pain in her left-hand pinky finger turned her shout into a gasp of pain. Before she had time to process the first break, crack went her ring finger. Jess's breath came out in bursts as her eyes teared up, the pain verging on unbearable. It felt like her pinky and ring fingers had been crushed at the joint. She heard herself whimper, but it sounded far away. Her thoughts wandered from the present terror and pain to grief over her poor ring finger.

"Please..." Jess pleaded, her face now wet with trailing tears.

"I thought you'd never ask." The words spoken so low she almost missed them. And then he began to talk and each time Jess tried to get up or say something, he broke another bone in her left hand. The strange man deftly wore her down until she didn't care about much of anything except wanting it all to end.

By the time Danny, the pimple-faced pizza boy, brought over their pizza and hard plastic cutlery, tears were streaming in a steady flow down her face. Head bowed, Jess didn't even glance up when he placed the slices on the linoleum table in front of them. His white sneakers took a step back as if to leave, then paused. The kid was hesitating.

He dismissed Danny with a perfunctory, "Her dog just died, so she's a little upset. You know how emotional women get." After another few seconds of being ignored, Danny's sneakers walked away.

Shortly after that, the stranger got up and left, whistling as he exited the pizzeria. She continued sitting in the booth long after the tears stopped flowing. The only discernible sounds in the pizzeria came from the easy listening station being piped through the speakers.

* * *

Danny's dream girl with the sad gray eyes and dark blond hair was still sitting in the booth and it was twenty minutes until closing. He'd checked on her an hour ago, after the guy she'd been sitting with left. Her head remained bowed. He had little experience with girls and no clue what to do when one was crying. He dropped off extra napkins and mumbled a "Um, here you go, miss. Sorry for your loss," all the while thinking she must have really loved that dog. Now the boss was getting antsy and had instructed Danny to clean the dining area in the hopes their one customer would get the hint and leave.

Paper towels and spray bottle in hand, Danny started on the closest booth and made his way around. He was cleaning the booth behind his dream girl when his shoe slipped, bringing his attention to the red trail of partial shoe prints on the floor. He'd stepped in something and was now tracking it across the gray ceramic tile. Luigi's customers weren't the most fastidious lot, so having to clean up the marinara sauce, or red sauce as the boss referred to it, happened more often than one would think.

"Great." Danny muttered and dropped the towels and spray bottle on the table before going to get the mop and bucket. On his way back, he noticed the red sauce was still dripping from somewhere under the booth. It had already traveled down the booth's length to the drain in the center of the floor. He bent down, his gaze retracing the sauce's trail to its origin.

Danny stared for a moment, trying to make sense of

what he was seeing. The source of the red sauce seemed to come from his dream girl.

* * *

No one saw Jess pick up the hard plastic knife and use it to rip a hole through her light cotton pants. Nor did they see her tear into the flesh of her upper thigh. The coroner would later reveal her cuts were hesitant at first, as if unsure of what she was doing, but grew bolder with each successive stroke. Jess traced the same path as her scar, as if digging through the layers of flesh would reveal something hidden within. She broke both hard plastic knives and was using a fork before anyone stopped her, but by then she'd already dug so deep she'd nicked her femoral artery. Even when Danny pulled the broken fork from her right hand and pressed a wad of Luigi's Pizzeria napkins to her wound to staunch the flow, Jess didn't say a word or even gasp in pain. It was like she'd already moved on.

It took five minutes for the ambulance to arrive, but by then it was already too late.

Within minutes the local police were swarming the pizzeria. Yellow police tape was already in place when onlookers gathered and shot questions at the stony-faced patrolmen guarding the scene. Little Murphy hadn't had this much action since the multi-car pileup on Highway ninety-three last winter and the locals were abuzz.

Of all the employees, only the kid working the front cash saw the man sitting with the victim before her death. Chief Turner was the senior officer on scene. Normally he'd let one of his investigators do the interview, but the victim was a friend of his daughter's. He found the teenager seated in the back office. There were bloodstains on his hands, his right sleeve and midriff of his yellow polyester shirt. There could have been more on his work pants, but the dark color hid them if there were. They'd have to collect his uniform before they released the kid.

Danny was shaking his head, muttering, "Who does that because of a dead dog?" under his breath.

"Danny? My name is Chief Turner. Can I ask you a few questions about tonight?" He waited for the kid to acknowledge him with a nod before continuing.

"So you found Jess after she'd cut herself?"

The kid's gaze dropped to the floor. He nodded.

"The guy she was with, did you catch his name?"

Danny shook his head.

"Maybe you overheard something they said—?"

Danny looked him in the eye. "I heard nothing. When I brought them their pizza the guy said she was upset because her dog died. I mean it was just a dog." The kid looked haunted. Although he sympathized, Chief Turner had to press on to get what details he could while they were still fresh in Danny's mind.

"Can you describe the man?" After a few seconds of silence, he continued. "Was he a teenager? In his early twenties? Late twenties? Thirties?"

The kid replied with a shrug.

The chief decided on a different tactic. "Did he look like he was around Jess's age?"

"Older." It wasn't much, but it was an answer.

"Ok. Did he look as old as me?" Chief Turner was in his early forties, so when the kid emphatically shook his head, he jotted down mid-late twenties with a question mark. Sometimes questioning a witness was like peeling back an onion, especially when they'd seen something traumatic.

"What did he look like?"

The kid only shrugged.

"Caucasian?"

He got a nod.

"Tall?"

Nothing.

"Short?"

Still nothing.

"Around my height?"

This time he got a nod-shrug combination, followed by a "Sure".

"Hair color?"

Another shrug.

That's when Chief Turner decided this interview was more like pulling teeth than peeling an onion. "Ok. Was he bald then?"

"He had on a tuque. And he was all in black."

Chief Turner nodded, then asked, "What about his features?"

The kid sighed and rubbed his hair in frustration, knocking off his Luigi's Pizzeria hat. "I don't know. I wasn't paying attention to him. He came in. Ordered a slice. Sat down. Chatted her up. Ate his pizza while she sat there crying. And left. I can't give you anything more because there's nothing more to give." The kid's voice rose in volume until he was nearly shouting. When Danny spoke again, his voice was shaky and barely more than a whisper. "What does it matter anyway? She killed herself."

Although Chief Turner agreed with Danny, this wasn't just any case. He gave him time to settle down again before pressing him for more, but the kid clammed up. From then on he responded with only Yes/No answers or a shrug. Shortly after that, the chief let him go. No matter how much he wanted answers, he couldn't force them out of the kid.

* * *

The reality was Danny had been far more interested in watching Jess that night than the guy she was with. Ever since she started coming to the pizzeria, Danny had developed a little crush on her. His chest tightened at the thought he'd never see his dream girl again.

On his way home, he found an empty Coke can and absently kicked it all the way back to his parents' house. It annoyed every resident still awake along Main Street, though Danny didn't notice or care. His thoughts were on the sad, fair-haired girl who always seemed to have the world on her shoulders.

Media trucks showed up to sniff out the dirt from the tragic scene, but to their disappointment, the police refused to give a statement until after they notified Jess's family. Two police officers went to Jess's mother's house to relay the news. Initially, Barbara was angry about the intrusion during her Monday movie night. The officers apologized but pressed on. The fact Jess was dead must have seeped through Barbara's rye soaked brain in to her consciousness because she started crying.

* * *

After a year passed and no further evidence came to light, they closed Jess's case, letting her cause of death stand as a suspicious suicide. The fact they couldn't explain who was sitting with her before she died or how the baby, ring, and middle fingers of her left hand got crushed forced them to use *suspicious*.

Chapter 2

Sam, Paul and Charlie Sittin' In A Tree

Five years ago...
It'd been well over a year since Sam laid eyes on her hometown, and it was as depressing now as the last time. Storefronts showcasing crumbling brick and peeling paint, broken park benches tagged so many time they were permanently tacky, and roads with so many potholes it made her wonder if the town's plan wasn't to ignore the downtown long enough to allow it to return to its natural dirt state. Murphy was like a worn-out Ford Pinto, too old to maintain efficiently and not charming enough to be worth the expense.

Most people who lived in Murphy gave little thought to the town. It held a steady population of over thirty thousand, most of whom either worked for or aspired to work for the local Campbell's factory, just like their fathers had before them. Their confidence and contentment in life was enviable, but their lack of aspiration for anything outside of Murphy was not.

Sam moved away the first chance she got and hadn't looked back until now. Recent downsizing in her company had made her redundant and the handful of interviews she'd landed since had led nowhere. Forty-two grand in debt and her meager savings would only cover expenses for another couple of months at most. To top it off, her fiancé dropped a bomb on their relationship a few weeks ago.

She felt like Humpty Dumpty, on the verge of a great fall, and didn't know if she could put herself back together again.

Rubbing tired eyes, she shut down the unwanted thoughts and shifted her attention to the sunshine coming through the bay windows of her family home. Drawn to the warmth, she crossed the dark living room, opened the door and stepped into the sunroom. The fresh fall air beckoned her to the windowsill. The late afternoon sun shone through the leaves, sending intricate lace-like patterns of light and shadow across the front lawn. Sugar maples lined the road and their fall turn made Fleming the prettiest street in town, alive with passers-by enjoying the warm evening.

Movement to the left drew her eye next door and smiled as a familiar figure walked up the drive. Harold Sarken, their neighbor for over twenty years. Sam waved when he glanced over. The tall, elderly man stared for a second before recognition split his face into a warm smile. Same old Harold face.

"Well, well, well... the lost goose finally returns home. You know you're supposed to head south for the winter, not north, right?"

Sam smiled. "Yeah, what can I say? I never played follow the leader well."

Although retired, Harry had worked for Campbells most of his adult life. Now when they weren't at their cottage, Harry could be found neck deep in a tractor engine.

Sam didn't understand his fascination with John Deere and chalked it up to being a guy thing.

Sam disappeared from the window and reappeared a minute later, jogging across the yard. She threw her arms around his tall frame and gave him a squeeze.

Sam pulled back, smiling up at the familiar dark eyes, trim gray beard and long weathered face. "What's up, Harry? How's life in the big city?"

"You know how it is. Too many meetings, too many conference calls with the bigwigs. Too many people trying to waste my time," Harry grunted, shaking his head. "How about you? Your life of leisure treating you well?"

"Well, it has been pretty busy. Tea parties, soirees, mandatory tee off times at the Golf Club," Sam quipped, but her amused expression waned. A few weeks ago, June had been diagnosed with cancer and was the reason Sam had come back. The fact her father's birthday was this weekend was more of a coincidence than anything else. "Harry, I'm so sorry to hear about June. How's she doing?" Sam asked.

"She's her usual bossy self. She gave me a good swift kick just yesterday for stealing a scone from the cooling rack. That woman can be downright miserly." Harry chuckled, but stopped when his gaze landed on her worried frown. "My June is a stubborn lady. If she says she's good, then she's good. The only way I'd ever be able to get her to rest would be if I tied her to the damned bed."

Sam breathed a sigh of relief, only then realizing she'd been holding it in. Although loath to admit it to herself, she missed the crotchety couple, and it scared her to think June might go through what her mother had, a cancer so virulent all Sam could do was hold her hand as it and the subsequent treatments tore through her body like a wildfire. It was cruel, and there hadn't been a damn thing she could do about it.

"Seen your father yet?" Harry asked, pulling her back.

Sam shook her head.

"Well, I'm glad to see you're back, Sam. We've missed you, girl. ALL of us." Though she cared about them, they'd never understand how hard it was for her to come back to Murphy. Whenever she made it home, her father was usually too busy to visit, and when he had some time their conversations were stilted and awkward. She knew her neighbors better than she knew her own father.

"So, when are you coming over for a meal? June would love to see you. I'll even make my famous chili," Harry prodded, his eyebrows so high on his forehead they almost disappeared into his hairline. Sam didn't have the heart to admit she didn't care for chili. The pride he took in serving it was enough incentive to hold her tongue and eat it like she enjoyed it.

"Hmm, how about Sunday?"

"It's a date. Just make sure you show up this time. You were almost a year late last time." Harry's eyes softened the pointed statement.

"Killer clowns couldn't keep me away. See you then, Harry." Sam gave him another quick hug and watched him disappear up his driveway.

Sam headed back to the house, a two-storey Victorian with a raised sunroom, old oak trim and doors with the original glass windows. Each side of the block held a row of well-kept older homes; trim lawns and mature trees in an array of fall shades. Looking around, she could see why someone who didn't know better would want to live in this charming neighborhood.

Murphy was known as the tomato capital of Canada

because of the sheer numbers grown here. Unfortunately, few outside of Murphy seemed to be aware of this prestigious title. But anyone paying attention to the obits over the years would have noticed something else Murphy excelled at. It held the record for the highest deaths by bodily harm per capita of any city in Ontario, the leading cause of which was recorded as accidental, but Sam knew better. It seemed no matter how ludicrous the circumstances of a death, ninety percent of the time it was deemed "accidental".

Her father had worked for the Murphy Police Force for forty years, and he'd broken the bad news to the families of more than a few of her high school peers. After the third one, Sam paid attention, asking him direct questions about the circumstances around these "accidents". Her father never talked about work, but with this he'd made an exception. Perhaps it was his way of protecting her from something even he didn't understand. Things like; someone drowning in a two-foot mud puddle, or unintentionally driving a car off a cliff twenty-five yards away from the road. Her favorite "accident" was when a neighbor strangled himself after his bedsheets became entangled in the overhead fan.

And then there was Jessica, her best friend and fellow dreamer. Jess's death couldn't be explained as anything other than a suicide, and no amount of mental gymnastics made it otherwise.

Jess's home life hadn't been easy. Sam would often swing by her house to walk her to school. She met Jess's mother, Barbara, once and at the time she was drunk or high, maybe both. There was a lot of shouting and expletives, and she shoved Jess on her way back into the house. But neither of them knew why Barbara was angry.

After that, Sam invited Jess over so often she became

18

more of a fixture than a guest. Sam also made her promise that if it got bad, no matter the hour, Jess'd come over. Which was why she couldn't wrap her head around the fact Jess hadn't tried to reach out to her. Jess's life was shitty. But she'd had a plan. It made little sense that she'd make it through almost four years of hell only to give up a year before her eighteenth birthday.

Sam re-entered the house and headed straight for the kitchen. She stuck her head in the fridge and upon spying the potato salad, pulled it out. It wasn't French fries, but it would do in a pinch. Fork in one hand and potato salad in the other, she headed for the sunroom.

The fall turn made the street look like it was on fire; the reds, yellows and oranges of the falling leaves like sparks flying off burning wood. Other than Harry and June, Fleming street in the fall was one of the few things Sam missed this past year. The other was her mother.

Her thumb sought her ring finger to twist a ring that was no longer present. Her chest tightened in response.

They'd met in the third year. Within a week, he was sitting beside her in class. Within a month, he'd asked her out. After a year, he'd asked her to marry him. Back then Paul was sweet and attentive, and she couldn't wait to begin their life together. They'd set a wedding date and even discussed kids. Sam wanted two, but Paul was set on three, so negotiations were ongoing. The trouble started after graduation when Paul was hired by a startup. She understood work came first, but after months of being on the back burner, lucky to see her fiancé once every couple of weeks, her patience had worn thin.

Then three weeks ago, on their way back from visiting Paul's family, he dropped the bomb. It had started with an argument about Paul canceling yet another of their dates, but escalated into a full-blown fight. Looking back, it seemed he'd wanted to fight. She got so frustrated by his stoic one-word answers and unwillingness to compromise that she threw her tight, headache-inducing glasses against the dashboard. The crunch of a hinge snapping off was over-loud in the car, but the silence afterwards was worse. The minutes ticked by until Paul's voice cut through the quiet.

"If I'm being perfectly honest, I don't know if I want to marry you, Sam. Your troubled childhood, lack of family, and tenuous relationship with your father are all red flags. And that violent temper of yours has me concerned." He paused for a beat before adding, "What if you lose control and hurt our kids?"

Dumbstruck, Sam sat and stared at Paul's profile as those four sentences replayed over and over in her head. It had only taken four sentences to destroy their relationship. To her horror, he continued.

"Besides, you're not Catholic and I want my children raised Catholic. So, I think we should take a break." Paul didn't take his eyes off the road once.

That's when she'd felt them. Invisible bands tightened around her chest, restricting her lungs from expanding. Recognizing it as a panic attack, she'd pressed her back against the seat, dug her hands into her thighs, and concentrated on her breathing until the worst of it passed.

The first time she'd had a panic attack, she was seventeen. Her dad woke her up to tell her they'd found Jess at Luigi's Pizzeria and it looked like suicide. She recalled little after that. Later, he told her she'd had a panic attack. Since then, she'd learned to recognize the signs. Although these were different situations, the overwhelming emotions were similar. Helplessness. Anger. Betrayal. And despair.

No one knew about their time out, not even her friend Helen. Logically, Sam knew she'd never hurt a child. Still, his ridiculous words wedged themselves deep within her psyche, allowing in self doubt. To say she was sad didn't come close to how badly she was feeling. She'd have killed to talk to her mom, which only made her feel worse.

Sam was so preoccupied she didn't notice anyone in the front yard until a man's voice interrupted her train wreck of thoughts.

"Beautiful day, huh?"

The voice belonged to a smiling stranger, his head and neck visible above the windowsill. She took a startled step back and almost toppled over the chair behind her. Fortunately, she caught the window frame before she went down. Unfortunately, the potato salad wasn't so lucky. It landed in a lumpy mess on the sunroom floor.

"Sorry to startle you, miss. I was just passing by and wanted to say hi. My name is Charlie." The man's smile broadened. In a town like Murphy, it wasn't unusual for someone you didn't know to greet you as they passed by, but it was odd for them to walk to a window fifty feet from the sidewalk and converse through a screen.

Sam studied the stranger for a moment. His blond locks so light they were almost white, his eyes the oddest shade of blue she'd ever seen, his straight nose, firm chin and perfect skin made for an appealing package. But his strange, over-large smile made her uneasy.

Sam hesitated so long it became awkward. Years of conditioning forced a "Hi" out of her, but she didn't like it. He seemed wrong, like a Pyrex baking dish with a hidden hairline fracture. When cool air hits the fault in the hot Pyrex in just the right way with the right amount of exposure, it explodes. It wasn't a common occurrence, but neither was this interaction.

"I noticed you admiring the trees and I couldn't resist coming over to see which one had you so enthralled." Charlie smiled, glancing in the direction her gaze had held not moments ago, before turning back to her.

"This time of year is beautiful," Sam replied politely, but kept her eyes trained on the stranger. She didn't like him one bit, but couldn't put her finger on why.

Charlie's eyes danced across her face before glancing down at her hands, his eyes pausing on her left hand before returning to her face again.

"However, now that I'm up close I can see you weren't so much mesmerized by the fall beauty as lost in thought. Some pretty sad thoughts, I suspect. You look like you just lost your best friend, Sam."

She was sure she'd never met him before. Not so odd in a town of close to ten thousand residents, but the fact he knew her name was very peculiar.

"Sorry, but do I know you?" she asked, curiosity winning out over wisdom. The question hung in the air. As if on cue, his expression transformed from pleasant to excited, if not downright giddy. The fine mesh of the window screen seemed too flimsy a barrier between them now.

"You know me, Sam. I'm the guy who will change your life. I know you're miserable, depressed even. So depressed, in fact, you even considered ending it all. Pulling the plug. Taking a long dirt nap. You feel like a burden to your friends. And who are we kidding, right? You are. Who really wants to spend time with sad Sam? Especially your best friend. That used to be Paul, your EX-fiancé."

Charlie paused and leaned in closer to the screen.

As if her feet had a will of their own, Sam took an involuntary step backwards.

Charlie's overwide grin widened even further before he leaned in to whisper. "Well, I guess he won't be missing you now, will he? Don't look so surprised. Deep down, you already know he'll be glad to be rid of you."

Sam was speechless. She'd just been sucker punched by an asshole she'd never even seen before. *Who was he, and how did he know her?*

"So, who does that leave? Helen, maybe? Nah. She's so wrapped up in med school right now that other than a tear or two, she'll hardly notice you're gone. Besides, she'll be relieved she won't have to make time for you anymore." Charlie leaned back, a troubled frown creasing his brow, and raised a hand to his chin in mock consideration of her predicament.

She knew better than to listen, let alone let anything this stranger said get to her. Still, she couldn't help but hear the ring of truth behind the awful words. Sam knew she wasn't herself lately and every time she called Helen she felt like she was pestering her. To top it off, Sam half suspected her friend had been avoiding her calls lately.

Charlie's solemn expression split into a grin as he leaned in towards the screen. The dread she felt about what he might say next left a metallic taste in her mouth.

"And why wouldn't you? Your fiancé broke your heart and used one of your greatest fears against you. Not only did he confirm what you've suspected all along, that you're unlovable, but he left you with the gift of knowledge. That he either truly believes you'll become an abusive shit like his father was, or at the very least your shitty childhood and low-rent family is tarnishing his vision of his own. Either way, he doesn't think you're worth the effort. And let's face it, with that temper of yours and your history, you aren't. If I'd had your lousy childhood, I would have offed myself years ago," Charlie assured her with a smile.

Watching him was like watching a game show host, the kind her grandmother used to watch when she was a kid. She'd hated those damn things. It was as if Charlie knew it too because his already wide smile broadened, so the edges of his mouth almost reached his ears.

She wanted to punch that grin off his face.

"Tsk tsk Sam, you must learn to check that violent streak of yours before it gets you into real trouble," Charlie scolded. Sam shook her head, wanting him to stop. Needing him to stop. But he kept talking. "Your peers bullied you, your teachers ignored you, your father tolerated you and the one person you counted on didn't help you when you needed her most. Do you remember, Sam? After you told your mother about the first incident with those older boys. She promised to pick you up after school and that promise lasted. What? Two weeks? Do you remember when that gang of boys caught you the second time? What they did to you? You weren't so lucky that time around, were you, Sam? To be honest, I'm surprised you've hung on this long."

"Stop saying my name! How could you possibly—" Sam hated the emotion in her voice. She stopped talking as soon as she saw the satisfaction bloom across Charlie's pretty face. She blew her breath out like a deflated balloon and squeezed her hands together to stop their telltale shaking.

Charlie's words flipped a switch in her head and illuminated memories she'd buried until now. The fear, rage, anger, humiliation and shame rolled over her in waves as it thrust her back in time. At school, bullying was a favorite pastime for the bored and uncreative, and Sam was an easy target because she didn't toe the line. It never crossed her mind to tell anyone about it. It felt like she'd be ratting someone out and she was no rat. However, when the older boys cornered her in the alley that first time, it was different. Although Sam got away unscathed, there was something about them that scared her. Something she didn't fully understand.

It was the only time she ever tried to tell her parents about the harassment. As usual, her dad was at the precinct, and her mom was in the home office trying to rally support for a position on the district school board. Back then it seemed like she was on the phone constantly chatting with potential voters.

Perhaps it was because she never told them about any of the harassment before, but when Sam told her mom about the boys who'd tried to corral her in the alleyway, the significance of what happened seemed lost on her. When Sam finished stumbling over her own tongue, her mother asked if they'd hurt her, to which Sam admitted they hadn't. Her mom gently led an embarrassed Sam out of her office, telling her to avoid them and she'd give her a ride home from school from then on.

Her mother's chauffeuring lasted a few short weeks until the election results came in and she won the position she'd been vying for. After that, she gave Sam rides when she could but asked her to walk home with her friends on meeting nights, which would turn out to be more often than not. With only one friend living anywhere close to her block, occasionally Sam was forced to walk home alone. It was just a matter of time before teenage boredom and opportunity coincided, giving the same boys another thrill as they ran her down again.

Only this time they did much more than scare her when they caught her.

She'd told no one what really happened that day, so how could this stranger know? Sam studied Charlie's face, but found nothing familiar there. She'd memorized the faces of all the boys involved and watched them mature into grown up bullies, sadists, rapists and worse. Charlie's face didn't resemble any of them. And even if Charlie somehow found out what happened to her as a kid, he couldn't know what had transpired between herself and Paul because she'd told no one, not even Helen.

Her face felt hot, but her clenched hands were ice cold. If she were a bomb, she'd have gone off already and taken Charlie with her. She hated him, and in that moment everyone else in her life, too. She couldn't deny she had dark thoughts from time to time and occasionally even debated on whether it was worth it to keep fighting. But she also knew she wasn't special in this. Everyone had their issues. She just always figured things would get easier as she got older, but so far that hadn't happened. Life just kept knocking her down, and she could feel the fight in her waning.

And what did Charlie mean when he said he'd change her life?

"So, Sam, are you ready to dance? Cause I'm dying to get my hands on a new partner," Charlie said, letting the last word hang in the air as he reached for the window frame.

Sam noticed two things simultaneously. The first was Charlie's expression. The creepy amusement was gone and in its place was stark hunger. Sam knew what lust looked like, and this was something entirely different. The second was the glint of metal off the object he pressed against the screen. Charlie slid his right hand along the lower right side and the screen peeled away like tissue paper. The icy fingers of fear slipped down the back of her neck.

The shark was about to get in the water with her now and she only had two options, get out of the water or disable the threat.

"No!" she screamed as she brought up her right hand, the one still gripping the fork, and struck out. It met resistance. Sam staggered back, away from the window. She heard tearing, and then the window was empty.

The stranger named Charlie was gone.

She glanced down at her now empty right hand. Sam thought she'd struck him somewhere in the face, but it happened so fast she couldn't be sure. He hadn't made a sound.

Sam just stood there for a second, unsure if she should be relieved he'd disappeared or more afraid because she didn't know where he'd gone. Except for the tear along the lower right side and the small hole mid screen, there was no evidence Charlie had ever been here.

Sam took deep a breath to calm down as adrenaline coursed through her veins. She edged closer to the window to get a better vantage point. Dusk had blanketed the street in darkness, but there was still enough light to see the yard was empty. On her way out of the sunroom, she bent and retrieved the bowl at her feet, leaving behind the lumpy mess of potato salad already on the carpet. She crossed the living room, locked the front door, snatched up her iPhone and then stared at it. She had no clue what to do next. The last five minutes were so absurd it would sound nuts if she tried explaining it to anyone else.

Help me because this guy came up to the house and talked to me. He mentioned things no one else knew about me and told me he could help me. He tore the screen with what looked like a knife and it creeped me out so much I stabbed him in the face with a fork. Oh, and the injured guy vanished, along with my fork. Yeah, that didn't sound crazy at all. Chief's daughter or not, if she went to the police with that story, she'd either end up in jail herself, or at the very least, completely discredited.

Feeling lightheaded and woozy, Sam sat in the nearest chair at the dining table, the mostly empty bowl of potato salad still gripped in her left hand.

That's when the fear, terror and violence of the encounter punched her in the gut and her stomach rolled.

Sam slid off onto her knees in time to get rid of the little that was in her stomach into the bowl before pushing it aside. She sat for a few minutes to get her bearings and try to make sense of what just happened.

Who the hell was Charlie? He knew way too much to be some rando.

She understood life wasn't fair and that some people had it harder than others. Jess used to call the lucky ones *clovers* and the unlucky ones *shrooms* because they could handle whatever shit came their way. Although Paul was not solely responsible for her current dark thoughts, he'd set the ball rolling. His words had picked off the scab covering old wounds, his actions had infected them, and now they were festering within. Part of her wanted him to take it all back, to tell her he didn't believe she'd ever be an abusive shit, but the realist in her knew the damage was already done.

Sam used to be proud to be a *shroom*. What doesn't kill you makes you stronger, right? Now she wasn't so sure about that.

Chapter 3

Dash To The Dance

"Hi Sam."

Her recent encounter with Charlie foremost on her mind. Sam was slow to recognize the caller. It was Paul. He sounded tired or bored, maybe both.

"Paul? Oh, thank god—" she began.

"I didn't call to talk about us. I'm just returning your call."

He was referring to the call she'd made a week ago. She did her best to keep the irritation out of her voice. "Fine. Listen, I'm at my dad's house and something strange h—"

"I'm not the one who keeps trying to talk. I told you I don't know how I feel about us right now. I need time to figure out what's best for me."

Sam counted to ten to calm down instead of what she wanted to do, which was bang her iPhone on the table. "Listen, this has nothing to do with you and I. Something happened tonight and I need to talk to you about it."

He sighed. "Fine. What?"

"Out of the blue, this guy named Charlie came up to the sunroom window and started talking—"

"Sam, I don't care if some guy hit on you—" he griped.

"Paul, he was a complete stranger, yet he knew things about me. Personal stuff. And he was scary creepy. Did you talk to anyone about me? About our fight?" Sam let the question hang there for a moment. His silence was all the confirmation she needed. "What did you tell them? He seemed to know a hell of a lot about my past and our breakup."

"No. The person I talked to wouldn't have said a word. It must have been someone you told," Paul stated matter-of-factly, as if that was the end of the discussion. It amazed her she never noticed how conceited he could be.

"Well, either you told Charlie yourself or the guy you talked to did, because I've told no one yet." She didn't add the reason she hadn't talked to anyone about their breakup was confessing it would have made it all too real.

"First, I don't know anyone named Charlie. And second, my friend is female, not male."

As far as she knew, Paul didn't have any female friends. He'd always been more of a guy's guy.

"Who the hell is she, Paul?"

Paul took his time answering. "She goes to my church. And she wouldn't have told anyone else. She's a good person and would never do that to me." The pitch of his voice rose with each word, his discomfort so palpable she could feel it over the phone. Not only had she never met this "close friend" of his, but the fact he'd defended her suggested their friendship wasn't merely platonic. Sam's stomach knotted as an enormous piece of the puzzle surrounding their breakup fell into place.

"Are you seeing this friend of yours?" The silence was

deafening. She choked on the knot of emotion now lodged in her throat, but forced it back down. It felt like she'd swallowed a golf ball. "How long?" Sam whispered.

"It doesn't matter how long."

"Weeks?" His silence forced her onward, regardless of the pain his answer would cause. "Months?"

"I said nothing because I knew it would hurt you." And that was that. He didn't deny it or even attempt an apology. Just facts. Paul continued talking, but she was no longer registering his words.

It never occurred to her Paul might cheat, but it made sense. The longer times between seeing each other. Canceled dates. The dirty wine glasses on the kitchen counter. Sam thought back to when things changed months ago. When he got more involved with church, started playing in the church band, joined a bike club, worked longer and longer hours at the office... all excuses to spend time with his new Catholic girlfriend?

She didn't know how long she sat there in stunned silence before a foreign noise broke through her fog. It sounded like a zipper coming undone. Her back was to the sunroom windows, to the source of the sound. Sam slowly turned towards it.

Perhaps it was because she was still processing Paul's revelation, but her brain was slow to make sense of what she was looking at.

The screen she'd stuck the fork through was now cut along its length and down the middle. Hands gripped its torn edges and were ripping back the panels like they were peeling an orange. Cold tendrils of fear snaked down the back of her neck as an all too familiar face appeared, now with a white patch covering his left eye... where she'd stabbed him with the fork.

31

"I'm back!" came Charlie's singsong voice. It took his lips curving into that ugly shark-like smile to break the spell keeping her rooted in place.

"Oh god, Charlie's back," Sam gasped as she shot out of the chair, stumbling over the bowl as she got to her feet.

Her panicked statement had two effects; Paul stopped talking long enough to ask, "Charlie? You mean the creep that hit on you?" It also energized the creep into action because his hands were now gripping the bottom edge of the window as he swung his knee up on to the screen free ledge.

"He's almost through the window. Oh, fuck!" Sam cursed as she ran to the front door. The door was as old as the house, built well over a century ago, and still used a skeleton key to lock it. The iPhone slipped from her fingers as she wrestled with the door's lock. She could hear a faint voice coming from the abandoned iPhone, which meant Paul was shouting. Not that it did her much good.

She knew baby-faced Charlie was intent on hurting her, if not killing her, given half the chance. She knew it when she maimed him, and she knew it now. Sam was up to her eyeballs in the shit now.

Charlie already had one leg and his upper torso through the window as she swung the solid oak door open. The over-large hunting knife in his right hand only added to her momentum. She slammed through the metal porch door without pause and leaped off the top step to the walkway. Sam flew down the dark street, her runners barely touching the cement before propelling themselves off again.

The streets looked deserted, and she had no idea where she was heading other than away from Charlie. She needed a plan, but the only thing that came to mind was people. There's safety in numbers when there's a predator around.

At the last minute, she turned left towards downtown. Her hesitation caused her to misstep, but she caught herself in time to avoid a header. She chanced a glance behind and immediately wished she hadn't. Charlie was only fifty yards or so behind her.

Sam scanned the houses. The plan was to find a crowd, but an open door to duck into was an alternative. A locked door between herself and Charlie would give her time to call for help, but it had to be a sure thing.

Some houses had lights on, but no one home. Movement in the front window of a brown brick on the left caught her attention, but it was just a cat shifting the drapes. Then someone emerged onto their porch a few doors further down. It was still far enough away she had time to plan how to get them inside safely. If she dashed up the front steps, she could use the element of surprise to shove them through the open door before they resisted, but it depended on her hostage's weight and how quick they were on their feet. They could holler and fuss all they liked once they were safely in the house. Better a cussing or a black eye to a stabbing.

Her excitement turned to dismay once she realized who the porch loiterer was. Mrs. Kinsley, a retired schoolteacher who'd taught her grade four well over a decade ago. Mrs. Kinsley had been one of Sam's favorite teachers. She was also senile, partially deaf, and on the heavier side, so attempting to drag her into the house against her will would be a challenge. There were just too many unknowns to take the chance.

Unfortunately, Mrs. Kinsley still had amazing eyesight and a perfect memory of her teaching years.

"Samantha Turner, what are you doing out this late? Isn't it past your bedtime?" Mrs. Kinsley shouted as she shuffled closer to the railing. "What would your parents think, you running amok in the dark," there was a pause and then, "and with a boy no less!"

Sam would have cursed had she had the energy. She needed to divert Mrs. Kinsley's vociferous attention away from them in case Charlie decided to veer off to dispatch their only witness.

"Everything's fine, Mrs. Kinsley. Buster got out again so we're just trying to find him," she shouted back, referring to a dog they'd had when Sam was in grade school. She was betting on the fact Mrs. Kinsley would remember their dog, who was infamous for escaping their backyard to follow Sam to school. Until her parents changed the gate lock. But Buster had had a good run for a while.

Not hearing anything more from Mrs. Kinsley, Sam chanced another glance back and, to her relief, saw her old teacher head safely back into her house.

She also glimpsed Charlie brandishing his knife. He was closer now, maybe forty yards away. *Sick bastard*, she thought with disgust.

A stitch nagged her right side. She alternated between massaging and pinching it to ease the pain. At the end of the block, she took a sharp right onto Erie Street, which headed straight through downtown Murphy. Although still a few blocks away, the neon lights of the Shanghai Dragon were a welcome sight. Decent food. Great lemon chicken. And people.

Head on a swivel now, she looked back only to see he'd gained more ground. Her stomach muscles tightened, aggravating the stitch in her side. She needed a new strategy but drew a blank. Only darkness welcomed her along the side streets, and most of the houses lining Erie were dark.

It reminded her of a Twilight episode where a man

woke to find the entire town's population had disappeared while he slept. *Maybe I'm still asleep and this crazy day is just my imagination working overtime.* She gasped as her stitch bloomed into a full-blown cramp, scaring away any possibility it was all a bad dream. Dreams were never this painful.

The street lamps were only a couple of hundred yards away now, which meant people and safety were close. *Charlie wouldn't be crazy enough to try anything in public.* But the more she thought about it, the less confident she felt. He'd been bold enough to climb through her front window when anyone on the street could have seen him. Doubt about her foolproof plan crept in, but it was the only one she had.

Excited shouts came from somewhere straight ahead. Then she saw them. A group of young teenagers walking towards the Shanghai Dragon from a side street on the opposite side of the road. The street lamps started just this side of the restaurant so they wouldn't be able to see her yet. Only one teenager bothered looking around for oncoming traffic before they all crossed the road. To their delight, the shortest kid of the bunch bounced off a parking meter onto his butt. They had a lot of fun at the little guy's expense.

She counted her blessings she was no longer a teenager, at the same time as cursing them for being teenagers. This lot was so self-absorbed she could have been running buck-naked down the middle of the street and they wouldn't notice.

The group was about to enter the restaurant. Sam was still a good half a block away, but close enough if she yelled, they should be able to hear her.

Sam opened her mouth to shout when something grabbed her hair from behind, yanked her back and slammed her into a wall so hard it knocked the wind out of her. Steel bands in the shape of arms enveloped her. One powerful arm circled her waist, pinning her left arm against her body while the other crossed over her torso, trapping her right arm down to the elbow and making it useless. Immobilized like she was, it would be next to impossible to launch an effective defense. His right arm, which was as strong as his left, pressed against her windpipe, putting pressure on her airway, choking her. She struggled against the binding arms, but they didn't budge. Icy fingers of fear gripped her as tightly as her pursuer was.

She was the fly, and the spider had her in its grip. The only sound she emitted was a strangled gasp as she watched the last kid disappear through the restaurant door.

Charlie's breath grazed her ear as he spoke, making her skin crawl wherever the light breeze brushed her. "I told you we'd get our chance to dance."

Sam shuddered and swung her head back hoping to catch him in the face. Her captor, being a head taller, moved his head out of the way in time to miss the blow. His right arm tightened, increasing the pressure on her windpipe. She stomped on his foot, but her running shoe didn't have the impact she'd hoped for. Charlie chuckled in response.

Bastard. They were in the shadows, so even if someone saw them, they'd only see a couple embracing.

"I love the chase, Sam. The fork was a little much, but I understand. I might have done the same thing in your situation. With the adrenaline pumping, that survival instinct kicks in and WATCH OUT! The lady has a fork." Charlie chuckled.

Gimme another fork and I'll show you just how much more damage I could do to you, you psycho.

36

"Oh, you've got me wrong, Sam. I'm much more than a simple psycho."

Sam stilled at the words spoken against her hair. She knew she hadn't said it aloud because she physically couldn't with the chokehold he had her in.

"I bet you don't even remember the last time you were happy or felt loved. Your mother is dead. Your father always loved his job more than either you or your mother. You now know your fiancé never loved you. He as much as admitted you were just a fill-in until the real thing arrived. You can't even hold down a job. What's left to hold on for? It's natural to fear the unknown Sam, but isn't the unknown better than what you have now? I know part of you thinks so. How often do you go to bed silently hoping to never wake up again?"

Sam shook her head, thrashed, and jerked as much as her confinement allowed to try to break free of him. But no matter how much she struggled, she remained pinned in place. Her struggles only made the arms holding her squeeze tighter, more painfully, like a spider cocooning its prey. Sam screamed her frustration, but all that came out was a wheeze. She didn't want to hear anymore of his nonsense because the dark, weak part of her that was so tired of fighting and struggling against life's bullshit had started listening. And it scared the crap out of her.

She felt the brush of Charlie's breath on her ear and tensed in preparation to slam her head back. Before she'd even completed the thought, his right arm tightened painfully against her throat.

"Though I love the fight," Charlie chuckled against her hair as he squeezed off her airway, "I can anticipate your every move before you have any chance of following thru." He only eased his hold once she choked.

"I'm actually here for your benefit, Sam. We both know you've thought about ending it time and time again, but there was always something holding you back, stopping you from taking that last step. Now you can finally be free. There's no judgement and no one here but you and me, so there's nothing in your way now. Your life has come to a head, you have no prospects to look forward to, your life sucks and will just get suckier as time goes on. Besides, considering your track record and how many worthless people are out there, you know you're just going to repeat the same mistakes over and over again... I'm here to help you. I'm a facilitator of sorts, here to make your deep dark wish come true."

Sometime during Charlie's little speech Sam had stopped struggling and hadn't even realized it. That he'd completely incapacitated her, that it was pointless to keep fighting considering the lock he had on her physically and now mentally, was creeping its way into her consciousness, showed just how tired she really was. She knew this because Charlie was making sense. His words had settled in and set up camp in her head, and even if she could speak aloud, she couldn't deny the truth behind them without lying. She'd learned a long time ago these were things you didn't talk about. Things you have trouble even admitting to yourself and would never disclose to anyone else.

So how could he know this shit about me?

Charlie's arm tightened across her chest. "But you can let your guard down now. I know you're tired, so why fight it? Deep down, you want to give up. Life is hard and every time you think it will give you a break, and perhaps you'll get your little piece of happiness, it all turns upside down again. There will always be someone there to let you down. Experience has taught you you can't rely on anyone. People will inevitably betray you, lie to you, and turn on you, so why stay?"

Sam tried not to listen to his crazy monologue, to tune it out, but she was his captive audience, so had little choice in the matter. She could feel herself reluctantly relaxing. Giving up and giving in.

It was so tempting. What's the point of fighting? I'm as good as dead anyway. The dark shadow of doubt, depression, and hopelessness melted over Sam's thoughts. She could feel herself become more pliable as she gave in to her fears and allowed her darkest thoughts full reign. She relaxed, allowing Charlie to mold her as he liked.

And just as the pressure from his embrace eased and became bearable, Sam felt it. A sharp piercing pain just under her ribs. Sam couldn't hold back her involuntary groan of pain and looked down at the source. Something silver was sticking out of her now, and that something was attached to Charlie's hand. It was the wicked-looking hunting knife he'd brandished when he'd climbed through her sunroom window. It slid out of her with surprising ease, like a knife through butter Paul would say, and the excruciating pain dulled to a burning heat. Her right arm now free, Sam automatically pressed her hand to the wound. It came away covered in blood.

The sight of the crimson liquid dripping off her hand was jarring.

Suddenly she saw everything, both the bad and the good flashed through her mind. There was a hell of a lot of bad, but she also remembered all the wonderful moments she'd had in her life. Like her mother before she got sick, Jess, Helen, Harry and June, and even her father. She remembered the happy moments. Although most were fleeting, they were still there. And just as Charlie was sliding the knife in again and the burning pain sliced a second path through her abdomen making her gasp, Sam felt something familiar. Something she hadn't felt in quite a while. Hope. Tears ran down her cheeks because she knew in that moment, without a doubt, that she didn't want to die. She wanted to live.

I want to LIVE asshole!

And then the pressure on her windpipe was gone. And before Sam could verbalize the thought, so was Charlie. Unfortunately, he left his toy behind. She could still feel the cold steel in her abdomen and really wanted to pull it out. But before she could, Sam's world tilted, and the ground came crashing up to meet her.

A moment later, she found herself staring at the stars in the night sky. They were beautiful.

Well, I've always wanted to do more star gazing but never seemed to have the time. Still crying, Sam would have laughed at the irony of the thought had it not been so painful.

She thought she heard voices arguing, but they sounded far away.

* * *

Justin needed a cigarette. The endless teasing over his collision with the parking meter was wearing on his nerves, and he needed a break. Unfortunately, Climmy followed him out of the restaurant probably to steal smokes off him again. The problem was he was down to his last cigarette.

"It's my last one, Climmy. Forget it," Justin said, pack in hand.

"Come on, Justin. I saw you buy a pack yesterday. There's no way you're down to only one."

"No, I bought them two days ago. And it's your fault I'm down to my last one asshole. You keep swiping them off me." Justin pulled his lighter out to light the cigarette dangling from his lips, but it vanished. Climmy snatched it up so fast he never even saw his friend's hand.

Justin was about to go after the thief when movement out of the corner of his eye caught his attention. It was out of range of the street lamps, so all he could make out was a glint of silver sticking out of a dark mass on the sidewalk. At first glance, he thought it was a trash bag, but something about it bothered him. After staring at it for a few seconds, he still couldn't make sense of what he was looking at and took a step towards it.

Climmy's laugh told him he'd lost his claim on the last Lucky Seven. Glancing back, he saw his friend already had it lit and was smoking it away. Justin hesitated for a moment as he considered reclaiming his property, but his curiosity won out. He tossed a "Fuck you Climmy" over his shoulder as he began walking towards the object holding his attention.

"Uh-oh, careful of those hydro poles, Beaver!" Climmy taunted.

He hated that nickname. It had a double meaning; he was the youngest of the lot, so the one referred to his slight size like Justin Bieber, and the second referred to his dark, curly hair resembling a certain part of a woman's anatomy. Who needs enemies when you have friends like these? They could be such dicks. Even so, he knew they'd help him if he was in a bind.

Justin only walked a couple of yards before he picked up his pace, first into a jog, and then into a full-blown run.

Dusk made it hard to tell what he'd been staring at, but when he made out what looked like a pale hand, he didn't waste any time.

Within seconds, he was standing over a young woman lying on the ground with what appeared to be a large knife sticking out of her abdomen. She had dark clothes on, so it was hard to tell how badly hurt she was. Justin figured it wasn't good, since she was lying there, not even trying to get up. It took her a minute to notice his presence, but when she did, her expression registered a mix of surprise and relief.

"Can you help me? I'm having a little trouble—" Before she even finished the sentence the kid was yelling at his friend to call an ambulance. Within seconds, someone with a shock of white blond hair appeared over her.

"No!" she gasped, and raised a hand to ward off the coming attack. It was only when the blond took a startled step backward she realized the person looming over her wasn't Charlie at all, but another teenager with a similar shade of hair.

"Holy shit Justin—," the blond said, his face now a mask of worry and fear.

"Climmy, you're upsetting her. Just go get help," the one named Justin said to the spooked kid who glanced back to his friend before disappearing from view. Justin leaned closer and talked to her in a soothing tone, reassuring her that everything would be fine.

Wow, I must be in a bad way if he feels it necessary to reassure me. The kid was trying and had she not been in so much pain, she would have thanked him for it. That's when Sam recognized who Justin was... the scrawny, dark-haired teen who had run into the parking meter. So there was hope for him yet.

Sam wanted to tell him so, but she was having trouble forming words. A couple more heads appeared over her, blocking her view of the stars, but it didn't matter. Someone had flipped the dimmer switch, and everything was fading out. The last thing she heard were sirens in the distance.

Chapter 4

The Mechanic & The Little Shop That Could

Present day Murphy

* * *

The light on the answering machine flashed like a beacon by the time Tim opened the door to his shop, Timothy's Auto. He'd stayed late last night to deal with all the calls, which meant these were all from this morning and it was only six-thirty. Business had been steady ever since he opened the shop, but now they were hard pressed to keep up with the work. Even though the local economy had never fully recovered from the last recession, it hadn't slowed down business. There was an increased demand for his shop's services, and he wasn't complaining. With all four of his employees being related by blood, marriage, or friendship, they were thriving on the demand.

Brandy, his Bernese, trotted past him, hopped up onto the black guest couch, and flopped down.

Tim sat down in the old yellow office chair and turned

off the answering machine. As if on cue, the phone rang. He recognized the number. It was Bob Perkins, and Tim already knew without answering why he was calling. Bob always complained about a mysterious rattle in the engine right around the time his vehicle needed an oil change or maintenance visit. Tim had never once heard a rattle in that engine. This was just part of their ritual. Bob would complain. Tim would tell him to bring it by. Bob would drop it off and ask Tim to do whatever he needed to. Tim would take a look, find nothing, and end up doing the required maintenance. Bob knew about cars. Being a grease monkey in his earlier years, he used to rebuild engines and take care of his own vehicles. Tim figured Bob was either physically incapable of taking care of his own car now, or he just didn't want to do it anymore. Either way, he seemed to need the excuse to justify it to himself. It was Bob's thing.

"Ayah Tim."

"Hi Bob. Rattle back?"

"Oh yeah, worse than ever. 'Specially when I use the brakes. You think you can help me out this time?" Bob code for please replace the brake pads because they're worn thin.

"I'm sure we can, Bob. And I'll check the brakes too since it'll be in the shop, anyway."

"That'd be great. Just great. As long as you're sure now. That rattle's a funny thing the way it keeps comin' back."

"It is. I'm sure we'll find the culprit one day."

"Ayah, hope so. See you in an hour." And that was that. Tim hung up.

The answering machine flashed "o3" on the indicator. Tim pressed play and scratched behind Brandy's ear who'd moved to his side once he'd taken a seat, and waited for the messages to start. Two were maintenance requests, and the third was Gertie stating she'd be late because of a grandchild issue. Judging by her tone, there would be hell to pay. Her teenage grandkids, Jenny and Justin, had lived with Gertie most of their lives and this wasn't the first time she'd had a "grandchild issue". Last time, Justin got caught vandalizing a car. He and his friends decided it would be a great idea to stuff it full of pickles. Extra garlic dill pickles. Tim thought the stunt pretty funny considering who owned said vehicle. His old math teacher and Justin's current vice principal, Mr. Brimley, whose awkward gait was reminiscent of someone with a pickle lodged up his hiney. And though he never found out the specifics on why Mr. Brimley's Mercedes got targeted, he was certain he deserved it. Brimley had a habit of picking on and humiliating the weaker students in his classes to a point where they'd either drop out or stop attending class. This was your classic case of a small town teenager finding a unique way of delivering justice with the added benefit of amusing himself and his friends.

"Timmies, Tim?" Toni asked, hands full as he shouldered open the shop door. Toni handed over one of the hot containers of coffee and settled on the chair across from him.

"Thanks," Tim smiled as he accepted the beverage.

Being a large fellow, Toni dwarfed the chair, which was a duplicate of the seventies throwback Tim occupied. It always amazed him the small spaces Toni could fit into. He also had the eerie ability of seeming to appear out of nowhere. Most people never heard the man approach until he was standing right beside them.

"I wonder if Mr. Happy will deign to grace us with an appearance today," Toni mentioned too innocently. Toni was referring to Tim's brother-in-law Mike, who was turning out to be a good example of why one should never hire family.

Tim sighed and ran an agitated hand through his hair. Sensing his upset, Brandy chuffed her disapproval. It was a rhetorical question, but since Toni had helped him by picking up some of the slack created by Mike's serial absenteeism, Tim felt he deserved an explanation.

"I don't have a clue, but today I intend to get to the bottom of what's been going on with him." Tim paused, then followed it up with. "Don't suppose you have any idea?"

Toni responded with a raised brow as he took another sip of coffee. He was a man of few words, which Tim appreciated. Toni was the last person Mike would open up to. Personality wise, they were too different to even approach something close to a friendship.

Predictable, dependable and hard-working Toni was Tim's right-hand man. They both grew up in Colberg County. They'd seen each other around for years but had never hung out. It was only later when they worked at Al's Autobody together that Tim came to call him a friend. The job at Al's was ok, but it didn't stay that way for long. The recession hit, resulting in pay cuts across the board, which only meant more work for less pay. They didn't like it, but Al promised it was only temporary. But after the economy recovered Al decided he liked the profits too much to keep his word. That's when Tim took the leap and opened his own shop. Not only did he take Toni, one of the best mechanics Al had on staff, but Gertie, the personality of the operation. Tim, Toni and Gertie were the head, heart and pluck of Timothy's Auto. Starting the business was one of the best decisions he'd ever made. Tim loved the independence it brought him even with the long hours. If something went wrong, he was the one who had to find a solution. The buck stopped with him and unfortunately, this was happening far too often because of Mike.

He'd taken Mike on as a mechanic over a year ago, but a couple months back he started showing up late for work and it had only gotten worse since.

Now Mike was barely there at the best of times and, to top it off, he'd started making mistakes. He'd signed off on a cruiser last week after repairing the transmission, but didn't screw it to the frame properly. Tim doubted Constable Lotts would have been too pleased to lose his transmission in the middle of an emergency. Luckily, Tim had started double-checking Mike's work after finding bolts lying on the ground after a tire change. Mike had told him they were just extras he'd grabbed from their stock. Suspicious, he'd asked the owner to come back under the pretense of checking the tire pressure and discovered it was missing a couple of bolts. He'd fixed the issue and talked to Mike about it, but it barely registered. Now the other two mechanics in the shop, Toni and Ralph, had started complaining about the extra time and effort they had to put in to make up for Mike's absence and shoddy work, and he didn't blame them. Tim had already given him warnings so their talk tonight would be more than a slap on the hand.

Deep down, he already knew he'd have to find someone to replace his soon to be ex-employee. Mike had never been one to handle criticism well and he had a quick temper, so Tim already knew their talk would not be pretty.

This was one part of ownership he wouldn't enjoy.

* * *

Mike didn't want to get out of bed yet. It was the same shit, just a different day. If he wasn't at work, then he was here with Paula nagging him to fix this or that. His job was ok, but it wasn't something he'd ever aspired for. Working for someone else didn't suit his personality or his wallet. Besides, he knew he'd do a better job of it than Tim. The guy had no business sense, as proven by the way he under-charged their customers for work that cost twice as much everywhere else, and underpaid his employees. Others assured him what he earned as a mechanic was fair, but it definitely wasn't enough to live on. His wife, Paula, worked as a part-time secretary at a local dentist's office, but her meager wages only covered the groceries and incidentals. Together, their income hadn't made a dent in their ever-increasing debt load.

He knew Lady Luck was to blame for that. He used to be the guy who walked in to the casino with a few hundred bucks and walked out with five to ten times that in winnings. Lately, though, he couldn't seem to catch a break. The thing that kept him coming back was the knowledge that no one was unlucky one hundred percent of the time. And when his luck changed, he'd pay off all their debts, every last dime.

Just thinking about his future winnings improved Mike's mood. Already he felt lighter and happier because today could be the day. Besides, he'd never win unless he played. They didn't have the money to lose, so he'd only wager a couple hundred dollars. If it didn't pan out, he'd leave. But if he got his big break, then all their financial stress and worries would disappear. And maybe then he'd be able to get a decent, worry-free sleep.

Mike could hear Paula moving around downstairs. They had a century home, and the floorboards complained with every step, so sneaking up on someone wasn't an option. He heard her climb the stairs and cross the hall landing. The creak near the door announced her entrance into their bedroom, the faint brush of her feet along the carpet before the bed shifted under her weight.

"It's after eight, hon. Don't you have to get to work?" Paula asked as she touched his arm.

Mike pasted on a smile and opened his eyes. "I'm up," he said, as he swung his feet onto the floor and headed for the washroom, giving her no chance to say anything more.

It was important to keep up appearances and remain positive otherwise he'd get distracted. He didn't bother telling Paula he was skipping work to go to the casino. She would only try to stop him. He had bigger priorities than repairing cars. He had to get them out of their financial hole.

He had told no one about their financial mess, not even Paula. His father always said, *If you got nothing good to say then keep your flaps zipped cause no one wants to hear it.* His father applied this anecdote to everything, including finances, and Mike prided himself on carrying on the family tradition. Paula had no idea how bad things actually were. She assumed they still had RRSPs and such, but he'd cashed in the last of those months ago. Today he'd get their money back and none would be the wiser.

Mike showered, shaved, and was out the door within twenty minutes. Whistling, he slid into the driver's seat of his car.

Today would be a mighty fine day. He could feel it in his bones.

* * *

It was a couple of days later when Mike still hadn't bothered showing up to work that Tim knew he had to deal with his wayward employee, whether or not he came in. The extra work was causing a real strain in the shop and it had to end.

He dialed Mike's cell, but it went to voicemail again. As a last resort, he called his sister's cell to see what was going on.

"Hey sis."

"Hi. Wait a minute you two... Tim, just a second." Tim heard shuffling and muffled words as Paula instructed his niece and nephew to take their shoes off. More muffled words, and then she came back.

"Sorry about that. The kids just came in with mud all over their shoes. What's up?" Paula was Tim's older sister by six years, but you'd never know it to talk to her. More often than not, Tim felt like the older brother.

"I don't suppose Mike is home sick today?" Tim asked. One could hope.

"No, he's at work—" Paula began. Silence reigned over the phone for a second before a few colorful expletives erupted through the receiver. He heard the kids squawk somewhere in the background followed by some muffled words, likely Paula telling them to go play in the living room. His sister's sigh told him she was back on the phone. "I don't know what's gotten into him lately." There was another long pause before she asked. "This isn't the first time, is it?"

Instead of responding to a question she already knew the answer to, he asked, "Has he been acting different at home?"

Her extended silence confirmed it wasn't just work he'd

been skipping out on. Without even seeing his sister, he knew she'd be tugging on her lower lip.

"Paula, tell me what's going on."

There was another bout of silence. He suspected Paula was debating on how much to tell him. Just when he thought he'd have to prod again, she spilled. It sounded similar to Mike's behavior at work. He would disappear for long stints of time without explaining where he'd gone or what he'd done. He was moody and unpredictable. Tim could hear the anger and disappointment in her voice, but there was also another emotion he couldn't pinpoint. In the next breath, she admitted she suspected he was gambling again. Although he didn't voice his next thought, he suspected Mike was doing a lot more than gambling. The dark circles under his eyes, moodiness, forgetfulness and general lackluster appearance suggested either drug or alcohol abuse.

"Paula, why don't you and the kids stay at my place for a while? I have the room. Besides, I would love a little more time with my niece and nephew." Even as he said it, he knew she wouldn't take him up on his offer. At least not yet.

"Aw! You're missin' your big sis, are ya?" But Paula's teasing sounded strained. She couldn't fool her little brother. "Thank you, but no. At least, not right now. The kids are supposed to go stay with mom and dad for a few weeks, so I'll just push their visit ahead and join them depending on how my conversation with Mike goes. I doubt he'll even miss the kids right now with the way he's been ignoring them."

"And I repeat, you know there's always a place for you and the kids with me, right?"

"Thanks. I appreciate it, little brother. I may take you up on it one day, but not now. Today I have to arrange for the kids to get out of Dodge and track down my wayward husband."

"Maybe I should be there when you talk to him. If he's been unpredictable, I don't want—"

"No Timothy." Whenever Paula used his full name, it meant the subject wasn't open to discussion. "I've never feared my husband in the past, and I don't intend to start now. I have to be the one to talk to him about this." Tim didn't like it, but she'd refused his help and he didn't know what more he could say to persuade her. Short of showing up on his sister's doorstep unannounced, there wasn't much he could do. As if reading his mind, Paula followed up with, "Besides, your presence might escalate things unnecessarily, especially if he feels like he's being ganged up on. I'll call if I need you."

"Paula—"

"I will call you if I need to." And that was the end of it. But before letting her go Tim made her promise to call him right after her conversation with Mike regardless of the hour.

* * *

Mike was on a high the moment he stepped through the double doors. The closer he got to the tables, the more bounce he had in his step.

"Hey Chris," Mike said in greeting as he nodded towards the familiar face standing at the door. The bouncer returned his nod, but not his smile.

The ding of a winner's bell on a slot machine drew him through the lobby, down the hall, and into the bosom of the casino. Back in his element, the bright lights and sounds of the slot machines working made his pulse quicken. Shouts and groans of people surrounding the craps and roulette tables told him who lost and who won. Mike brushed his hand over the empty card tables as he walked past. The soft forest green felt tickled the pads of his fingers. Every time a new deck replaced the old, it gave off a subtle new deck smell, and it excited him. Even the solid dark colored walls and ceiling, meant to be boring and forgettable to keep people's attention on the games and grease the flow of money, comforted him.

Mike savored his surroundings, letting the familiar sounds and smells wash over him as he stepped onto the busy multi-colored carpet. Although the noise might irritate some, he felt like he was home. If he could, he'd pull up a cot and sleep right here, in the center of it all. Next to the triple seven slot machines, snuggled up against the black-jack table.

He saw an opening at a poker table and took it. More than once, Mike had regretted not following his instincts, and this was one day he wouldn't regret. He took the seat between a portly fellow with a shiny crown, broad features, sporting a beige golf shirt, and an elderly grandmother with a shock of white curls and soft features who appeared to be sitting on her own walker. The dealer smiled at him as he settled in his seat, but the other four players barely spared him a glance. The last card had just been dealt.

"Son of a Gerbilfucker!"

More than a little shocked to hear the sweet looking elderly lady to his right curse like a sailor, Mike quelled the giggle that bubbled up. At least he wouldn't be getting her cards. In the world of poker, there's usually somebody winning but always many somebodies losing. As long as you sat by someone on a losing streak, there was less chance of the losing streak hitting you.

Barely able to contain his excitement, Mike took two bills out of his wallet and placed it on the felt. The platinum haired dealer took his money and gave him his chips. Mike knew most of the dealers, but didn't recognize this one. Must be new, because he was smiling. A lot. These guys rarely smiled.

The game was *Let It Ride*. The dealer dealt each player, including himself, three cards from the deck then discarded the first card in his pile. The remaining two cards completed everyone's hand. Mike lifted his cards to reveal a pair of queens. Suppressing a smile, he tucked his cards under the chips he had in play and sat back. All but Mike tapped their first bet back. Now he felt it. The rush and excitement of knowing he'd double his money tonight made him feel like a king. When the dealer revealed his first card, four of the players tapped out and took their second bet back.

Tension palpable. It took forever for the dealer to flip over the second card. The reveal drew a few groans, but the best response came from his right, yet again.

"Fartknocker! These cards are tap dancin' on me last nerve!" Spat the elderly grandmother.

A server with long, sun-darkened legs and exotic eyes came by. Mike ordered a gin and tonic. Normally, he didn't drink this early in the game, but tonight was different. He was in a groove and nothing would stop the moneyfall. With a wink, the dealer tripled the chips he had in play and dealt again. Mike evened out on the next two hands but doubled up on the third with two pairs. He was still on the positive side of the game, so all was good in his world. This was not the case for everyone. The middle-aged golfer to his left had had enough and walked away.

Mike's stomach knotted. The change meant the dealer's hand would change.

The next few rounds went well. He came out even on one hand and doubled up again on the second. He glimpsed his exotic server, his Lady Luck, again. Mike could practically feel her long dark legs wrapping around him as she caught and held his gaze. He had a semi, but wasn't sure if it was because he'd won the last few hands or because of his Lady Luck's flirtations. Either way, he'd be sure to repay his exotic server for her luck. Mike had three decent hands in a row, and he gave his server a healthy tip to thank her when she brought him a fresh drink. In response, she brushed up against his arm with her breasts as she reached over to grab his empty glass, giving him a delightful view of her cleavage. The little minx did it on purpose. His semi became rock hard as most of his blood migrated to his joint.

That's when he lost his first hand. The next half hour was uncomfortable as he waited for the blood to flow back to his extremities, and the losses just kept mounting. It wasn't long before he lost everything he'd won. Sooner than he thought possible he was dipping into his credit to gain back what he'd lost over the last two hours, but his luck never returned.

Having been slapped in the face by Lady Luck once again, he left the table to find his exotic server. She was checking out the high rollers at the slots. Those who played two or more machines at once, feeding them hundred-dollar bills like they were candy. The longer he watched her flirt with them, the more he wanted her. The sashay of her hips as she walked, the way the material of her red dress tightened over the best parts, the naked curve of her back where it dipped down to her buttocks, the way she placed a perfectly manicured hand on an older man's arm then leaned in to whisper something in his ear. She was good. Occasionally, she'd glance over at him, tracking his movements whenever he'd move to a new spot. He could tell she wanted him, too.

Mike was an attractive guy. He knew it. Women knew it. He'd never had a problem getting a woman into bed, or out of bed. Occasionally, he'd forget to remove his wedding band, but that didn't deter the majority. In the beginning, he felt guilty about cheating, but not anymore. God wouldn't have given him these looks if he wasn't supposed to use them to his advantage. He was meant for bigger things than working as a mechanic in a shitty little town like Murphy. He just needed people to stop getting in his way so he could get there.

His phone vibrated again. He ignored it. It was either Tim or Paula looking for him, and he didn't have time for their clingy nonsense.

After a few more losses at different tables, Mike had had enough and retired to the bar to watch the crowd while he waited for his Lady Luck's shift to end. People always reminded him of ants doing this and that without taking a pause to see the big picture. He watched the ants move around the tables, some winning, most losing, everyone focussed solely on the game in front of them. Using his thumb and index finger, he put a few of the most annoying ants in his line of sight and pulled the trigger. When his Lady Luck stepped into view, Mike pulled the trigger as she neared him. Her laughter tinkled, like glass hitting the floor.

Her shift finally done, Mike accompanied her back to her apartment. He needed to blow off steam from his heavy loss today, which he partially blamed on his exotic Lady Luck. Her disappearance coincided too conveniently with his losing streak. She owed him. In the end, she wasn't a bad lay, but afterwards, when they were still lying naked in bed, she laughed. He asked what was so funny, but instead of answering, she only laughed harder. It reminded him of the high-pitched twitter of a hyena. After another couple minutes of listening to her idiotic high pitched cackling, he'd had enough and hit her over the head with the penguin shaped bookend from her side table. She stopped laughing.

The blood oozing from her head wound cut a dark path through her curls before blending in to her red sheets. If he looked at her at just the right angle, she looked like she was sleeping. Most of the books the bookend held up slid off on to the carpeted floor, but a couple remained on their sides on the nightstand table. One of the two titles read *The Art Of Being Happy* and Mike's last thought before he left the small, dingy room was that she did die laughing.

Chapter 5

Murphy, The Best Little Hell Hole Anywhere

His breath caressed the back of her neck, making the fine hairs dance. In different circumstances, this would have been a pleasant sensation, but this was far from that. Her skin crawled wherever the warm air landed, sending chills down her spine. Try as she might, she couldn't move her arms or escape the wall at her back. She could feel the sweat rolling off her forehead as her body shook. Déjà Vu hit her hard as she tried again and again to get away from her restraints.

A dog barked off in the distance and it made her ache for her golden retriever, Buddy.

That's when she heard the voice again. The one who visited her most nights. "You remember me Sam... I'm the guy who's gonna change your life—"

A scream built in her throat as she thrashed with renewed fervor to get away from her assailant, but before she had the chance to bellow out her frustration and fear, a wetness on her face distracted her. She stiffened, trying to figure out what was happening. Did she get hurt? Was that her own blood dripping down her face? Again, something wet ran along her face, but this time she caught a whiff of something. Before she finished the thought, Sam sputtered awake and found Buddy frantically licking her right cheek.

"Ugh. Buddy, stop." Sam turned her face away and tried to put up her hands to fend off the doggy tongue coming at her again, but her arms wouldn't budge from her sides. Breath caught in her throat, she swung her gaze down to find a cocoon of bedding wrapped around her, trapping her arms. She was in her own bed in her own apartment.

Sam sighed and laid her head back down again. Buddy leaned on the side of the bed and whined, telling her the nightmare had freaked him out, too. After struggling with the sheets, she pulled a hand free to rub fur face's muzzle.

"Sorry, big fella. I didn't mean to scare you. Thanks for waking me up." Buddy chuffed in agreement, dropped his front paws off the side of the bed, and sat on his haunches to watch her.

Nightmares had plagued her ever since Charlie's attack. For the first couple of years, she'd had them nightly. Now, after five years, their frequency was down to a few times a week. Unfortunately, this past week was the exception. She'd woken up in a cold sweat almost every night and it was all because she was going home.

Her father's retirement party was this weekend and she still couldn't imagine him not being Chief Turner anymore, though deep down she knew it was for the best. The job had taken its toll on him. He could never leave work at work and always took it to heart when a case went unsolved. So when he couldn't find the perpetrator of his own daughter's attack, it nearly did him in. Being the protector of an odd town like Murphy, where the number of weird accidents and outright suicides outnumbered car accidents and heart attacks combined, would be hard on anyone with a conscience. And although Charlie was not a figment of Sam's imagination, he might as well have been considering how he somehow vanished after that.

Sam had danced with the devil and survived, and she had the scars to prove it. Of their own volition, her fingers found the rough ridge of one of the knife wounds on her pelvis. With scary precision, Charlie had found her fault lines and skillfully whittled her down until she gave up and gave in. Once an idealist at heart, she'd always held fast and firm to the idea that everyone was essentially good and, if given the opportunity, most people chose to be decent. She no longer believed that. Even with the negative repercussions from that night, Sam was grateful to be alive. One big positive to come out of her attack was it cured her of any depression she'd felt over the break off of her engagement. It removed her blinders and revealed her ex as the narcissist he was.

Getting into another relationship was low on her priority list, especially after her ex and then Charlie got thru with her.

The nightmares were another reason having a relationship seemed impossible. A woman in her late twenties with night terrors as severe as hers would be too much baggage for most sane men to handle. At least, that's what her last boyfriend told her over a year ago as he dashed out the door.

Impatient now, Buddy barked and headed for the door. When she didn't move, he came back to sit by the bedroom door and whined again. When Buddy stressed, he did the same thing Sam did, headed for the kitchen. Only instead of food, the only thing he could get his paws on was water. He must have drank way too much of it thru the night and was paying dearly for it. If Buddy could cross his legs, he'd be doing it right now. He was already up and pacing again.

"Ok Buddy, I'm up. Just let me get out of this bloody bed," Sam sighed as she sat up and pulled her other arm free. She stood and tugged at the top sheet still wrapped around her. After struggling with it for a minute or two, making no headway, she'd had enough. Her last big tug brought her right foot clear off the floor. Unable to regain her balance, she toppled backwards hard on to her ass only then realizing the sheet had tangled under her right foot.

Buddy stopped his pacing to look at her and whined again as if to say, *Stop goofing off. I really have to go!*

"Ouch... no sympathy for your master, huh, dog? Fine. I'm coming, I'm coming. Hold on to your fur," Sam said as she got up. After a quick glance in the mirror confirmed the dark cotton pants and t-shirt she wore were passable, she walked from the bedroom, through the open concept apartment to the front door, rubbing her sore right cheek as she went. "Remember this when you're dragging me down the street for the perfect potty spot. If I can't move tomorrow, I'm blaming you."

Slipping her feet into the runners by the entry, Sam opened the door and had to shield her eyes from the bright light. Once her eyes adjusted, she took in the beautiful summer day. Joggers, running with conviction, as her trainer would say, passed by them. Two months ago, Sam got coerced by a colleague in to running the Run-For-A-Cure marathon. Sam ran all the time with Buddy, so figured a marathon shouldn't be that much harder and it was for a good cause. She also thought it would give her a goal to work towards, one which would help her shed her winter weight. She already regretted agreeing to do it after talking to people who'd run it the previous year. Comments like "I was lucky to finish", "I'd rather go to the dentist than run that thing again" and "I quit after the fourth hill because I thought I was having a heart attack" motivated her to get a personal trainer that she now trained with a couple times a week. It wasn't so much the distance that killed runners, but the hills and valleys on the course made for some treacherous inclines. As a result, a surprising number of participants quit midway through.

Sam allowed Buddy to drag her down the street until he found his perfect patch of grass. Once he'd done the deed, she led him back to the apartment. She'd slept in later than she planned so there was no time to waste. Buddy would have to wait until they reached Murphy for his walk.

Sam drove past the Circle K Minimart at the corner of Talbot and King. The store that once marked the outskirts of town now looked overwhelmed by big box stores and chain restaurants. To say Murphy had changed in the last five years would be an understatement. The grim, unpleasant downtown core, a stark contrast to the hustle and bustle presented in the recent development surrounding it, remained mostly the same. And though new businesses now outnumbered the old two-to-one, to her Murphy would always be the same hopeless, depressing town she'd grown up in.

Although she'd been back at least a dozen times over the last five years, she still had to force herself to drive the highway back to her hometown, every turnoff a temptation to hightail it back to Toronto. With her mother gone and her now widowed neighbor, Harold Sarken, living in a busy retirement community on the other end of town, the Chief was the main reason she came back. For the better part of her life, she'd had an awkward relationship with him, but they'd grown closer over the last few years. Perhaps almost losing his daughter was a wake-up call.

As a kid, she'd never thought of her parents as a power couple. In her father's case, the other woman was his job. As the youngest police chief appointed to the force, home was just somewhere he slept and visited from time to time. Her mother must have tired of the empty house because as soon as Sam enrolled in school full days, she went back to work as a high school administrator. She worked her way up, took night classes and joined the district school board. Self-reliance was something Sam learned early on from both her parents.

And on Sam's part, she did her best to focus on school and dodge the worst of the harassment, but it was difficult. Grade school came as a real shock because she, over every other awkward goofy kid in the schoolyard, was always the favored target. Only twice did she go to her parents for help, but the first time, with a six-year-old's reasoning and a six-year-old's vocabulary, the severity of the situation got lost on them. Their only advice was to either ignore it or go get a teacher.

But Sam was no tattle-tale, so she'd dealt with it the best way she knew how. When she was young, she'd often cry. Occasionally, the teachers would reprimand the instigators, but it was a temporary reprieve. As she got older, she'd tried ignoring it, and more often than not the kids would get bored and move on. Later, when the harassment started up again, the teasing was harsher and much more aggressive. Then one evening in grade six a group of older boys followed her home after school. The first time she got away unharmed. Unfortunately, she wasn't so lucky the second time around and returned home badly bruised, beaten, bleeding, humiliated and ashamed.

64

It wasn't the first time she'd come home with injuries, nor would it be the last. However, this time was different. That night her parents were late getting home, so they never found out the extent of what happened. Unfortunately, the long-sleeved shirt and pants she'd donned, which remained her go-to outfit until the worst of the cuts and bruises healed, didn't hide the bruise on her temple or the fat lip. When pressed she excused her injuries as a stupid school-yard tussle and dropped it. Her parents had made it clear years ago that they were more interested in their careers than in her. Sitting down and telling them what she'd been going through over the last six years seemed moot after what had just happened. Besides, as a family, their communication skills sucked, so to expect anything different could only lead to disappointment on top of everything else.

But her dad's cop instincts must have kicked in because even in the face of her silence he did the one thing that would end up helping her in the long run. He started teaching her basic moves to defend herself. And then a few months later, he started taking her with him to the gun range to practice. Over time, she became quite the marksman. The gang of boys never chased her home again and although the schoolyard bullying never fully ceased, there was a marked difference compared to what happened in the past. Any harassment from then on seemed more disorganized and opportunistic.

But as fate would have it, years later, an affable psycho named Charlie set his sights on Sam, making her a target once again. Although as ridiculous as the idea sounded, Sam couldn't shake the feeling she was a magnet for the worst kind of people. But just as quickly as the thought popped into her head, she pushed the ridiculous notion away.

"This is definitely not the time to get paranoid," she chided herself.

Like the town, she'd also changed in the last five years, but unlike the town's crumbling core, hers was composed of a hard kernel of embittered strength. Gone was the girl who felt she deserved the hatred and abuse she received from her peers. Gone was the girl who blindly believed someone's words over their actions. Gone was the girl who backed down and gave up when she should have fought harder, longer. That girl died five years ago.

As she drove past the Shanghai Dragon, she couldn't hold back a shiver. It was early September, and the day was uncharacteristically hot, but it still didn't warm her chill. It ran too deep to be warmed by a mere sunny day. Unnerved by a sudden feeling of vulnerability, Sam put her hand on the automatic window lever but suppressed the urge to put them up.

"Jeez, Sam, will you get over yourself already? You act like you're the only one ever targeted by a psychopath outside the Shanghai Dragon," she muttered, and then laughed. She laughed so long and hard she had to pull the car over before she ended up getting them in an accident.

All the while Buddy regarded her, his head cocked to the side as if to say, "WTF?" His perplexed expression made Sam laugh even harder until there were tears streaming down her cheeks. He must have had enough of her near hysterical behavior, because he whined at her in disapproval. It was only when a paw touched her forearm, along with a second drawn out whine, that she forced herself to stop laughing.

"Ok, ok. I'm not gonna lose it, at least not today big fella," Sam said, wiping away her tears. Buddy chuffed his agreement and waited until the car started moving again before dropping his paw and sticking his snout out the passenger side window.

"Tough crowd," she sighed and patted Buddy on the head. Sam had stopped at the police station on her way in. His retirement party was tomorrow, and they wanted more photos for the presentation. Sam was the only one who knew where they might be, so Lieutenant Bobby recruited her to search them out. The more embarrassing, the better were Bobby's exact words.

When she turned her car down Fleming Street, the quaint charm of her old neighborhood struck her once again. It didn't look at all like the long, desolate and scary street she'd ran down that dark night five years ago. Sam pulled into the driveway, put the car in park, and took a moment to settle herself. As always, the house looked the same. Same cement stoop leading up to the front door. Same metal screen door with the tear on the bottom right-hand corner. Same gray, dreary side porch which always collected wasps in the summer. Her gaze skittered along the roofline and came to a halt on the sunroom. The only difference there was the one window had a newer screen replaced after her attacker tore it to shreds.

"Ok, let's get on with it, shall we?" Sam muttered and got out of the safety of her car. She avoided looking at the sunroom as she let Buddy out the passenger side and mounted the steps to the side porch. Sam swung open the screen door and paused for a second before stepping up onto the porch. A wall of heat wafted over them. *This I remember*, she thought with irritation, waving off a wasp buzzing too close to her ear.

Buddy snapped at another wasp hovering over his muzzle.

"I feel your pain, Buddy." She put her key in the front

door lock, her hand on the doorknob, took a deep breath and she and Buddy stepped into the cool dark house.

Sam halted just inside the front door to allow her eyes time to adjust to the darkness. Not so for Buddy. She saw a streak of white heading through the dining room and into the kitchen at the back. His enthusiasm relaxed her. Ever since the attack, Sam wasn't comfortable being in her family home, but having Buddy with her made it bearable. She didn't have any illusions about thinking the big softie would defend her if something like Charlie happened again, but that didn't matter. It was enough he was here with her.

Eyes now adapted to the dark, she could see the familiar interior of her family home. Same dark dining room set, same paneling on the walls, same brown sectional and tree trunk coffee table in the living room. The furniture was at least twenty years old but looked barely used. Not a shocker, considering her father was a workaholic and any socializing he did was at work. Sam's gaze drifted to the front windows and beyond to the sunroom. Icy fingers tickled the back of her neck as memories of that night flooded her. Although she couldn't control the fear, she could control her response to it. She pushed down the all too familiar panic and forced herself forward in search of the photo albums.

Chapter 6

The Oil Change

Mike showed up around noon on the fourth day looking like hell. Tim wasn't surprised. If he had to guess, he'd say Mike was suffering the repercussions of a late night bender.

As promised, Paula called Tim after she'd talked to Mike. She confronted him about everything; his absence from work, where he went at night, and the disappearance of the money from their joint savings and RRSPs. He didn't deny any of it, but he didn't explain or apologize either. Mike just kept repeating the words *it's all gone* as if a deep scratch was etched in his mind, forcing him to skip back to this one thought.

He snapped out of it once it finally registered his wife was about to take the kids to stay with her parents for a while. Mike's erratic behavior escalated after that. The next moments were a bit of a blur. Somehow, her arm was in his hand, his grip tightening painfully as he shook her. It was when he drew his free hand back, making his ill intentions clear that she regretted not having Tim present. Luckily, their youngest, Riley, called out her name, taking the wind out of Mike's sails. He let his arm drop as he spilled into the chair sitting behind him. Head bowed, he asked her to leave. She didn't wait to be asked twice.

His sister admitted to him that was the first time she'd ever felt afraid of her husband. It wasn't so much the fact he'd raised a hand to her. That just pissed her off. It was the hate she saw in his eyes when he was about to do it that scared the crap out of her. She couldn't shake the feeling that had he followed through, he may have just kept swinging. Paula didn't know the person sitting in her kitchen last night, but it wasn't the man she'd married.

Mike was not a violent guy, but after his reaction to Paula last night, Tim didn't know how he'd react to their talk.

A sudden bout of shouting alerted him to a problem in the shop.

"Jesus Ralph. Just let me borrow your fucking air ratchet for a half an hour," Mike shouted.

"No friggin' way. You ruined my last Proto air ratchet and not only did you not bother replacing it, but you didn't bother even telling me about it until I needed it for a job. I'm not letting you touch my tools again," Ralph shouted back.

"Fuck you, I did. That was months ago—" Mike roared, red faced. They'd started their argument a good fifteen feet apart, but Mike had closed half the gap between them already. He gripped a wrench in his right hand, holding it more like a weapon than a tool. Tim didn't like it one bit.

"Six weeks ago. Remember, it was one of the last times you were here on time?" Ralph pointed out standing his ground. Ralph had every right to hold his ground, but why today?

"Fuck you, Ralph! See if I let you borrow any of my

tools next time one of your gear ratchets gets sheered," Mike yelled back, still closing the distance so now they were only a few feet apart.

"Fine by me." Ralph shrugged, eyeing him.

"Hey guys. Cool it," Tim said, stepping between them, and then turned to Mike. "Take a break outside. Get a coffee, whatever, but cool down. Then come see me." Mike stood there for a moment, white knuckling the wrench as if debating his next move.

"I'll remember this, fucknuts," Mike ground out as he glared first at Ralph and then at Tim.

Tim noted his clenched jaw and the bulging vein in his forehead before Mike turned and left the shop. Both of them exhaled in relief once the door closed.

"I know he's your brother-in-law and all, but he's losing it Tim," Ralph said, eyeing the door Mike exited thru.

"Yeah, that escalated way too fast," Tim replied, staring at the same spot before turning back to Ralph. "One way or another this ends today."

Tim hadn't intended to fire his brother-in-law today, but what happened next depended on Mike. He'd planned to talk to him about the jobs he'd screwed up, the number of days he'd missed, and give him a written official warning so he understood another incident would cost him his job. And maybe give him a few days off so he could get the help he needed to deal with his gambling problem. But now he wondered if it was wise to give Mike another chance at all considering what he'd just witnessed. Brother-in-law or not, he couldn't allow Mike to resort to physical violence and start a brawl in his shop. He needed to talk to his lawyer to find out his legal options before their chat.

* * *

After Sam found photos she figured would pass for funny as hell, she and Buddy headed for the police station to hand over the incriminating pictures to Bobby.

Stuck at a red light that was taking forever to change, all she could do was people watch as pedestrians walked past enjoying the sunny day. A little girl in an aqua princess-cut dress holding the hand of a woman, likely her mother, were forced to walk around a couple of people standing in the middle of the sidewalk before disappearing into the mini-mart.

Her gaze bounced back to the two men blocking the sidewalk. They stood outside TIMOTHY'S AUTO SHOP, deep in conversation. One wore gray coveralls like a mechanic would wear, and the other had on a golf shirt, black dress shorts and a baseball cap, like he'd just walked off a golf course. His hat had KILLER ON THE COURSE embroidered across the back of it.

Sam stared in stunned silence. It wasn't the words on his ball cap she found alarming, but the shock of white-blond hair peeking out from under it and what she could see of the man's profile.

A horn blasted from behind, startling her out of her abstraction. She looked up at the now green traffic light. She was blocking traffic. A glance in the rear-view mirror showed at least a half dozen cars waiting behind her. *Well, tough shit.* Sam turned her attention back to the two men, but it was already too late. Ball cap guy had turned away, so she no longer saw his profile. And then another car joined in on the fun and blasted his horn. Now two horns blared, one after another. They'd found a way to make their already obnoxious honking into an even more annoying rhythm. With no other choice, she gave up her vantage point and took a left on the next street to circle the block.

By the time she returned, the mechanic was alone, leaning against the brick wall of Timothy's Auto. Sam wanted to ask him a few questions concerning his friend, but something about him bothered her. His pose suggested relaxed but his body exuded tension. One hand white knuckled a coffee mug, while the other was clenched at his side. His tense jaw line squared off.

Sam opted to get an oil change at Timothy's Auto instead and pulled up to one of the two closed bay doors she'd driven past on her tour around the block. Less than a minute later, the automatic door rose, allowing her Honda admission. Sam slid in, threw the car into park, let Buddy out of the back and headed for the room with the MAIN OFFICE printed on its door. She took the empty seat in front of the desk as Buddy laid down on the floor to her right. Within minutes, a tall, slim, dark-haired man came in and settled in the chair behind the desk. She didn't recognize him, but his name tag read TIM and he had an air of authority about him. The owner of Timothy's Auto, perhaps?

"So what can we do for you today, Miss—?" Tim asked. He had a pleasant face, warm eyes, and a nice smile, which made her feel a little calmer.

"Sam. Sam Turner," Sam said, returning his smiled. "I was hoping to get an oil change?"

Tim looked up when she said her name and searched her face. She could see he was trying to work out where he knew the name from. It was fascinating watching him work it out. His expression went from quizzical to confused. He opened his mouth to ask a question but stopped as what she guessed was the realization of who she was dawned on him.

I think I made the poor man speechless, Sam thought, sympathizing a bit. A victim of one of the few unsolved attempted murders to happen in Murphy was sitting in the chair across from him. He seemed to struggle with what to do or say next.

"Yes, that Sam Turner. The one who was attacked five years ago. Can you fit me in for a quick oil change? Or should I come back another day?" It sounded more abrupt than she'd intended, but it got the ball rolling. Tim wasn't the first one to recognize her name and associate it with that night.

Tim's eyes widened with what she could only assume was shock. She waited, but the awkward silence seemed to stretch on forever. *Oh dear, I think I broke him.* Sam breathed a sigh of relief when he spoke again.

"Yes, we can fit you in for a quick oil change," Tim replied tightly, looking down at the schedule on his desk. "In about thirty minutes. That good?"

"Yes, thank-you." Sam replied and then sat there, unsure of how to broach the subject of the two men she'd seen conversing not five minutes ago. "One of your mechanics was outside on a break. What's his name?" Tim's eyebrows shot up a good half an inch at her question. "I saw him talking to someone I recognized. I would have approached him myself, but he disappeared before I had the chance."

Tim sat back in his chair with a sigh before running a hand through his hair. "That would be Mike, but I have to talk to him in a few minutes myself, so..." he murmured more to himself than to her, before he shook his head and finished with. "Sorry, would you mind waiting in the guest area while we work on your car?"

The strain in his voice at the mention of Mike told her their talk would be much more than a casual conversation. How could she tell this stranger to be careful because —

because of what Sam? The mechanic might throw his coffee cup at him? Even though she knew it was ridiculous, she still felt on edge. So much so she had the overwhelming urge to get back in her car and leave the garage as fast as possible.

But she stayed.

Tim had already risen from his chair. A polite way of saying *I've got work to do, so please go away now.*

Seeing no way around it, Sam stood, looked him in the eyes, and just said it.

"Listen, you have to be careful and watch out for anything odd. I know this sounds strange but I have a terrible feeling. I've had it ever since I saw your mechanic talking to the guy I recognized out front." Buddy whined, likely in response to her anxiety, but it punctuated her point perfectly. She placed her hand on his head to calm him. Tim was eyeing her with suspicion now, but it didn't faze her. She'd stopped worrying about what others thought of her years ago.

"Ok. Not sure what you're talking about—" Tim said. His expression was one of bewilderment, mixed with a hint of fear, and perhaps a little disappointment. She knew she sounded like a nut job, but Sam couldn't tell him what she didn't know.

"I don't know either, otherwise I'd tell you but—" She paused, searching for a better way of explaining the sickening feeling in the pit of her stomach warning her something was just not right. But there was nothing more she could say to make him believe her. "—just be careful."

And with that, she and Buddy exited the office and took a seat in the guest area, aware of Tim's gaze following her. The room she sat in had two good size windows facing out into the shop and a window facing the office she'd just exited. It allowed her a good vantage point to see much of the garage. She could see a tall mechanic walking towards a car in the bay diagonal from her and if she leaned forward and to the left, she could just make out another mechanic working on a vehicle to the right of the sitting room. Neither was the one she'd seen outside. Out of the corner of her eye, she saw Tim still seated at his desk, watching her. Sam snatched up a magazine off the side table she was leaning over, sat back in her seat, and opened it to whatever page. It allowed her to watch the garage from under hooded eyes. Though she had no clue what she'd do if something happened. She could throw the Time magazine she was pretending to read and give him a paper cut. Then Sam remembered the pepper spray in her bag.

The shop was noisy. A drill. Drawback from an air compressor. An engine being turned over. Tim left the office and walked over to the tall, wide shouldered mechanic working on an old truck in the bay to the left. The man was huge and she couldn't help but think he'd be the perfect stand-in for the Friendly Giant. After they exchanged words, the Friendly Giant glanced her way.

Oh great, they're discussing me. Probably something along the line of *Please keep an eye on the crazy woman over there.* It was bad enough when those who knew her looked at her in sympathy. She could just imagine the looks she'd get now if word went around that she was touched in the head. Sam rolled her eyes at both men and went back to pretending to read her magazine as she continued to scan the garage.

Mike was nowhere to be seen, but she also hadn't seen a coffee mug sail through the air, so didn't take it as a bad sign. It was only after reading the same page for the third time that a foreign noise caught her attention, making her head snap up. It sounded like thumping, but she couldn't be sure. Nothing seemed amiss. The two mechanics were still there. The Friendly Giant was bent under the hood of an old Chevy to the far left. When she leaned forward and looked right, she could see the other mechanic was still working on the Volkswagen.

Sam sat back and stared at the magazine in her hands. Something about the mechanics bothered her. No, not both. Just the one. She leaned forward again to get a second look at the mechanic on the right. She remembered him having gray sprinkled in his dark hair and a heavier build. Although this mechanic was a similar height and hair color, he looked slimmer now and his hair was missing the gray.

Sam held her breath as she waited for him to raise his head. When he did, she recognized him as the mechanic she'd seen outside. Mike. He dipped his head to lean in the car's trunk again. The older mechanic, who'd been working on this car minutes ago, was nowhere in sight. Odd. Mike held a long screwdriver in one hand and a tire iron in the other. It was when he turned away from the car and starting striding to the other side of the garage that alarm bells went off in her head. He was heading straight for the Friendly Giant whose head was presently buried under the hood of the old Chevy. Mike looked like a man on a mission, and considering he held both tools like they were weapons, it didn't bode well.

Sensing a shift in mood, Buddy was already on his feet at attention. Sam held up her hand, palm down, and whispered, "Buddy, stay." Fur face sat back down.

Pepper spray in hand, she pushed the door open to the garage's bay area and headed towards the back of the Volkswagen on her right. Mike had his back to her, so he didn't see her leave the guest area and approach the car. She found the missing mechanic sprawled across the front seat. His head was a bloody, pulpy mess. Sam dragged her attention away from the horrifying sight back to Mike in time to see him disappear behind the Chevy. Her angle to the truck and its raised hood blocked her from seeing anything more.

That's when the owner of Timothy's Auto shop reappeared on the opposite side of the garage. He emerged through a side door at the center of the bay area. Unfortunately, he spotted her as opposed to Mike who was still concealed behind the open hood of the truck. Damn. He'd caught her sneaking around the garage bays, an area off limits to customers, with a can of pepper spray in hand.

"Excuse me? What do you think you're doing!" Tim demanded as he took a few steps towards her. Mike took advantage of the distraction and emerged from behind the hood. He had his right arm raised, the one gripping the tire iron, and bore down on Tim.

"Behind you!" Sam shouted to Tim.

Frenzied barking could be heard coming from the waiting room.

Tim either heeded her warning or caught the movement out of the corner of his eye because at the last second he turned towards Mike, lifting his right arm. Too late. The tire iron caught him on the temple. Fortunately, it looked like the worst of the blow deflected off his raised forearm.

She was already making a run at Mike, pepper spray raised high in her right hand, as Tim crumpled to the cement floor. The irritant connected with Mike's right eye, but he turned away too fast for her to reach his left. She had no alternative but to backpedal to get out of the tire iron's reach, which he swung in a wide arc towards her.

Her right heel caught the edge of a metal tie and she went down hard on her backside. She couldn't stop the momentum of her fall. Sharp pain radiated through her back and over the back of her head as they connected with the cement floor. For a split second she saw stars, but the approach of the tire iron hurtling towards her again chased them away. She attempted to roll left out of its path, but wasn't fast enough. The iron bit her hard in the right shoulder. The resulting agony eclipsed anything she'd experienced before. She cried out in pain.

She almost wept in relief when she heard a fierce growl come from behind, followed by a flash of white as something jumped over her. Buddy had somehow escaped the guest area. She heard Mike scream, followed by the sound of a heavy metal object hitting the cement floor.

Sam felt around for the pepper spray she'd dropped. Her left hand bumped into something that rolled. Her fingers followed it and folded around the cylindrical shape. Relieved to have found the canister, she forced herself to sit up, gritting her teeth through the sharp pain the movement caused. What took mere seconds felt like an eternity, but finally she made it upright again with the pepper spray extended ahead of her. She wasted no time pepper spraying his face again.

"You bitch!" Mike screamed in outrage. He rubbed at his eyes with his left arm as Buddy furiously tugged on his right arm to keep him off balance. Disoriented and half blind, Mike kept trying to stand, but was pulled back down by Buddy again and again. His disorientation wouldn't last long. She knew if she wanted to keep the upper hand and survive this situation she had to work quickly.

Tim groaned. He lay a few feet to their left. She felt like groaning with him. Although her head and shoulder throbbed, she no longer saw stars. She got to her feet and sprayed the bastard in the face a third time as she walked past. Mike screamed more obscenities. She ignored him and grabbed a roll of electrical tape off the wall. While Buddy still had a hold of his right arm, she grabbed his left hand and spun the tape tight around one wrist and then tried to bind it to his other wrist but Mike resisted. Her right shoulder pulsed with pain with every movement, and she didn't have the strength in it to force them together.

"Stop resisting or I'll pepper spray you again." She threatened and after a few seconds he relented, allowing her to pull his arms together with the tape. Even with her bum shoulder she bound his wrists tight enough he gave her a satisfying grunt of pain.

"Ok Buddy, let go." Sam commanded. She had to repeat the command a little firmer a second time before he released Mike's arm. "Good boy."

"Get up", Sam commanded and waited as Mike struggled to stand. Obviously having trouble coping with the irritant in his eyes, he kept rubbing his face against his arms. She hoped it hurt like hell. He staggered as she led him to the guest area where she'd been sitting only minutes ago. It was an enclosed room with three windows, one door, seats, and a water cooler. There was only one access point, no obvious weapons, and she'd be able to keep an eye on him in here. Sam led him to a chair where he sat without saying a word. Grabbing her iPhone from her purse, she took a chair with her as she left and jammed it under the door's handle to prevent him from escaping. Then, she called the police. After confirming they were en route, she headed back to check on everyone else.

Tim was conscious and pushing himself up against the wall. She went to the mechanic she'd nicknamed the Friendly Giant, who'd been working under the hood of the truck to her left. He was lying unconscious on the ground with the long screwdriver Mike had been carrying sticking out of his right side. Sam felt his neck for a pulse. Upon finding a strong rhythm, she headed back to check on the older mechanic lying in the convertible.

She stopped when she reached the vehicle, taking a step back as she took in the scene. The damage done to his face made him unrecognizable. Although she knew her CPR and First Aid training were sorely inadequate for the severity of his wounds, she had to try to help him. Luckily, her training kicked in, overriding her instinct to get as far away from the poor mechanic as she could, and started going through the motions of helping. She felt his neck for a pulse, but couldn't find one. There was so much blood and tissue damage, what was once a face was now just a bloody mass. After locating the area where his mouth should be but detecting no breath, Sam used her fingers to clear away any obstructions that might block his airway. She gave up when she figured out she was just pushing teeth aside, a few of which fell out. Upon closer examination, she made out indentations around the side and top of his head. Mike hadn't just broken the mechanic's face, he'd beat on his entire head. That's when she noticed a portion of his skull caved in on the left side. There would be no coming back from that.

Until then, Sam had been working on adrenaline. But now that the immediate threat had passed, the horror of it all filtered through into her consciousness. She stared at the blood on her hands, then back at what remained of the older mechanic after Mike had gotten through with him. Without warning, her stomach churned violently. She barely had time to step away from the seat and clear the car to vomit what was left of her breakfast on the garage floor. She stayed like that for a few minutes, head down in a partial crouch to allow her stomach to settle and the buzzing in her ears to stop. It was only when she felt a hand on her shoulder, which she jerked away from, did she realize how scared she really was. The hand belonged to Tim and saw her fear mirrored in his face. The sharp pain her straightening caused her shoulder made her grimace.

He must have said something when he approached, because he was looking at her expectantly. Not getting a response from her, he repeated the question.

"Where's the mechanic you saw outside — Mike?" Tim asked, eyes wide with fear and perhaps a little panic.

"I locked him in the guest area," Sam responded, glancing there. Only part of the guest area was visible from where they stood, and Mike was nowhere in sight.

They approached the door to the sitting area together. Once the interior was in full view, she simply stared as she tried to make sense of the scene before her. She'd left Mike sitting with his hands tied in front of him in a locked room. The door was still shut, with the chair wedged under the handle. But he was no longer sitting on a chair. He was hanging. From the ceiling. Twitching.

Just hangin out, she thought wildly and almost laughed, but stopped herself. *Oh, that's not good.* Knowing the inappropriate joke must be a sign of shock or hysteria.

Tim pushed aside the chair wedged under the handle, swung open the door, and ran into the room. Sam followed close behind. He grabbed Mike's upper legs to support his weight. The makeshift noose wasn't made of rope. It was made of several thin, black, shiny plastic strands. The tape she'd bound his hands with? There was a small wad of it on the floor by the chair she'd sat him in. He must have wrapped the tape in loops over the ceiling support frame. It had twisted tight against his throat, and the only way that could have happened was if he'd stuck his head through the loop and spun himself. They'd never be able to remove the tape from his neck in time to save him without cutting it.

They both must have come to the same conclusion because even as Sam ran for his office, Tim was shouting, "The scissors are in the top right-hand drawer!"

Buddy, who'd been sitting outside the guest area, followed her into Tim's office.

"Sit, Buddy!" Sam said as she rounded the desk and frantically opened drawers. Upon finding the scissors, Sam yelled a "Stay boy" at him, who was still sitting on his haunches by the desk, before closing the office door behind her. She didn't want Buddy loose in the garage when the cops arrived. A young, overzealous cop amid this carnage might mistake him as a threat.

Scissors in hand, Sam flew through the guest room door, grabbed the toppled chair at Tim's feet, jumped up on it and cut the tape above Mike's head. Once they lowered him to the ground, she worked at cutting away the many layers of tape around his neck. It was much harder to do because of how tightly wound it was against his throat. Even after cutting away several layers of his makeshift noose, he still wasn't breathing. And the purple hue to Mike's lips was a concern. More than a little panicked, Sam picked up her speed.

The swoosh of the door swinging open behind them signaled someone's entrance into the guest area. Focussed on trying to remove the rest of the plastic noose restricting Mike's airway, she paid little heed to the newcomers until the shouting started. Even then, it took a moment for her to comprehend that the police were actually shouting at her.

"I repeat, put the weapon down now!"

Looking up, Sam saw several police officers surrounding

them with their guns. On her. *Jesus, they think I'm the threat.*

That's when she noticed the blood on her hands and shirt from when she'd tried to help the other dead mechanic. And whether the blood on Mike's throat was from transference or a small nick in his skin mattered little to the officers pointing their guns at her. Sam dropped the scissors.

Without warning, hands shoved her from behind, sending her sprawling onto the thinly carpeted cement floor, and smacking her chin. Her left arm took the brunt of the downward impact. Something heavy pressed down on her back, making it difficult to breathe. She couldn't help but wonder how many of them were leaning their full weight on her. Tim was shouting at them to stop. A frenzy of barking came from Tim's office and Sam counted her lucky stars she'd had the forethought to shut Buddy in there. Although the massive weight at her back didn't completely disappear, it let up slightly when she started to choke under it.

Although a little pissed about the strong-arming, she couldn't really blame them either. Because of her father, Sam understood the use of force better than most. Split-second decisions had to be made based on what they saw upon entering a scene. From their viewpoint, some woman covered in blood was holding a lethal weapon to a prone man's bleeding throat. Not a good look.

Up to now, things were pretty quiet until one overzealous officer cuffed her hands behind her back by yanking her right wrist back and upwards. Her pain-filled scream rending the air eclipsed the sickeningly loud pop of her injured right shoulder. Everything blurred as the agony in her shoulder overwhelmed her. She could hear people around her arguing, but their words were lost on her. The next thing she knew, she was up on her knees with her hands cuffed in front. Her gaze swept down to her right shoulder, now jutting out at an odd angle. She averted her gaze to avoid looking at it. To say her shoulder didn't feel right was an understatement.

A hand took a hold of her arm, forced her to stand and move forwards. The movement brought with it pain, but she bit back on it. At the door, Sam stumbled, but the officer's grip on her arm and the back of her neck steadied her, preventing her from going down. The officer guided Sam in to the garage. As they passed Tim's office, a snarl drew her attention. Buddy had his hackles up, his focus trained on the officer escorting her.

"He really doesn't like you," Sam murmured as she started turning her head towards her police escort. The only response she got was a tightening of his grip on the right side of her neck. A finger dug in close to her injury causing a shot of white hot pain down her arm. She sucked in a pain filled breath but didn't give him the satisfaction of crying out. Sam agreed with her pup's assessment. This officer was a real jerk.

Most of the local police and OPP officers they passed barely glanced her way, and the few that saw her didn't recognize who she was. That didn't surprise her. The Ontario Provincial Police officers, or OPP for short, were only called in when Murphy found itself shorthanded, so most wouldn't know she was the Chief's daughter. As for the local cops, a lot of them looked like newer recruits and she hadn't hung out at the police station in years. Besides, at some point she'd lost her hair clip, so her hair hung like a curtain hiding her features. They walked past a cop and two medics who were working on the Friendly Giant lying in

85

front of the Chevy. He still had the screwdriver sticking out of his side. When they emerged from the garage, at least a dozen police cruisers and emergency vehicles were parked haphazardly along the road, blocking any access from the street. The officer was guiding her toward the closest cruiser parked by a cluster of community mailboxes.

"Do you know where Chief Turner is?" Sam asked, turning to look back at the officer, but stopped midway when the pain reminded her to stop twisting. When only silence met her question, she tried again, but a little louder. "Can you take me to my father, Chief Turner? Or at least tell him I'm here?"

They'd reached the cruiser, and the officer already had the back door open. The painful pressure on her shoulder disappeared now that he'd released his hold on her neck. Without warning, a hand grabbed her by the throat and slammed her back against a wall. The ugly familiarity of this situation made her panic, but the unyielding hand at her throat didn't allow an effective resistance. The more she struggled, the more his grip tightened around her windpipe until her breath was coming out in a wheeze. Because of the location of the cruiser, the height of the back door, and the way he'd positioned her, no one would see there was a struggle going on. To her disgust she was, once again, stuck in her tormentor's web and helpless to do anything about it.

Déjà Vu hit her hard especially when his breath grazed her ear.

"Did you miss me, Sam? Hmm... you must have. Otherwise, why come looking for me?" Charlie chuckled and twisted the cuffs, making her shoulder burn. Sam clenched her jaw, but didn't utter a sound. "I'm touched. I have to dash, but we must catch up soon. Oh, and before I forget, I still owe you something."

A flash of silver caught the light as his right hand swung down and stabbed something into her upper thigh. Her scream came out as a hiss of air in a longer wheeze.

Dragged back kicking and screaming to five years ago when Charlie had her pinned much like now, only then it was a knife protruding from her abdomen. The flash of silver was a fork now buried so deep in her thigh the tines weren't visible, but the handle's design was familiar. Unable to bear the sight of the fork sticking out of her thigh, Sam ignored the pain, grabbed its handle and tugged. Once it pulled clear, the fork slipped from her numb fingers, the metallic tang echoing on the pavement.

Her tenuous hold over the panic threatening to bubble over slipped. Gasping, her chest hurt from drawing in too little air. That's when she felt more than heard him chuckling against the back of her neck. The small callous act pissed her off so much it drew her attention away from her panic and fear to the swell of anger and hate she had for Charlie. Her rage grew with each breath he brushed across her skin. She was no longer hyperventilating.

"Tsk, tsk, tsk Sam. There is so much anger and hostility in that head of yours. I could help you direct it to a more... productive and satisfying end, you know." And with that threat hanging in the air, Charlie shoved her into the backseat of the cruiser. Sam landed on her wounded shoulder and heard more than felt her head smack against the far door. Only pain accompanied her into the dark.

Chapter 7

Hospital Pain

S am woke with a start. The pain registered first. In her shoulder. Back of her head. On her backside. At her temple. Upper thigh. On her chin. The fact she was lying in a hospital bed registered next. She slowly scanned the room, half expecting Charlie to pop out, but the only things in the room were two empty hospital beds and a sheet drawn across the third. Maybe she'd dreamed the last crazy bit about Charlie arresting her.

The ache in her right shoulder drew her gaze down to the right. They immobilized her arm and shoulder in a sling. *Well, that's not good,* she thought. She touched the back of her head, wincing when she found the tender spot, the result of her head smacking against the cement floor of the garage. She wiggled her feet, moved her legs, moved her left arm, her wrist, and wiggled all ten digits. The ache in her upper right thigh, and the tenderness on her backside and her knees from hitting the cement floor smarted, but overall nothing unbearable.

She looked down at her left thigh again in apprehension. Sam lifted the sheet away and pulled the hospital robe aside to reveal the dressing. She grasped the edge of the bandage, intending to pull it off, but hesitated when she heard voices approaching. Instead, she pulled the sheet back up to cover her thighs.

Her father and a woman she didn't recognize stepped into her room. The stranger was tall, with dark eyes and dark hair tied back in a tight bun making her angular face and features more severe. Still, the look worked for her. She walked with an air of authority, so likely an officer of some sort. Her father's face lit up with relief upon seeing her.

"Perhaps we should have named you Trouble instead of Samantha since you always seem to find it," Chief Turner said as he approached her bed and gave Sam's left hand an affectionate squeeze. His eyes looked a little shiny, but it may have been a trick of the light.

"Jeez, thanks." She grumbled, but did her best to return his smile.

"I'm just glad you're okay, Sam." His voice sounded a little gruff. "They found you passed out in the back of a police cruiser. You took a good blow to the head." He paused, waiting for Sam to nod her understanding before continuing. "Your right shoulder is dislocated. The doctors reset it but it looks like you'll need physio because it's a bad tear. There's another contusion on your temple. And the strangest thing, they found what they think is a fork wound in your upper thigh..."

So it hadn't been a dream at all. Charlie had been there, up close and personal, disguised as an OPP officer. Fuck.

"... do you remember when that happened?" Chief Turner asked, but Sam had no clue what he was asking about now.

"Sorry. When what happened?"

"The fork wound. We figure it must have happened

when you were fighting with that mechanic, Mike. According to the angle of the puncture, the person who stabbed you must have come from behind or above you. Did he get behind you at some point?" Sam didn't know what to say because the truth was too unbelievable, even for her. So she nodded, hoping that would be the end of the questions concerning the fork.

"Jesus Sam, you're lucky. I taught you better than that. You could have got yourself killed with that kind of mistake." Again, her dad looked worried.

"I'm fine." Sam replied, shutting down further discussion. He looked like he wanted to say more, but nodded before turning to the woman standing beside him.

"This is the incoming Chief of Police, Superintendent Kabowski. She's in charge of the murder investigation and has a few questions for you. They have asked me to step out. Do you feel up to answering them?" Sam was still reeling from everything that had just happened so answering questions was the last thing she wanted to do. However, it wouldn't look good if the police chief's daughter refused to cooperate in an investigation.

After a few more seconds of silence passed, Superintendent Kabowski's eyebrow popped up as if to ask: *Why are you stalling?* With little choice in the matter, Sam nodded her consent. He gave her hand another quick squeeze before leaving the room. Kabowski already had a pen and pad of paper at the ready.

"Although this is an informal interview, anything said here can still be used as evidence if a crime has been committed. Would you like a lawyer present?" Sam's eyebrows shot up at that last question, but after a beat shook her head. She had nothing to hide and the sooner she finished with the formalities, the closer she'd be to getting the hell out of Murphy.

Kabowski nodded and continued. "The owner of Timothy's Auto filled us in on some of it, but since he was unconscious for a time, he thought you'd be able to fill us in on the rest. Can you tell me what happened?"

"Wait... how are the others doing?" Sam asked.

"Tim is fine. Just a mild concussion, and a bruised forearm. The big fella named Toni who was stabbed with a screwdriver is still in surgery. Doctors said his chances are good. The others are dead."

Kabowski stated it in such a blunt, matter-of-fact manner that Sam winced. She didn't know these men from Joe, but she still grieved for what happened to them. None of them should have died. She knew it, and Kabowski knew it.

"So Mike died?"

"Yes. Friend of yours?" Superintendent Kabowski asked, eyes narrowing ever so slightly.

"No. I'd never met him before today." Kabowski was analyzing her responses, looking for tells that she might be lying. It would be hard for anyone to understand how she knew something bad was about to go down at the shop. She'd have to keep the explanation simple, but before getting into what would undoubtedly be a long conversation, she had to find out who had Buddy.

"What about Buddy, my dog?"

"He's at the station. Seems like a pretty dog-friendly environment. They were more than happy to keep him for you."

Sam sighed. Unfortunately, because of her warning to Tim, she'd have to fess up about why she'd decided to get the oil change. She knew if she lied to them and got caught in the lie, she'd look suspicious, so she had to choose her words carefully. The reality of what had happened was so farfetched she had no intention of telling Kabowski everything.

"I was heading to the station to drop off some photos for my father's retirement party. When I stopped at the stoplight at Erie and Hickory, I noticed a mechanic from Timothy's Auto talking to someone I thought I recognized. I circled the block to get another look, but by the time I returned he'd gone. I got an oil change, figuring it might give me the opportunity to talk to the mechanic. After I pulled in, Tim said it would be a thirty-minute wait. When I asked after the mechanic outside, Tim told me his name was Mike but that he needed to talk to him about something. So Buddy and I waited in the guest area. Tim left the office to talk to one of the other mechanics, Toni I think you called him. Not sure where Tim disappeared to after that. I saw the older mechanic working on the Volkswagen.

"A few minutes later I heard thumping noises, but when I looked over again, I saw a mechanic leaning into the trunk of the car. I thought it was the older mechanic at first, but after I took another look I saw it was the one I'd seen chatting outside, Mike. Then he left the car and strode across the garage holding a long screwdriver and a tire iron. Something about Mike's behavior bothered me, so that and the fact the older mechanic was missing made me want to investigate. I grabbed my pepper spray and headed for the car he'd just left. I found the older mechanic lying in the front seat. His face and head were a mess. I looked back in time to see Mike disappear behind the hood of the truck where the other mechanic, Toni, had been, but I didn't see or hear anything.

"I started walking towards them when Tim came

through the side door and yelled at me. Mike took advantage of the distraction and ran at him with the tire iron. I shouted a warning to Tim, but Mike was closer and hit him over the head before Tim had much of a chance to react. I'd already started running at Mike and peppered him, but he turned his face away avoiding most of the spray. The next thing I know I'm dodging a tire iron, but in the process I tripped and fell backwards, smacking my head on the floor. I must have let go of the pepper spray at that point, because it was no longer in my hand. Mike swung the tire iron a second time and caught me on the right shoulder. Buddy somehow escaped the guest area because the next thing I saw was a flash of white fur jumping over me to get at Mike. I finally located my pepper spray and sprayed Mike full in the face this time.

"While he was otherwise engaged, I looked around for something to tie him up with and found some electrical tape, which I bound his hands with. I then confined him to the guest area by wedging a chair under the doorknob so he couldn't escape. Then, I called the police. Tim was already stirring, so I checked on Toni, who I found with a screwdriver sticking out of his side but with a strong pulse. So, I went to check on the older mechanic lying in the other car. I couldn't find a pulse or heard any breath sounds. I tried to clear his airway in case it was blocked, but eventually gave up. That poor man—" Sam shuddered as she recalled the obliterated face of the older mechanic. "—and then I threw up. Shortly after that, Tim came over and asked after Mike. We found him hanging from electrical tape in the guest area, so Tim held him up by his legs while I went to get the scissors from his office. I cut Mike down and was cutting away the tape twisted around his neck when the police arrived. They told me to drop my weapon, so I dropped the scissors." With the amount of detail she gave, there should be no doubt Sam was telling the truth.

There was a long pause as Kabowski furiously scribbled down what she'd just heard.

"So when did he stab you in the leg?" Kabowski asked. When she got no response, Kabowski looked up from her notepad, eyes narrowed. "You told your dad that Mike got behind you and stabbed you in the thigh. When did he get behind you and do this?"

Sam sighed. Already caught in a lie, she covered it as best she could.

"Actually, I only agreed with what my dad said. I never said Mike got behind me. Mike was above me after I fell back and hit my head. That's when he stabbed me with the fork."

"That's a pretty big detail to leave out of your story." Kabowski deliberately used the word story as opposed to statement insinuating Sam was weaving a pleasant tale for their benefit.

Even though she knew she could take whatever this bitch dished out, she still felt the tension tighten the muscles in her neck and shoulders and forced herself to relax.

"So he came at you with a tire iron, at which point you fell backwards and hit your head. He then stabbed you with a fork and then hit you in the shoulder with the tire iron."

Sam nodded. The fewer words she said the better.

"Why?"

"Excuse me?"

"Why did he bother with a fork?" Kabowski asked as she tilted her head. The movement reminded Sam of an owl. A hostile, intelligent, bitchy owl. Right then, Sam hated owls.

"How would I know wh—"

"Ok then, where did he get the fork from?" Sam shrugged, but Kabowski pressed on. "You watched him. You were right there for the whole thing, by your own admission, tracking his movements. Did he pick it up off the shop floor? Did he take it out of his pocket? Did he start eating pie in the middle of the attack?"

Sam felt her face grow hot with anger, but there was little she could say.

"I think it's interesting that your retelling of the events from today was so detailed, yet you didn't mention the fork once. You got stabbed with the bloody thing, but not a word about the incident. I also think it's strange that he'd bother using a fork when he still had the tire iron in his hand. I mean, a tire iron would have incapacitated, but a fork?" Kabowski continued to stare at her but Sam remained closed. It felt like their stare down lasted an eternity, but must have been less than a minute. Kabowski dropped her gaze to the notepad again.

"Another thing—" Superintendent Kabowski said, flipping through her notes before pausing on a page. "You said you saw Mike talking to someone you recognized, but when you came back around, the guy was no longer there and that's when you got an oil change." She looked up, her gaze assessing, before she added, "Why didn't you just approach Mike and ask him about the other guy while he was still on his break?"

"I didn't know him. And he looked—" *Angry, unpredictable, a little crazed, like he was about to go on a rampage,* was what she was thinking but instead said. "tense. So I got an oil change in the hopes I'd get the chance to talk to him in the shop."

The Superintendent nodded as if understanding what

Sam was saying, but she knew better than to allow herself to be lulled into a false sense of security. "You didn't approach him because you thought he looked 'tense', yet according to the warning you gave Tim, you thought Mike was much more upset than that, right? And I quote, 'You have to be careful and watch out for anything odd. I have a really bad feeling.' Can you explain what you meant by that?"

Sam almost groaned aloud. When she responded, she kept her face and tone as neutral as possible.

"What I meant was exactly what I said, nothing more or less."

"But you said you didn't know Mike, so I assume that means you'd never met him before today?"

"That's correct."

"Yet you thought something bad would happen just by glimpsing some random guy you say you didn't know. And it so happens that something terrible did happen. That's quite the coincidence, don't you think?" Kabowski pressed.

Sam returned her stare, but said nothing.

"So your bad feeling compelled you to get an oil change." Kabowski paused for effect, no doubt to emphasize how ridiculous the statement sounded before continuing. "I, too, have had feelings before... like it's a bad idea to eat that extra hotdog or it's a bad idea to have that last drink. But I've never had a bad feeling that led to a murder."

"Neither have I, hence why I felt compelled to get an oil change when I didn't need one."

Kabowski nodded in understanding. "Uh-huh. So, do you believe yourself to be a psychic, Ms. Turner?"

Sam didn't respond to her question, feeling it didn't require an answer, but the Superintendent continued to stare at her expectantly.

"Ms. Turner..."

"Yes."

"Can you answer the question, please?"

"No, I don't believe I am a psychic, nor do I believe in psychic ability."

"So this 'bad' feeling you had, which motivated you to get your oil changed, was...?"

This time, Sam didn't hesitate with her response. "Instinct."

"Ah. Well, that's quite the talent you have there then. Being able to sniff out a killer before they act. Correct me if I'm wrong, but isn't that the reason you stabbed a guy named Charlie in the eye with a fork five years ago?" Superintendent Kabowski flipped through her notes again and read from the page, "Ms. Turner stated she stabbed the suspect named Charlie in the right eye because she felt threatened. That she believed he intended to kill her. Hmm. And now, five years later, you get stabbed in the thigh with a fork during your fight with Mike." She directed a hard stare at Sam as she asked. "So again I ask you, why do you think Mike would bother with a fork when he already had access to many better, more lethal tools in the shop, including the one he held in his hand?"

Sam could feel her heart racing and her ire increasing. She was being treated like a suspect as opposed to a victim, and it wasn't sitting well with her. What she wanted to do was punch Superintendent Ka-Bitch in the mouth, but knew that was probably what the cop wanted. A nice neat arrest and perhaps even pin accessory to murder to show how hard they're working for the taxpayers in keeping the streets safe. She understood their frustration and was sure there was pressure on them to find anyone else involved. However, if they intended on arresting her, they'd have to work much harder for it. She didn't bother to confirm or deny the last statement because she didn't need to. The Superintendent had her statement written right there in front of her.

Having figured out she wouldn't get a response from Sam, the Superintendent continued. "Some things about your story don't add up. I thought you stated the reason you went in was to find out who Mike was talking to?" The Superintendent scanned her page again, nodded as if confirming it to herself, and looked back to Sam.

Cornered. Now Sam had to fess up as to whom she thought was talking to Mike. She'd wanted to avoid bringing up Charlie in this conversation because no matter what she said, she knew it would sound suspicious. Feelings and intuition were not good reasons to get involved in a homicide, so anything she said would put her on shaky ground, but now it seemed unavoidable.

"Fine. I thought the man Mike was talking to was Charlie, but I wasn't a hundred percent sure. I went back to confirm it, but he'd gone by then. If I saw anyone talking with Charlie, I'd be concerned." Sam muttered and laid her head back on the pillow only to wince and raise it again when it came into contact with the wound on the back of her head. The Superintendent looked like she was about to ask Sam to explain, but she beat her to it. "Charlie has a way of talking to you. He can be very persuasive and when he pursues you, he is... relentless. I knew the moment I met him he was—" Sam racked her brain for a descriptor, but nothing came to mind. "—evil. I knew it wasn't good, whatever was going on." Though it really was the best word to describe Charlie, Sam knew no one else would understand unless they were unlucky enough to meet him. *Pure. Fucking. Evil.*

"You think it was this 'evil' Charlie again? That he just

reappeared here; five years after the fact, on the same weekend you roll back in to town, standing in front of a shop at the same time you happen to drive past. Wow. That is quite the coincidence, Ms. Turner."

"You don't have to pause for effect. I know how ridiculous it sounds." Sam sighed, leaned back again and winced once again when her wound hit the pillow.

"Fine. Let's say in this scenario that Charlie came back. Are you suggesting he could talk Mike into... what? Killing everyone in the garage?" The Superintendent looked at Sam for the longest time and Sam returned her stare. Sam had nothing more she could add to the conversation, nor would she play Kabowski's game. After a few seconds of silence in which she could practically feel Kabowski's stare burn a hole in her skull, she heard her close the notepad with a resounding snap. "Isn't it true you've cried wolf a few times in the last five years? And each time you were wrong?"

Sam had called the cops twice when she'd thought she'd seen Charlie, but both times led nowhere. By the time officers responded to the scene, he was long gone. "It was twice, and the responders didn't get there in time. The person I thought was Charlie was long gone by the time they arrived."

"The person you thought was Charlie? According to your statements, you were sure it was him both times, correct?"

Sam nodded.

"Then why did you say 'thought'?" Sam didn't have a response, not that it would have mattered if she had. She realized then that Kabowski was here to do one thing and one thing alone, discredit her. Cops didn't like loose ends and Sam was a very loose end. The smartest thing she could do was to stop talking.

"Wow, you must be so disappointed in us, then. I mean, according to you, we've dropped the ball. What? I guess this makes it four times now." Kabowski let the point sink in before continuing. "The cold hard facts are that no one but you saw Charlie that night and according to my records, no one has seen him since. Don't you think that's odd since, according to your statement, he has platinum blonde hair and is likely blind in his left eye because of the injury he sustained from you that night? I mean, a guy like that would be hard to miss, especially in a small town like Murphy. A one-eyed, platinum blonde, six foot, sprinter, with abs like Adonis?"

Sam knew what Superintendent Kabowski was trying to do, and unfortunately it was working. She could feel her face flush with anger. No one had ever said it to her face before, probably because she was the chief's kid, but she knew that's what many thought. That likely included her father. He wanted to believe her, but the facts were lined up against her. And if they couldn't rely on her as a credible witness, then what else from her statement about today's incident or from five years ago was reliable? The problem was that there were no fingerprints on the knife he'd used to stab her with; the trajectory of the knife according to her wounds was such that, although improbable, they could have been self-inflicted; and there were no witnesses to corroborate the attack.

She exhaled to calm down before answering.

"First, I never said he had abs like Adonis. I believe my exact words in my original statement five years ago stated he was incredibly strong and fit. And believe me I know how it sounds. Why do you think I didn't mention the fact I thought it was Charlie I saw talking to Mike beforehand? All I can tell you is what I saw and what motivated me to get the oil change. And I have no clue why no one but me has ever seen Charlie." Sam rubbed her forehead in aggravation. "Maybe most people don't survive seeing Charlie. Or perhaps he's too smart to be caught in public. I don't know." They both knew she was reaching, but she didn't have a better explanation and she much preferred this one to the alternative, which was that she was crazy.

"Or maybe he's a ghost," Kabowski said, the sarcasm dripping off every word. Sam could have killed her. Oh, she did not like this woman at all, and Kabowski had made it clear the feeling was mutual. At the very least, Kabowski didn't trust her, and at the worst, she would try to pin part of the responsibility of what happened at the auto shop on Sam.

"Last thing I need you to do is sign this statement stating you will not talk to the press until after we've notified the victims' next of kin." She held out the clipboard, which had what looked like a standard nondisclosure form attached to it, and handed her the pen. Sam took them, glanced over the document, and signed it with her left hand.

"I thought you were right-handed." Another test. The Superintendent had her sign it to see her handedness. And it confirmed they considered her either an unreliable witness at best, or a suspect at worst. Great.

Sam handed back the clipboard with only the slightest pause. "I'm ambidextrous. When I was seven, I broke my right arm in two places so had to learn to use my left hand. I'm naturally right-handed but am pretty good with my left too." Now she wished she'd said yes to a lawyer when asked.

"Hmm. Ok Ms. Turner, I think that's it for now. But

rest assured I will want to talk to you again soon. Anything else you'd like to mention before I leave?"

"No," Sam replied, but thought. *Even if I had more to say I wouldn't tell this witch hunter.*

"Because it looks like you have bruising around your windpipe and there's nothing in your statement to explain an injury like that. Did Mike do that?"

Sam couldn't hide the surprise from her face, but just as quickly shuttered it. Considering the last five minutes of their conversation, she would not be volunteering any more information about Charlie to her.

"No," was the only answer she gave again.

"Well then, I see this conversation has come to its natural end. Here's my card in case you think of anything else. I'll be in touch." And with that, Superintendent Kabowski turned on her heel and exited the hospital room.

Grateful she was alone again, Sam laid back, careful to avoid her head wound, and tried to relax. Her right shoulder ached, and the tension in her back made it worse. Or perhaps the pain meds were wearing off. Either way, she was not comfortable.

Very aware of the throbbing pain in her leg where she'd been tined by a fork, Sam drew back the sheet to expose her upper thighs and peeled back the bandage to reveal the wound. There was no mistaking what had caused the four evenly spaced puncture marks. The surrounding skin was shiny from a topical antiseptic balm and the wound looked angry. *But who could blame my leg for being angry after being stabbed with a fork?* The fact she was putting human emotions on her leg made her laugh a little.

"What's so funny?" a voice asked as the curtain next to her bed drew back. Tim, also sporting a hospital gown, was sitting on the neighboring bed.

Startled, Sam jumped and immediately regretted it. The sharp pain shooting through her shoulder and head made her want to throw up. She swallowed hard, closed her eyes and breathed deep to try to clear the nausea threatening to embarrass her.

"I'm so sorry. I see now I should have done that differently. I was feeling like a peeping Tom but didn't know how to make myself known without startling you. Do you want some water? Or a nurse?"

Sam shook her head, but kept her eyes closed. After a few more seconds passed, she whispered, "Just... give me a sec." She heard movement from the bed and the soft patting of feet as he walked around the room.

"I'm putting a glass of water in your hand."

As soon as she felt the cool glass in her hand, she raised it to her lips and swallowed. It seemed to do the trick, and she felt better moments after drinking the cool liquid. Sam opened her eyes expecting to see the ceiling but found Tim's concerned face hovering over her mere inches from her face. She started in surprise. Again.

"Jesus, I can't believe you did it again. You should wear a bell or something." Sam grumbled after a moment, eyeing him with irritation as he straightened up.

"Maybe you can get me one." Tim stated, his expression a combination of regret and maybe a little amusement. "Listen, I am sorry about Superintendent Kabowski. I didn't know what to tell her when she asked what happened other than the truth."

"So you heard everything."

Tim nodded.

"Well, I have nothing to hide. It's just hard to explain something you don't understand yourself." She paused before adding. "I'm so sorry about your colleagues."

Tim's expression turned raw for a moment before he shuttered it. The display of emotion was fleeting, but it touched her. "Did you have any idea what would happen? I know you said you didn't to Kabowski but—" Tim let the unfinished sentence hang there.

"No. I didn't know anything would happen for certain. I'd had a similar feeling when Charlie first appeared on my dad's lawn and then he came through the sunroom screen after me." Sam paused for a moment unsure if she should ask her next question or not. "Did you have any inkling Mike might be capable of doing what he did?"

"God, no! He had personal problems, but I've never known him to be violent. Just before he came to work, his wife Paula, my sister, took the kids to our parents' for a break. He had a gambling addiction, which was supposedly under control, but he must have relapsed. He lost all their money. And he'd been missing a lot of work. I'd planned on talking to him about it just before he—" Tim trailed off as he shook his head.

"Your brother-in-law? Jesus, I'm sorry, Tim." Sam didn't know what else to say. His brother-in-law just went postal in his own shop. And now his sister was a widow. Tim dropped his gaze and rubbed the back of his neck. Sighing, he brought his gaze back up to Sam's.

"I feel bad for poor Janet." He must have caught her questioning expression, because he explained, "Sorry. Janet is Ralph's wife, the other mechanic who died."

The other mechanic with the caved in face. Sam shivered. "What he did to Ralph didn't suggest anger but unadulterated rage."

Tim remained silent for a minute then admitted, "They had their moments, but it always blew over. Then today they argued, and it got tense. Had I thought—" Tim shook

104

his head. "What happened today was not the Mike I knew. Thank God Gertie took the day off work."

"Gertie?" Sam asked.

"Our receptionist, but don't let the title fool you. She does everything except fix the cars and she can be shrewd when needed. She would have confronted Mike right off the bat and likely got herself killed."

Sam nodded in understanding. Tim clearly cared for his employees and would likely rack his brain from now until kingdom come on how he should have been able to prevent this from happening.

"So this Charlie guy tried to kill you five years ago?"

Sam nodded.

"And you saw him talking to Mike just before everything started?"

"As I told Kabowski I thought so, but by the time I returned he'd disappeared."

Tim nodded and said, "I guess we'll never find out, since Mike's the only one who could have told us that. Jesus, Paula's gonna be a wreck."

Tim touched his right temple where he'd been clocked as he looked down at her lap. When he didn't look away after a few moments, she looked down at what fascinated him so. His gaze had settled on her mysterious thigh injury where a fair amount of skin was on display as well. Sam blushed a little and pulled the sheet back up to cover her thighs.

"Sorry I... is that the fork wound Kabowski asked about? Mike did that?" She didn't want to lie more than she had to. And for whatever reason, it seemed important not to lie to Tim. So instead, she changed his focus. She wanted to find out what he thought of her OPP escort, anyway.

"Did you get a good look at the officer who took me from the guest area?"

"Some young asshole cop. I couldn't believe he put his full weight on your back and then twisted your bad shoulder. He may have even kneed you once. I swear if I hadn't been held back I would have decked him." Tim gritted his teeth as he recalled the events.

"Platinum blond, athletic build, boy next door features and blue eyes?"

"Well, I didn't get a look at his eyes and can't say for sure he had boy next door features but everything else sounds about right. Why? You know him?"

Sam turned quiet as she processed everything. Tim's testimony confirmed she wasn't crazy. Charlie had waltzed into the thick of it, impersonated a cop, played with Sam and waltzed back out with no one but her being the wiser. *Oh, he was good.* Sam's stomach twisted. She swallowed hard, refusing to allow any of its contents freedom. Tim searched her face like he wanted to say something. The nausea passed, allowing her to divert the conversation before he questioned her further.

"Well, it's a good thing you didn't go after him. He was aggressive enough he may have shot you just for interfering." Tim would take what she said as a joke, but she knew better. Charlie would have enjoyed killing Tim.

A few seconds of silence passed before Sam noticed Tim's shoulders shaking. The man was chuckling, and it pissed her off. She knew her irritation had to be visible, but instead of shutting him up, it only made him laugh harder. Sam glowered at him.

Then she thought about everything they'd been through in the last twelve hours. Stalked by a killer who she took down with fur face, using a can of pepper spray, and some electrical tape. Then her arresting officer, who also happened to be the psycho that nearly killed her five years ago, dislocates her arm. And instead of getting thanked, she's treated like a suspect by her father's replacement as chief. Her body was one giant ache from head to foot; her forehead, back of her head, neck, shoulder and right arm, back, butt, thigh, knees, even her left foot she rolled when she tripped. And what surprised her most was the bloody fork wound hurt more than any other injury. That's when Sam laughed as well. Because the alternative, like crying or screaming, was not an option.

"When I caught you sneaking between those two cars armed with what looked like hairspray, my first thought—" Tim laughed.

"Let me guess... Oh god, there's a crazy lady on the loose in my garage?"

"No. My first thought was, 'Wow, great legs.' My second thought was, 'It's too bad because the woman is crazy.' And my third, although brief, thought because a tire iron was hurtling towards my head was, 'Oh shit, she was right and what the hell does she think she can do with a can of hairspray!'"

Tim must have caught her look of dismay. "I'm a guy! My natural instinct is to look at your legs before anything else, including any weapon you might be wielding."

Sam rolled her eyes. "I don't care if you were looking at my legs, my ass, or whatever. I grew up around the precinct, so I've heard and seen it all. But hairspray? Really? You think a police chief's daughter would resort to hairspray as a weapon against an armed killer?" Sam looked at him incredulously.

Tim put his hands up in placation. "I have no defense for myself. It was the first thing that popped into my head when I caught you skulking around. If it helps, I will never doubt your choice of weaponry again." Tim smiled. He paused before continuing, his voice taking on a more serious tone. "Anyway, thank you, Sam. Toni and I would not be around right now had you not gone with your gut. I promise I will listen next time you have a hinky feeling."

Many questioned what happened to her five years ago and her tête-à-tête with Superintendent Kabowski reconfirmed what she'd suspected all along, that most everyone, including the cops, believe she'd lied about what happened to her back then and Kabowski believed she was lying now. So although she'd never admit it, what Tim just said meant a lot.

"Now I have to get back to my room. Paula is bringing the kids so they can see their uncle Tim is alive and fine." Tim turned to leave but then swung back to her and asked, "Can you meet me for coffee? I'd like to talk to you again before you leave town."

"I'd like that." She wanted to talk to him alone where there wasn't the possibility of an extra pair of ears listening.

"You can call me at the shop. All the calls are being forwarded to me until the shop reopens. You're staying at Chief Turner's place?"

Sam nodded and with that Tim did a one-eighty and left. Sam had to choke back a laugh as Tim walked away, his bare white ass visible in the space between the gown edges, which flapped apart with each step. Obviously, Tim didn't embarrass easily.

Certain he'd gone, Sam's hand drifted up to touch the tender flesh at her throat, still sore from Charlie's chokehold. Needing to see it, Sam pulled the sheet back the rest of the way, swung her legs over, and slid off the bed into a standing position. She didn't get dizzy, a good sign in her books. Sam held on to the mobile I.V. stand with her left hand and walked gingerly to avoid jostling her right shoulder. Once in the bathroom, she switched on the light and looked up. Her shoulder length hair hid the worst of the bruising, leaving only a hint of it visible along her throat. Sam traced the slight discoloration along her windpipe back towards the much more tender, angry bruising at the side of her neck where his fingers dug in. Kabowski must have got a glimpse of it somehow... and that's when Sam remembered her brief attempt to lean back on the bed. The bump on the back of her head was so tender she lifted her head off the pillows again. The action must have shifted her hair, revealing the bruise to the cop.

The bruises were Charlie's calling card. Sam only hoped she'd be better prepared next time around. Yet even as she thought it, she knew how unrealistic it was. How could she ready herself for someone who was unpredictable, insanely bold, stupid strong, and had the unsettling ability to know what she was thinking before she acted on it? All in all, Charlie seemed more like a comic book super villain than a simple psychopath.

Superintendent Kabowski could question her until she was blue in the face, but Sam's answers would remain the same. If Sam saw Charlie talking to anyone, it could only mean bad news.

Chapter 8

The Chief's Turn

They released Sam from the hospital a day later under strict orders to leave her shoulder immobilized in the sling for a minimum of three weeks and then physiotherapy. When her dad came to pick her up, seeing Buddy barking at her from the backseat made her happy. Sad but true, she'd missed her mutt. A lot.

Upon entering the house, the first thing she saw were the yellow daisies on the dining room table along with coffee mugs, dessert plates and a platter of cookies waiting for them.

"Is there someone else here?" Sam asked, looking around and then behind her in case someone had followed them in.

"No. This is just for us." Her dad pulled out a seat at the table. "I figured you'd like a good cup of coffee and some chocolate chip cookies after suffering hospital food for a few days. Sit."

Sam obliged, figuring they'd sit in companionable silence for the next half an hour or so but then her father opened his mouth and started talking. He talked about the neighbors, who remained, who had moved away. He talked about work, who would retire next, and the changes that would happen because of his leaving. Her father lived and breathed his job, hence why his looming retirement felt so strange to her.

He'd never been a big talker, so to see him set the pace of the conversation in this fashion was... well... a little disturbing. The entire scene reminded her of when she used to sit and chat with her mom, but instead of coffee and cookies, they had tea and biscuits.

The longer he talked, the more aware she became that something was up because this wasn't her father. It was like he was skirting around the real topic he wanted to broach. She let it go on for a bit longer, but once the conversation turned to gossip, she stopped him.

"Ok, what's up? I know there's something on your mind." After a few moments of silence, she pressed on. "Just spill it. Your attempt at small talk is a little disconcerting." Sam softened her words with a smile.

His attempt at returning her smile looked pained. Something was definitely bothering him.

"I'm sorry Sam. I should have insisted on staying in the room when Superintendent Kabowski questioned you, but I never thought—" Sam hadn't told him anything about their conversation, so either he'd been listening in or someone told him Kabowski had raked her over hot coals. "I know she was rough on you. Calling you out about Charlie and questioning whether you lied—"

"Wait, how did you find that out?" Sam interrupted.

"Tim, the owner of Timothy's Auto. I stopped him in the hall at the hospital after Kabowski left, and he told me what happened. I didn't know she'd go after you like that."

Sam sighed, wishing Tim hadn't said anything. "You

can't protect me from everyone." Sam paused, debating on whether she even wanted to ask her next question. She should have asked him this years ago, but had been afraid of his answer all this time. "Dad... she mentioned some people thought I lied about what happened that night. Does that include you?"

He looked a little stricken by her question. "Sam, even when you were little, you weren't prone to exaggeration or telling tales like other kids your age. I pulled strings and had cops all over the region keeping an eye out for your attacker, but he never resurfaced." He shook his head, still looking miserable.

Sam nodded and paused before continuing on. She had broached this topic before, but he'd never been receptive and shut down the conversation before it even started. "I have another question for you, though. Remember the guy seen talking to Jess the night she died? Can you dig up his description again?"

"Sam, Jess committed suicide. I understand how hard that was for you to accept, but she did. She was still alive and cutting into her own leg when they found her. It's not a crime for someone to talk to her before she killed herself."

"But her fingers, most of them were broken on her left hand. That's not normal."

"There was no proof that whoever sat with Jess was the one that broke her fingers. There were people less than fifteen feet away from her the entire time, so she could have yelled for help or got up and left, but she didn't. And considering her abusive home life, there's no way to know for sure when that happened. Her mother even admitted to hitting Jess that night." Her father paused again, then said, "Besides, we never got a reliable description of her companion. The kid from the pizzeria told us the guy she was with was 'average' to all of our questions except for the fact he 'may' have had blond hair under his tuque. He also said they acted like a couple. I just don't think the kid was paying attention."

Sam shook her head. "Jess would have told me if she'd been seeing someone. And she wasn't suicidal. Depressed, yes, but she knew she only had to deal with Barbara for another year and then she'd have been free. She would have said something to me if she was contemplating suicide."

It was her dad's turn to shake his head. "That's not necessarily true. If she was depressed, she may not have said a word, especially if she was serious about ending her own life. But I know you know this already."

She couldn't deny the logic, but no matter what anyone said, Sam knew Jess's death was not a simple suicide. "Dad... this guy is something else. You don't understand how manipulative, brutal and predatory he can be. I thought perhaps my attack was a one-off, but I'm having a hard time believing that with what just happened." Chief Turner looked at her for a moment before answering.

"On the rare occasion I have met people who I know in my gut are guilty, but finding evidence to prove it is something completely different, especially since no one else saw him..." Chief Turner looked down at the table for a minute all the while drumming his fingers. When his drumming stopped, he looked back up at her, his expression resigned. "Do you honestly think the guy you saw standing outside talking to Mike was the man who attacked you?"

"Definitely."

"It was five years ago. Maybe you don't remember him as well as you thought..."

Sam looked him in the eye and said, "I'd bet my life on it. It was Charlie."

Chief Turner nodded, as if he'd known what her answer would be all along. "Ok then. I'll have my boys in blue keep a look out for anyone who fits Charlie's description. In the meantime, you stay out of trouble from now on. If you see anyone who looks like him, gimme a call and I'll make sure someone's there within five."

"I appreciate that, but you're officially retired next week. You won't be able to call the shots there anymore."

The outgoing Chief Turner nodded as if in agreement, but his next softly spoken words said something different. "They'd regret it if they didn't." And then he changed the topic. Sam thought perhaps she'd misheard him for a second. But no, he'd said it. Her pop was playing hardball and Sam had to smile.

* * *

Sam tapped her fingers on the laminate countertop and stared out the kitchen window at nothing as she waited for her morning dose of black gold to finish brewing. It was the third day after being released from the hospital and she was already climbing the walls. The last couple of days had been relaxing, uneventful, and downright boring. The boys in blue having confiscated her iPhone, there was only so much daytime T.V. a person could handle and Sam had hit her limit on her first day home. Even Buddy was getting antsy. Being let out in the backyard was a poor substitute for the runs she and Buddy were used to taking every morning. The icing on the cake was that running would be out of the question for at least the next twelve weeks because of her shoulder. That was a little depressing. Her boss had been understanding, but she had to head home within a couple of days and get back to her routine, minus the run that is.

Working for a busy advertising company gave her a steady paycheck, but it also meant her graphic designs were in high demand, so she didn't have the luxury of taking another week off.

The coffeemaker beeped, telling her the coffee was ready at the same moment the landline rang. Annoyed at the interruption to getting her morning fix, Sam answered the phone.

"What?"

"Someone hasn't had their morning coffee yet." She immediately recognized the laughing voice coming through the receiver as Tim, the half-naked wiseass from the hospital and owner of Timothy's Auto Shop.

"Yeah. I'm not human until after my first cup," Sam responded with about as much humor as a wet rag. *Tough.*

"Well, I called to ask if I could stop by with some lunch at noon, but perhaps I should call back in fifteen instead. After you've had a cup and sheathed your claws."

"I'm going a tad stir crazy here. I've already watched enough Maury Povich to last a lifetime. Lunch sounds good."

"Ah. Not a big fan of taking time off, huh?"

"Well, certainly not when it's in Murphy and having been told I have to take is easy."

"Not a fan of your home town either, huh?" Her silence was answer enough. "Wow, that's two for two. You do need coffee."

"Coffee makes me civil. See you at noon." Sam replied and hung up before Tim said another word. He made her nervous, which made her edge even edgier. She was starting to like Tim, but really she didn't want to. Not just because he was a local. But she still didn't feel ready to get involved with anyone after her last relationship disaster. Pushing away any further thought on the subject, she poured herself a cup of coffee and hugged it to her, smelling the aroma and sighing as she took her first sip.

* * *

It took a couple of days, but Chief Turner tracked down the only witness to Jess's alleged suicide, the kid who was working at the pizza shop that night. He didn't expect to learn much more from this interview. Perhaps if he asked the right questions, he might draw out details they either missed or seemed insignificant back then. Danny Owens now lived two towns over in Carling and worked as a chef at a local French gourmet restaurant.

The restaurant was long, narrow, and dark, making it look deceptively small. With the number of tables he counted in passing, it was obvious they could fit quite a few customers in the space. When he asked after Danny Owens, the girl wiping down tables near the front pointed towards the back where a slender, dark-haired man in chef whites stood at the counter. Now in his mid-twenties, Danny no longer resembled the scared, pimple faced kid he'd interviewed over a decade ago. He was dicing vegetables, tomatoes, it looked like. A variety of colorful fruit and vegetables peppered the surrounding counter. He looked up from his prep work as Chief Turner approached. Recognition registered on Danny's face, and he didn't seem happy about it.

Without a word, Danny put down the large chef knife, grabbed a towel to wipe his hands off and led the way through the restaurant kitchen, out the door marked Exit to the back alleyway. Once outside, he leaned against the graffiti covered red brick wall next to the door and pulled a pack of cigarettes from his pocket. After offering one to Chief Turner, which he refused, Danny pulled one from the pack and stuffed the rest back into his shirt. He stuck the cigarette in his mouth, lit it, and took a long drag. The entire time, Danny's hands shook ever so slightly. Chief Turner waited. As the seconds stretched into minutes, he wondered if Danny had recognized him from a decade ago, or if he thought the cops were here for another reason. Perhaps Danny read the Chief's growing impatience in his body language, because just when he was about to break the silence, Danny finally talked.

"I wondered how long it would take before someone asked me about that night again," he began. "I had nightmares for years afterwards. All that blood... it just kept running through my fingers regardless of the number of paper towels I pressed to her leg," Danny said in a far off voice. "And her fingers." He shuddered as he took another drag.

"Danny, I came to ask you about the man sitting with her just before Jess—" Chief Turner asked, letting the question trail off.

"—killed herself." Danny replied bluntly. He shrugged and said, "I told you guys everything I saw back then."

"Well then, tell me again."

Danny shook his head. "It was a long time ago—"

"If that night is as vivid to you as what you've said so far implies, then answering a couple of questions shouldn't be a problem," Chief Turner said, cutting him off before Danny had a chance to refuse.

Danny looked up, frustration written across his face. For a moment, it looked like he might refuse to cooperate. Then he sighed and his agitated expression changed to one resembling sadness. "They looked like they were together.

Intimate even. At one point I came over because she looked upset, but the guy said her dog just died. She didn't say a word to me or even spare me a glance, so I left. It looked like he was comforting her." Danny stared ahead as he recalled the moment, clearly still affected by that night. Then he dropped his gaze and took another long drag from his cigarette.

"Did you hear what they were talking about? Anything?"

Danny shook his head. "No. There was music playing in the background, and they had their heads close together. No way I'd have been able to hear anything they said to each other." Danny looked down and shifted his feet. He looked so vulnerable it reminded Chief Turner of the fifteen-year-old Danny he'd interviewed ten years ago.

"You noticed nothing amiss right after the guy left?"

"No. I mean, she looked upset, but the guy told me her dog died, so I assumed that's what she was crying about. It was only after I noticed the trail of blood on the floor... there was so much blood."

Chief Turner nodded. Danny shifted his feet again and dropped his gaze. It looked like he wanted to say something more, so Chief Turner waited. After a couple more minutes of silence, he decided a nudge might be necessary to get him talking.

"Is there anything else you can remember from that night, even something you think is insignificant?" Chief Turner prompted. Danny shifted his feet again. The shifting feet could be attributed to nervousness, but the dropping of his gaze had more to do with anxiety or fear.

"The guy that was with her—" Danny seemed to have a hard time finding his next words. "I was just a kid, so I brushed it off as my imagination working overtime

118

because of what happened to the girl, but to this day I haven't forgotten how creepy he was. I mean, it's been ten years yet I swear if I ever saw him again I'd run in the opposite direction. Everyone else be damned," Danny said, shaking his head as if even he had a hard time with what he said.

Chief Turner considered him for a minute. Danny behaved like a man who was well and truly scared. Not so strange for someone having recently witnessed a violent death like Jess's, but for a bystander to feel this way a decade later was odd.

"Danny, can you describe him again to me? In as much detail as you remember."

Danny shrugged and took another drag before he began. "He was dressed all in black. He had a dark tuque on. Mid twenties, maybe younger. He looked average. Average height and average weight. Not sure what more I can tell you."

"You mentioned he was Caucasian. Did he look like he had a summer tan like myself or was he more pasty..."

"Pasty white."

"Hair color?"

"Maybe blond... from the little I saw under his hat it looked blond." Again, he shifted to his other foot and flicked his cigarette.

"Dirty blond, yellow blond?"

"Light blond, almost white."

"Did he have a paunch?"

"He didn't have a noticeable belly or anything, but the guy had a dark jacket and pants on, so I couldn't say for sure."

"How tall. You said average, so what? Five-foot nine inches?"

"He sat most of the time, but when he first came up to the counter, I'd say five-eleven or even six feet."

"Ok. And what about the color of his eyes?"

"Cerulean blue," Danny replied automatically. After a brief pause, he continued as if needing to explain his definitive answer. "I had no idea what color Cerulean blue was until my wife painted the living room. And of all the different colors and shades she could have picked, she chose fucking Cerulean blue." Danny dropped the nub of his cigarette and rubbed it out with his foot before looking up again. "At one point, I swear those creepy Cerulean blue eyes of his changed to black. It was one of the most disturbing things I've ever seen."

Chief Turner pulled out the sketch of Sam's Charlie and handed it to Danny. He accepted it, but after barely a glance, he handed it back as if it hurt him to handle it.

"Yeah, that's him."

Danny opened the back door to leave, but before he escaped, the Chief hit him with one last question.

"Danny, each time you've described this guy you said he was average, but according to the details you gave me, like the platinum blond hair, the cerulean blue eyes, the pasty white skin, his height, and this sketch all suggest he wasn't average at all. So why, when I asked you to describe this man, did you keep referring to him as average?" Throughout his question, Danny kept one hand on the door to keep it ajar, as if on the ready in case he had to flee at a moment's notice.

Danny shrugged and said, "That's how I remember him." He crossed the door's threshold but paused long enough to look back at the Chief. "I had nightmares about that night for years afterwards. And I meant what I said earlier. If I ever see that guy again, I'm running in the opposite direction like the devil's on my heels." Then Danny disappeared back into the restaurant pulling the door shut behind him.

Chief Turner stared at the closed door for a few minutes as if in doing so, the beaten and weathered painted steel surface might reveal more clarity about that night. When nothing came to him, he started walking up the alleyway, back towards his car as he pondered this new turn of events.

He definitely got more from his witness now than they had ten years ago. Danny's smoking habit and constant shifting showed he was nervous, but as far as Chief Turner could tell, he wasn't lying. Now he had to figure out if or when he would tell Sam about this. She was already obsessed with Charlie, so to tell her that the guy with Jess the night she died matched Charlie's description... he didn't know if that would help or hinder her.

All he wanted to do was to protect his daughter, yet it was becoming clear to him he couldn't, or at least someone would not let him.

Tim arrived at noon on the dot, holding a brown paper bag, which she assumed was their lunch. He wore a lot more than the last time they met and Sam had to admit to herself she was a little disappointed.

"So we're brown bagging it today? Let me guess, peanut butter and jelly sandwiches? Perhaps some juice boxes in there as well?" Sam said, eyes twinkling as she raised an eyebrow quizzically. She couldn't care less what he brought over. It was just nice to have the company for a change.

"And what if I did? Is the big city girl too good for pb & j sandwiches and juice boxes?" Tim parried back, but like her, humor danced in his eyes.

"Are you kidding? Give me an apple juice box and anything with peanut butter and I'm a happy girl. One of my favorite snacks growing up, apple slices and peanut butter." Talking about it brought to mind the combination of tangy sweetness moderated by the creamy peanut buttery goodness. Suddenly, the small hungasaurus inside her stomach growled. Loudly. Sam's face pinked up. Of course, Tim noticed both.

"Nice, Turner. I'll have to try that sometime. There are a few apple trees in my backyard, so you never know. If you play your cards right, I might even let you pick some," Tim said with a suggestive, exaggerated wink.

Memories of the apple trees they had years ago flooded her. The ripened apples were always worm infested, so they'd sit and rot on the branch only to drop in the fall and become wasp infested. Sam must have grimaced, because Tim's smile turned into a perplexed frown.

"Sorry. Your mentioning the backyard apple trees reminded me of the ones we had when I was a kid. They were always infested with worms in the summer and wasps in the fall." Sam shuddered.

"Yuk. Well, I take care of my apple trees, so that doesn't happen. A little care can go a long way with fruit trees."

"Well, that's a different story, then. I'd love to come over and pick apples."

"It's a date then. Shall we say late October when they're ripe?" Tim replied, to which Sam raised her eyebrows. "Don't worry, Turner, you'll get those apples. I have little doubt you'll still want my company by then."

Sam's eyes widened. "Wow, that's a bold statement to make, considering we just met."

"Perhaps. But I already know you like me, otherwise you wouldn't have bothered joining me today." Tim grinned back, and Sam couldn't resist laughing even as she shook her head at him. Oh well, so he knew she liked him a little. They were adults, after all.

"So, I figured you and Buddy might have cabin fever by now, and since it's a nice day, I thought perhaps a mini picnic would be a good idea?" Tim suggested, searching her face for a response. "Yes? No?"

"Oh God, yes!" Sam said, already slipping on her shoes. She was about to call for Buddy but found him already sitting pretty right beside her. "Obviously, I'm not the only one feeling stifled in here." Buddy was already wagging his tail before she clipped the lead to his collar.

"Guess I made the right call then," Tim said with a satisfied grin and held the door open for them before following. Once down at the sidewalk, Tim had them make a left.

"Where are we heading?" Sam asked, enjoying the sun on her face. She took Buddy's lead with her left hand, which meant Buddy was on her left, leaving Tim to take her right.

"Wait, I have one request before we go," Tim said. Sam stopped, and Buddy sat at her feet with a silent command. "Let's not talk about the incident at my garage. Tomorrow is fine, but not today. Between dealing with insurance, police, Paula, Janet and worrying about Toni, the last few days have been hell. I just need a break from—"

"Ok," Sam said, and that was it. They started walking again. Although an older neighborhood, Fleming street remained one of the prettiest in town. The homes were well maintained, and the mature trees dotting the lawns lent a good amount of shade to begin their walk.

"We could take a walk by the river towards Gander

Park. They've been restoring some of the historic buildings there I thought might interest you," Tim said, smiling. "Plus, there's a nice spot to eat by the river." Sam nodded. Even Murphy had its pleasant areas.

"So, why did you open your own shop?" Sam asked. "That couldn't have been easy to do."

"Out of necessity. Believe me, it wasn't an overnight decision or a painless move to make, but it was the right move. The only other decent size shop within a hundred-mile radius where a licensed mechanic can find full-time work is Al's Autobody, and I had had one too many run-ins with Al to work there any longer. So I opened my own."

"Personality conflict?"

"Hmm. If by that you mean an untrustworthy and opportunistic employer, then sure. Big Al was unrealistically demanding and took advantage of his workers, but the clincher came when he told me to apologize to a client for doing what he'd instructed me to do."

"I take it you didn't apologize?"

"I did not. In fact, I ended up typing up my notice of resignation and handing it to Al an hour after he reprimanded me in front of said client," Tim shrugged. In the past, Sam had worked for employers who had shady work practices. She'd learned to watch her back, so she understood Tim's frustration with his previous employer. Sam whistled, shaking her head.

"He must not have been too pleased about that."

"No, he wasn't." Tim replied with a smile, as if reminiscing about it. Glancing over. "And what about you? I take it you work in Toronto?"

"Yeah. I'm a graphic designer. It can be fun, but lately it's been more stress than anything else." Sam's thoughts went to her job, which she didn't want to think about. What had once been an enjoyable work environment was now full of stress and monotony as more and more work was being downloaded onto the junior executives, which included Sam. "So you were born and raised here?"

"No. I grew up in a community thirty minutes south of here, near Colberg. I moved to Murphy for work fifteen years ago and have been here ever since."

"A community? That means it isn't even big enough to be called a town. Wow."

"I am a small-town boy," Tim replied with a grin. It was so infectious that Sam couldn't resist grinning back.

"No, you mean you're a farm boy!" Sam said, chuckling. And a comfortable silence ensued for a few minutes.

"May I?" Tim asked. He'd pulled a yellow tennis ball out of his pocket and held it up, waiting for her reply. She grinned and unclasped Buddy's leash. Tim threw the ball to the side of the path to which fur face obliged, chasing it down enthusiastically before coming back with it in his maw.

"Buddy's pretty well behaved. Trained him yourself?" Tim asked, after throwing the ball again.

"Yes. But he's got a great temperament, so training him was easy." Sam rubbed Buddy's head affectionately when he returned to her side this time.

"How'd you learn to—?"

"From the age of about twelve onward, I spent a lot of time around the station waiting for my dad to finish work for the day. Often he was busy dealing with this emergency or that, so I'd hang out on my own until he finished. Most of the cops ignored me, but a couple of them were nice and would sometimes let me hang out with them. Bobby trained potential candidate dogs for police service. I found it fascinating, and I guess I picked up some of his training techniques." Sam shrugged.

"Which leads me to ask, why didn't you follow in your dad's footsteps?" Tim asked. Sam was already shaking her head before he'd finished his question.

"Nope. Never wanted to," Sam replied too fast. When Tim raised a curious eyebrow, she said, "Ok, so you had your stipulations for today, and now I have mine. No more career or dad talk. Fair's fair."

They continued their walk, talking about their mutual appreciation for running, dogs, nature, and the changes to Murphy over the last five years. Sam was pleasantly surprised at how much she enjoyed their mini picnic. The main reason was the company, but the route they'd taken passed by some rejuvenation projects, which showed the effort being put into Murphy. It was long overdue and something she hadn't seen happen in a very long time.

Buddy and Tim got on like a house on fire and she couldn't resist laughing at Buddy's antics as he ran, dove and jostled to catch the tennis ball Tim threw. By the time they returned to the house, Sam was more than ready to get off her feet.

Before leaving, Tim asked if she'd join him for breakfast the next day, and before she knew it, she'd agreed. She hadn't had a proper greasy breakfast in so many years she had to fight the urge to go rooting through the fridge in the hopes of finding a package of bacon. However, the moment she stepped into her family home, the only thing on her mind was how exhausted she felt. Without another thought, she headed to what was once her bedroom. She figured she'd just rest her eyes for a few minutes to recharge. Sam fell asleep within seconds of her head hitting the pillow.

* * *

Awoken by a loud banging, Sam shot straight up in bed. Disoriented, it took a few seconds to remember where she was and why her shoulder hurt so much. Sighing, she instinctively looked for Buddy, but Fur face was no longer lying on the floor beside the bed.

Another bang, but this time it sounded more like the clang of a pan. What little fog still clouded her mind was scared away by the adrenaline now pumping through her veins. The sounds drew her from the bedroom into the dining area, where she found the table set for two. The noise came from the kitchen where it looked like the Chief was attempting to make dinner. She couldn't remember the last time she'd seen her father cook.

"Do you need help?" Sam asked in the kitchen entryway.

"Nope. Just sit. I'll be right there." He speared what looked like a roast and put it on a large serving plate.

Sam headed back the way she came to freshen up in the bathroom. When she returned, she found him already seated, bowls of julienne carrots and mashed potatoes, and a plate of carved roast waiting for her.

"The meal looks great," Sam said, taking a seat and eyeing her dad. "Not even retired yet, and you're already bored enough to cook dinner for us."

"What? I've cooked dinner for you before," he stated, sounding surprised, if not a little offended. He'd already piled food on his own plate. She was surprisingly hungry herself and took a hearty helping of the roast beef, potatoes and carrots.

"Harrumph, you haven't cooked a meal since... Well, I can't even remember it's been so long," Sam laughed and dug in with gusto. The food was good. Perhaps he could start a new career as a cook if he got bored with retirement.

"See what you're missing up there in the big city? If you came to see your poor old man more often, you might get more of these home-cooked meals."

"Using the guilt card! Nice. Really nice. Keep in mind I come and see you just as often as you come and see me." Sam pointed out, raising her eyebrow at him. "Now, if I knew I'd be getting meals like this every time I visited, you might see me more often."

"Tsk. Tsk. I will burn it next time," he replied gruffly, making Sam laugh.

Silence reigned as they dug into their meals and in no time flat they'd finished. Sam cleared the table while her dad put on the coffee. Armed with mugs full of steaming coffee and a plate of cookies, they sat back down at the dinner table. For a few minutes, a comfortable silence prevailed, and then the talking started. Topics ranged from the Leaf's latest season, whether they'd draft so-and-so, and how the town councilors had voted to approve the new wage hikes to municipal employees. The more he talked, the more it sounded like he was babbling again. A sense of Déjà vu passed through her. Eyes narrowing, she scrutinized the Chief as he spoke, picking up on the forced laugh and tightness around his mouth.

"Spill it," Sam interrupted, cutting him off mid-sentence, something about how not to cast when fly-fishing.

He stopped speaking but raised his eyebrows, feigning ignorance at what she was getting at.

"I know you have something to tell me because you've been talking nonstop since we sat down for coffee and dessert. So say what you need to say."

Though he didn't deny it, he said nothing at first. Sam

waited. Her father stared back at her, then nodded as if agreeing with something that was said. It's what he did when he had to broach a difficult topic. Sam's stomach knotted in apprehension. He sighed, a cue that he was ready to tell her what was on his mind.

"I tracked down the witness to Jess's suicide today," her dad explained, meeting her gaze. "He confirmed the composite of Charlie resembled the man who sat with Jess that night at the pizzeria." There was a brief pause before he continued. "However, I don't think his answers are a hundred percent reliable."

Sam just stared at him for a full minute, processing what he'd just revealed. A range of emotions surfaced, but the strongest one at the moment was anger, and she asked incredulously, "What do you mean you don't think his answers are reliable? So, what? You think he lied? What could he possibly gain from that?"

"No, I think he believed what he said was the truth. But it happened over ten years ago when the witness was only fifteen. We can't depend on his memories being accurate, if they ever were."

"Why would you say that?" Sam tried to keep her voice neutral, but her question sounded more accusatory than curious. It hit too close to home, and she was having a hard time not taking it personally. She knew it and her dad knew it, too. To his credit, he didn't waiver from the facts, which helped her keep it together. He looked as frustrated as she felt, but continued trying to explain.

"He seemed scared. Paranoid even. It's been over a decade yet he behaved like he'd experienced it only yesterday. Besides that, there are too many inconsistencies in the details he remembers from that night."

"Fine, I'll bite. What inconsistencies?" Her voice sounded hollow, even to her.

"In both interviews, Danny said the same thing. Jess's mystery man was an average looking Caucasian male wearing dark clothing and a dark tuque. Average weight. Average height. Average guy. Period. It was only when I asked him detail oriented questions like what shade of blond was his hair, how light was his skin tone, and had him answer yay or nay to a range of heights did I find his answers didn't line up with what one would consider average. Even after I pointed this out to him, he still said he remembers Jess's companion being average."

Her dad shook his head as if in doing so would make all the inconsistencies disappear, and then added, "He also said the guy had Cerulean blue eyes, which is not only the furthest from average a color can get, but it's also physiologically impossible. If he saw irises of that color, then they must have been contacts. But I can't rely on his testimony because in the next sentence he stated they changed color, which can't happen, contacts or not. His testimony is unreliable." Sighing, he pinched the bridge of his nose, a clear sign he was suffering from a headache.

"What color did he say they changed to?" Sam asked.

"Does it matter?" Sam's expression must have told how serious she was because without another word, he pulled out a little notepad from his front shirt pocket and flipped it open. "He said, 'I swear those creepy Cerulean blue eyes of his changed and went black. It was one of the most disturbing things I've ever seen.'" Then he flipped it closed and shoved it back into his shirt pocket.

Sam felt the heat in her face as her anger mounted. Although she wouldn't be able to make him understand, most of what her father found out today corroborated her suspicion that Charlie was responsible for her best friend's suicide over a decade ago. Ironically, what made Danny an unreliable witness to her father was what confirmed it for Sam because she'd experienced it firsthand. The irrational fear verging on paranoia years after the fact. The weird Cerulean blue eyes that changed color. The witness's reference to creepy. Charlie had creepy down in spades. However, she agreed with her father on one thing; she didn't understand the witness's need to use the word average regarding Charlie. It was the strangest part of their entire conversation.

Feeling an overwhelming need to break something, Sam got up and paced.

"Sam, I was on scene the night she died. I was there for every interview. I was the one who told Jess's mother she'd passed. But even if we'd got a more accurate ID of her companion, it wouldn't have changed the outcome. I went over the case with the coroner myself and there was no doubt in anyone's mind. She tore through her femoral artery herself."

Sam continued to pace. She'd told no one the full story or what she thought Charlie was capable of, being able to pull the worst out of a person at their weakest moment. Her dad would never understand the full significance of Charlie's presence the night Jess died. Perhaps no one else ever would.

"You're making me dizzy with all your pacing. Can you please sit down for a minute?" His expression looked pained, and it was enough to make Sam do as he asked.

"Fine," she said as she sat back down. She gripped her coffee, but unlike usual, it didn't make her feel any better.

Sam stared into the dark liquid and wished she could go back a decade and be there with Jess that night. Maybe it would have changed her outcome. Yet even as she thought it, she knew he just would've waited for another opportunity. And that made her sad.

"Your mother and I were fond of Jess. Her suicide hit us hard, too. But the pain it caused you..." Her dad's voice rose as he said this, betraying an otherwise calm exterior. He reached out and squeezed her hand. "You know we would have done everything we could for Jess, right?"

Pulling her hand away, Sam released the tension in her shoulders and said, "I know." And she did, but it changed nothing. Now more than ever, she knew what she had to do. Charlie had to be stopped. Going after her was bad enough, but the fact he'd killed her best friend when she was still only a teenager...

She made a promise there and then. Even if it took everything she had, she would see Charlie rot in hell or die trying.

Chapter 9

Revelations

The next morning, Tim picked her up in his old blue Ford pickup, a throwback from the early eighties, but a well-maintained classic. It suited his farm boy image.

"So, breakfast at the best greasy spoon in Murphy?" Tim asked, looking over at her.

Sam sat there for a moment before it dawned on her. Grinning, she shouted, "Angelo's!" She hadn't been there in years and could already feel her mouth water at the thought of it.

"You are a Murphy native!" Tim chuckled, putting the truck in gear.

Sam watched Tim drive. Handling the gears with ease. Taking the corners a touch faster than he should. Shifting down to slow the truck as they neared intersections. It was obvious he enjoyed driving. It was when he looked over and caught her watching him that she redirected her gaze out the window. They were driving through a neighborhood she didn't recognize. Followed by another, and another.

"Wow, she has changed, hasn't she?" Sam said as they

drove by house after house that were carbon copies of one another. Obviously constructed by the same builder, they all looked like they'd come off a manufacturing line. The only difference being the particular shade of beige they chose for the brick and siding. And, of course, the door color. Sam imagined what the neighborhood conversations entailed. *Why Beatrice, I love that shade of brick you chose. It goes so well with the red maple you have out front. Your red door is to die for!*

"The mere idea of living in one of these cookie cutter houses makes me wanna hurl." It was only when she heard Tim chuckle she realized she must have said that last part aloud. His ensuing silence meant either he agreed with her or he found her opinion on the topic amusing. Either way, he didn't let on.

"I am curious. Why do you call Murphy a she?" Tim asked, glancing over.

Sam was so surprised by the question, she didn't respond at first.

"I mean, Murphy is a much more male sounding name, so I would have naturally leaned towards the male pronoun as opposed to the female," Tim explained.

Sam blinked. "To be honest, I never thought about it before. Perhaps it's because the heart of the town is its people and these people have kids who will either create a more robust town or leave and create more towns and cities. So, in order for cities and towns to stay alive, they must remain fertile." For good measure, she added, "Either that or I'm a misandrist at heart and believe the world revolves around women." She smiled sweetly back at Tim whose own smile waned.

"Good to know, Turner."

Shortly after that, the tacky neon sign showing they had

reached their intended destination came into view. The restaurant's sign comprised a caricature of a portly Italian gentleman bent at a ninety-degree angle at the waist, looking sheepishly around his derriere, holding a giant dish of pasta. The light outlining one of his buttocks, and half his smile had burned out. Sam recalled the last time she'd been here the "o" in Angelo had been burned out, so it read Angel's Diner. Now it only read as AN EL 'S DINER, making it so much funnier.

The interior looked the same. Red vinyl booths with black piping, a worn black counter lined with old-fashioned red stools, and a checkered black and white tile floor, although the white looked more gray now after decades' worth of wear.

Well, at least some things never change. She found that notion oddly comforting. They chose a window booth halfway between the front and back doors. The server took their orders, and Sam and Tim made idle conversation until their meals arrived. The breakfast was good, but the steaming cup of coffee was better. No one made coffee like Angelo's. Sam closed her eyes as she hugged the mug in her good hand and savored the smell of the black brew. When she opened them again, she found Tim staring at her in fascination.

"Wow, you really like your coffee. Do you always handle your first cup in the morning with such reverence?"

Sam often hugged her coffee cup in the morning, but she wasn't about to admit it. Sam took a sip, savoring the black gold as it traveled down her throat. Happiness started with a good cup of java.

"It's Angelo's coffee." Sam replied finally, as if that explained it all.

Tim picked up his mug, sniffed it, took a sip. Unimpressed, he put it back down with a shrug.

"I've never been envious of an inanimate object before, but I'm pretty jealous of that cup right now." Tim said, eyeing her hands.

Sam blushed, put the cup down, and cleared her throat. Tim chuckled before adding, "You and my sister would get on well. She loves her coffee too and is quite the bear without it. She always stops drinking it once she knows she's pregnant, so I knew weeks before she told any of us because of how irritable she'd become."

"Yeah, I'd probably like her a lot." Sam laughed. Never having had siblings of her own, she'd always been a little envious of those that did.

"You would. You'd also like my niece and nephew. They're spoiled but smart. Luckily, they seem to have gotten my sister's easy-going personality as opposed to Mike's—" Tim let the sentence trail off and then sighed. "I just don't understand how he could have gone from the Mike I knew a few weeks ago to what we witnessed a few days ago. He was never the most amiable guy, but the Mike I knew wouldn't have been capable of... Jesus... bludgeoning someone to death." Tim grimaced as if picturing Mike's handiwork on the older mechanic. "I just don't get it."

Since yesterday, Sam had debated on how much she should tell Tim. She barely knew him, but for whatever reason she trusted him. If she let him know what really happened at his shop, it might kill their budding friendship. But if she didn't trust someone, what she knew could end up killing her. She'd been isolating herself and looking over her shoulder for so long now that she struggled to think of any other way of being. Either way, a part of her would be relieved she'd told someone even if he didn't believe her.

"I think the question we should ask is, how did Mike get to such a dark place? Did something traumatic happen to him to set him off or is it possible he was... pushed?" Sam paused. Tim's brow knit into a web of unease as he processed her words, but she continued. "My gut tells me Mike got a push or even a shove to do what he did. You said he had no history of violence. So for him to have had such a rapid decline in just a few weeks, there had to be a trigger. What set off his psychological break?"

Tim looked confused, and Sam didn't know what else to say. Having had firsthand experience with Charlie, she had little doubt how manipulative and persuasive he could be. She was no psychologist, but she had minored in behavioral psychology.

"So if it was Charlie you saw talking with Mike, then you're saying it's possible that Charlie may have somehow coaxed Mike into action?" Tim stared past her as he processed this new information. Then his eyes refocused on her face. "So he persuaded someone else to do his dirty work because, why? He was afraid of getting caught?"

"No, I don't think he's afraid of getting caught." Sam replied, shaking her head. "Charlie's not your average bear. He would have enjoyed manipulating Mike into doing it. He hunted me down, and I am not talking figuratively here. He hunted me down as if I were prey. But it didn't stop there. Once he has you in his grip, he works over your psyche as well. He talks and talks and talks some more and he doesn't let up until his words make sense. He seduces the small, dark part of you that wants the pain to stop."

Tim's look of alarm almost ended the conversation there. But she knew if she stopped now she'd likely tell no one the truth. "I'll try to explain what happened to me. I'm not proud of this period in my life, but if the truth gets me closer to catching this guy, then so be it."

Sam took a deep breath and began. "I was in the middle of a nasty breakup with my ex-fiancé. I loved this man, or at least I loved the man he presented himself to be, and I thought he loved me. We had planned a future together, set a date for our wedding, where we'd live, even the number of kids we'd have... the whole bit. He was a partner in a start-up, and I understood his work came first, but it got to a point where I was lucky to see him twice a month. We had an argument and by the end of it he stated he doubted me in ways I was unprepared for. He ambushed me, and the seeds of doubt he planted concerning my character were devastating.

"I found out later that the real motivation behind our breakup had to do with his desire to move on to someone new. However, being honest about his infidelity conflicted with his good guy persona, so instead he blamed me for the demise of our relationship. Telling me I'd become too needy, that my temper was out of control and I might hurt our future kids, and on and on just so he could leave the relationship guilt free and ask a girl he'd recently met at church to marry him instead. He'd done a real number on me and though I didn't know it at the time, I became severely depressed. To top it off, everything else in my life went to crap. I'd lost my job, my friends were so busy and preoccupied with their own lives they didn't have time for me, my school debt was overwhelming, my mother was gone, and my dad and I were barely speaking. To say my perspective was skewed would be an understatement."

Sam took a breath. She'd never spoken about this to anyone, and saying it out loud was as terrifying as it was liberating. "Charlie appeared out of nowhere at a point when I was so tired and depressed, I'd begun daydreaming of a way out from all the pain and self-flagellation. He chased me down, held me captive, and kept at me. I remember him referring to himself as my 'facilitator'. This stranger knew things about me no one else knew. He talked about how easy it would be for me to give in and give up on everything and everyone. He poked at past wounds until they were open and bleeding again. He focused on those I loved, twisting and magnifying any issues that were there. He emphasized how much worse life would get for me if I stuck around. Essentially, he took my worst fears combined with the knowledge of the most intimate details of my life, past and present, and kept at it, and kept at it, and kept at it some more until I believed the only way out of my misery was death. By the end, I had completely given up and wanted out. And that's when he stabbed me. Repeatedly."

Tim stayed quiet as he processed all she'd said. The mere fact he didn't get up and walk out straightaway she took as a good sign.

"So are you saying you believe this guy wanted your permission before taking your life?" Sam didn't miss the subtle rise in Tim's pitch by the end. He didn't wholly believe her, but that was ok. Sometimes she even had trouble believing it and she'd lived through it.

"Charlie could have taken my life right when he caught me, but he waited and worked me over until I gave in and gave up on everything. But he had me in a choke hold so I couldn't have said anything even if I'd wanted to." Sam thought a moment longer before shaking her head. "Maybe something in my posture let him know. I don't know."

Tim's expression, his lowered eyebrows creating a crease between his narrowed eyes and his pulled up lips, perfectly illustrated his incredulity. If they'd been talking about any other subject, she'd probably find it amusing, but laughing was the last thing on her mind. Feeling uncomfortable, Sam dropped her gaze but continued on.

"Now maybe you can understand why I've never told anyone the complete story in all these years. I only told the cops what they needed to know to catch him. That I'd had a brief conversation with Charlie at the house, after which I stabbed him in the eye with a fork because he threatened me. Later, I was talking to my ex on the phone when I heard something behind me and discovered him climbing through the screen. He chased me downtown, caught me near the Chinese restaurant and stabbed me before getting scared off by kids down the block." She paused before meeting Tim's eyes again. "I know what happens when a victim's statement is so ludicrous it's unbelievable. The case is either dropped outright or gets put on the back burner. Then, after an appropriate amount of time has passed, gets filed away. And good luck if the perp gets caught, and it goes to court. The defense would have a heyday with what I told you, and he'd get off on the grounds that the victim's testimony was unreliable."

Tim watched her for a long time before answering. Sam had to clasp her hands in her lap to stop from fidgeting, reminding herself she didn't care if this guy believed her or not. He no longer looked stricken, but now wore a guarded expression.

"And now?"

Sam looked at him for a few seconds, thinking he'd say something more, but when nothing came, she bit. "Now what?"

"How do you feel about life now?"

Sam smiled. "Well, at this particular moment, it kinda sucks. I have a concussion, a dislocated shoulder and someone just tried to kill me. Again. If I was a more sensitive person, I might think I had a target on my back."

"I think you do. But you're too stubborn to give in and die." Tim chuckled, then went still. Concern flashed across his face. "You know that was meant to be funny, right?"

Sam smiled, waving it away. When Tim relaxed again, she said, "If I was smart, I'd leave Murphy, never come back and forget Charlie ever existed. The night he attacked me, a light switched on and I knew, without a doubt, how much I wanted to live. And I guess someone upstairs was looking after me because one minute Charlie was stabbing me and the next he was gone."

Tim's eyebrows rose almost to his hairline. "Wait. Are you saying that during your attack you had a change of heart, asked him to stop stabbing you, and he did? Because that would have been pretty considerate of him, given he was trying to kill you."

"No. Remember, I couldn't talk—" she began, but her words trailed off as she turned her thoughts inwards.

Tim was right. What kind of psychopath goes to the lengths this guy did and then stops before the job is done? She knew it hadn't been an act of mercy or even pity that stopped him. So why? Was it fear of getting caught by the nearby teenagers? Thinking back on it that made little sense. They'd been in the shadows and Charlie had been well hidden behind her, so even if the teenagers had glanced over, they'd only have seen the silhouette of a couple embracing. Besides, it would have taken him mere seconds to finish the job, so... why hadn't he? Earlier that night, he didn't seem to care who saw him as he broke in her front window, and he didn't hesitate to chase her through the neighborhood into downtown Murphy.

And how has Charlie remained so elusive? Sam

couldn't blame Kabowski for calling her out on whether she actually saw him because it would be impossible for someone as distinctive looking as Charlie to remain hidden in small town Murphy.

Yet again, Sam revisited those last moments of her attack. She remembered a feeling of calm and hope sweep over her as the knife slid into her abdomen for the second time. In that moment, her passion to live was overwhelming, but he still had her by the throat, so saying it aloud wasn't an option. And then he left, knife still stuck in her gut, as if he'd heard the thoughts she'd been screaming at him. Charlie knew things about her she'd never said aloud to anyone and there were times during her attack she swore he was responding to her thoughts as she was thinking them.

"Hey! Talk to me. I can see your thoughts are racing, but I can't read your mind." Tim touched her hand to get her attention, but she pulled back without thinking. She forced a smile, but Tim didn't look very reassured by it.

"You're right. It makes little sense. Why would he stop? This guy went to great lengths to kill me. It was... predatory is the best way I can describe it. He crawled through my sunroom window, for God's sake. Chased me down for half a dozen blocks. Caught me seconds before a group of teenagers would have seen me. All I wanted to do before he messed with my mind was bash his pretty blond head in, but I couldn't do or say squat because he had me by the throat. And he enjoyed playing with me, too." Sam shivered at the memory and rubbed her arms even though her chill had nothing to do with being cold.

Tim stayed quiet for a moment, processing and then asked, "So what stopped him, then? Obviously, you don't think it was a sudden onset of guilt."

Sam's only response was a decided harrumph.

"So, what about fear? Did he think he might get caught by those kids? Or perhaps someone else was present but didn't come forward?"

Sam shook her head. "Not that I saw."

"So either Charlie decided to let you live, or he thought you'd die from your wounds, so saw no need to continue," Tim suggested. It was an explanation, but a weak one. A part of her knew that wasn't why Charlie stopped, but the alternative was so far-fetched and scary she couldn't say it out loud. The mere thought that anyone, but especially someone like Charlie, might know what you were thinking when you were thinking it was downright horrifying. Sam rubbed the ache in her temple.

Even calling Charlie a person felt wrong. He didn't act like any person she'd ever encountered, or even an animal. Her gut whispered to her, telling her Charlie was something else, foreign and dark. He was the thing that went bump in the night you hoped you'd never cross paths with.

But I had. Twice. And now I was... what? Planning on pursuing him? Sam was so wrapped up in her thoughts again that it took the squeeze of her hand to bring her back to the present. Unprepared for the contact, she almost upended the mug she held.

"Hey, you ok? For a minute there you looked terrified," Tim said with concern. His hands now safely wrapped around his own mug.

Sam nodded and then asked, "Sorry, what did you ask me before I spaced out on you?"

"Why would Charlie get Mike to do what he could do himself? His M.O., at least with you, was hands on. And if Charlie is as bad as you say and is skilled enough to have escaped detection this long, then you'd think he'd want to enjoy it firsthand, wouldn't he?" He rubbed the furrows in his forehead again.

Sam studied her mug of joe for a moment, hoping Tim might bring up the obvious. That Charlie actually was there to witness his work, but when it didn't come up after a few minutes, Sam knew it was either fess up or shut up. Right now, Tim was all she had in her corner. Unfortunately, it meant she'd have to tell him about the cop who wasn't a cop at all. *Here goes nothing.*

"And what if Charlie was there?" Sam asked watched him from over her mug. Tim looked at her, perplexed. Sam pressed her meaning. "What if Charlie was present to witness his handiwork at your auto shop?"

"What are you saying?" Tim asked. The intensity in his stare was a little disconcerting, but she forced herself to return his gaze. He needed to see what she was about to tell him was the truth.

"Remember the cop that handcuffed me and escorted me out?"

Tim nodded. "The one I wanted to haul off and kick the living shit out of for—"

"Yes, that one. T-H-A-T was Charlie." Sam knew he'd be upset, but how upset depended on how he took the news. At the very least, he'd be pissed she'd withheld this information. But at worst, he'd be upset because he thought she was well and truly crazy.

"What!" Oddly enough his outrage calmed her. It implied that, at least to a certain extent, he might believe her. "Wait, why didn't you say anything at the time?" His voice, considerably lower than a second ago, was still loud enough to carry. She resisted the urge to shush him and continued on in a low voice, hoping he'd follow suit.

"I never had the chance to look at him, so had no idea it

was him until we reached the patrol car. Then he made sure I couldn't shout out."

"Then why didn't you at least tell someone when you woke up?"

"You mean why didn't I tell Superintendent Ka-Bitch that Charlie successfully disguised himself as a cop, arrested me and then escorted me out of the crime scene to a squad car, where he put me in a choke hold, threatened me, and stabbed me with a fork, before throwing me into the back-seat with enough force to knock me out." Sam let him digest her words before continuing. "She'd already decided that I made up the bit about Charlie up, so revealing that was out of the question." The contempt she had for Kabowski bled into her tone.

That she was the only one that ever saw Charlie wasn't only frustrating, it was downright aggravating, but as she pondered this for the umpteenth time it finally dawned on her that that might be the point. It might be part of his game. He wants her to realize how vulnerable she is. That he could kill her whenever he wanted and no one would be the wiser, because she's the only one who's seen him. Charlie didn't want headlines or acknowledgement for his kills. And then Sam remembered something Harry, their old next-door neighbor, often said, "The devil has the patience of a saint, the cunning of a fox, the slyness of a snake, and is as heartless as any politician." She'd always assumed Harry was talking metaphorically, but now had to wonder if he hadn't been talking from experience.

Tim studied her. She did her best not to squirm under his scrutiny. At one point, it looked like he would say something, but then his expression cleared. At least he hadn't walked out yet.

"Why do you think no one but you have ever seen him?" Tim asked.

"Perhaps he doesn't want anyone else to see him."

"Jesus... he's not superman. People don't have the type of skill you're implying here." Tim insisted as he pushed a hand through his hair. "If everything you're saying is true, then this guy must be brilliant and crazy, or he's Houdini. Besides, why would he risk getting caught just to threaten you again?"

"I guess he's crazy then."

When Tim continued watching her, waiting, she leaned in. The diner was virtually empty and although she was certain no one had heard their conversation, she wanted to keep it that way. "Murphy has a pretty small police force and often the OPP are called in to help when the camp-grounds are busy. Labour day weekend is the last big party weekend before the students go back to school. They needed the extra bodies to handle the crowds expected to descend on Murphy, so they called in a few OPP officers to help. Disguising himself as an OPP officer and being one of the first responders to the scene... it was the perfect way in. Murphy cops wouldn't recognize all the OPP assigned because there's so much rotation in the force. Besides, no sane perp would be crazy enough to disguise themselves as a cop and put themselves in the thick of it."

"And here I was hoping for Houdini," Tim said tightly. "So if what you say is true... And I'm not saying it is because there are so many improbable, if not impossible, leaps you've taken here, I'd have to be crazy to believe it all. However, let's say for argument's sake it is and I am. Do you think he's actually a cop or just impersonating one?"

"My gut screams he can't be a real cop, but there's no way to check, anyway. And from some of the research I've read sociopaths and psychopaths gravitate towards positions of authority, so occupations in law enforcement or the military would be attractive to someone like Charlie. These days, the psychological evaluations potential candidates must undergo tend to weed these out. But the highly intelligent, functioning psychopaths are still likely to get through."

"Sorry, functioning psychopath?" Tim asked, eyebrows knitting together in confusion.

"Functioning psychopaths are individuals that are smart enough they can give the correct responses reflecting society's expectations of them when asked, even though it's not what they'd actually do if there were no consequences. They're talented actors, giving the audience what they want to hear, but once the curtains are drawn, they'll do what suits them best," Sam answered simply.

Tim's eyes widened before he asked, "So why didn't you follow in your old man's footsteps?"

"Having an interest and having a career are two different things," she replied with a shrug.

Tim continued to look at her, his eyebrows raised in question, but she ignored it. In her experience, focusing on the dissatisfactions in life just made people more dissatisfied, and talking about them made them more real. She wasn't ready to face such a life altering change yet even if it meant she'd be happier in the long run. When she didn't budge on the topic, he pressed the point. "Fair's fair, Sam. We talked about Mike and Charlie, so cough it up."

"Fine." Sam rubbed her eyes with her free hand and leaned back in her seat. "I saw what the job did to my father. How much he sacrificed for it and how much we involuntarily sacrificed for it as well. Sometimes we wouldn't see him for weeks on end. He'd come home after we went to bed and was gone before we woke up. And if we were lucky enough to be blessed with his presence, nine times out of ten he wanted to be left alone because he was still working on a case. The job was the other woman and my mother got pretty lonely. I think a big part of why she kept herself so busy was to avoid thinking about it. I didn't realize how unhappy she was until much later, but by then she was already sick. After she died, I was so angry all I wanted to do was get the hell out of Murphy."

"Away from your father you mean."

"Yes. But away from Murphy as well."

"Grass is always greener and all that." Tim suggested gently.

"Something like that." Sam needed a change, but now was not the time to think about it. "So—"

"Maybe we should try to figure out where Charlie might show up next." Tim raised an eyebrow and let the idea hang there.

"Hmm, so you think I might have an idea? You do remember it took five years before I ran into him again? I'll be about as useful in tracking him down as a cup of decaf."

Tim chuckled, but continued on, undeterred. "Considering the number of wagging tongues in town, we'd have heard if he lived anywhere near here. So, since you seem to be the only witness who's seen him..."

"The only thing we have to go on is he may eventually revisit Murphy. His sketch would have been circulated and checked against the national criminal database five years ago. Considering how elusive he's been to date, I doubt he's been added to the database since then, but I'll ask my dad if he can check. I don't trust Superintendent Ka-Bitch to bother looking. And I'll see if I can get someone to check if there's an OPP officer matching Charlie's description. But again, my gut says he's not working for them." Sam rubbed her right shoulder unconsciously, then added, "I have to head back to Toronto within a couple of days. A week is all I can afford to take off of work, torn shoulder or not."

"Guess that means I'll be staying here and keeping an eye out for anyone matching his description. Adonis right?" Tim asked, with a brief glint in his eye.

"You forgot Houdini," Sam replied, and wondered if she'd ever find out who Charlie was. She may never even see him again. One could always hope.

Chapter 10

Tim and Harry, Buds for Life

Days later, when the cops informed Tim no one would be allowed back on the shop premises for another few days, all he felt was relief. Tim didn't scare easily, nor did he believe in ghosts or curses, but after witnessing the aftermath of his brother-in-law's rage-fueled breakdown, he just couldn't see anyone working there after that. And with two out of three of his mechanics dead and the last seriously injured, he'd have to find more help. Just thinking about it made Tim nauseous. He considered them more like family than employees, so replacing them would be... well... impossible.

"Damn." Tim tugged a hand through his hair as he felt a weight brush up against the back of his legs. Brandy always knew when he was upset.

Kneeling, he scruffed Brandy's neck and waited for her to tilt her head to look up at him. "Looks like we're going to have to find a new shop, girl. You good with that?" After a brief pause, she chuffed in agreement, her soft brown eyes serious. Tim gave her a quick hug before standing again.

Though most of his clients would understand why the

shop was closed, there was always the handful of emergencies that would need to be addressed in the meantime. Luckily, he had a full set of tools in the back of his truck and most of the equipment he needed on hand for the majority of jobs. Plus, he wanted to stay busy. Keeping his mind and hands active might help stave off the gruesome memories that kept replaying in his head, with the added benefit of distracting him from thinking about the strangely resilient Sam Turner.

The day flew by in a blur. It started with a brake job, followed by a headlight bulb replacement, an exhaust fix, a couple of brake replacements, and a rear light replacement damaged by eighty-four-year-old Mr. Gurdy when he backed into a mailbox post.

Tim's last job of the day was a house call. Harold Sarken, one of his regulars who'd become more of a friend than a client, had left a message on the work phone a few days ago to say he couldn't get his yellow 1969 Oldsmobile started.

Harry's Oldsmobile was a thing of beauty, and being a lover of the classics himself, he understood his passion for the vintage car. Tim had gotten into the habit of going over to help Harry with his classic, though their meetups usually ended up being more a chance to chat than anything else. He'd been meaning to get over there for a while now, but with Mike's absenteeism and the sheer volume of work at the shop, he'd never found the time.

Grabbing his phone, wallet, and keys, Tim opened the door and turned back. "Brandy, come!" was all the encouragement the Bernese needed. Now glued to Tim's side, Brandy followed him out into the warm fall air. Once at the truck, Tim opened the back door wide, allowing the big black dog to leap into the backseat.

Harry lived in a little bungalow in a newer retirement community on the other side of town. He'd moved there shortly after his wife, June, passed away a few years back. Tim had only met June once, but she'd seemed like a great lady. Harry wasn't one to put his emotions on display. Still by the little he'd said in passing, Tim knew Harry still sorely missed June.

The tall, gray-haired man leaned heavily against the canary yellow 1969 Oldsmobile presently parked in the driveway. Tim parked on the street out front and approached.

"Harry." Tim smiled as he approached.

"Tim," Harry returned with a nod. Taller than Tim, the man looked like he was in his early sixties, though he knew he had to be a good ten to fifteen years older than that. He only hoped he'd age as well as Harry seemed to have.

"The old girl giving you issues again?" Tim asked as he glanced over at the car. Pristine paint job, gleaming chrome, and black trim. She was a beauty.

"Yup, another hiccup in the road, it seems," Harry nodded. "She turns over but won't start."

"Sorry I couldn't make it here sooner—" he began, but a wave of Harry's hand stopped him mid-sentence.

"I know what happened. An apology for being tardy after something as horrible as what happened at your shop is ludicrous. And you should fire anyone expecting one," Harry insisted without looking at him.

With nothing more to say, Tim opened the door, slid into the driver's seat, and turned the key. Just like Harry had said, she turned over but wouldn't start. Reaching down, he pulled the hood latch and got out. Once he'd leaned in with the immaculate hood above him and the gleaming engine below, Tim sighed. Just being under the hood with his hands on this fine a piece of machinery calmed him. It didn't take him long to find the issue. The fuel filter was completely clogged, not allowing any fuel to the engine. Tim stared at it for a moment. It was an easy fix and one that shouldn't have happened, considering Harry kept his car in such pristine condition. Odd, he hadn't figured this out himself.

Tim straightened and walked around the hood of the car. Harry had drifted over to Tim's truck to fuss over Brandy. The back door was open and he could see Brandy lying prostrate on her back in absolute bliss as Harry rubbed her belly.

Shaking his head, Tim walked to the back of his truck to grab a replacement filter. He could hear Harry talking to Brandy, but his voice was too low to make out the words, so gave it little heed. Once he replaced the fuel filter, the engine started without a hitch.

"Good job." Harry smiled as he came parallel to the driver's door.

"It was just a clogged fuel filter," Tim replied, giving him a sidelong glance.

"Huh. Well, I'll be damned," Harry replied, pushing his bottom lip out over the top in question. Even so, Harry didn't sound surprised by this news.

"Yeah, I'm a little surprised you didn't find it yourself," Tim commented, raising an eyebrow.

"Well, we all get it wrong one time or another." Harry smiled. "You have time for a beer?"

Tim hesitated for a beat. He didn't have to be anywhere after this and it'd been a while since he'd had the chance to shoot the shit with Harry. The man was full of surprising information, especially about Murphy. "Sure. That'd be great."

"I'll get Brandy a bowl of water. I may even have a few dog biscuits around here somewhere."

Tim smiled as he returned to the truck to let Brandy out. Apparently, Harry wanted Brandy's company as much as his own.

With Brandy on his heels, Tim followed Harry through a side door into the garage and whistled. This was the first time he'd been in Harry's garage, and it was gorgeous. A black, red and gray tiled floor, gray cabinets and work table across the back, and a red bar fridge in the corner by a sink. A dark chestnut bar table with four stools sat in the middle of the right parking spot, leaving just enough space to park the Oldsmobile on the left. Tim drifted over to the hand-made cabinets and worktable.

"Wow, this is gorgeous, Harry. You finish this yourself?" Tim asked, admiring the workmanship on the cabinets, before stopping in front of the ten-foot long, four-foot deep, two-inch thick solid-oak worktable. The gray stain revealed so many rings of growth, the tree this slice came from must have been ancient.

"Oh yeah. It took some time, but it was worth it."

Warm to the touch, Tim brushed his fingers along the worktable's surface to see if he could feel any of the hundreds of years of ridges along it. "I would occasionally help my father out in his workshop. He built most of our furniture. I remember the work being painstaking, but holding that finished product in your hands was so satisfying. How did you get your hands on such a gorgeous piece of oak? I thought these were nearly impossible to get."

"The tree that came from wasn't harvested in the traditional sense," Harry replied. But when Tim raised his eyebrows in question, Harry just shook his head. "That story will take longer than a beer to tell my friend. Let's save it for another time. Take a load off."

Tim reluctantly pulled his hand from the oak surface and headed for the bar table. He took a seat on the furthest stool and Brandy sat to his right on the tile floor with her front legs crossed. They both watched as Harry took a bowl and a bag from a lower cabinet, filled the bowl with water, grabbed a big biscuit from the bag and put it and the water bowl down in front of Brandy. Brandy first stared up at Harry and then over at Tim, waiting.

"She's so polite." Harry smiled down at her a moment before turning to head back to the fridge.

"Ok Brandy, take it," Tim told her and watched as the Bernese inched forwards and started nosing her treat.

Harry returned with two beers in hand, placed one in front of Tim, and took the seat across from him. Harry must have pushed the garage door button because the right side garage door slowly rose to reveal the sunny driveway. The cool air felt good against his skin.

A comfortable silence reigned for a few minutes. The only sounds came from the faint hum of a vehicle passing through the neighborhood, the occasional bang of a door, and Brandy crunching away on her treat. But finally, Tim figured he should break the silence. Having lived and worked in Murphy his entire life, Harry knew practically everyone. Tim thought if anyone knew of a suitable vacant building, it would be him and asked, "I don't suppose you know of a vacant building suitable for an auto repair shop?"

"Nope. But I can send some feelers out for you if you're in the market."

"Yeah, that would be great, Harry. It's time for a change."

"No doubt," Harry replied and waited until he met his

gaze again before adding, "What happened at your shop was a tragedy, Tim. No one should ever have to go through such a thing. Your mechanic, tall fella named Toni, I think? He gonna be ok?"

Tim breathed out for a moment before answering. "Yes, physically, he'll be okay. But it'll be a while before he comes back... if he comes back to work. I wouldn't blame him if he wanted to find work elsewhere after what happened."

Harry nodded. "He'll come back. If he has as good a head on his shoulders as I believe, then he'll be back. Not a lot of owners are as dedicated or as considerate to their employees as you."

Tim blinked and felt his eyebrows rise of their own volition as his gaze turned to Harry.

"People talk Tim. I heard what you did. Not something a business owner, big or small, usually does for his employees."

Tim shuttered his expression, but he needn't have bothered. Harry had his gaze fixed on the scenery outside.

Fucking small town. But Harry was right, people talk. He'd already set the death benefits when he started Timothy's Auto, but the decision to give his employees, or their families for Ralph and Mike, full salary and health benefits for another few months, was his. He knew it would be a tough go for a while, but it was the least he could do. They weren't just employees.

He just didn't know if he could forgive himself for somehow missing, or worse yet, overlooking the danger signs. His brother-in-law had been a problem for weeks before he'd gone on his killing spree, and it was Tim who'd kept giving Mike a pass. Maybe if he'd suspended Mike earlier, he and Ralph would never have argued, and Mike would never have...

"Stop blaming yourself. You likely couldn't have stopped it." Harry's voice startled him out of his dark thoughts.

Swallowing the lump in his throat, Tim refocused his gaze back on Harry, whose expression was decidedly grim. He didn't have to wait long for him to continue.

"I once knew someone a lot like Mike. Blamed everyone but himself for what was wrong in his life, always had an excuse for not being able to dig himself out of the hole he created. And instead of taking any of the help offered to him, he embraced his dark side and allowed it full rein. He, too, ended similarly to Mike."

"This person you're talking about... he was a friend?"

"At one time, he was a good friend. And then he wasn't." Harry shrugged in sadness. "Point being no one but Mike is responsible for what Mike did. And I don't mean any disrespect, but what happened at your shop could have been far worse."

Tim narrowed his eyes and opened his mouth to ask just how he thought it could have been worse, but Harry beat him to the punch.

"For example, you could all be dead right now as opposed to two of your mechanics. In my friend's case, he took his family with him."

Harry's words punched him in the gut, his body curling in at the thought of what could have happened to his sister Paula, and his niece and nephew, Reese and Riley. Cool air swept through the garage, bringing a chill with it. The sun was going down, so the air was cooling off.

"Jesus, that's... fucking awful," Tim spat, still feeling sick.

"Yeah, it was. At the time, I had similar thoughts to what I suspect you're dealing with. How had I missed the warning signs he could do something like this? Could I have prevented it? Did he do this on his own, or was someone influencing him?"

"Sam mentioned she saw someone talking to Mike outside just before..." Tim's voice trailed off. What more could he say? That Sam thought there was a psychotic killer running around Murphy messing with people, pushing them to kill? Even saying it in his head sounded ridiculous.

"Well, like attracts like, right? Even if that were the case, it was his decision and his alone to turn to violence and murder," Harry replied sadly.

A long pause ensued as the truth of Harry's words sank in. Having sensed the men's shift in mood, Brandy got up and kept alternating between the two of them. Currently, Brandy was up against Tim's leg while he absently scratched her chest.

Harry took a long pull from his beer before setting it back down on the table. "So how is Sam?"

"It'll take time for her shoulder to heal, but she'll recover," Tim responded automatically, relieved at the change in topic. The familiarity in the use of her name was unmistakable. "You know Sam Turner?"

"I hope so. We were neighbors for practically her entire life. Except for the last few years, Sam used to come over to visit us all the time."

"Really? You haven't seen her much since you moved here?"

"Been longer than that. Sam rarely comes back to town anymore. She came back less and less after her mother passed, but then after her attack... we're lucky if she comes home at all anymore." Harry shook his head. "Even as a youngster, Murphy was never easy on her. When someone shines as brightly as our Sam, it can attract bad things."

Tim stared back at Harry for a moment, processing several things at once. The fact Sam hated her hometown was no surprise, but the fact "bad things" had been happening since she was young was new. And now he knew someone with inside knowledge of Sam. Tim was itching to ask Harry more, but held his tongue. Harry had pushed back his stool, showing he was about to get up. It seemed their little tête-à-tête had come to its natural end.

Giving Brandy a last scratch, Harry rose and led them out the open garage door towards his truck. The sun was setting, and the view was gorgeous.

"Thanks again for coming by to fix the girl today, Tim." Harry smiled.

Tim nodded, but he didn't believe a word of it. He knew Harry knew how to fix it. It didn't matter though, as Tim felt like he may have gotten more out of this repair than Harry had. Smiling, he said, "Anytime, Harry."

Opening the back door, he stepped aside to allow Brandy to jump up. Once he'd shut the door, Tim reached out a hand to shake Harry's hand. His grip strong.

The old man nodded and then said, "Make sure you keep that pretty lady by your side. She may be a happy, go-lucky pup, but she'll protect you when it counts."

Tim watched as Harry retreated to the garage before getting in behind the wheel. As he drove, Tim replayed parts of their conversation over and over again in his head, including his parting words, which felt more like a warning than random advice.

Chapter 11

Back In The Big City

Sam couldn't stay in Murphy any longer. She'd never taken time off in her life, so after almost two weeks of resting, she was ready to go back to her apartment. Besides, the increased frequency and urgency of calls from her project manager told her they were getting antsy to have her back.

Chief Turner offered to take care of fur face while her shoulder recovered, but Sam refused. She couldn't imagine not having Buddy with her. When her father insisted on driving them the couple of hours back home, she didn't argue. She knew he'd offered the ride out of concern, but it also insured she came back to Murphy. With no way to get her car home, she had to return to get it back. Sneaky.

What happened at the auto shop had a strangely cathartic effect on Sam. Her worst fears had come true. She saw Charlie again. Someone tried to kill her, again. This should have sealed the deal for her ever returning to Murphy, but instead it dulled the sharp edge of her fear. She'd survived a second attack and although she didn't understand why, someone or something was looking out for her.

Once home, Sam threw herself back into her routine. Commuting to work and shopping locally became a necessity as opposed to an option. Luckily, both the subway and the local market were just down the street from her apartment. She kept in touch with Tim, talking to him once a week, which soon turned into twice a week or more. Her father kept her updated on the search for anyone resembling Charlie's description. So far, the favors he'd called in hadn't turned up anything, but that didn't surprise her.

Sam tried walking Buddy at their usual time, but that didn't work out so well. After being attacked by a mixed breed Rotti last summer, Buddy had a wariness for male black dogs. As luck would have it, the first pooch they ran across was a poorly trained black lab cross who beelined it for them. Buddy jerked his lead a few times in response to an ensuing struggle for dominance, jarring her shoulder. After that, she switched to walking him much earlier in the morning to avoid the unwelcome canine meet and greets. Sadly, running Buddy wasn't an option, so she asked her neighbor, Steve, otherwise known as Mr. Grumpy, if he'd mind taking Buddy with him occasionally. She knew he ran because she and Buddy often passed him on their way out. He looked ready to refuse when a cute blond appeared beside him who, upon seeing Buddy, dropped to her knees and fussed over the fur ball. Buddy obliged, wagging his tail, loving the attention. That's when Mr. Grumpy surprised Sam with a "Sure, why not?"

At first, Steve only took Buddy with him a couple of times a week. However, Buddy must have melted some ice around Steve's heart because by the time Sam started physio, he was popping by to take Buddy on his run almost every day. He'd even started pleasantries with Sam. Any friend of her dog was a friend of hers.

"That's my pup. Even an old grump like Steve couldn't resist your charms," she whispered as she scratched Buddy behind the ears. Sam got an affirmative "Woof" and nudge for her efforts. As Sam left for physiotherapy, she gave Buddy strict rules to remain vigilant and leave her new Merrells alone. Although he was well past the chewing stage, he wasn't beyond gumming up new shoes. For reasons beyond her understanding, he loved the new leather smell that came with purses, shoes, or belts. Last time she bought a belt, it went missing for an entire year. She found it hidden in the lining of his dog bed. Clever bugger.

She took the number two bus to the physiotherapy and rehab center. Physio was excruciatingly painful, especially with Nurse Ratched at the helm, Sam's nickname for her physiotherapist Nancy. The woman had a no-mercy battleaxe attitude, not to mention she looked a little like Louise Fletcher, the actress who played Nurse Ratched in *One Flew Over The Cuckoo's Nest*. Nancy took it all in stride and often laughed when Sam called her that. Scary when she wanted to be, Nancy didn't faze her. Sam didn't scare so easily these days.

Pain meant it was working. At least, that's what Nurse Ratched responded with to anyone who dared complain. And Sam had to admit her merciless approach was working. After less than a month, she had a lot more mobility and strength in her shoulder. Nurse Ratched figured it would be another eighteen sessions before Sam could return to normal activity levels. Sam kept a countdown of the number of sessions left after each appointment. It made her feel better knowing the torture wouldn't go on indefinitely.

Then she could go back to Murphy to retrieve her car and get her freedom back.

Sam got to know a few of the other patients while in the waiting room. Pat, the flamboyant grandmother with chronic neck issues because of a head-on collision with a car years ago. The car won, although Pat would argue she gave the Honda a run for its money. Katie, the quiet gymnast and once aspiring Olympian before the fall that left her in a wheelchair. Now she only aspired to walk again. And Bernie, the surly ex-construction worker, who was dealing with the repercussions of backbreaking labor over the last 30 years.

Right from the beginning, she and Pat got on like a wild-fire. They'd chat, joke, and hassle the physiotherapists who dared to doddle within earshot of the waiting room. With each subsequent session, more and more people began hanging around the waiting area, joining in on their conversations.

It turned out that beneath Bernie's crusty exterior lay a wicked sense of humor. And the teasing and camaraderie even drew the sullen Katie out of her shell until she, too, was smiling and putting in her sarcastic two cents. The four of them often brought everyone to tears, the howls of laughter reaching as far as the businesses next door. They only found this out when the hygienists from the dental office on the right poked their heads in to find the source of such mirth. Sam looked forward to seeing her comrades in pain three times a week.

Nurse Ratched really lived up to her nickname today, forcing Sam to push past the pain. By the end of each round of exercises, her shoulder ached from her neck down to elbow. It took everything she had not to lie down where she stood and take a nap.

Exhausted, Sam headed for the change rooms to get dressed, a challenge with her shoulder, but she made do. She paused in front of the locker mirror, her eyes drawn to the damage done to her body. Her scars looked less angry than before. Her fingers traced the raised and puckered skin of the old knife wounds on her abdomen, mementos from her first run in with Charlie, and allowed her gaze to drop to the tine-shaped scar on her thigh from their second encounter. She couldn't help wonder if there would be a third and if she'd be lucky enough to escape with only a scar the next time around. Three strikes. The mere thought of a third encounter made her stomach muscles clench and hands sweat. Keeping an eye out for Charlie had become almost as much of a habit as breathing.

Sam checked the wall clock and hastened to finish dressing and get to work. On her way out, she stopped at the front desk to pay and set up her next session. She didn't recognize the red, curly-haired receptionist attending to the person in front of her. Slow and ill mannered, Sam already knew it wouldn't be a fast process. It didn't help that her voice had a high nasal screech similar to *The Nanny* actress Fran Fine.

"How do you want to pay for this again?" the receptionist asked, her voice verging on a screech. Sam had already told her twice to put eighty percent through her health insurance and the other twenty she'd pay by cash, but the girl wasn't getting it.

"My health insurance covers eighty percent of it. Yes, that's the card in your right hand. Use that and then I'll pay the difference in cash." Sam gritted her teeth as the redhead sighed in exasperation, obviously upset she was being so put upon. If that wasn't bad enough, the woman then yelled across the room at someone named Sally. A burly lady with short brown hair and hawkish features materialized beside the receptionist.

"What now, Joan?" Sally asked, irritation etched in every plain of her face.

"This woman wants me to put eighty percent of this bill through her insurance or something. I don't know how to do a partial charge to insurance," the redhead complained, holding out the card in front of her like she might catch something from it.

Sam did her best not to let her irritation show, even though all she wanted to do was hunch forward like a troll and growl at the receptionist. She didn't think that would go over well, so kept her lips pursed to keep any nasty comments from slipping out.

"We have shown you how to do this, Joan, many times already." Sally sighed as she directed the receptionist on what to do.

Sam prayed for patience as the girl attempted to ring the payment through a third time under Sally's guidance. The Fran-esque quality of the red-headed receptionist's complaints tap danced on her last nerve. She forced herself to look away rather than resort to yelling at her and saw Katie being escorted to the back doors by a nurse. A blond was talking to her physiotherapist. Her eyes skittered to Katie as she disappeared through the exit, then darted back to the man. Sam stared. Try as she might to get a better look at him, a partial side profile was all she got. The platinum blond hair, his build, what she could see of the guy's profile bore a striking resemblance to Charlie. Then he laughed. Even at this distance, the sound creeped her out. Before she even realized what she was doing, her feet were carrying her towards the man in question.

"Hey, I need your signature. Excuse me!" The receptionist's nasal screech increased in pitch with each word. Sam put her hand up in acknowledgement, but kept walking. By the time she made it out the back exit, the nondescript black SUV had already pulled away from the curb and into traffic.

Sam re-entered the center and sought the physiotherapist the man spoke to, but because of patient confidentiality, she got very little. Also, the red-haired receptionist's squawks had crescendoed to painful. Knowing she wouldn't get anything more from Katie's physiotherapist, Sam headed back to deal with Joan before everyone's eardrums exploded.

After that, Sam was so busy at work, the rest of her day flew by in a blur. However, no matter how busy she got, Katie and her Charlie lookalike danced in the back of her mind. Her last session was in three days, which coincided with Katie's next appointment. She didn't know what she'd say to the depressed teenager, but she had to warn her somehow. Sam was not looking forward to that conversation. The one person trying to help often drew the skeptic's gaze first, but perhaps that was the point. If what you're doing is painful enough, then perhaps it'll make a difference.

The next three days flew past, as did Sam's final rehab session at the clinic. Sam did her best to concentrate on Nurse Ratched's instructions, but her gaze kept drifting towards the waiting room to search for Katie.

On their first session, Nurse Ratched, having noticed the deep bruise caused by the tire iron, asked Sam how she'd injured her shoulder. Sam told her the truth. Nurse Ratched hadn't mentioned it since until now.

"And Turner—" Ratched said, grabbing Sam's attention as she stood to leave her office for the last time, "let the police tackle the bad guy next time. Unless you miss me so much, you want to come back and visit." Ratched grinned, baring her teeth ever so slightly.

"I might be a masochist, but I'm not crazy. I hope to God I never have to see your smiling face again, Ratched," Sam returned with a grin before heading for the reception.

After confirming Katie hadn't canceled her physio appointment, Sam sat down and waited. After another hour of no Katie, she gave up and left. Once home, Sam went straight to bed and curled up with Buddy. Although she hoped Katie had acted like the typical teenager and just missed her appointment, a part of her suspected something had happened to her.

A few days later, Katie's family informed the clinic Katie had died. Sam was still in touch with Pat, who called her that night to let her know. Katie'd hung herself by her medal two nights after she'd last seen her.

Everyone close to Katie knew about her depression, so they didn't question whether it was anything more than a suicide. And perhaps her suicide was inevitable. Going from aspiring Olympian to partial paralysis would depress the happiest person. For all intents and purposes, Katie's physio had just started. She hadn't even had enough time in to see how much mobility would return had she stuck it out. But if Charlie was involved, Sam knew he'd at the very least expedited the kid's suicide.

Besides, hanging herself by her medal was quite the dramatic exit for a depressed teenager.

* * *

The next morning, Sam began searching for answers about what happened in the days leading up to Katie's death. Being the daughter of a cop, she knew how to get the information she needed and took the next two days to investigate the family and what role Charlie may have played in Katie's life.

The Parson's housekeeper, Marie, a short, dark-haired lady in her mid-forties, answered the door when Sam came to pay her respects. Marie's red-rimmed puffy eyes and reddened face showed how distraught the housekeeper was over her charge's death. It took very little coaxing to get her to open up. According to Marie, Katie's new psychotherapist, Dr. Lea, who sounded like a dead ringer for Charlie, only seemed to make her charge feel worse. The housekeeper often referred to Dr. Lea as the "Devil" throughout her telling of the events preceding her charge's death.

Katie was clinically depressed and her doctors suggested a psychotherapist would be beneficial, giving her someone outside the family to talk to. But instead of helping her, Katie became more moody and withdrawn after each session she had with the new therapist. According to Marie, these sessions seemed to bring out a new depth of sadness in Katie that scared her. She tried bringing it up to the Parsons but her concerns fell on deaf ears. They told her they just had to trust in Dr. Lea's process. Then it was too late.

Marie always helped Katie in the evenings with the more challenging activities, like giving her a hand with her bath and helping with her prescribed stretches. As usual, Katie retired to her room after dinner, but when it reached midnight and she still hadn't heard from her charge, Marie went to her door to inquire if she needed anything. Her first knock was met with silence, so she'd knocked again, but still nothing. After the third knock, she'd opened the door to find

Katie hanging limp and lifeless at the end of her bed, strung to the top railing of her bedpost by her medal.

Sam already knew what Marie would have walked in on. Katie's eyes red with burst blood vessels, bulging grotesquely from a pale face. Her tongue swollen from a lack of oxygen pushing out her bottom lip. To Marie, it would have looked like a demon had taken her charge. And maybe one had.

Unchecked tears streamed down Marie's tired face by the end while Sam sat there helplessly. She couldn't do much to ease Marie's grief. Once the housekeeper settled down, she thanked her for her honesty and silently vowed to kill Charlie if she ever had the opportunity. Before leaving, she asked if her psychotherapist was around when Katie took her life. The housekeeper shook her head, saying he'd already gone home for the day.

On her way out, Sam turned to ask Marie one last question.

"Sorry, but you wouldn't know Dr. Lea's first name?" Sam asked.

"I overheard Mrs. Parson refer to him as Richard once," the housekeeper murmured before bidding her goodbye and closing the large, solid oak door.

Sam just stood there, staring at the closed door for a moment, thinking about the name. Something about the name bothered her.

Dr. Richard Lea.

Richard Lea.

Rich Lea.

C-H-A-R-L-I-E.

Son of a bitch.

It would have been heartbreaking for a young girl who had so much potential to have it all taken away in a split second by one bad landing. Even if Dr. Richard Lea left before Katie hung herself, it didn't shake off his guilt one iota. The more victims that turned up, the more she thought this might be Charlie's pattern. Although Sam couldn't ask his other two victims since they were both dead, she'd bet her life each of them felt just as hopeless as Sam had so many years ago.

Like an addict trying to find his next fix, Charlie hunted down the depressed, hopeless, and broken.

The next day, Sam scoured the news for other incidents involving a man fitting Charlie's description, but nothing turned up. So far, she seemed to be the only one still alive that could link him to anything.

The more she thought about it, the more she knew Charlie had made a mistake with her. He would come to rue the day he let her live.

Chapter 12

Bill, The Good Teacher

Bill Morris was a teacher at J.P. Murphy High School. He taught geography and geology and considered himself to be one of the better teachers on staff. Bill had a wife, two kids, a yellow lab, a gray SUV and a two-story house in the suburbs. Bill was an average, middle-income guy living an average, middle-income life. No big life dramas. No secret meetings with a girlfriend on the side. No real money problems weighing him down. No work politics. He rarely, if ever, complained. A great neighbor to all, helping when they asked or even when they didn't. Bill was a fine contributor to the community.

Every day he'd get up at 5:45 am, take the dog for a walk, come back to shower, shave, get dressed, have breakfast with his family, then head for work. Bill would get to his classroom, coffee in hand, with fifteen minutes to spare. He wore charcoal or dark brown slacks with a blue or beige and white striped shirt, black socks, and brown loafers. Sometimes he changed it up with a pullover, but only when he felt a bone chilling day coming on. Bone chilling was a great analogy for so many things; like those cold, rainy days when you never seem to warm up, or his mother's stare right after she found out his father had cheated on her, or how he felt right after he dreamed about doing unspeakably violent things to his own family.

The scary thing was, he wasn't sure where these thoughts came from. He wasn't a violent man or prone to fits of rage. His kids were average students with average lives who disappeared in their rooms after dinner and often whined about not having the latest this or that gadget until they wore him down. And his wife, Joanie... well, Joanie was Joanie.

They met in college and dated for three years. As an English major, her goal was to become the next New York Times best-selling author. As a Geology and Earth Sciences major, he'd set his sights on working for a big gas company like Shell or Esso one day. His family liked her and her family liked him. Both of them had the same core values, from politics, to religion, to the number of kids they wanted. They were perfect for each other. They got married, got pregnant and had two kids.

Joanie never wrote a short story, let alone a best-selling piece of literary brilliance. As the kids got older, he expected she'd look for a job, but she never did. When their eldest, Lizzie, was old enough to babysit her little brother, he sat Joanie down to talk to her about it. She balked at first, but by the end of the conversation, she assured him she'd start applying for work. A year later, when Joanie still had found nothing, Bill took the matter in to his own hands. There was an opening at their family dentist for a part-time receptionist, which would be as good as hers if she got in touch with them. That night, Bill couldn't wait to get home to tell Joanie, but instead of relief or appreciation, his news was met with anger and outrage. Usually Bill backed down from a fight, but this time he held his ground and pushed back until she admitted the truth. She'd never intended on finding a job. Then, in the same breath, she stated her work was raising their two kids and he couldn't put a price on that.

Bill never got his dream job. The few interviews he landed over the years went nowhere. Bill could tell, even as he answered their questions perfectly, that they were only humoring him. He was competing against younger PhD grads, so to them he was old news. As the years passed and his dissatisfaction grew, it was hard not to feel a little resentment. It was Joanie, and by extension Lizzie and Chris, who'd prevented him from getting his PhD. Bill planned to continue his education the fall after they'd married. They had already accepted him into the PhD program, but that summer Joanie got pregnant. As the sole breadwinner, he was forced to continue working. When Lizzie was past her toddler stage, he'd planned to go back to school and let Joanie bring home the bacon for a while, but she got pregnant again. After two "accidental" pregnancies, Bill got a vasectomy. Joanie had steamrolled him twice and still he'd stayed.

His life was not what he'd envisioned for himself twenty years ago. Although he had moments of dissatisfaction, he'd always been able to shake them off with a good sleep. Lately, though, he wasn't shaking off anything and his negative feelings towards his family were escalating. He now saw Joanie for what she really was... a lazy, selfish opportunist. Bill was just her meal ticket. And the apples hadn't fallen far from the tree because Lizzie and Christopher were duplicates of their mother... persistent little shits when they wanted something, but often ignoring him otherwise.

Bill was trapped. Divorce wasn't an option. Not just because it was a sign of failure, but Joanie hadn't worked in well over fifteen years, so he'd end up paying big time on spousal and child support for a family he felt less and less love for with each passing day.

No, divorce was not the solution he was considering.

His subconscious thoughts were much darker than that and though he could push them down when he was awake, they'd begun intruding on his sleep. He knew this because, for the first time in his life, he remembered his dreams, and they were as vivid as reality. He'd wake up in a cold sweat, nauseated, and gasping for air like a drowning man. He couldn't believe he'd dreamed about hurting his family, but night after night, he did.

What scared him most wasn't the fact they were getting more violent, but that, as time went by, he didn't feel as horrified by them as he had the night before. Just like his family who often wore him down to get what they wanted, his subconscious was wearing him down to get what it wanted.

Bill was being conditioned from the inside out.

* * *

Bill shifted in his sleep. His dreams often began the same way.

He was in the den grading papers. He'd heard the doorbell ring a minute ago, but thought nothing of it. It was probably for Lizzie. His daughter was quite popular, so there always seemed to be a revolving door of kids coming in and out of their home.

Shouts from somewhere in the house broke the silence.

"Bill! Dad!" His wife and kids screamed. Bill was up

and at the door within a second, but what he saw as he swung the door wide made him freeze. A stranger was in their house, chasing Joanie, Lizzie, and Chris. He held a metallic object in his right hand that caught the light. A knife. And he was gaining on them. They fled up the stairs, their pursuer hard on their heels.

The spell keeping him rooted to the floor broke, and Bill started moving again, chasing after them. He reached out to grab the blond attacker, his right hand successfully grasping the man's shirt. The stranger wrenched himself free, pulling Bill off balance. His right foot slipped from under him, bringing his right knee down hard on the stair. A fierce pain pierced his upper shin and knee. Bill didn't know how much damage the fall did him, but the crunching sound didn't bode well. He had trouble getting his leg to move the way he wanted it to. Bill saw his family make it to the master bedroom mere steps ahead of their blond assailant. Bill already knew it wouldn't be enough lead-time for them to get the door closed. The blond pursuer was forcing it open.

"No... leave them alone!" Bill roared. Ignoring the pain shooting up his right leg, he forced himself to move. The few seconds it took him to hobble up the rest of the stairs and down the hall felt like hours. The blond man had already ducked in to the bedroom. He felt a surge of terror as the door slammed. Bill reached the closed door, but it wouldn't open. He twisted the handle and banged on the door, all the while shouting for them to open up.

"Get away from me!" He heard Joanie scream. Bill tried slamming his shoulder into it, but it wouldn't budge. They had a century home, so most of the doors were the original solid oak, including their bedroom door. He'd always taken pride in that feature before. Now he hated it. Joanie's drawn out pain-filled scream sent him into a panic. He flung his shoulder into the door again. It held fast, but his shoulder was the worse for wear. Then his kids started screaming. He redoubled his efforts until the doorjamb finally gave way. He stumbled in to room, his shoulder badly bruised, maybe worse. What he saw made him freeze. Joanie sat in the middle of the bed, her back against the headrest. It was the same position she took at night if she wanted to have a talk, but a few things spoiled that innocent image. The odd angle of her head. Her glazed, open-eyed stare.

Lizzie's screams drew his attention away from his dead wife to the verandah where his kids stood. The sliding glass doors were wide open and the blond stranger was advancing on them. Lizzie had Chris behind her, shielding him with her body as they backed away, but they'd come up against the railing. She had her forearms up to ward off the blows but the blond was relentless, slashing at her every few seconds, laughing at every downward blow and fresh cut he made on his daughter's forearms.

Bill's rage swelled, his vision blurred red, and he roared as he advanced on their assailant. Bill raised his right arm up, the one gripping the knife, and swung downwards with all his pent up rage and fury.

Only it wasn't the blond assailant in front of him any longer. It was Lizzie. He watched in horror as the knife in his right hand, committed to its downward left-to-right arc, slashing across his daughter's throat...

"No!" Bill gasped, and sat straight up in bed. His entire body, soaked in sweat, shook and his right shoulder, the one he'd rammed against the door in his dream, ached. At least his dream didn't nauseate him this time. He looked over to see Joanie lying beside him, snoring softly. Unlike himself, Joanie had always been a solid sleeper. Still, it surprised him she hadn't woken up. On the best of nights, Bill might get five to six hours sleep, but lately he'd been lucky to get a couple. He looked down at his still trembling hands to verify they were clean and blood free. Bill slumped back in relief, only then realizing how rigid he'd held himself, his muscles aching now that they were slack.

Chapter 13

Peter, Peter Student Eater

Peter Vance hated his school with a passion. His fellow students reminded him of lemmings, following each other around without an original thought between the lot of them, and the teachers weren't much better. They didn't have a great affinity for him, either. To say Peter wasn't well liked at Murphy High was an understatement. He had a few acquaintances, but their interactions didn't reach beyond a nod here, or a question there. He walked to school alone. Sat in class alone. Ate lunch alone. And walked home alone. Though not exactly sure why others gave him such a wide berth, he could guess. He wasn't handsome or even cute. He wasn't athletic. He wasn't funny or outgoing. He wasn't academically inclined. His parents were all of these things. They were attractive, athletic, successful people, and they were as alien to him as his peers were.

Sometimes he fantasized he was, in fact, an alien sent to live among humans to teach them something important. And when he came of age, his purpose would reveal itself and he could finally do what he'd been sent here to do.

Unfortunately, reality was more prosaic than that. No one cared about him, and he never learned to care about anyone else.

Peter's parents seemed happy enough. They were the extreme opposite of the helicopter parents of his peers. Gone before he got up in the morning, they usually returned well past dinner, so he seldom saw his parents anymore. Busy, successful and popular, they were in high demand and made little time for Peter, especially now that he was no longer a cute kid they could show off to their friends. There wasn't much cute about him now.

At seventeen years old, he was all angles and awkward edges. His mother liked to call him gangly. His father didn't call him anything at all. Last year they forgot his birthday. Peter never mentioned it to them and they never let on they'd forgotten. It was like his birthday had never happened that year. They did not know what was going on in his life, nor did they seem to want to know. Perhaps it came down to simple biology. Peter was nothing like them, and they knew it. They were not the same, therefore they deliberately left him behind. As a senior, they should be interested in their son's plans after high school, but neither of them had even broached the topic with him. Perhaps they already knew he wasn't passionate about much of anything.

Anything except Miss Kelly, his French teacher. He'd do anything for her. Beautiful, kind, intelligent, and he was pretty sure she was fond of him as well. Why else would she offer to help him all the time? She was always happy to see him, went out of her way to talk to him, and she'd even touched him on his shoulder when she came over to help him last week.

For the first time in a long time, Peter buzzed with excitement. Today was the day he would reveal his feelings to Miss Kelly. Peter had a little hop in his step as he walked to class.

* * *

Peter remained after class for his semi-regular tête-à-tête with Miss Kelly under the guise he needed help. Of course, he needed the help, but he couldn't give a donkey's twat about French. He was there for one reason only: Miss Kelly.

She looked pretty in a light pink skirt and a white blouse. She had her black hair pulled back at the top, but some stray strands hung down to curl along the back of her neck and along her collarbone. He couldn't help but stare, enthralled by the way her blouse pulled here and there straining the buttons as she spoke and gestured at the backboard. He loved the way she used her hands to illustrate her points. Peter tried to concentrate on her words, but he was utterly lost. She was trying to teach him about the rules around the use of the superlative. Peter kept nodding and repeating what Miss Kelly said, hoping she wouldn't question him further. However, this tactic only lasted so long before she started asking him questions in French about the material she'd just gone over. Perhaps his far off, dreamy expression gave him away. Peter was stumped and could only shrug as she peppered him with questions until Miss Kelly had had enough.

"Peter, it's like you're not listening to a word I've said. I don't mind helping you, but if you aren't even going to attempt to understand the material, then you're wasting my time." She stood there staring at him for a second, waiting for a response. After a few minutes of silence, Miss Kelly shook her head and turned towards her desk. She started packing up her books, muttering in French under her breath.

Peter panicked. The last thing he wanted to do was piss off the woman he loved. He had to tell her the truth. *Well, it's now or never,* Peter thought, and got up from his seat and approached her desk.

"I'm sorry Miss Kelly. I'm distracted because I have something on my mind," he said, stuttering over his own words. "The thing is, I..." But what he wanted to say evaporated again.

"Mademoiselle Kelly," Miss Kelly reminded him without looking up as she continued packing. Peter wanted to tell her how much he adored her, but his tongue just wouldn't form the words.

Not knowing what else to do, Peter stepped into Miss Kelly's path. Being a head taller than his French teacher it would force her to look up at him. When her startled eyes rose to meet his, he reached for her, but all his fingers found was the soft material of her blouse before it slipped from his grasp as she did a quick two-step backwards.

"No Peter! This is not appropriate behavior," she snapped, face beet red now.

Peter dropped his hands but continued forward, his tone beseeching. "Miss Kelly, we don't have to pretend anymore. I realize we have to be discreet, but I'm a senior now, so soon it won't matter that I'm one of your students. After I graduate, I'll be able to take care of you. Don't you see? I... I love you." Peter smiled tentatively, putting his hand out again.

Eyes wide and lips parted in surprise, Miss Kelly retreated but with the blackboard at her back, Miss Kelly was running out of room.

"You don't have to hide your feelings for me anymore.

The way you smile at me. Always offering to help me. Your interest in me personally, wanting to find out what's happening in my life. It's all an excuse to be around me, and I feel the same way about you. Don't you see, Miss Kelly? We'd be perfect together!" Her stricken expression was almost comical, like she'd run into a glass door at full speed not realizing it'd been there all along. Peter understood she might be a little embarrassed because he'd figured out she had feelings for him. That and the fact she'd be concerned about their relationship hurting her career if they weren't careful.

He saw something akin to panic cross her face as she shook her head. If he wanted to say anything more, he'd have to be quick about it. "I'd be discreet," he rushed on, "and I don't care if you're a few years older..."

"Stop!" Miss Kelly shouted. She had her hand raised palm out as if to ward him away, her panicked expression now replaced with anger.

Confused, Peter paused, his right hand still stretched out towards her.

Laughter to their right drew his attention to the two girls standing at the front of the room. He hadn't heard the classroom door swing open, so didn't know how long they'd been standing there. Peter felt a surge of anger at their intrusion, relieved he wasn't the only one. *Now they'd get it,* he thought, and waited for Miss Kelly to chastise the snooping teenagers.

"Peter, you are one of my students and are failing my class. I have no feelings for you other than I'd like you to pass my course. That's all! I offer several kids help, as you can see." She stated as she nodded towards the two smirking girls standing by the doorway. "It means nothing other than that, helping students that are having trouble

182

with French," she said, gesturing toward the girls to come in and sit down.

Peter took another step towards her, but Miss Kelly just stood her ground and eyed him like he'd grown a set of horns and hooves.

"Peter, leave now. And from now on, you will have to ask your questions and get the help you need during class hours." Miss Kelly turned away and walked to the far side of her desk, asking the girls to take a seat in the front row.

The girls sauntered over and took their seats, laughing in his face as they walked past. The first one, Elizabeth Morris, or Lizzie as her friends called her, whispered loser under her breath just loud enough so he could hear it. The other, her friend Christine something-or-other, rolled her eyes at him. Peter disliked most everyone at school, but he had a special hate on for these two and their little clique. Obnoxious, these spoiled brats had nothing better to do than make fun of everyone and anyone they deemed unworthy. And the rest went along with it. Being an expert at blending into the background and making himself too inconspicuous to be bothered with, they usually ignored him. Unfortunately, he may have just made himself interesting enough to get their attention.

Miss Kelly, ignoring him now, began talking to the two girls in French. Both Lizzie and Christine wore broad smiles as they waved him goodbye. Peter took one last glance at the woman he'd just poured his heart out to, yearning for some sign of hope, but she wouldn't acknowledge him. Another bout of laughter reached his ears as the classroom door swung closed behind him.

A slow curl of anger unraveled within. The burn of acid in his throat, a bodily reaction to the building rage that had nowhere to go. He needed to find a toilet and barely made it to the men's bathroom before he heaved up the contents of his stomach. What he retched up was something foreign, bitter and dark. Wiping his mouth with the back of his hand, he stared at the bathroom wall as he hung on to the dirty toilet rim. Along with a lot of graffiti, a peeling, faded image of their high school logo had been stuck to the wall beside the toilet. Obviously someone thought the sticker looked better here being sprayed by student waste rather than on the bumper of a car. Peter couldn't agree more.

He felt weird. Like a piece of his heart had just dissolved into bitter black muck and slid down to take residence in his stomach. Peter grabbed for the toilet again as another bout of nausea rocked him. Considering how much he'd retched up so far, soon there wouldn't be enough of his heart left to keep him alive. The thought was soothing.

* * *

The snide remarks, laughter and finger pointing began the next morning.

Lizzie and Christine proved they'd been busy over the last sixteen hours. A hush fell over everyone as he passed in the hall on his way to homeroom, but then the tittering started. He ignored the gawking, giggling and finger pointing, but the sneers and outright laughter were tougher to ignore. When Peter got to his homeroom, he heard his name spoken in hushed tones and whispered comments.

His homeroom teacher, Mrs. McBride, was a doughy, gray-haired teacher with pinched features who had an affinity for large floral prints. Although she appeared grandmotherly, no one would ever describe her as such. Miserly yes, but not grandmotherly. Peter didn't mind Mrs. McBride. As teachers went, she wasn't the worst at J.P.

Murphy High School and she usually left him alone. It was in her class where the real harassment began.

"Psst," someone hissed to Peter's left. He ignored it and continued writing notes from the blackboard.

"Peter!" the person hissed again. And again Peter ignored him, but it caught the attention of others within earshot. He could feel multiple sets of eyes on him now. He figured if he refused to play their game, they'd eventually get bored and leave him alone. At least, that's what he hoped.

"Hey Pete, are you going to confess your undying love to Mrs. McBride as well? I'm sure she'd be game to ride a young stud like yourself!" The same person hissed. The comment set off a round of giggles and titters from the surrounding students. Peter recognized the voice as David Hess, a jock and more often than not the instigator in their group.

"I'm sure she'd be a WHALE of a good time there, studly!" That sounded like Ryan Dendridge, the group joker. His comment earned him a round of outright laughter from at least a half a dozen students.

"Peter, how does it feel being the only senior who's still a virgin?" another person sneered on the heels of the last comment. Peter white knuckled the side of his desk, his pen pausing mid-stroke. He almost lost control but knew it would be ten times worse if he engaged with them.

"Enough! Now be quiet and get back to work!" Mrs. McBride growled, glaring in Peter's general direction.

Although the outright comments and laughter stopped, whispered jeers and chuckles at his expense still erupted here and there. It all fed the hatred simmering deep within. The overriding thought he had as he traveled from class to class being harassed and guffawed at was he'd

185

never forget this day or those involved, especially Lizzie and Christine.

It was French class when his anger edged into a simmering rage. Every set of eyes in the class watched him, waiting. Whispers, snickers and the occasional giggle reached his ears, but no outright comments. At least not until the royalty of the student body showed up. And then the humiliation began in earnest.

"Hey Virgin... aren't you going to ask Miss Kelly out? Oh wait, you tried that already, and she shot you down!"

"Yeah, maybe she likes them young. I hear some teachers are into that kinda thing."

"Peter, Peter is such a sucker, has a hot teacher but can't fuck her..."

"What's wrong Peter? Did the big, bad French teacher huff and puff and break your heart in two?" another taunted.

"Enough!" Miss Kelly said upon re-entering her class-room, silencing the possibility of any further comments. She wouldn't look at Peter, but he watched her from under hooded eyes. Not once throughout the entire fifty minutes would she even glance his way. She ignored him and the class dragged on. For the first time, Peter looked forward to hearing the bell chime indicating the end of Miss Kelly's class. Though the perpetrators were hidden by the herd of students exiting class, he heard a few more snide remarks thrown his way on the way out. Everyone left except for a small group of students chatting in French. They'd taken seats in the front, making a semicircle close to Miss Kelly's desk. He hoped, unlike yesterday, he'd be able to talk to her without interruption. Peter remained in his seat, biding his time for an opportunity to speak with her.

He figured the real reason she'd reacted so poorly to his

confession yesterday was because Lizzie and Christine had interrupted them. The teacher's code of conduct clearly stated that teachers could not get involved with their students and to do so would be grounds for termination. Had they been alone he was certain she'd have returned his feelings. He had to get her alone. Miss Kelly was the only person who'd ever given him the time of day. She had to like him.

So lost in thought, he didn't notice when the animated chatter stopped. Someone cleared their throat, bringing Peter's attention back to the front to find all eyes on him. What had he missed? He leaned back in his seat and fidgeted with discomfort.

"I repeat, only students involved with the French club can remain, otherwise you must leave this classroom!" Miss Kelly announced in an overly loud voice. She made the declaration sound generic, but everyone knew it wasn't. Peter was the only one left in the classroom other than the French Club kids. He started putting his books away, but must have moved too slowly.

"That means you, Peter," Miss Kelly stated, eying him pointedly.

Peter got up and exited the classroom, all the while staring at Miss Kelly. She refused to look at him as he walked out, which angered him more than anything else he'd endured today. She'd treated him like he was nothing more than an annoying kid.

The reality of the situation sunk in. Peter had lost the one thing he'd felt anything for, Miss Kelly. He would make one last ditch effort, and if that didn't work, then all bets were off. He'd see them all go to hell if he could.

* * *

* * *

That afternoon, Peter waited for Miss Kelly until five p.m., after the French Club finished. She followed the last student out and was walking toward the back exit, where the teachers parked. Peter followed, catching up to her before she went through the first set of exit doors. He grasped her arm.

"Miss Kelly, can I talk to you in pri—" Peter began, but released her arm when she turned on him and shook off his grip.

"Peter, we have nothing to talk about," Miss Kelly said, cutting him off and took a giant step away from him. The little light streaming through the back door windows illuminated enough of the dark alcove they stood in to reveal her irritated expression. But that couldn't be right, because she cared about him. She had to.

"Peter, as I told you yesterday, you are my student and I am your teacher. That's it. I'd give the same help to any other student who needs it. You are not special in any way, shape or form to me," Miss Kelly stated, brow furrowed and lips pulled tight across her teeth. Peter had seen this expression once before when she'd chastised a student for insulting her, but this was the first time she'd directed it at him. Her expression softened as she continued. "I'm sorry if you've misinterpreted any help I've given you as anything more than a teacher aiding a struggling student, but that's not my problem. In the future, if you need anymore help with French, you must ask in class because I can no longer help you outside of class hours." Miss Kelly turned on her heel to leave.

"I know you feel something for me, Miss Kelly. Please let me—" Peter pleaded, his hand grabbing for her arm again. She shrank away from him, but wasn't fast enough. This time when he didn't release her, she jerked her arm away. Her expression showed her fear, but it was replaced with a look of disgust as she rubbed her upper arm where he'd gripped her.

"Enough! Don't seek my help after hours. Don't wait for me outside my classroom. And don't follow me ever again." This time she poked a finger in his direction as she said, "And you will not touch me again or I swear I'll have you expelled Peter."

Then Miss Kelly left.

He watched her leave, heels clicking on the sidewalk as she walked away and another enormous piece of what remained of his heart dissolved and slid down into his stomach. Even with only a partial heart left, he still felt the pain. Sadness that yet another person he'd reached out to had rejected him. Hurt that the woman he loved could treat him with such contempt. Helpless because he couldn't do anything about it. Overwhelming despair because he was tired of struggling and fighting. And for what? Why did he have to struggle so hard against everyone and everything?

He pressed his head hard against the cold pane of the window in the door. The cool glass felt good on his forehead. Peter tapped his head on the window. The tapping gradually graduated into thumping until it turned into pounding. Peter pounded his head on the tempered glass to the beat of his heart. The pain in his forehead throbbed, and the salty copper taste of the wetness running down his forehead, along his nose to his lips told him he was bleeding, but he didn't care. The physical pain was a welcome distraction from the emotional pain he felt. He would have pounded his head indefinitely had it not been for the tap on his shoulder from someone standing somewhere behind him.

Peter swung around to face the intruder, tense with hands fisted. But it was only the janitor. Peter's shoulders slumped in relief.

"Looks like you're mighty upset about something," the janitor drawled, looking him over. His gaze paused on his forehead before coming back to his eyes. "I don't suppose it's about a girl?"

Peter studied the man in the blue jumpsuit for a minute. His voice made him sound older than he looked. He had light hair, either platinum blond or white gray. He assumed platinum blond because this guy didn't look old enough to have gone gray yet. His boy-next-door looks and wrinkle free face hinted at later twenties. The blue jumpsuit was nondescript. He had a name tag with CHARLIE printed on it, and his right hand held one of the biggest brooms he'd ever seen. He guessed this guy must miss the corners if all he used was this broom.

Although the janitor's posture was relaxed, Peter felt uncomfortable. He supposed part of it might be he wasn't used to having to talk to people, and this stranger was forcing him to talk. The other part was the janitor's position had him cornered, making it hard for Peter to remove himself without either bumping or knocking him aside. The janitor's body, the broom he held, and his distance from Peter effectively wedged him between the door and an over-size garbage can.

Peter mumbled a quick "Sorry" and attempted to walk around him. Only the janitor didn't budge. Now he felt trapped and more than a little irritated. The janitor was grinning, but there was nothing funny about the situation Peter could see unless he was getting pleasure out of making Peter squirm. He'd had enough crap for one day and had to resist the urge to smash the janitor's face in and get himself expelled.

"Listen, buddy, get the hell out of my way. I need to get home," Peter said as he shouldered his way past the janitor. Rude, yes, but effective because Peter was now free of the corner.

"Why the rush? You know, the only thing waiting for you at home is an empty house and a microwave dinner."

Peter paused and swiveled his head back to eye Charlie the janitor again. "Yeah, me and every other student here." And continued up the hall towards the front exit.

"Perhaps, but most parents don't treat their kids like boarders or leave for weeks at a time without notice... it's almost like they don't even like you."

Paul stopped dead in his tracks. Wary now, he turned back to assess Charlie. *Who was this guy? How the hell did he know this stuff, and what the fuck did he want?* He was about to ask, but Charlie beat him to it.

"You're wondering how the hell I know this? Oh Peter, I know much, much more than you could ever even imagine." And then Charlie the janitor grinned, a wide toothy grin that reminded Paul of a big bad wolf parody he'd seen years ago.

The janitor knew his name, but he'd never told him what it was. He supposed he should feel unsettled by that, but oddly enough he didn't. He felt calmer now than he had all day, though he couldn't put his finger on why. The anger he felt had gained strength all day and crescendoed into rage after his final tête-à-tête with Miss Kelly. The rage remained but now simmered on low beneath a blanket of calm.

What was happening internally is what had happened to him externally years ago. By all appearances, he looked like a normal teenager, but everyone else seemed to know better, hence why he'd been ostracized since he started high school. Now his psyche was catching up with everyone's expectations.

Peter was rapidly losing the ability to care about anything or anyone else. People reap what they sow and he was an excellent example of nurture versus nature. No one cared what happened to him, and that complete lack of love by anyone had created him. At that moment, he hated everyone without exception, even the janitor. However, this Charlie fellow piqued his interest.

"Come on. We can chat as I give you the grand tour of your school. You wouldn't believe all the nooks and crannies this place has. You could hide just about anything here, and no one would be the wiser."

And then the janitor named Charlie gave Peter a tour of the school unlike any other.

* * *

* * *

Peter's education...

Peter took his usual spot on the bench by the soccer field to eat his lunch. The culinary delight of the day was tuna. The only reason he knew it was his lunch was the post-it pasted to it declaring it "Peter's lunch." But the mayo tasted tinny and old. Unfortunately, this wasn't the first time his mother had handed off her old lunch to him. He suspected she'd bought the sandwich for herself but got so busy she forgot to eat it so it sat where she'd dropped it. Unopened on her desk, in the hot sun most of the day, hence why it had that lovely tinny taste. Waste not, want not, she probably thought when she popped it into a lunch bag and left it in the fridge in the morning for him. As usual, she was gone before his alarm went off.

"Thanks for nothing," Peter said in disgust. He hated that all too familiar feeling of disappointment in his parents and put the half a sandwich he'd taken a bite out of back in its wrapping with the rest of it then squeezed hard, making a tuna and bread ball wrapped in cellophane. He whipped the spoiled tuna-dough ball at the soccer goal and right into the net. *Score! With any luck, the goalie would step on it later and get a stinky tuna encased cleat.* Peter smiled at the thought.

This bench was a semi-regular haunt for him. Peter found the best way to avoid letting his anger get the better of him was to avoid people as much as circumstances allowed. Hence why he ate in the yard as opposed to the cafeteria, where most of the herd congregated for lunch. But this strategy was no longer effective now that he'd become the gossip du jour. Over the last few days, not only had anger become his constant companion, but the cattle had begun to seek him out.

He saw a couple under the big sugar maple tree to the left of the field. If he had to guess, he'd say it was Robbie Swayne and Jane Dinsmore. They were an item these days and Robbie was pretty easy to pick out in his shiny silver jacket. Robbie strode around school like he was the bomb, but to Peter it just looked like inflated tinfoil. The girl leaned against Robbie, his left arm wrapped around her shoulders. There was a large bulge in her bright red top. He figured it had to be Robbie's hand stuck down the front of it, but hard to tell from this distance. Peter was far enough away that they could have peeled off their jeans and done it right there by the tree, and all he'd be able to make out would be the contrast of their clothing against pale skin. Like most everything these days, he quickly lost interest in the couple.

Peter's personality had always leaned towards the somber end of the spectrum. Even before the Miss Kelly incident, no one would have mistaken him for a positive, hope filled person. However, of late, darker, more disturbing thoughts had clouded his mind and without the usual diversions to distract him these darker influences were gaining ground. One of his favorite pastimes was reading, but now he had trouble focusing on the stories. He also enjoyed gaming, but he hadn't picked up a controller in months. Peter didn't want to be here anymore. It was like the town was gradually eating him alive, tearing the flesh from his bones, chewing his tendons like liquorice and slurping up the little fat he had like pudding. Consuming all the best parts, and spitting out the gristle and bone left behind. Peter felt the pounds sloughing off as each day passed. Now he needed a belt just to keep his jeans from sliding down.

On the rare occasions when they talked, his father liked to remind Peter that "These were the best days of his life and he better appreciate them because it wouldn't get any better."

"Peter, Peter pumpkin eater has no life, and is such a good bleeder. For Miss Kelly he really fell, but had no chance cause he's an imbecile," came a singsong voice from in front of him. He didn't have to look up to know which asshole was singing. Good ol' aluminum boy had sought him out.

Peter looked past him. Not one to be ignored, Peter felt a sharp blow to his right foot. He squinted up at Robbie. He expected to see Jane somewhere behind him, but she was nowhere in sight.

"Did you get a nice eyeful there, perv?" Robbie asked, looming over him. He fit every jock stereotype; all brawn, no brains, and a bully to boot. Robbie was also as perverted as they come, but the irony of his accusations would be completely lost on him.

Peter had no illusions. He knew life wasn't fair. He also knew this dimwit had no idea just how good he had it.

Try being in my shoes for a day and see how fast you crumple like the empty can of diet Coke you resemble, Peter thought. He knew it didn't matter what he said to Alcan man. If Robbie wanted to kick Peter's ass, he would do it without thinking twice. That's when Peter saw an image in his mind's eye of a can of Diet Coke kicking the shit out of him and it struck him as so funny he let out a small giggle.

Robbie must have heard it because one moment Peter was sitting on the bench and the next he was laid out on the ground behind it. His jaw and lower left cheek throbbed from the sucker punch he'd received, and his head and butt hurt from the impact of hitting the ground. Peter was pissed, but the laughter and guffaws from somewhere to his left pissed him off even more.

"Wow, the power of steroid use," Peter coughed. He knew provoking him while still lying prone at Robbie's feet wasn't the best idea, but deep down Peter understood it didn't matter what he said or did. The assholes of the world, at least in Murphy, would always find a way to justify beating the crap out of him. So why bother fighting it?

"You weird-ass motherfucker!" Robbie shouted. Peter felt sharp stabbing pains everywhere Robbie's boot connected.

After Robbie grew bored and left, Peter remained where he lay, on his side in the dirt, breathing. All but one of the sharp pains had abated to dull aches, but he'd be sore for a while. Mesmerized by the dirt swirling on the ground in front of his nostrils with each exhale, it took him a minute to register the shadow standing above him. He refocused his gaze on the dark work boots in his eyeline. Peter didn't bother looking up. He already knew who owned the work boots.

The janitor loomed over him, but didn't say a word for a few moments.

"Taking a dirt nap, Peter?" Charlie chuckled, breaking the silence. "Perhaps this will be the impetus you need to understand that down in the dirt is where the others should be."

"What are you doing here? Shouldn't you be cleaning a toilet or something?" Peter grumbled.

"Hmm. Someone woke up on the wrong side of the ground. You know I'd be pretty shitty at my job if I lolly-gagged around, feeling sorry for myself like you are right now."

Peter rolled from his side onto his back, groaning a little when the ground connected with his bruised tailbone. He was in a foul mood and didn't appreciate Charlie poking at him as if they knew each other.

"As a janitor doesn't lollygagging kinda come with the territory? I thought a big part of your job was to sit around and pretend to clean up other people's shit. Speaking of which, the boys' washroom by the library needs cleaning after what Tom Laretti did to it." A long pause ensued. Long enough, Peter thought perhaps Charlie had walked away. But when he opened his eyes, the dark work boots were still there.

"Young, misguided, sad, Peter... most of my job is what I do in the background. The stuff that no one ever sees. Besides, I consider myself more of a facilitator than a janitor." Then Charlie did something unexpected. He lifted one of his boots off the ground and pressed it into Peter's newly bruised ribs. He increased the downward pressure until Peter cried out.

"Get the fuck off me!" Peter's hands wrapped around Charlie's boot, trying to push him off his aching ribs, but his efforts didn't seem to have any effect at all because the pain Charlie's boot caused didn't ease in the least.

Charlie's lips curled into a wolfish smile. He continued talking in a low voice that only Peter would hear. "Listen up Pete, because I'll only say this once. Your father was right. You better appreciate the good times now, kid, because it won't get any better. Your shitty little life's a nightmare and I'm not sure why you bother getting up in the mornings other than to get your ass kicked. Life is full of choices, but all the avenues open to you just keep leading back to the same shitty path, you meek little mouse." At that point, the pressure on his ribs increased until Peter shouted out in pain, certain he felt something snap. Then the pressure let up again.

"Here's the clincher kid. Life's a bitch and everyone dies, but at least you can choose when you go and how many you take with you." And then Charlie was gone. Peter sucked in the breath he'd been holding through his haze of pain and expelled it in a moan as he laid his head back down on the ground. Once the intensity of the pain diminished to an ache, he gingerly touched his ribs until he found what he was looking for. There was a small ridge. *Yep, definitely a break. Motherfucker!*

As he laid there waiting for the pain to ease, he couldn't help but think about Charlie's words. He hated this fucking life and all the fucking people in it. There wasn't one person left he gave two shakes of a shit about and that included his own weak ass. No one cared what happened to him. Most onlookers seemed to enjoy his humiliation. Even the silent non-participants condoned it, otherwise they'd say or do something. All of them were cattle, waiting for their next instruction. Do this, go there, line up for the nice people, sit down at your desks... get slaughtered here.

I might be the meek mouse today, but just wait and see what I become tomorrow. The hint of a smile curved Peter's lips. For the first time in a long time, Peter felt something akin to hope. He had something to look forward to, and that was enough to motivate him to carefully pick himself up off the ground.

Yep, his future was looking brighter already.

Chapter 14

Zoey And The Wicked Wolf

Zoey had had it. She'd barely dodged a set of scissors swinging dangerously close to her head twenty minutes ago, and enough was enough. The sneaky bastard snuck up on her while she was at the water fountain. Fortunately, she caught Robbie Swayne's reflection in the tap in time to sidestep him. A good thing too, because the way he'd swung those scissors around he would have cut more than her hair had she not ducked in time.

Having a known medical condition like chronic migraines had its benefits. She left school early, complaining of an onset.

The root of her problem stemmed from the Jackson Street jackasses. Two years ago a group of high school boys with pea-size brains decided it would be a great idea to perform stupid stunts such as seeing how long they could hang on to the back of a moving car, or skateboard into a brick wall and compare injuries, which they then posted on YouTube. The founders of this brilliant endeavor lived on Jackson Street, hence the name, and of course they'd copied the premise from the infamous *Jackass* series of movies.

Their latest stunt, a scavenger hunt, had them running around the school scavenging for target items. Unfortunately, someone in their troop decided it would be a great idea to include Zoey's blue hair as one of their most prized items. She'd been dodging scissor and clipper wielding teenage jackasses for the last few days and her harassment quota was maxed out.

Considering what she'd experienced in Murphy over the past few years, Zoey expected the unwanted attention, but this stupid stunt hit an all new low. What floored her most was seeing Sean in the thick of it. Of all the boys swarming around high school, Zoey thought Sean had the greatest potential. When she'd first met him, he had an opinion, didn't always go with the status quo, could hold a decent conversation, and was nice. Zoey wouldn't call him a friend anymore, but she never thought he'd screw her over either. Until now.

As she made her way home, she noticed someone fall in step beside her. So lost in thought, Zoey didn't know how long the person had been shadowing her. Zoey looked up, expecting to see a familiar face, but found a stranger. It was odd, and it startled her.

People who don't know each other just don't walk side by side. And in the off chance it happens, the newcomer always drops back or speeds ahead. Not this guy. He just kept walking in step with her. To an onlooker, they probably looked like friends walking home together.

After another few uncomfortable minutes, Zoey changed direction and headed back to the store she'd just passed expecting the man to keep on walking, which he did. She wanted to put some distance between herself and the stranger, so she loitered at the magazine rack. The clerk kept glaring at her, but she ignored him. After about five

minutes of perusing *People* magazine and not bursting into
flames from the nasty looks the clerk shot her way, she put
the magazine back on the rack, chose a pack of gum at the
counter and exited the store with her purchase.

Not seeing the man, she started for home again. A light
breeze ruffled her blue locks and sent a chill down her back.
The sun, hidden behind a cloudy sky, wouldn't have the
chance to burn away the gloomy haze settling over Murphy.

The day matches my mood perfectly. Tugging her jacket
closed against the cool air, Zoey hugged herself, but her
chill remained.

The unwanted negative thoughts from the morning
began intruding on her consciousness. The straw that sent
her home was witnessing Sean brandish a pair of scissors as
he laughed with his friends who then pointed in her direction. His laughter died when their eyes locked, the mirth in
his expression replaced with... what? Guilt? Shame? He
looked like he wanted to say something. Maybe *Sorry but I
couldn't resist the urge to be a lemming anymore,* or perhaps
*Deep down I was always a jerk, you just didn't want to
see it.*

Who knows and who cares? But Zoey was still angry at
allowing Sean's stupidity get to her. She knew he'd changed
since he'd gone over to the jackasses. Now he seemed like a
lost cause.

Although deep in thought, Zoey became aware of the
crunch of footsteps to her right. She looked over and caught
a glimpse of the same dark runners worn by her unwanted
companion from earlier. Nice shoes, she thought, but still
rude to walk alongside someone without being invited. He
must have waited for her while she'd been in the corner
store, which made this guy downright creepy.

Zoey sped up, but her creepy companion matched her

pace. At almost three quarters of the way home, she didn't want this guy knowing where she lived. Not that it would be hard to find out in a small town like this one with so many wagging tongues. Still, instinct told her caution was best here. Zoey stopped dead in her tracks and waited. Mr. Creepy took a couple more steps before stopping and turning back to face her.

Zoey broke the silence with, "Who the hell are you, and why are you following me?"

The stranger smiled, transforming his creepy image into more of a boy-next-door one. He almost looked pleasant. Almost. The smile was a little wide, and it didn't reach his eyes. Zoey had enough experience with superficial niceties to know the difference. This was different.

"My name is Charlie. You seemed a little blue and thought you could use a friend."

Zoey caught the play on words and didn't like it. His widening smile told her he thought himself quite clever, but he was old enough to realize his approach would unsettle a lone teenage girl. This guy was either playing games or out of touch with reality. And far too persistent for comfort. Zoey took the direct approach.

"I don't want you to walk with me, Charlie," Zoey stated bluntly.

"Well, that's not very friendly, is it? Besides, I'm not walking with you. I'm walking beside you. We both just happen to be heading in the same direction," Charlie said, using his hands to illustrate.

"Fine then, I don't want you walking anywhere near me, Charlie. I'll stay here while you continue on your way," Zoey said as she dropped her school bag, crossed her arms, and planted her feet. Unsure of where this encounter was heading, she tensed, ready for a fight. This guy weirded her out.

Charlie looked at her for a minute, then smiled, said, "Ok Zoey, have it your way," and walked away.

Zoey stood there, staring after the receding figure. It took a few moments for her to realize what had bothered her about his last statement. He'd called her by her first name. She didn't know this guy from a bar of soap, so how did he know her name? Zoey stared after him, but restrained the urge to call him back to ask. Her sense of self-preservation wouldn't let her. It's also when she noticed what looked like a pair of scissors peeking out the top of his jeans pocket.

"Motherf—" but someone calling out her name cut her soft curse short.

Zoey glanced to the left to find John Peterson sticking his shoulder and dark baseball-capped head out the passenger side window of a blue Honda Civic. The driver was harder to make out, but she suspected Sean Grindal was in the driver's seat. John was a founding member of the Jackson Street jackasses. Considering the day she'd had so far, their sudden appearance on her street in the middle of a school day seemed par for the course.

"Zoey, how are you?" John asked, smiling. John had never said more than two words to her before.

Step right up and check out the girl with the blue hair, the one and only one in Murphy. She'd be happy to let you slice off a sample for your scavenging pleasure! Zoey would have bet big money he held a pair of scissors in his left hand, but she refused to scurry away like some timid rat.

"It's funny how popular I've become today. People who have never deigned to talk to me before are suddenly my friends. So... are you my friend now, John?" Zoey cocked her head to the side, waiting for a reply.

John looked a little startled by her talk back, but his tentative smile lasted mere seconds before his face split into a grin. "Sure, I'll be your friend. Why don't you come here and hang out with us? We could even give you a ride home."

"Hmm. I doubt you're interested in my sparkling personality or the fact I can hold a decent conversation. From what I hear, you don't hang with a girl unless you intend to fuck her, which means you spend about, what? Two minutes max with her and then you're back with your buds? You've gained quite the reputation, John. So much so it's like you're trying to prove something. So I wonder, are you that guy? The one that needs to prove how manly he is because, in reality you're afraid to let your gay flag fly?" Zoey paused as John sputtered. "Well, let it fly B-U-D because we're all friends here, right?"

John was turning an interesting shade of red. Zoey didn't care. She saw through his crap and knew for all his huff and puff that he was a coward. She didn't feel this guy was an actual threat, at least not at ten after two in the afternoon on a quiet residential street. Zoey had had it and wasn't in the mood to put up with any more bullshit.

"Since I'm not one of your *buds* and considering what I've overheard you call me when you think I'm not listening, like *alien* or *reject from the blue man group*, I'm assuming you're not here to fuck me so what exactly do you want John?" she said, staring at him. A vein pulsed in John's darkened face, and his arm tightened as he gripped the outer door handle. But just when she thought she may have underestimated him, his grip loosened. Zoey was almost disappointed to see him relax. Although she was sure he'd be able to overpower her if he wanted to, she knew she'd get in a few good strikes. She knew enough self-defense moves to know where to hurt a person, even someone as big as John.

"Next time, freak. We'll catch you when there are fewer eyes around," John growled, his gaze fastened on something beyond her. He then tucked his baseball-capped head back in the car and they drove away.

Zoey glanced over her shoulder to see what had spooked John into leaving. She was afraid she'd see stalker boy behind her but found it was the clerk from the corner store. He was still looking over in her direction. She lifted her hand and waved at her unlikely hero. The clerk looked at her for another few seconds, shook his head and waved her off like he'd wave at an irritating fly buzzing around his head. *Well, maybe not such a gracious hero,* she thought wryly as she picked up her schoolbag and headed for home again.

Wary now, because of her two back-to-back run-ins, Zoey had her head on a swivel as she continued home, but no one intercepted her. It seemed both her new friend John and stalker boy had left her alone for now. Her mind raced over the day's odd events and she couldn't help wondering if it was a full moon.

She'd reached her house and was crossing the lawn when she noticed a faint scent that reminded her of lazy Sundays. It was the smell that drifted up and teased her senses into coming downstairs to join the land of the living most mornings. It was coffee, and not just any coffee, but a Tim Horton's coffee. She could identify that aroma anywhere.

Her excitement evaporated when she rounded the corner and saw who held the Timmies coffees. Stalker boy. The hairs stood up on the back of her neck. She stopped walking to debate her options. He was blocking her path to the side door. She could either approach and face crazy head-on or walk back the way she'd come to the corner store. Although the troublemaker in her would love to see the look on the clerk's face when she reappeared in his store, she was getting tired and just wanted to get inside her house and forget about today. Besides, stalker boy was being persistent enough he'd likely follow her. Zoey opted for door number one and prayed Charlie was a harmless nut. As a precaution, she dipped her right hand into her bag and found her keys. She then palmed the key chain and slipped a key between each finger as she approached. A crude weapon, but at least she had something if needed.

Charlie grinned as she neared him. She came to a halt just outside his reach, but close enough she could see the color of his eyes. They were an odd color, not aqua but not a sky blue either. The combination of his blond hair, fine features and the blue of his eyes made him look angelic, almost. His wolfish grin marred the effect. He held out one coffee. She reached over with her left hand and took it. She had one foot in the rabbit hole already, and he wasn't allowing her any room to wiggle out.

Charlie was leaning up against the side door, blocking her way into her house, so she mirrored him and settled against the passenger door of her dad's pickup. Charlie watched her as he took a long draw from his Timmies, but Zoey just held hers. She'd learned a long time ago not to take candy from strangers, and Charlie was the strangest of them all. She debated on asking him to leave, but she'd already tried the direct approach and look where that got her.

Zoey waited for him to say something, but he seemed far too interested in his coffee to bother. The cup of coffee, now uncomfortably hot in her hand, had to remain where it was otherwise she'd have to give up her crude key weapon. Besides, a hot beverage could be a useful weapon, so she did her best to ignore the mounting discomfort. Zoey waited for Charlie to get on with the conversation, but only an uncomfortable silence ensued.

Unable to bear this weirdo's company any longer, Zoey broke the silence first. "Charlie, or whatever your name is, I've had it with the stalker routine. Can you just tell me what you want? And please don't gross me out by saying you think I'm cute or something like that cause you look old enough to be my father." In reality, Charlie didn't look old enough to be her father, but Zoey didn't care. She didn't want him hitting on her. Her day had been pretty shitty so far, and she was ready to pack it in.

Charlie didn't speak right away. His smile and laid back stance as he took another sip of coffee told her he was savoring her discomfort as much as he was his coffee.

"I told you before, I thought you could use a friend. And considering what I saw after our brief dialogue, I was right, wasn't I? With a friend like me you could go places Zoey... or should I say Chelsea." Charlie took another draw from his coffee, letting the fact he knew her real name sink in. His expression changed, becoming leaner and meaner, but still held a whisper of a smile. "Although I will concede I am technically old enough to be your father, I couldn't possibly have filled your dad's shoes. I mean, the way your father took down your entire family... it really was a work of art. You gotta give your old man points for efficiency. Using only a baseball bat on your mother and twin brothers. He had real potential," Charlie remarked with obvious admiration.

Zoey's mind reeled with information overload. All she wanted to do was remove the satisfied expression from

Charlie's face, but she was having trouble putting this in motion. The easiest way would have been to throw the hot coffee on him, but the shock produced by his words stunned her so badly the coffee slipped from her numb fingers and drop in an ineffectual puddle at her feet. She could hear a high-pitched keening sound coming from somewhere close by. It stopped as soon as she snapped her mouth shut, making her realize she was the source of the noise.

"How? Why are you—" Zoey tried to say something intelligible, but her brain wasn't cooperating. The confusion and anger brought on by his surprise assault overwhelmed her. She could feel herself shaking, but was helpless to stop it.

Although most people would have heard about the Deroras family five years ago, no one knew who she was. No one except the officers who responded to her nine-one-one call and Family Services that put her in the custody of her mother's sister. The media became so bloodthirsty for any fresh scrap of dirt they could get on her parents that her aunt and uncle decided moving was the only way to ensure some normalcy for Chelsea and themselves. Once they got official custody of their niece, they changed everything for her. Each of them took their middle name as their first, dropped the "son" from their last name to become "William" and her aunt and uncle became her parents from then onward. They moved over a thousand miles to start again in the little town of Murphy and only stayed in touch with their most trustworthy friends. Both of them went from working for the government to working for themselves doing what they loved most, working with dogs. Most people didn't understand how to train their own kids, let alone their pets, so Wag the Dog Daycare & Obedience School flourished. Zoey helped with the business part-time and loved it almost as much as her "parents" did.

Though she had never admitted it to them, picking up and leaving everything behind was the best thing they could have done for her. Not only did she come to feel like they were an actual family, but it allowed her to feel normal from time to time.

Zoey was the lone survivor of the Deroras family massacre and no one outside her inner circle knew this. Until now. Was it possible for someone to find out where they'd gone? Obviously, the answer was yes, but they'd have to be pretty motivated to go to that much effort. Zoey's stranger danger flag was flying high now. Charlie was not some harmless stranger, nor was he a local. If he'd been a local, Zoey would have seen or heard of him by now. That's the price you pay for living in a small town. Everyone knows everything the day it happens, so the only way to keep anything a secret is to have no witnesses and never speak of it, not even to your best friend. Zoey curled her hands into tight fists and waited for the shaking to abate. Once she felt calm enough, she let her words fly.

"What do you want, you C-R-A-Z-Y F-U-C-K-I-N-G P-S-Y-C-H-O-P-A-T-H!" Zoey shouted. Not a smart or eloquent move, but it garnered a response.

Charlie was in front of her so fast she rocked back on her heels, only to come up hard against her dad's Ford pickup. Charlie's position effectively pinned her right hand to her side, leaving her key weapon useless, his face mere inches from hers. Because of his proximity, it was hard not to look into his face. His breath reeked of coffee and some sort of spice. Rosemary perhaps. His striking blue eyes were downright creepy up close. They seemed to take on a life of their own. Charlie leaned in closer, shoving her right arm against the window, pinching it painfully. She refused to give him the satisfaction of acknowledging the pain and gritted her teeth. But the pressure he put on her arm only intensified until a pain-filled moan escaped her compressed lips. And then it eased.

"I'm here to help finish what he couldn't." Charlie tilted his head as if in consideration. "Tsk, tsk, tsk... don't worry Zo-eeeey, you may still get your chance to punch the smile off my face because I G-U-A-R-A-N-T-E-E we'll be seeing more of each other soon." And then he was gone.

She never saw where Charlie went, or the approach of their neighbor, Mrs. O'Grady. Her eyes were wide open, but nothing was registering. Zoey shouldn't have been surprised to see their nosy neighbor. However, a butterfly landing on her arm would have startled her at this point.

"Zoey, what are you doing home so early? Shouldn't you be in school? Oh, I doubt your mother would be happy about this!" Mrs. O'Grady had scolding down to an art form.

Normally Zoey would smooth things over with a white lie or two, but in this moment she couldn't care less what her neighbor thought or did. Mrs. O'Grady must have taken in her ashen face, strained expression, and lack of response because the next thing she knew she'd switched from reprimanding her to neighborly concern. Mrs. O'Grady insisted on helping her as she took Zoey's keys from her bruised right hand and unlocked the side door entrance. She then escorted her into the house and had her take a seat at the dining room table. She heard the elderly lady chattering away as she bustled around the kitchen putting the kettle on to make tea, but Zoey was so preoccupied with her own thoughts that it barely registered.

Thoughts of another girl with another life and another family not so long ago.

* * *

That evening Zoey and her aunt and uncle had dinner together, and as was their ritual, each took turns talking about their day. She enjoyed hearing about their accomplishments with this or that dog, or frustration with a stubborn canine, but tonight Zoey had difficulty focussing on their conversation. When asked about her day, she rattled off what they covered in class, leaving out anything to do with the ridiculous scavenger hunt or her encounter with the stranger named Charlie.

The reasons for keeping her tête-à-tête with Charlie to herself made perfect sense. The most obvious being, what could they do about it? If someone wanted to hunt her down, they would, period. If this Charlie guy did, in fact, want to finish what her father hadn't, then what would stop him from finding her again? Monsters are real and living among us. They could be a stranger, the clerk at the local grocer, a neighbor, a friend, or even a father.

Another reason was her aunt and uncle were happy in Murphy. They'd already uprooted their lives once for her, leaving behind friends and jobs they enjoyed. It had taken years for them to establish their business and new friendships. How could she ask them to move again? It was doubtful they'd be so lucky in the next town they found.

Besides, she didn't want to run anymore. It felt like she'd been running since the night her family died. She was tired. If Charlie knew something about it, Zoey wanted to find out what it was. Could be another piece in her fucked up family puzzle. She needed to know why her father murdered them, the ones he supposedly loved most. The standard "your father had a psychotic break due to stress" didn't cut it.

Truth was, she just plain didn't want to tell them about Charlie. For now, the why behind her resistance to tell them would have to drift around in her subconscious.

When Monday rolled around, Zoey considered skipping school, but in the end decided against it. Although not ready for another encounter with Charlie, she couldn't stay home indefinitely either. She'd just have to make sure she wasn't caught alone again. With that in mind, Zoey chose the most popular, but least favorite, route to school. She didn't relax until she reached the high school grounds. So far, so good, she thought.

She glimpsed Bonnie making her way up the sidewalk and beelined it for her. Although not a close friend, Bonnie was someone she'd occasionally chat with. Known for preferring older guys, she'd likely know if there was a new available guy in town. Bonnie glanced over as Zoey caught up with her.

"Hey Zoey," Bonnie said.

"Hey," Zoey said. "You go to Kelsey's party this past weekend?"

"Oh yeah. You missed a good one, Zoe. Kelsey got so smashed she let Lizzie dye her hair green. This awful puke green color. By the way, a few of the guys asked after you." Zoey knew which guys Bonnie was referring to and their interest in her had nothing to do with them crushing on her. After dodging multiple assassination attempts on her blue locks last Friday, Zoey had boycotted all parties until the scavenger hunt was over.

"Maybe the next one." Zoey replied, nodding. "Listen, I don't suppose you've seen anyone new around town?"

"Hmm... only the new postie. Not much to look at but seems nice enough," Bonnie replied with a shrug. Bonnie was referring to the new postal worker, Arthur Bellio or Art, as he insisted on being called. Zoey had met him when he brought his chocolate lab, Ruby, to doggy daycare a few weeks back. Art was a short, dark-haired, ruddy faced Italian with a pleasant disposition. And the complete opposite of Charlie.

"No, the guy I'm thinking of has platinum hair, blue eyes, a slim, muscular build, and tall."

Bonnie shook her head. "Nope. Sounds yummy though. Someone you're interested in?"

"You might say that," Zoey said. Bonnie cocked an eyebrow, curiosity written all over her face. Zoey was interested in him, at least in his whereabouts, but she wasn't willing to talk about creepy Charlie to anyone, least of all Bonnie. When Zoey volunteered no more information, Bonnie shrugged and let it go.

"If I hear anything, I'll let you know," Bonnie nodded. There was a brief pause before Bonnie gasped, grabbed her forearm to pull her around to face her. Bonnie's eyes were as big as saucers and Zoey braced herself. "Did you hear what happened to the French teacher?" Bonnie exclaimed, her voice rising on the last two words. Although Bonnie had always been nice to her, she liked her gossip.

Bonnie rolled her eyes at Zoey's confused expression. "Wow, it's all over the school. I swear, sometimes it's like you live under a rock or something!"

"I left early on Friday," Zoey explained. She usually ignored gossip. Most of it was either exaggerated versions of the truth or, at worst, blatant lies, leaving one or both parties involved hurt or embittered.

"A few nights ago Christine and Lizzie heard Peter tell

Miss Kelly he loved her! I guess Miss Kelly freaked out on him."

Zoey nodded, hoping that would end the gossip gab. *Who cares if a student has a crush on a teacher? It's bound to happen.* Zoey was more surprised this was the first they'd heard of it. Young, slim, petite, attractive, and she could speak a romantic foreign language, Miss Kelly was the epitome of every teenage boy's fantasy.

"God, Peter is so strange. He finally gets a crush on someone and it's his freaking teacher. He'd be lucky to have a shot with any girl at our school. Even Sue Malloy has better taste than to date the likes of him, but to try for a teacher! Hello! Earth to Peter! Anyone home?" Sue Malloy took after her father and tended to dress more like a truck driver than a teenage girl.

Being a bit of a drama queen, Bonnie's impassioned speech didn't surprise her, but Zoey understood why Peter had a crush on Miss Kelly. She was probably the only female who'd ever given Peter the time of day at school. Of course, he had no chance with her and he should have realized she'd be off limits being his teacher and all, but the guy had to be lonely. Anyone who paid even a little attention to what was going on around school could see that.

Zoey felt sorry for him. Peter was the classic loner, and she understood being a loner herself. The difference was although solitary by nature Zoey still forced herself to go to some parties, sit with friends at lunch and chitchat because it's what society expected. Besides, you needed someone in your corner. If you break from the social norm and don't have any support, even if in doing so you're trying to avoid being seen, you inevitably draw negative attention to yourself. People don't like what they don't understand and they don't understand outliers. It reminded her of the Sesame

Street song Big Bird sang... *One of these things is not like the others. One of these things just doesn't belong. Can you tell which thing is not like the others?* The other would be Peter Vance.

Zoey stopped dead in her tracks. Less than a couple of yards in front of her sat Peter. And beside him stood a janitor, but it wasn't the usual older man who they knew and disliked. Their school janitor was a grizzled, gray-haired, smelly grump who, according to the dirty name tag he wore, went by the name Larry. Zoey had always thought it strange they never reprimanded him for his lack of personal hygiene considering they hired him to clean their school. This was a much slimmer man with either white or platinum blond hair sticking out from beneath a dark blue ball cap. His back was towards her. She couldn't tell if it was her stalker, but something about him gave her pause.

Zoey murmured an excuse to extricate herself from Bonnie's rant and, without waiting for a reply, headed towards Peter. She'd only taken a few steps before someone grabbed her arm, bringing her to a halt.

Sean Grindal, the driver of the ass-mobile from yesterday and ex-friend extraordinaire. Zoey stopped, but pulled her arm free of his grasp. She'd never enjoyed being manhandled and Sean was no exception, old friend or not.

"Sorry Zoey... I just want to talk," Sean said, putting his hands down. "Listen, I'm sorry about yesterday. I didn't know why John wanted me to ditch fifth period and drive him around. He told me to turn down your street and boom, you were there. He assured me he only wanted to talk to you, otherwise I never would have stopped."

Zoey waited for him to say something more, but when nothing came, it infuriated her more than if he'd said nothing at all. "Sean, are you seriously trying to tell me you thought he wanted to socialize with me? When has John ever stopped to chat with me?" Zoey had time to cool off over the weekend and she had, but now she was getting pissed off all over again. Friday had floored her for many reasons, but seeing Sean behind the wheel of John's getaway car was a new low for him. Now he was trying to tell her he didn't know what John had been up to? How stupid did he think she was?

"I didn't know, otherwise I would never have driven him," Sean insisted.

"Jesus... I saw you waving the bloody scissors around Friday!"

"Yeah, I'm sorry about that. But I told him to leave you alone, Zoey. And that I wouldn't be involved with the scavenger hunt any longer." Sean's pained expression seemed genuine enough. Still, Zoey didn't understand why Sean cared what she thought anymore.

"Hmm... well, congratulations. You finally found the balls to speak up and have an opinion that contradicts those jerks. Kudos on your choice of friends, by the way. Speaking of which, I see your buddies coming down the hall towards us right now. So I guess we should go back to ignoring each other again?"

Sean looked like he wanted to say something else, but after a few moments of silence, Zoey left. She was halfway down the hall before realizing Peter no longer sat on the bench against the wall. She scanned the crowd but didn't see the janitor either. The halls continued to empty as students disappeared into their homerooms. Frustrated, Zoey headed for her locker.

Another fun-filled day at Murphy High and it's only just begun.

Chapter 15

Dream A Little Dream

That night, Sam dreamed about Mr. Morris's geology class. He was teaching the concept of tectonic plates. Sam only ever took one geology class because it was a requirement. Odd that her first dream about Murphy High landed her in this class.

She was doodling in a notebook when she noticed strands of blue hair lying across her right shoulder. She looked back down at her hands as they worked on the lined paper. Porcelain white and slender with a tiny cross tattoo on the back of the thumb. Nope. Not her hands. A coat of light silver blue polish over neatly clipped nails. Definitely not her shade. Her gaze dropped to the delicate bracelet, a flock of silver birds circling her right wrist. A beautiful piece, but again, not Sam's style.

She was wearing a fitted black t-shirt with stenciled on white wings, black jeans and dark ankle boots. Clearly not a Barbie doll, she thought. Who was this girl?

The glint of silver from her wrist caught her eye again. It was such a unique piece, odd for a teenager to wear to school. The chain of birds flew toward a larger piece, the focal point of the bracelet. Dozens of tiny birds flew in a circle around four or five birds clustered wing to wing in the middle. The girl let the pencil drop from her fingers to the desk, opting to play with her bracelet instead. Nervous habit? The center circle flipped over, and Sam got a glimpse of the fine print on the back. "Deroras" was the only word she caught before the girl stopped fidgeting with it and raised her right hand.

Deroras. Sam didn't recognize the word. A family name?

The girl sat that way for a few minutes, hand raised, waiting for Mr. Morris to address her, but he never did. She was being ignored.

She stood, threw her notebook into the bag hanging on the back of the chair, slung it over her shoulder and headed for the back door. It wasn't until Mr. Morris stepped in front of her she stopped.

"I repeat... Miss William, where do you think you're going?" Mr. Morris asked, staring her down.

"To the washroom," the teenager stated. As she stood there, Sam felt the girl's jaw clench. She did not like her geology teacher.

Mr. Morris shook his head and pointed back towards her seat.

She just stood there, staring back at her teacher. Sam could feel the internal struggle in the teenager's tense shoulders and clenched jaw. The girl glanced at the door again. Just when Sam thought she might make a dash for the door anyway, she relaxed. Her shoulders rounded down, and her jaw slackened before turning to go back to her desk.

The teenager sat but remained tense. She didn't even open her notebook to keep up the pretense of note-taking. Something kept drawing her attention back to the door because she kept taking furtive glances at it. The third time she glanced back, Sam saw what held her attention. Someone was standing in the hall, looking in. The only thing visible in the darkened hallway was the shadow of someone's head and shoulders. What she saw on the girl's next glance left Sam stunned. There, framed in the door's window, stood Charlie. His lips peeled back into that awful, shark-like grin, and his eyes sparkled with a blue flame.

The girl was already on her feet, hurrying towards the back of the room. Mr. Morris stood on the opposite side of the class, so try as he might, he wouldn't be able to block her exit this time.

"Miss William, get back to your seat! I won't tell you again, young lady!"

Ignoring the order, she stayed her course. She'd almost reached the door when the face vanished. Running the last few steps, she swung the door open and stepped out into the hall.

"Zoey William! If you leave this classroom, don't bother coming back! You can take yourself right on down to the principal's offi—" Mr. Morris shouted, his last few words lost under the swoosh of the closing door.

Sam reeled. What sick game was Charlie playing at with this girl? Zoey William, Mr. Morris had said. She didn't recognize the name. And why did Zoey feel compelled to follow this sick fuck? Sam wanted to yell at the teenager to stop following him, but as a mere observer there was nothing she could do.

Zoey pursued Charlie, clad in what looked like a janitor's uniform, down the hall. She had to jog to keep up with his long strides. He turned left down a corridor. By the time she came around the corner, he'd already reached the end of the next corridor, turning right this time. He paused, as if to ensure she was still pursuing him, then disappeared around the corner to the right. The teenager jogged the rest of the way down the hall, rounded the corner, and found no one there. Sighing in exasperation, Zoey continued down the hall at a dead run, but stopped when she reached the end of the corridor. The hall was empty and silent, the only sound her own heavy breathing.

Although the layout of the school was familiar, a lot had changed since Sam had frequented these halls.

Suddenly Zoey's breath blew out in alarm, bringing Sam back to what had the girl so agitated. She was standing under one of four exits out of the school. It looked like the east side exit, but where there used to be a water fountain now stood an eyewash station. That's when she noticed what had Zoey so upset. Someone had chained the handles of the exit door together with a padlock, barring anyone from getting in, or out, of the school. Zoey touched the chains, the steel cold to her fingertips.

Desperate to know the time, Sam urged Zoey to look up above the exit doors where the wall clock used to sit, but the girl didn't raise her head. Instead, she reached into the bag slung over her shoulder and slid her hand along the bottom until it hit a flat rectangular object. Pulling it out revealed an iPhone. Zoey touched the screen, displaying the time and date. It read 2:27 pm on Friday, October 17th. Tomorrow.

Zoey hit the phone icon and dialed 911. She waited a minute with the phone against her ear, but when nothing happened, she looked at her phone again. One bar, so although low, it still had a signal. She tried redialing the last number, but still nothing. Cursing, she dropped the phone back in her bag and headed down the hall the way she'd come. She'd only taken a few steps before a loud popping sound made her stop. Then another pop, followed by screams and shouts. It sounded close. She started jogging, picking up her pace as she went. Sam wasn't sure if Zoey was running towards or away from the gunfire, but she could feel the teenager's fear. Her sweaty palms, fast heart-beat, and the rush of blood like thunder in her ears. Zoey was in the red zone.

Suddenly dragged backwards, it felt like the girl's hair was being ripped out of her scalp. Zoey tried to twist and fight off her attacker, but each time she reached out, someone wrenched her by the hair in the opposite direction. Her hands grasped at the hands and arms that held her, but they outmaneuvered her, not giving her the opportunity to get a grip. At one point, Zoey lost her footing, putting her off balance. Sam hoped it would pull both Zoey and her assailant down with her, but no such luck. Her attacker held his footing and responded by twisting her hair viciously, pulling an involuntary cry of pain from the teenager. A sharp burning sensation shot through the lower right side of Zoey's scalp, followed by a warmth trickling its way down her neck. Her assailant had ripped a chunk of her hair out.

That's when she heard a familiar voice again. "As I said a few days ago, it's time to finish what your father couldn't." Charlie purred against Zoey's ear.

They were standing by a door. Zoey cringed away from the sounds coming from the classroom. Charlie chuckled as he grabbed the classroom door handle, swung it open, and shoved her inside.

Zoey staggered forwards pin wheeling her arms in an attempt to stay upright, but the momentum of the shove didn't allow her time to recover. The desk came up to meet her, fast. Her hands cushioned the impact, but she still crashed into it hard, smacking her face on the tabletop's edge as she fell. The side of Zoey's face and temple screamed in pain and her cheek felt odd, like a piece of it had detached from the whole.

Someone sobbed nearby. Sam became aware she was lying in something wet. Turning her head to the side, she opened her eyes and found a face staring up at her. Sam didn't recognize her, but Zoey must have because she murmured the name "Lizzie". Looking down, Sam could see Zoey's hands and chest were wet with blood. Lizzie's blood by the look of her empty stare and all the crimson fluid on and around the dead girl's body.

Sam felt Zoey's panic peak, but instead of losing it, the teenager looked away from Lizzie's face and slowly regained control. Her relief was short-lived as a pair of Docs came into her line of sight.

Oh God, please go away.

"Thanks for dropping in, Zoey. We can always use a fresh set of eyes."

Her gaze traveled from the Docs, up the dirty denim-clad legs, over a blood red t-shirt with the words RAMONES ROAD TO RUIN emblazoned on it, to the smirking face of a teenage boy. Sam had no clue who this kid was, but Zoey did because her already taut muscles tightened even more the moment she locked eyes with him. The teenager looked to be about Zoey's age, with dirty-blond hair and shiny gray eyes. Dark circles framed each bloodshot eye. But the most notable thing about him was the shotgun he held in his hands. It was a Canuck over under shotgun. She recognized it because her dad owned one just like it. It was an expensive piece and not a common gun to see around, especially in the hands of a crazed teenager.

Then Zoey whispered a name. *Peter.*

With little point in playing possum, she placed her

hands beneath her and began pushing herself up when a wetness on her face gave her pause.

Really wet.

Unsure of where it was coming from, she brought her knees up and shifted to the right to stand, but it put her off-balance and felt herself falling...

Chapter 16

Back To Murphy

Sam awoke with a start and groaned. Everything ached. Her face felt wet. She panicked for a moment as she tried to figure out where she was and why her face was drenched. Then she heard a dog whine. Buddy. He must have tried to wake her up. He sat a few feet away, whining at her. The hard bedroom floor was at her back, the covers tangled around her legs. Somehow she'd made it to the floor without waking up, but knew her body would sing its regrets later for having done it. Buddy was giving her an unusual amount of space compared to the usual doggy breath in the face routine, and she suspected she may have accidentally kicked him in her sleep.

"Sorry, Buddy... it was a terrible night. Come here, boy."

Buddy chuffed in agreement and slowly came over for a scratch behind the ears.

After disentangling herself from the sheets, Sam went over to the kitchen table, grabbing a notebook and pen from her desk along the way. She didn't want to forget the details of this dream.

Although logic told her the dream resulted from stress

so held no real meaning, it didn't sit well to just let it fade from memory. Sam jotted down the details she remembered; Mr. Morris's class, the layout of Murphy High, the names of the kids Zoey had whispered, the name Deroras, and the time and date displayed on Zoey's iPhone. October 17th at 2:27 p.m. Today's date. And it was already 7:02 a.m. She'd planned on heading back to Murphy this weekend, but that was still two days away. The longer she stared at the date and time, the more uncomfortable she became.

Determined to ignore her hinky feelings for once, Sam shook her head to clear her mind and thought about making coffee. She needed her morning elixir to get her through what would undoubtedly be a long workday, and the last thing she needed was the distraction of last night's weird dream to slow her down. Her mind was set on treating this day like any other. She pushed her chair away from the table, intending to head for the Keurig, but Buddy's drawn out whine caught her attention.

"Ok Buddy, I'm coming." She looked over, expecting to see him sitting with his lead in his teeth, something he often did if he had to go when Sam was moving too slowly for his taste. But instead of his lead, he sat with her overnight bag lying in front of him. The last time she'd used it was when they'd gone to Murphy eighteen weeks ago. He must have dragged it out from its resting place under her bed and dropped it there. A little befuddled, Sam stared down at the bag and then at Buddy. After another minute of perplexed silence, Buddy barked at her, went to the door and returned to sit by the bag again. That was Buddy speak for I want to go out, but the usual prop was not her overnight bag. Thinking perhaps he was a little confused, Sam got up, retrieved his lead from the side table, and waited for him by the front door. But he sat where he was, perfectly still, staring back at her in the middle of the room.

"Come on, Buddy. Time to do your business," Sam coaxed, but Buddy continued sitting by the bag. Odd, because Buddy never needed prompting to go outside.

"Time for your walk, Bud. Come here." Using the word *walk* never failed. She even opened the door. Another cue they were going now, but he didn't budge. This was definitely not normal Buddy behavior. Not only did he not want to go outside for a walk, but he seemed to be purposely ignoring her command.

"Buddy, I don't have time for this. Let's go!" Sam used her commanding tone to tell him she meant business this time. It elicited a response, but again, not the one she expected.

Buddy stood, walked a couple of feet towards her and barked once in disagreement. He then circled back, grabbed her overnight bag in his mouth, dropped it a couple of feet in front of her, and sat back down again, staring up at her expectantly.

Sam gaped.

Buddy waited, holding her gaze as if waiting for her feeble human mind to catch up to what was going on.

Thinking you have an exceptional dog and knowing you have an exceptional dog were two entirely different things. Now she knew Buddy was, without a doubt, one of a kind. Sam dropped to one knee and picked up the bag he offered. "So you want me to go back to Murphy, do you?" Sam asked.

Buddy rose but kept looking at her.

Sam's brow knit as she thought about what she'd said, then restated her sentence. "You want US to go back to Murphy?"

Buddy barked twice, tail wagging. Definitely an affirmative.

"How about I go and you stay with Steve for a couple of days?" Sam asked, testing the waters of these newfound super dog abilities.

Buddy whined, barked once and sat down again, but this time with his back to her.

Well, look at that... I have a dog that can actually communicate with me. With all the weirdness that had occurred over the last few years, a super dog shouldn't be that big a shock. But Sam was dumbfounded. However, she didn't have the luxury of time to explore this new revelation with the minutes ticking by so fast. Sam settled for patting Buddy on the head and reassuring him he'd be coming with her lest he found a more imaginative way to pout. "Don't worry, Buddy, you're coming with me. Gimme a few minutes to get ready, then I'll take you outside."

With that, Buddy stood again and barked twice.

Even though she'd tried to push it aside, Sam's hinky feeling intensified with each minute that slipped away. For better or worse, they'd be heading to Murphy this morning. With no time to dawdle, Sam packed an overnight bag and took a four-minute shower. She'd only packed two days' worth of clothes so threw in a couple of extra t-shirts and pairs of underwear for good measure. On the way out the door, she grabbed the notes she'd jotted down earlier, along with her purse, iPhone, and Buddy's lead.

Sam and Buddy caught the first cab she flagged down and settled in for the two-hour ride. The cab was dingy, but she needed to get to Murphy fast, so waiting for another wasn't an option. Initially, the cabbie refused to take Buddy, but after negotiations and an extra fifty to sweeten the pot, he grudgingly accepted the unwanted passenger. Silence reigned and Sam counted her lucky stars she got the one cabbie in the city that didn't like small talk.

Sam dug around in her purse for her iPhone. She had a couple of calls to make en route. The first was to Tim to see if he wouldn't mind meeting them at her father's house who was supposed to return from his annual fishing trip up north sometime tonight. In the meantime, she needed to pick up something from the house. She wasn't looking forward to the second phone call. Telling her boss she wouldn't be making it into work for a few days would be hard enough, but telling him it was because of a dream she had wouldn't go over well. She settled for a half lie and told him she had to go back to Murphy to deal with some unfinished business to do with the incident at Timothy's Garage. If he wanted to fire her for her recent absenteeism, then so be it. She'd given blood, sweat and more than a few tears to the company over the last five years, often working late to meet deadlines and skipping vacations to work on projects deemed urgent. Finding Charlie had become much more important than any work her company had lined up for her.

Whatever he was, Charlie was a threat to everyone he came into contact with, and the possibility of catching this reoccurring nightmare trumped everything else.

The high school would be their priority, but after that they'd have to wing it. For whatever reason, Charlie seemed to have an affinity for her hometown, and she needed to find out why. Sam knew at some point she'd meet Charlie again. The one advantage she had was he seemed to enjoy his game of cat and mouse with her. She just hoped her luck didn't run out, that he wouldn't tire of it anytime soon. Maybe next time she'd gain the upper hand for once. One could only hope.

* * *

The more Tim found out about Sam, the more he liked her. He knew he was in trouble when he couldn't resist asking around town about her. People seemed to be divided into three camps concerning Sam Turner. Many felt bad for her and seemed to take pity on what had happened. Others thought the trouble didn't start until she arrived back in town, so she must have brought it on herself. And a small but surprising number thought she was the one behind the murders and, police chief's daughter or not, she should be the one strung up for it. It didn't matter to this minority that there were eyewitnesses who stated otherwise.

And he couldn't seem to shake the feeling there was something familiar about Sam. He gravitated towards her even with all the craziness surrounding her. Tim already knew he would help Sam because, if nothing else, it meant he'd get to spend more time with her. He couldn't blame her for wanting to leave Murphy with all that had happened here, but that was the thing with Sam. She acted more like someone on a mission than a victim. She'd faced incredibly violent, life-threatening situations twice now and still refused to back down from her search for the one responsible. And if what she said was true about Charlie, it meant they were all in trouble.

Although Tim kept an ear to the ground about Charlie, no one matching that description ever turned up. Then, a day ago, Mr. Kotts, a postie who's been around forever, mentioned there was a new janitor at the local high school. Tim planned on checking it out today. That was until he got the call from Sam asking him to meet her at her father's house first thing. The strain in her voice and the urgency in her words told him she likely had another one of her feelings. Today might wind up being a bad day and the last bad day with Sam ended with two of his mechanics dead, another injured, and him in the hospital.

Now all he felt was apprehension.

Tim called his new shop, now located on the other end of town, to tell them he wouldn't be in today. Harry had been as good as his word and helped Tim find a new location. He'd talked to someone who knew someone else who had a building available that once housed an auto repair shop before Al's Autobody put them out of business. Vacant for the last ten years, it took a little work to get it back into working order, but other than a couple of lift replacements and new automated garage doors, most of the work was superficial.

Tim was relieved to see Toni return. Until he fully recovered from his injuries, Toni assigned himself to oversee the new mechanics Tim had hired. One was pretty green, but a bright kid. The other was a seasoned mechanic, another dissatisfied employee he'd poached from Al's Autobody, so he wasn't concerned about the work not getting done. At the last minute, he also hired on Gertie's problem grandchild, Justin. They needed the extra help for odds and ends around the shop, and Tim figured if they kept the teenager busy, he'd have less time to find trouble. As for Toni, he didn't enjoy sitting on the sidelines playing babysitter, but he did it anyway, which is how Tim knew his Italian brother from another mother must be in a fair amount of pain.

He also asked his neighbor, Mrs. Waznek, to check in on Brandy throughout the day and feed her in the evening if he wasn't back by then. His neighbor adored Brandy and often jumped at the chance to dog sit. Tim was certain if something unfortunate happened and Tim met an untimely end, Brandy would have no problem finding a new owner. Both Toni and Mrs. Waznek would volunteer to take his spoiled pup as their own. The only question would be who'd get her in the end. Toni was bigger and faster, but he suspected Mrs. Waznek could be sneaky when it suited her. The thought of Toni and Mrs. Waznek duking it out made him chuckle.

He noticed the time and pushed the morbidly silly thoughts away. Sam would arrive at her dad's place within twenty minutes, and he'd promised to meet her there.

She didn't trust many people, but who could blame her? People were either scared of her or indifferent, and many still questioned what really happened to her. Yet for all her determination and skill, self-preservation didn't seem to be one of her strong suits. He wanted to help her with that weakness. He wanted Turner to stick around for a while.

Tim was already in the driveway, leaning on the open door of his truck by the time they pulled up to her father's house. Sam practically leaped out of the backseat in her desire to get out of the cab. Buddy followed suit, but then gazed up at her, fidgeting with excitement as he waited for permission to go.

"Oh go on," Sam said, releasing him.

Buddy chuffed once and trotted over to greet Tim.

She paid the cabbie what she promised, along with a little extra. True to form, he didn't look her in the eye or say a word. Being careful not to touch her hand, he took the offered money and then backed towards his car and left.

The strange behavior gave Sam a chill, making her think of the old woman yelling expletives at passers-by outside

231

her apartment last week. She mostly used classic swear-words, but occasionally she'd throw in a curve ball and shout something more original, like Monkeyfart or Rhinoceros scrotum. However, when Sam walked past, the bag lady did something even more peculiar. She backed away and shouted, "Bad Juju!" at her over and over. When Sam looked back over her shoulder, the old biddy was still pointing at Sam's retreating figure shouting "Bad Juju!", ignoring everyone else walking past her. Maybe she did have bad juju.

Pushing the negative thoughts aside, Sam looked up as the cab pulled away and locked eyes with Tim. It was a bit surprising how happy she felt seeing him again. If his broad smile said anything, then it looked like the feeling was mutual. Sam couldn't resist grinning back at him.

"Hi crazy," Tim said by way of greeting.

"Hi gullible," Sam shot back.

"Cabbie didn't take to you, huh?" Tim asked, having noticed the man's reticence to interact with her.

Sam shrugged as she approached and replied, "I guess my lucky charms didn't work this time."

That's when Sam noticed Tim's large companion sitting behind him in the cab of his truck. That had to be Brandy, Tim's Bernese Mountain dog. The name Brandy was so incongruous with the dog's sheer size, Sam couldn't help but chuckle. Although the pup had the distinctive Bernese white and brown patches on her head and chest, they were practically swallowed up by the immensity of her black fur. It was quite apparent by Buddy's excitement that he didn't mind her mostly black coloration. Buddy sat by the truck in front of Tim, positively vibrating with anticipation as he stared at the unexpected furry newcomer. The big mostly black dog looked pretty excited too, but her gaze kept shifting from Tim to Buddy and back to Tim. Well trained, too, as she didn't try to jump down or even crowd her owner.

Oh, this was going to be fun, Sam thought with amusement.

"I thought I'd wait for you for formal introductions. Sam, Buddy, this is Brandy. Say 'Hi' Brandy," Tim said and Brandy barked once, tail wagging.

"So I have to ask... how did you come up with the name Brandy?" Sam asked in amusement.

Tim nodded, a half smile hovering over his lips. "I learned too late not to let your four-year-old, adorable niece know you've got a puppy until after you name it," Tim laughed. "Is it ok if they greet each other?"

"Oh yeah. As you can probably tell by the fact he's positively shaking with excitement, Buddy hates other dogs." Sam chuckled.

"Down Brandy." Was all the encouragement Brandy needed. The dogs were all over each other in an instant. Sam would have loved to watch them play, but having arrived later than she wanted, she left the trio to their greetings and headed into her father's house.

Only intending to be there long enough to grab her things from her dad's safe, Sam dropped her bags by the front door and bee lined it for the basement. The gun safe was hidden under the bar in the entertainment room. She'd always thought it funny he stored his Smith & Wesson right beside his Grey Goose vodka. The location had everything to do with the fact her mother never wanted guns stored anywhere near the family areas. However, Sam knew her dad had at least one gun stashed somewhere else in the house, likely the bedroom. She didn't know a cop alive that didn't have a sidearm more readily available, just in case. As the clean-up crew to the rips and tears in the community, cops saw the worst society had to offer on a regular basis. It's not hard to understand why most are cynical, disillusioned, and protective.

Something they'd never let on to her mother was when her father started taking Sam to the gun range. At the time, he'd also promised to tell her the gun safe combination if she hit the bull's eye dead center six times in a row. To his delight, he discovered she was a natural. He gave Sam the gun safe combination a month after she turned seventeen. As far as her mother was concerned, father and daughter went fishing a lot, but during most of their "fishing trips" they'd end up at the gun range instead of on the lake. Sam didn't have the passion for fishing like her father, but they still went occasionally to keep up appearances.

Sam stopped at the top of the stairs, noting the stairwell and landing to the back door looked brighter than usual. Eyes drawn to the culprit, she noted the back door was ajar, showing an inch or two of screen. Strange. Did her father forget to lock the back door before he left? She jogged down the five steps to the landing and pulled the door open. Splintered wood on the inside of the doorjamb told her someone had kicked it in. The fact someone had broken into the house hit her at about the same time she heard the creak of a step behind her. Sam swore under her breath for exposing her back to the stairs when she hadn't checked them first. She knew better than that.

Sam tensed in anticipation for a blow from behind, ready to drop to the ground any second. Then she heard the familiar chuff, closely followed by Tim shouting her name. Sam sighed in relief as Buddy reached her side.

"I'm by the back door!" A moment later, Tim and Brandy appeared at the top of the stairs.

"Someone broke in," she said, nodding towards the door. Sam was already on the second step down from the landing before Tim caught her arm, forcing her to pause.

"Sam, you can't go down there. Whoever broke in could still be here. We need to call the police," Tim stated staunchly.

"We don't have time to—" Sam said in exasperation. She knew she was being careless in her hurry, but the urgency she felt earlier now bordered on panic. Instinct told her to get to the school now, because something terrible was about to go down. And after the dream she'd had she wasn't about to go unarmed. She also knew whoever had broken in was gone, but she couldn't rationalize instinct to someone else. Luckily, she didn't have to argue with him or resort to more drastic measures like knocking him upside the head.

Buddy decided for them by disappearing downstairs, followed closely by Brandy.

Blowing out a sigh of frustration, Tim grunted, "Please, just stay here."

"Ok. But only because you asked so nicely," Sam said sweetly.

Tim rolled his eyes but didn't do a very good job of hiding the smile tugging at the corners of his mouth as he followed the dogs downstairs. It didn't take Tim long to confirm what she already knew... that no one was in the basement.

"Ok, the coast is clear. But you won't like what they took."

Sam, already halfway down the stairs by the time Tim shouted, jogged the rest of the way down. He stood in front of the now empty gun case. It's where her dad stored his antique shotguns. It looked like the perp smashed the front window and took them. Too bad, because the gun case was an antique as well.

"Well, the good news is the guns they took were antiques for display only. So, although valuable, they'd never be able to shoot."

And then Sam noticed something that made her heart drop. The back wall of the cabinet wasn't flush. *Fuck.* Reaching through the broken front door, she pulled the lip of the back panel of the antique gun case open the rest of the way to reveal the large gun locker behind it. Reaching for the locker's door handle, Sam tugged it open to reveal... an empty case. *Fuck. Fuck. Fuck!*

Years ago, her dad had replaced the back of the antique gun cabinet with a secret door to hide the gun locker he had bolted into the wall behind it. Obviously, someone had found out about the hidden gun locker and either got a hold of the locker's key or picked the lock, and took all three hunting rifles. Sam's guess would be they picked the lock. There were only two keys to the gun locker. She had one, and her dad had the other. She still had her keys and was certain she'd have heard if he'd lost his, which left picking the lock. Also, the key to the antique gun cabinet was next to the key to the gun locker. If the thief had the keys, logic dictated they would have used the key to unlock the antique gun cabinet's door instead of creating unnecessary noise by smashing through the extra thick glass of the cabinet and possibly alerting a neighbor to the break in.

"The bad news is someone somehow found out about my dad's gun locker, broke into it, and took all three hunting rifles as well. And they were definitely in working order."

He always stored the artillery in the smaller gun safe behind the bar. It held the handguns, bullets and gun shells. She could see they'd tried their best to find some, though.

The front of the gun safe was marked up and dented. It looked like the frustrated thief had taken a hammer to the front of it with conviction.

"Wow. Whoever did this has a lot of pent up rage," Sam said as she skimmed her fingers over the gun safe's damaged surface. Sighing, she concentrated on the lock, dialing in the same combination he'd given her ten years ago. It rewarded her efforts with a satisfying click as the lock released the deadbolt. She swung it open and took out the thirty-eight snub, loaded it, and slipped an extra clip into her purse. Compact, easy to conceal, yet still powerful enough to pack a punch. The thirty-eight snub was her own gun, given to her when she turned eighteen.

"You can't be serious, Sam. Do you even know how to use that thing?" Tim asked from somewhere behind her. His comment didn't surprise her, but it wouldn't change her mind about taking the gun. To date, she'd had two deadly run-ins she'd survived, and she wasn't sure her luck would withstand another one.

"Yes, and yes."

Sam wasn't about to go into detail about how well she handled a gun, or apologize for taking it. And the more she thought about it, the more she didn't want Tim coming. Not because she couldn't use his help, but she didn't want to worry about him if something went down. And considering someone had just stolen her dad's hunting rifles, there was no doubt in her mind now... today was going to be a terrible day. She closed the safe door and re-engaged the lock, all the while thinking about what she could say to Tim to get him to go back home.

"Thank-you for meeting me here. You don't have to come with me, but I have a favor to ask. I'd appreciate it if you could keep an eye on Buddy for a couple of hours while

I go check on the school. Normally I'd leave him here, but with the back doorjamb damaged, I won't be able to lock the doors. And you never know if whoever broke in earlier will come back," Sam said, but Tim was already shaking his head.

"Nuh-uh. You're not getting rid of me that easily, Turner. In for a penny, in for a pound, right? Besides, like you, I have to see what's happening at the school. Hopefully, your dream was just that, a bad dream. However, if it's more than that and something goes down—" Tim let the sentence hang there, unfinished. He didn't have to say anything more because Sam already knew how he felt. Even though it was absurd to take a dream seriously, she'd be wracked with guilt if something happened at the school and she'd done nothing to stop it. She also hoped her bad feeling was just good, old-fashioned indigestion this time.

He ran an agitated hand through his hair before continuing. "Well, we better get this show on the road before we run out of time and turn into pumpkins."

* * *

They waited for the cops to arrive on the stoop outside. The first responder was Constable Douglas, which suited Sam just fine. He'd only been on the force for four or five years, so wouldn't be as jaded as the more experienced officers and perfect for this job. Although lanky, she could see he had put on muscle since the last time she'd seen him. To her, he still looked a little awkward in his uniform, but she was biased. Having known Douglas as Aaron most of his life, she had to remind herself to call him by his last name.

"Morning, Douglas." Sam smiled as the officer approached them.

"Morning Sam. Tim." Douglas nodded. "I thought it odd you called this in. Your dad off on one of his fishing retreats again?"

Sam nodded, smiling. "He headed to Kirkland Lake hoping to catch the big one this time." Her father had been going to this fishing camp for the last dozen years with one goal and one goal only, to get the biggest fish of the season and win Kirkland Lake's Big Kahuna contest. For several years now, he'd come home with runner-ups, but never the highly prized granddaddy. The winner got his picture in the local paper and the coveted trophy that stated so-and-so caught The Big Kahuna. Thousands of fishermen flocked there annually, hoping to win it. Sam didn't understand the draw, but being a self-confessed non-fisherman, she likely never would.

"Oh yeah, the Big Kahuna." Douglas smiled. "He's been going up there for a few years now, eh?"

"At least a dozen now. He's determined to win it one day. You fish?"

"Only when my dad can't get his buddies to go with him. I'm more of a hunter than a fisher. You?"

"Nah. I'm not big on fishing either," Sam replied, grimacing. Douglas nodded in understanding.

"So Sam, you just up for a visit, then?" Douglas asked, scrutinizing her face. Small talk was over. Sam knew the drill.

"Yes, and no. I came to retrieve my car but will probably stay the weekend."

"So someone drove you here?"

Sam shook her head. "I took a cab in this morning. I'd just dropped my bags by the front door and headed into the kitchen when I noticed a lot of light in the stairwell. When I went to investigate, I found the back door open." Sam looked directly at Tim as she continued. "I saw someone running away through our backyard. He had on a gray sweatshirt, jeans and a backpack and climbed the back fence like it was nothing." Tim's expression turned quizzical, but he said nothing.

- "Can you describe his hair color? Build? Eye color? Any discerning features?"

"He had a gray ball cap, but from what I could see of his hair, it may have been blond, but that could have been his shirt collar. I only got a glimpse of his profile when he glanced back, but he looked young. Like a teenager. No distinguishing features I recall. Average height. Slim build." Not wanting to inadvertently get an innocent kid arrested, Sam made sure her description was as nondescript as possible. She just wanted the cops to have enough cause to visit the high school.

"Just one perp?"

"Just one that I saw."

"Do you know if he took anything?"

"I'm not sure what all he took, but everyone in this town knows this is Chief Turner's house. The only thing of real value other than tools would be his gun collection. After we found someone had broken into the house, we came back outside to wait for the cops."

Douglas nodded again. "You have anything else to add?" Douglas directed the question at Tim.

"I was outside with the dogs when most of this took place," Tim said, shaking his head. Satisfied, Douglas moved away from them to speak into his shoulder radio and call for backup. Sam had planted the seed. Now all they could do was wait and see how it played out.

"Nice play Turner. Do you think they'll send someone to check the high school out?" Tim said.

"Let's hope so, Hooch," Sam said as she watched the young officer talk to dispatch. It took her a minute to notice Tim staring at her, his expression incredulous.

"I don't know your last name, so I improvised," Sam said, and shrugged.

"It's Cox. Tim Cox."

Sam just looked at him for a minute, waiting for the punch line, but none came. Now she looked incredulous. "And you thought Hooch was worse? Jeez, man, no wonder you called your shop Timothy's Auto."

"But a dog. You made me the dog sidekick—"

Sam just shrugged and stated the obvious. "Dogs are loyal. Smart. Courageous. And man's best friend. You could do worse." Tim's mouth hung open slightly and she couldn't resist putting her index finger under his chin to lift it back up.

Ninety minutes had passed by the time backup arrived, and Douglas and his partner finished searching the property. They found no one in the house, but the gun display case had been smashed and was now empty, as was the gun locker behind it. After asking Sam a few more questions, they confirmed that the three hunting rifles and two shotguns were taken. In the meantime, Douglas requested a uniform to check on the high school. Just before they left, Douglas gave Sam a thumbs up, which meant the school checked out fine. But Sam still couldn't shake her hinky feeling. Buddy's whining reinforced this as he pressed himself against her leg, a habit he had when he was stressed or scared.

"You still have that feeling, don't you?" Tim looked like he already regretted asking. Whatever showed on her face was all the confirmation he needed. "I'll pack up the mutts. We can drop them off at my place on the way," he said as he headed for his truck. Both Brandy and Buddy followed close behind.

Sam glanced at her watch again, and her heart sank. "I'll be right back." She disappeared into the house to retrieve her purse. They had a little over an hour left before their time corresponded with her dream's time. Sam saw the back door still hung ajar, but there wasn't much that could be done about it now. She locked the screen, closed the door as much as the damage allowed, dashed back up the short set of stairs and grabbed her purse on the way out.

It was time to meet the teacher...

Chapter 17

School Hell

Bill wore dark brown slacks, a beige and white striped shirt, a beige sports jacket, brown socks, brown loafers and had a double size Red Bull in hand as he stepped into his classroom. He normally chastised his kids about drinking these types of high caffeine, high sugar content drinks, but this morning it couldn't be helped. He needed to stay awake. Nightmares had plagued him the entire night, and he never really fell asleep. The dreams felt far too real, and that scared the hell out of him.

Student chatter hummed through the classroom. As usual, no one paid him any heed, but it didn't bother him. Sleep deprivation should have put him in a bad mood, but not this morning. Bill wouldn't say he was happy, but today there was less pressure behind his eyes. He felt lighter. Bill closed the classroom door and waited for the announcements to begin.

The day went by turtle slow and quickly sapped away what little energy he'd had. The students came and went in waves as each period started and ended with the toll of the bell. Bill felt his light mood seep away with each passing minute until he felt as disinterested today as most of his students did every day. Bill had no illusions. He knew geology wasn't everyone's bag of stones, but he liked to think he was a good teacher. Or at least he used to be. Today, however, he just went through the motions because he was just so damned tired. When the door closed behind the last student leaving his fourth period, Bill collapsed into his chair. He had fifth period to himself.

He wanted another coffee to see him through the rest of the day, but whatever they used in the teacher's lounge always tasted burned. Bill pulled the stack of assignments sitting on his left in front of him and started grading. Not fifteen minutes into it, he had to stop. The assignment in front of him, handed in by a tenth grader, Gerard Bishop, was so bad he'd likely never forget Gerard's name. Obviously, the kid didn't want to be in his class, and Bill didn't want him as a student.

Bill didn't even realize he'd shut his eyes until his head snapped back up. He'd dozed off. Sighing, he rubbed the back of his neck again. The weariness in his muscles made everything ache. He should be on the sixth paper instead of the second, and only a good night's sleep would help. Since that wasn't a possibility at the moment, a catnap would have to do. The clock on the wall read 1:45. Plenty of time for a quick shut-eye. He leaned back in his chair, stretching out his back and neck as he did so. A catnap would be short enough he wouldn't have the time to dream. Bill closed his eyes and let his body relax, telling himself that five minutes was all he wanted. Catnaps were never a problem for Bill, as he always woke up of his own volition.

* * *

Bill popped open his eyes and shot forward in his chair. His hand, outstretched in front of him, was the only thing that stalled his forward momentum and prevented him from bashing his head against the desk. A hill of unmarked assignments, askew now because of his hand's interference, still stacked on the desk in front of him. The seats in his classroom remained empty. The wall clock read 1:46. It'd only been a minute since he'd shut his eyes. So what woke him up?

Agitated, Bill rose from his chair, stretching out his back as he wandered towards the classroom door. Swinging it open, he took a step into the hall, but everything was quiet. After a minute of silence, Bill reentered his classroom, letting the door swing closed.

A loud popping sound halted him mid-stride. Bill turned back, reaching a hand out to halt the door before it completely closed. The noise, reminiscent of a car backfiring, sounded like it was coming from inside the school, not out. Bill walked back to the middle of the hallway and looked in both directions, but there was nothing. No further noise. No movement. Nothing out of the ordinary. After a few minutes of silence, Bill started heading in the direction he'd thought the sound came from on his left. Past Mr. Redna's physics class. Past the girls' washroom. Past the utility closet. He stepped under the GO LIONS GO! banner in the middle of the hall. He could feel it in his bones. Something was off.

A door to his right crashed open and students started streaming out, slamming into and running over one another in their haste to escape. More loud popping sounds and a few students collapsed in the doorway, blocking the door from closing. Kids continued to run past him, bumping into his shoulders and arms as they fled, but Bill continued moving forward against the panicked tide.

Bill stepped over the body of a girl with a red smeared ZOMBIES RULE t-shirt blocking the exit and paused inside the doorway to assess the situation. The shooter, dressed nondescriptly in a dark hoodie, black jeans and runners, had his back to the door so Bill couldn't see his face. He held a rifle aimed at a group of teenagers huddled in the back corner by the windows. Bill heard the sounds of weeping and the low murmuring of a male voice. The owner of the voice stood closer to the shooter than the rest and appeared to be talking to him. By the look of his hand gestures, the brave teenager was attempting to placate the guy with the gun. If Bill were a betting man, he'd place big money that this kid was about to get a face full of metal. Just after he had that thought, up came the rifle and bang, right in the face. The kid's right eye, the only one left intact now, rounded in shock as he slid down the wall.

One girl screamed. Bill figured she'd be the next to go. Sure enough, the shooter raised his rifle again, only he took out the weeper instead. Well, that was a surprise. The screamer's screams increased in pitch.

Bill supposed he should be scared, but felt nothing. Not fear. Not anger. Not even sympathy for the dead kids he'd passed along the way or the terrified teenagers the shooter had rounded up in the corner. It was like someone hit the mute button on the remote but instead of getting rid of the sound; it rid him of all emotion. Some hostages stared at Bill while others shouted at him for help. The shooter barely glanced at him before turning his attention back to the kids.

The gunman said something to the huddled teenagers as he raised his rifle again. That's when a girl standing next to the screamer slapped her, but still she screamed. It wasn't until the slapper hauled back and punched the screamer that the shrieking finally stopped.

Bill headed towards the shooter. Why hadn't he been shot down yet? He must have heard his approach because the gunman turned to face him just before Bill would have reached him. What he saw stopped him dead in his tracks.

There, standing in front of him, was the platinum blond guy from his nightmares. His grin so wide and his teeth so bright they blinded Bill for a moment. Enraged by the sheer pleasure he saw in the stranger's expression, Bill grabbed the blond by the shoulders and shoved him hard. He glimpsed the butt of the rifle before an excruciating pain exploded in his head. The blow sent him reeling. He lost his footing, sending them both over the desks, where they landed in a heap on the tile covered cement floor. Bill hit the ground first, taking the brunt of the fall. He felt a lot of pain in his back, his butt and especially in his right elbow on which most of their combined weight fell. With the wind knocked out of him, he was slow to react and the body on top of him was moving fast. He tensed in anticipation of the coming blow, only it didn't come. That's when he felt a shift as the shooter adjusted his position, jerking Bill up off the floor by the lapels of his sports jacket into standing then pulled him in close until he was less than a foot from the blond's grinning face.

Then the grin spoke. "What's wrong Bill? You upset because I'm having a hell of a good time?" He pulled Bill's face even closer until he was a mere few inches away. His damp breath fanned his cheek. "Or because you are?"

Bill roared and shoved him back. The shooter stumbled, his grin faltering as Bill got a hold of the rifle. He swung it around, taking aim at the blond's stupid grin, the muzzle an inch from his teeth. Without thinking twice, Bill pulled the trigger, shooting the grin off the blond's face. He dropped like a rock. Gazing down at his handiwork, Bill was awestruck at how satisfying it felt. He had little a chance to savor the moment though because one kid began to wail. The screamer again. The tiresome noise sorely tempted him to swing the rifle in her direction.

They should be thanking me for killing the shooter, Bill thought with disgust. He looked down at the shooter again and sucked in a breath. His world tilted sideways as he realized the person he'd shot wasn't the blond from his dreams at all, but some other kid. His unfortunate victim only had half a face left, the still intact side spattered with blood. Something about the partial face tickled his memories. His hands shook, and the headache, which had only been a dull ache, sharpened into the beginnings of a migraine.

The screaming, which seemed so distant a minute ago, came back into focus. And it was the most irritating, obnoxious noise he'd ever heard.

Incensed, Bill raised the gun and aimed it at the screamer. Eerily, she reminded him of his daughter. Without thinking twice, Bill pulled the trigger and felt another wave of satisfaction as she, too, hit the ground. The ensuing silence was pure bliss.

After only a few seconds, the yelling started anew. He swung the rifle towards the unknown source of noise, recognizing the girl as the one who'd punched the screamer earlier. Her blue hair made her memorable. His finger tightened on the trigger until he noticed something different about the screams. She wasn't screeching nonsensically like the last girl. Still, he had trouble making out what she was saying. It was like she was shouting at him through a thick pane of soundproof glass. Bill had to concentrate on the movement of her lips to make out her words.

"—shot your own kids, you bastard!" The blue-haired girl shouted at him again. Bill looked back down at the still gunman.

No, it couldn't be.

The shooter looked young enough he might be around the same age as his son. The hair, the same light ash blond. Bill bent down and unzipped the black sweatshirt to reveal the kid's t-shirt. What he saw gave him pause. The shirt, an old concert t-shirt from the early eighties, was the same one he had. He'd grown out of it years ago, but it being one of his favorites, he couldn't bring himself to throw it out and ended up giving it to Christopher instead. It even had the small blue stain on the bottom right side from a felt-tipped pen he'd dropped on it years ago.

Bill rose to his feet and stepped around the kid that looked like his son before continuing on to his other piece of handiwork. The now quiet screamer was lying facedown a few feet from where the other students still huddled in the corner. All except for the blue girl. She stood a few feet to the right, staring daggers at him as he approached. Her fists were clenched and she looked pissed.

Join the club, Bill thought. The screamer had the same ash blond hair as his son. It spilled across her face, hiding most of it from view. She also had a dark red spot blooming from the left side of her chest. Bill stopped in front of the body and used the muzzle of the rifle to push the hair out of her face. *Her fixed stare was a dead giveaway.* Bill almost laughed aloud at his unintended pun. The girl definitely looked like his daughter.

Bill knew he should feel pretty torn up right about now, but he just couldn't quite get there.

His grip tightened reflexively on the rifle as he caught a movement in his periphery and looked up in time to see a flurry of blue hurtling itself at him. Before he could do much more than raise his rifle to block the attack, he was shoved back hard. It felt more like the sheer momentum of the thing's fury had thrown him back.

No, not a thing. A girl. The blue-haired girl.

Bill stumbled backwards and before he caught his balance, he tumbled ass over head over a desk.

Bill realized his mistake too late. He instinctively tightened his grip, bringing the shotgun in tight, hugging it against his body as his fingers clenched. Bill heard the report of the shotgun at the same time he felt it. The explosive pain in his jaw, mouth and head as the bullet traveled through it followed by a distinct cracking sound as his head bounced back on the nape of his neck.

Bill awoke with a jerk. Still disoriented from his dream, he was slow to realize why students were filtering through his classroom door in twos and threes, chatting to one another when there was so much carnage. Why was everyone acting so normal? It wasn't until his eyes swept the floors and doorway again that he realized it was still a regular school day and he must have slept through fifth period.

He exhaled, trying to relax his tightly wound muscles and ease the knots cramping his stomach. The only evidence of the dream he'd had was the pounding in his head. Bill reached into the top drawer of his desk for his stash of Advil. He'd been depending on the little maroon pills a lot lately, popping at least half a dozen a day. Not finding them, he reached deeper, but instead of pills, his hand closed around something foreign, cold and metallic. Bill drew his hand back and saw he now held a gun. It was an old military issue Governor, just like the one he'd inherited when his father passed. But that was impossible because his dad's gun still sat in the safe at home. Bill slowly turned the gun until it faced right side up. Bill swallowed hard as he read the initials engraved on the base. TM, for Theodore Morris. His dad's handgun. He must have brought it to school with him, only he didn't remember doing it.

That's when Zoey William, the girl with the blue hair, walked through his classroom door. Same girl from his dream, the memory of which came crashing back to him. He remembered everything, including feeling nothing about killing his own kids.

Bill watched her from under hooded eyes. His grip tightened on the gun he held hidden in his desk drawer. Realizing what he was doing, he carefully released the cool metal and drew his hand out of the drawer, but paused when his fingers brushed against a small box. Grasping it, he pulled it out for a closer examination and saw it was a box of cartridges for the Governor. Advil forgotten, Bill returned the small box, closed his desk drawer, and stood. His right hand felt uncomfortably empty, so he grabbed the measuring stick off the chalkboard to hold on to as he taught his last class of the day.

I'll whip these kids into shape even if it kills them, Bill thought as a smile curved his lips. Bill hadn't smiled in a long time. That power nap had done him good.

* * *

"Peter, Peter student eater, I'll take so many lives, life will be that much sweeter," Peter chanted as he set to work, putting the final touches on his homeroom display. He wanted everything perfect for his fellow students. He couldn't wait to see the look on their faces. His favorite people had this class next. He was looking forward to playing a game with them.

Peter had taken full advantage of Miss Kelly's free period to have a little chat with his favorite teacher about their dysfunctional, codependent relationship. At first she'd resisted listening to him, but after a little coaxing and cutting, she seemed okay with it. Initially, the conversation did not go well. She was determined to lie about the fact that she'd led him on. Peter was a perfect gentleman, even forgiving her for changing her mind about her feelings for him. After all, one of the first things he'd learned from his own mother was that it was a woman's prerogative to change her mind. His mother changed her mind all the time, promising she'd get him this, or they'd do that together. She more often than not changed her mind in the end. But he always forgave her for it because she always admitted the truth. That she'd forgotten or didn't have the time to give. But Miss Kelly was a whole different can of worms. She'd insisted on lying to him, telling him she'd never had feelings for him. When he told her that wasn't good enough, she'd resorted to yelling. Her irrational behavior left him with no alternative. He decided to save her from herself by removing that which allowed her to lie, her tongue. And it worked. She settled right down after that. With the added bonus, she could no longer lie. He wished he'd come up with that solution a lot sooner. It would have saved him a lot of heartache.

He and the janitor had a little tête-à-tête yesterday and

came to an understanding. The first thing Peter asked Charlie was why he'd broken his rib. His response had been simple.

"Often people need motivation to wake up from their stupor. For some, it's loss. For others, it's the fear of being alone. For you, it's pain. You have never had anything to lose. You've always been alone, therefore you have no one to disappoint. You needed to realize that the only thing this life offers you is pain. As you've learned the hard way, you can't run away from it because it will only track you down. Most of your brief life, you've avoided people and look where that's gotten you. Picked on, beaten up and outcast. And the worst part is now you expect it." Charlie let him digest his words before leaning in as if to tell him a secret. "Pain is all you know, Peter. Isn't it about time you gave some of that pain back?"

Charlie's words hit home, and suddenly everything made sense. The fact he'd never fit in anywhere or with anyone. That he never seemed to be all that good at, or interested in, anything had led him here. He was the outsider, and the only one capable of doing what needed to be done today. Exacting revenge on all the fucking bullies, master manipulators, and two-faced bitch liars who'd rained pain down on so many at school.

Peter felt better, if not lighter. Things were simple now. Charlie grinned, and Peter couldn't help but return the gesture.

And then the janitor took young Peter under his wing and taught him everything he knew about keeping the cattle indoors, the cops outdoors, and his best chance at avoiding a takeover from some overzealous teacher or student. Peter was a quick study, at least in this, and soaked up everything the janitor advised.

Chapter 18

The Collision

"Have you thought about what we'll do once we get to the high school?" Tim asked, glancing over. Now only five minutes away from the school and both of them were a little agitated. Tim's tell was his white knuckling the steering wheel.

"Other than looking as inconspicuous as possible, no, I haven't." Instead, she'd been focused on remembering the details of the dream, so she knew who to track down, protect, and perhaps even incapacitate if it came to that. "I don't think we'll be approached, but if we are, then we'll tell anyone that asks that I'm considering working here as a teacher and wanted to check out the high school before applying."

"What about people who know you?"

Sam shrugged and said, "I don't think it'll be a problem. I left Murphy right after high school, went away to college, and never looked back. So except for a handful of locals and my father's friends, no one else has seen me for years or knows what I do for a living."

"You might be surprised. Many people took an interest

in you after your attack. People your father barely knew approached him to ask after you. He's kinda proud of you, Turner." Tim glanced over again, looking for a reaction, but when she gave none, he went on. "From what I understand, he has been known to brag about you."

Sam remained quiet as she processed Tim's words. Not surprised to hear people, even strangers, were curious. She'd seen enough examples of how morbidly curious people could be when she was recovering. Strangers recognized her from the photo plastered in the papers. People would sit and whisper to their friends as she walked past, but the bold ones would appear by her side, as if they were great friends to ask her how she was doing.

What surprised her was to hear that her father was proud of her. She knew he loved her in his own way, but he was never much for affection, and compliments were rare. She suspected he'd always been disappointed she'd never gone into law enforcement. And he had never admitted he was proud of her, at least not to her face.

"So tell me, why do you hate Murphy so much?" Tim asked. He must have caught Sam's perplexed expression because he put his hand up in placation. "I know you have more reasons than most to hate Murphy with what happened to you five years ago and then again at my garage. But I get the distinct impression your dislike for this town runs much deeper than that."

Sam paused before she spoke again. "Let's just say there have been a lot of odd accidental deaths in this town," Sam said, emphasizing the word accidental.

"If you're implying what I think—" Tim hesitated.

"What I'm saying is there are a lot of *accidental* deaths in Murphy that at face value should win Darwin awards, but if you look at the circumstances of each, most just don't add up. The more logical explanation being suicide is so taboo that no one wants to talk about it, including my father."

"Wow, that's something I didn't want to know." Tim sighed, shaking his head. "How about we continue this conversation later? After we confirm everything is fine at the high school."

Sam didn't bother responding. What more could she say? She didn't like this town. An exceptional number of bad things happened to people in Murphy and no one talked about it. Not even her father. If any town had *Bad Juju*, it was Murphy.

In that moment, fate reinforced this idea, making it iron-clad in Sam's mind. A bone-jarring impact seized their truck, followed by the sounds of grinding metal on metal. It seemed to come from all around them. Squealing tires as brakes were applied far too late to do anything but send vehicles spinning out of control. A scream that sounded far away but must have come from within the Ford. The engine revved and for a split second, a surreal floating sensation overtook and suspended both of them before slamming them back down to reality with such force that Sam now knew all too well how crash test dummies felt.

Momentum taking over, Sam's head snapped sideways, slamming into the side door window. She heard a loud crack as something hard hit something harder. A loud buzzing followed up the impact, making her wonder if the sound came from her skull or the window. Sam reached up to her temple to find the source of the pain blossoming through the right side of her head. It felt wet and warm to her touch and only magnified the pain, making her stomach roll. Sam pulled her hand away and focused on breathing for a few minutes, trying her best not to be sick. The nausea waned at about the same time as the volume on the incessant buzzing dialed itself back to a dull hum.

The truck had come to a halt across the intersecting road and now faced east towards a row of houses. Her gaze focussed on the front fender of a car she saw through the windshield. She followed the line of the sedan to the passenger side window, but the webbed cracks in the glass from where her head smacked the windowpane distorted her view. The overwhelming urge to see the rest of the vehicle had her trying to put her window down, but pressing the button didn't work. Tugging on the door handle, she swung it open and attempted to exit. Something restrained her. Gazing down, she saw the culprit. Her seatbelt. Undoing it, she spilled out of her seat onto the pavement and stared at it. Her eyes roamed over the car's body, coming to rest on what caught her attention. A huge gash ran down the entire side of the car. It looked like a giant can opener had been used on the back half of the driver's side. The windows were shaded, but the shadow of a form was slumped over the wheel. Her first thought was to go over and check on the driver, but a low moan drew her foggy attention back to the truck she'd just exited.

Tim, she thought hazily, staggering back towards the Ford. He'd been driving them to the high school when something hit them. Something big.

Tim was leaning back in the driver's seat, his head against the headrest with his hands in his lap. If she didn't know better, she would have thought he was taking a nap, but his hands ruined that illusion. They were clutching his left leg, holding on for dear life. And although his head leaned back against the headrest, she could see the tendons in his neck standing out in strain or in pain. His moan chased away the fog still clouding her mind. Sam leaned in to examine the leg he clutched. She saw some blood, but not much else. His hands blocked her view.

"Tim, let me see." When he didn't respond, Sam put her hand on his arm. His breathing was rapid and shallow, and she didn't like his pallor.

"Let me see!" she said firmly, pulling one of his hands away. Her breath caught in her throat. Something was stuck in his thigh. It looked like a jagged piece of metal had gone through the driver's door and into his left leg. She couldn't see where it came out though, or if he was hurt anywhere else.

"Tim, look at me," Sam said. When she still didn't get a response, she repeated his name, getting louder each time until he opened his eyes.

"Are you hurt anywhere else?"

There was a pregnant pause before he shook his head and muttered through a clenched jaw. "No. I don't think so. But my leg... hurts like a bitch."

Sam, careful not to touch his legs, leaned over him and stuck her head out his open window to get a look at the metal shank pinning him to his truck. Even seeing the end sticking out his door, she couldn't make sense of where it had come from. She sat back in her seat.

Sam didn't like his slow responses, rapid breathing or shivering. All signs of shock. She couldn't do much about the piece of metal in his leg, but she could try to prevent the worst of the shock. She swiveled in her seat to look in the back of the truck. The movement was too quick, causing her vision to swim. She closed her eyes and took a deep breath to slow her heart rate before opening her eyes again. What she saw gave her pause. Another much larger piece of jagged rusty metal had embedded itself in the back of the cab. Suspended a foot off the floor, its trajectory would have skewered them both in the back if it had been another few inches to the left. As it was, this would have been where the dogs sat had they brought them along. Sam spotted what she was looking for. Grabbing the blanket from the cab's floor, she pulled. It gave way easily enough. She wrapped his upper torso with it. The mild smell of dog still clung to the fabric.

"Ugh.... that smells like dog."

"Sorry, but it's the only thing we have to keep you warm."

Hearing Tim complain about the dog smell comforted Sam. It meant part of him was still with her and she silently thanked her lucky stars they'd decided to drop both dogs off at Tim's house.

Although Buddy was happy to hang out with his new friend Brandy, he hadn't been pleased about being left behind. He'd had a doggy fit once Tim closed his front door. There was a lot of barking, howling and a noise that sounded suspiciously like something breaking at which point Tim looked over at her, his expression the perfect picture of "What the hell?" Agitated and pacing, Buddy would pop up in one window, then another, and then back to the original window again. Back and forth he went, along with the occasional barking fit. Almost as perplexed as Tim, the only thing she could think to do was reassure him she'd pay for any damages.

The wail of sirens approaching, along with shouts came from somewhere behind them. A glance at her watch told her only another forty minutes before show time. She turned to leave but Tim grabbed her hand forcing her to look back at him.

"You can't go to the school, Sam. Not alone."

Sam shook her head. "Nope. Not until I know you're ok."

"Not at all Sam. If something goes down, you won't have any backup to help you—" He stared at her, his face a mask of worry until another bout of pain hit him. He squeezed his eyes shut as the intensity of his pain etched lines across his face.

More shouts and cries came from the street. She squeezed his hand before pulling away. Sam stepped out of the truck but wasn't at all prepared for the scene that rolled out before her when she looked back into the heart of the crash. Luckily, she had a hand on the truck, otherwise she would have ended up on her ass. It was all too much to take in at one time. To process the chaos before her, she had to take it in piece by piece, like a giant jigsaw puzzle.

This road turned into a highway, so the speed limit here was much higher than usual, which explained the severity of the damage. Two tractor-trailers seemed to be at the center of the disaster. A blue semi lay on the left side of the road up against a telephone pole, which was now at a forty-five degree angle to the ground, with what looked like a Fiat pinned between the blue semi's cab and the pole. The Fiat, now squashed like an accordion, would have had no survivors. The blue semi's dump truck trailer lay on its side across the better part of two lanes. A few of the larger pieces of scrap metal still rested in and just outside of the trailer. She saw the top of a red cab from the other tractor-trailer. It must have struck the blue semi's trailer from behind, accounting for some of the uncontrolled momentum resulting in such destruction. Its trailer still stood right side up but blocked a substantial portion of the lanes. She couldn't see around the trailers, but had little doubt there would be a few casualties hidden behind them as well.

A couple of cars appeared to be stuck under the red semi's trailer. Considering the roofs had been sheared off, it would be a miracle if anyone survived from either vehicle. Metal pieces of various sizes, shapes, and color littered the road. It was clear theirs wasn't the only vehicle struck by flying scrap metal. Another half a dozen cars sat between the trailers and Tim's blue Ford, and all but one looked to have been peppered with metal pieces. She and Tim had fared better than most in this accident. The one car that appeared miraculously untouched by the metal knives had all four doors open. If she had to guess, she'd say the family currently huddled together on the side of the road had come from that car. They were holding on to each other like their lives depended on it, and she didn't blame them. To be honest, she'd like to join them.

Some pedestrians were wandering through the accident scene. A woman with only one shoe stumbled up the road. Her torn blue skirt revealed veins of blood running down the backs of her calves. She appeared to be searching for something. Sam looked away. She didn't want to find out what that something was.

The other wanderer, a man who looked like he'd just walked out of an Abercrombie and Fitch catalogue, looked unhurt. He was mumbling something as he stumbled down the middle of the road, perhaps fifty feet away. Obviously suffering from shock, he walked, turned, and walked back the way he came, grasping something in his right hand. It looked like a small, brightly colored baseball bat, but the shape wasn't quite right. Strings trailing from it, one of which looked like it was unraveling on the ground. No, not unraveling, but dripping and leaving a trail behind. Sam's eyes widened in horror upon realizing

261

what this poor man was dragging around with him. Sam pulled her eyes away from the man that had just lost everything.

Whether it was the shock from what she'd just seen or the aftereffects of the strike to her head, Sam knew she was about to puke or pass out. Hopefully not both.

"Oh, no—" was all she got out before she slid to her knees and retched. It kept coming until there was nothing left but dry heaves. By the time she finished, her head throbbed, and the buzzing returned in full force. Leaning back against the truck again, she kept her eyes closed. She wanted to help those poor people who were in various states of shock but knew, in this moment, she couldn't.

She heard someone calling her name. As the buzzing inside her head became more bearable, she realized the shouts were coming from somewhere close by.

"Sam!" Much more urgent this time. Tim was shouting her name.

The sirens, loud now because of their proximity, showed the emergency crews had arrived on scene. Counting to ten, she pushed herself up and looked towards the heart of the disaster again. Police officers, paramedics, and firefighters scrambled across the road. Some held small red boxes, which she assumed must be handheld emergency kits. She felt a little wave of relief when she saw paramedics had already descended on the two dazed pedestrians. She stood there for a minute, hoping to catch someone's attention, and waved at the first firefighter running in their general direction. Certain he'd seen her, she slipped back into the truck to check on Tim.

He was leaning forward, attempting to look around, worry and a good amount of pain knit his brow. He looked a little better, too. Pale, but ok.

"Sam, what's going on out there? I heard you—" Tim waited a few seconds before asking, "Is it that bad?"

"It's pretty bad. Several vehicles were involved, including two semis, one of which was hauling a load of scrap metal. That's what hit us. The emergency crews are here now. I flagged one down to come over to help you."

"You mean coming to help us. You don't look good. That gash on your temple—"

Sam nodded. She wasn't about to argue with him, especially in his current condition. It looked like Tim wanted to say something more; however, their rescuers appeared, saving Sam from having to lie to him. One way or another, she'd go to the high school no matter what anyone said.

Two firefighters came to their aid. After a cursory appraisal of the metal piece protruding from Tim's leg, they called over a couple of paramedics. Taking in the scene, one paramedic split away from the driver's side and rounded the truck. Sam climbed out of the passenger seat to allow the paramedic in. After a brief discussion, the four of them decided to transport Tim along with the door in case the metal spear had severed an artery. The firefighters went to work carefully removing the truck door, while the paramedic in the passenger's seat turned to her. She told him she was fine, but he ignored her assertions and poked and prodded at her head wound.

The grinding of metal on metal as the firefighters cut through the metal door created so much noise, the only reason Sam heard anything the paramedic said was because he was shouting it directly in her ear. "You have... concussion. You need to go... hosp—" Thankfully, the noise drowned out the rest of the paramedic's words.

The grinding noise stopped. The firefighters had removed the door from its hinges and were now loading it and Tim onto a makeshift gurney. Considering all the hand gestures, it looked like they were discussing how best to transport him to the hospital. There wasn't anything more Sam could do to help him. Although she felt guilty about not saying something to him before they took him to the hospital, she couldn't take the chance of the paramedics insisting she go with them.

Everything that had just happened to them would be for nothing if what she dreamed came to pass and she did nothing to try to stop it. If she hadn't come back to town early to check out the school, Tim wouldn't have been involved in this accident and gotten hurt.

"Now or never, Sammy," she muttered to herself. She slipped away from the truck and headed in the school's direction. At one point, she thought she'd heard her name being shouted but didn't stop or turn around to find out. She only had one thing on her mind and that was how little time she had left to crash her old high school.

At 2:00 p.m. Mrs. Waznek headed over to check on Brandy, her favorite four-legged neighbor. She had kind eyes, stood five feet tall, and had her white hair tied back in a bun. With a bounce in her step, she made her way to Tim's back door. She'd brought two doggy treats this time because she wanted Brandy to do a trick, like roll over or play dead. She'd seen Tim get her to do it from time to time. If she did the trick, she'd get two treats.

Years ago, Tim had given her a key. She used it now like she had on so many occasions. Once unlocked, she swung the back door wide. To her amazement, a large white retriever dashed through the opening. So surprised by the unexpected escapee she couldn't suppress a shout of alarm in reaction to the beast's exit, which almost bumped her off balance in its haste to leave. She counted her lucky stars that Brandy didn't follow suit, otherwise Mrs. Waznek was sure she would have ended up on her rump in the middle of the sidewalk. As it was, she'd dropped both doggy treats in the skirmish, which were now lying a few feet away from Mrs. Waznek's feet and being stared at by her favorite charge, Brandy.

A few white tendrils of hair had come loose from her bun. She pushed them back over her ear with a huff and regarded Brandy with kind gray eyes.

"At least you still have your manners, Brandy."

Brandy tore her eyes from their vigil on the dog biscuits, looked Mrs. Waznek in the eyes, and whined. Clearly Brandy felt unduly tortured by the proximity of the treats. Mrs. Waznek couldn't resist her doggy pout and smiled at the hopeful dog.

"Fine, go ahead," was all she had to say. Brandy barked once, beelined it for the biscuits and within seconds, the treats disappeared.

After closing the back door behind her, she decided she'd have to call Tim about the strange dog that had escaped from his house. That is as soon as her heart stopped racing. That's when she noticed the state of Tim's living room and proceeded forward. What was once a lamp had been broken into hundreds of shards on the hardwood floor. Tim's brown metal blinds now rested in twisted ruins over the windows. The lovely oak front door had scratch marks around the door handle, like something was frantic to escape the house.

"Uh-oh. I think your rude friend is going to be in big trouble." Mrs. Waznek would have whistled if she knew how. Brandy, who now sat beside her, looked up with beseeching eyes and whined. After it elicited no response, Brandy trotted over to the mess, sat down and, looking Mrs. Waznek in the eyes, she whined again. If she didn't know better, it seemed like Brandy was trying to ask her to help with the retriever's mess. Ridiculous. Mrs. Waznek shook her head as if shaking away cobwebs, but responded, anyway.

"Sorry Brandy, but even my domestic skills can't fix this mess." And with that, she picked up the phone to call Brandy's owner and give him the strange news.

Chapter 19

Time To Meet The Teacher

S am reached the school twenty minutes before the time in her dream, but it was already too late. The front doors, chained from the inside, wouldn't budge past an inch. Desperate now, she did a loop around the school to check the rest of the doors, wasting another few minutes. Even the gym door, which was normally left unlocked, was chained. Not good.

Years ago, the school became the target of regular break-ins. Rumors surfaced the school had become part of a coming-of-age ritual for local teenagers to break in and steal something from the school without getting caught. Theft became so prevalent and costly the school board hired a security firm to assess the high school and advise them on how to make it more secure. Their first suggestion, to install an alarm system complete with cameras and metal detectors at the doors would have cost the board several thousands of dollars to implement. Instead, they went with the third suggestion and installed bars on all the windows of the main floor for less than a tenth of their original estimate. The bars did a good job of stopping the midnight break-ins. However, the overall amount of theft only decreased by a quarter. The thieves got savvier and starting stealing during school hours instead of after hours.

Sam had to find a way in. After completing her second circuit around the school, a solution came to her as she looked skyward. A set of windows ran along the bottom of the hallway on the second floor. If she scaled the bars, she might reach them, but at least one of them had to open for this to work. Luckily, one window pane protruded out more compared to the others. Grabbing the security bars, Sam began scaling the main floor window. She was about to clear it when she heard a shout.

"Hey you! Get down from there or I'll call the cops," someone yelled.

Sam froze. The voice tickled her memory, pulling her back to her teenage years when she had to listen to authority figures like teachers. But those days were long gone. So instead, she forced herself to relax. Although not happy with the idea of being charged with breaking and entering, it solved the problem of how to get the cops here.

"Good. Call them," Sam shouted back.

A shuffling below her feet told her the speaker was trying to get a better look at her. Focussed on the task at hand, she didn't bother looking down. She'd found the window in question ajar by an inch and was attempting to force it open.

"Well, I'll be damned. I thought I recognized that voice and poor attitude. Samantha Turner! I heard you'd moved to the big city. How are you doing?"

Sam cringed at the full use of her first name and leaned back to get a better look at the stranger who obviously wasn't a stranger peering up at her. Mr. Nosey had his face pressed up against the glass distorting the right half, but even so she recognized him instantly. Mr. Redna, her old physics teacher. He had changed little. From the red hair now salted with gray and crowned by the bald spot on the top of his head, his blue sweater vest, down to the brown loafers. She never liked physics, but had always thought him a decent teacher. He never gave up on her, even though she'd been a lost cause on the subject.

"Oh. Hi Mr. Redna. I'm pretty good, I guess. Just... hangin' out," Sam replied dryly.

Mr. Redna nodded before asking, "Uh-huh. Life in the big city treating you well then?"

"Yes, thank you. You'll be happy to hear I have a golden retriever now."

Mr. Redna would often bring up his dog Skylar, also a golden retriever, when he taught physics. He'd be in the middle of teaching them about some law of physics and gave examples of how it applied in everyday life, and the examples often included Skylar. It was pretty funny.

"Oh yeah? That's great. Just great. You'll never want for companionship if you have a golden by your side. They really are the best." Mr. Redna paused a moment before continuing. "Sam, do you mind if I ask you a question?"

"Sure," Sam responded as she turned back to continue shoving open the stubborn pane above her head. Their whole conversation seemed so surreal that nothing would have surprised her at this point.

"Why are you climbing the school?"

Sam paused, debating briefly on what to tell him. Explaining why she was scaling the side of the public high school would be difficult without telling him something. Sighing, she bent down low enough to catch his eye. "Can you do me a favor and call the police like you threatened to? Tell them all the school doors have been chained from the inside so no one can get in or out. There's someone in this school that wants to hurt a lot of students."

Mr. Redna's red sandy brows rose in disbelief, his eyes as round as saucers. A pregnant pause ensued, at which point they could have heard a pin drop.

"Excuse me?" Mr. Redna asked, his voice barely above a whisper.

More than a little surprised he wasn't moving already considering all the high school shootings in the news over the last few years, she decided on a more direct approach. He needed to take her seriously.

"I apologize in advance for being harsh as I always liked you as a teacher, Mr. Redna, but I said... CALL THE FUCKING POLICE NOW!"

When he still didn't move, she knew one thing that would get a reaction out of him. Sam drew the gun from her pocket and brandished it in his line of sight. Mr. Redna's eyes widened with a combination of surprise and fear and backed away from the window.

Great, yet another person who's convinced I'm crazy and dangerous. The entire town will have me committed before the weekend has even begun. She thought grimly as she shoved the gun back in her pocket and grasped the edges of the casement above her head to continue her assault on the window.

Sam favored her left shoulder to avoid straining her right one, which was still tender from her last run-in with Charlie. She eyed the opening above her head. The casement swung out and was now open as wide as its design allowed. She should be able to squeeze her head and shoulders in, but barely. Tricky. Even if she stood on her toes on the upper ridge of the bars, she was still too far below the opening to gain the leverage she needed to guarantee she wouldn't lose her grip and fall backwards. The fall itself wouldn't kill her as long as she didn't land on her head or neck, but she'd definitely be broken in a few places.

That's when she noticed the ridge in the wall where it transitioned from standard red brick to the white cement preformed blocks. The ridge should give her an extra foot of leverage, enough to get her head and shoulders through the lower half of the window.

Taking a breath, she stepped up on the ridge, slid her hands up through the window and began trying to get her shoulders through. Although a tight squeeze, with enough maneuvering, she got them through the small opening.

Sam's relief was short-lived upon realizing the hardest part still lay ahead. With only the smooth tiled floor in front of her, there was nothing to hold on to to pull herself the rest of the way up. After a lot of pushing, pulling, straining, she cleared the window. Breathing, she lay there for a moment to assess herself. The pain in her right shoulder was back, and a throbbing in her temple meant the injury to her head was not in a happy place either. She could already hear Nurse Ratched's voice in her head, scolding her for pushing herself too much.

Hopefully, her old physics teacher held up his end and called the cops. It wasn't until after Sam reached the school that she'd realized she had no way to call the police. Her cell phone was in her purse on the floor of Tim's smashed up Ford. She often kept her phone in her back pocket, but of course, not today.

* * *

Ever since she'd got up this morning, Zoey couldn't shake the sense of dread hanging off her like a second skin. She woke up exhausted, back wet with perspiration, body aching as if she'd been running all night and knew it had something to do with the dream she couldn't quite remember. The hairs on the back of her neck still stood at attention by the time she had to leave for school. And just when she'd decided today would be a good day to play hooky, her aunt and uncle surprised her with a ride to school. The one day she wanted to stay the hell away from the school was the first day in months they'd waited to give her a ride in. Talk about kismet.

To her relief, class after class went by without incident. It was only when she headed towards her sixth period classroom, geology, that the hairs on the back of her neck tickled her with their insistence something wasn't right. Zoey looked around just as Peter brushed past her walking down the hall towards the back of the school. Peter had always been a lagger, but there was purpose in his stride now, which didn't sit well with her. But what disturbed her more was the smile he wore. In all the years she'd known him, Zoey had never seen Peter smile. All it took was a split second in the hall to erase any relief she'd felt that the day might turn out fine. It wasn't until someone bumped her out of her thoughts that she stopped staring after Peter and forced her feet to move towards her next class. Once there, though, she couldn't shake the feeling that something bad was heading their way. So distracted by her thoughts, she didn't notice class had started. The smack of a ruler across her desk brought her full attention back to see an irritated Mr. Morris standing in front of her desk.

"Miss William, can you tell us one type of boundary on tectonic plates?" A few titters erupted around her.

Last class, Mr. Morris had been talking about plate tectonics and how they shifted under the continental shelves. Some of it was interesting, especially when he referred to the modern day examples of their after-effects. However, that was yesterday. Now all she could do was stare back at Mr. Morris. Angry, his already-red face turned another shade darker right before her eyes.

Well, this is a little unsettling, Zoey thought as she watched a vein in his forehead twitch and his hand tighten on the ruler he held. She had the distinct impression what he really wanted to do was bash her head in with it.

"For the third time, I asked you to name the three boundaries at tectonic plates..." Mr. Morris ground out between clenched teeth as he swung his measuring stick down again, barely missing the student's hands on the desk next to hers.

Zoey's instincts screamed to get away from Mr. Morris. It didn't make any logical sense because of all the teachers she had, he always came across as even and mild tempered. Until today, that is. Her gut shouted a clear and present danger stood in front of her, and she needed to get as far away from him as possible. But how? She couldn't just walk out of the class, could she?

After less than a couple of seconds of internal debate, she did just that. Zoey rose from her seat, grabbed the bag hanging off the back of her chair, and walked out of the classroom. All thirty-one pairs of eyes stared after her, thirty of which wishing they could do the same.

"Zoey William where do you think you're—" Mr. Morris began, but the rest got cut off by the classroom door swinging shut behind her. Prematurely exiting class would likely mean a detention, but at this point she was too scared to care. She'd learned a long time ago that it paid to follow her instincts, and she wouldn't ignore them now.

Her bold exit must have shocked him into momentary

inaction because he didn't follow. So frightened, Zoey practically ran down the hall and around the corner. She thought she heard the swing of a door opening behind her as she cleared the corner. She ducked into the first empty classroom on the opposite side of the hall in case he had pursued her. Only the room wasn't empty. Mr. Redna stood by the windows, his gaze fixed heavenwards. He seemed to be in the middle of a rather animated discussion with himself. If she wasn't so scared, she'd have found his rantings to a higher power amusing. Luckily, his preoccupation allowed her to duck into one of the enclosed lab desks without being noticed. Hide and seek was another skill she'd gained under unfortunate circumstances. Zoey pressed her shaking hands between her legs to still her tremors and settled in for the forty minutes she'd have to wait there before the end of class bell rang.

The subtle sound of a door swooshing open, the same door she'd just entered from not a minute or two ago, made her inhale sharply. The approach of a soft tread paused just behind the desk she was under. Zoey froze like a rabbit sensing a predator nearby.

"Say, can you call out? I haven't been able to, which is weird because I just called my wife not a half an hour ago," Mr. Redna asked. The sound of rubber-soled shoes shuffling along the tile floor got louder. Then the shuffling stopped, and a pregnant pause ensued. "I'm sorry, but is that a—"

The crack of gunfire ringing out erased whatever else Mr. Redna was about to say, followed closely by a thump as something solid hit the floor. After what seemed like hours, the soft tread receded followed by the swoosh of the door swinging open, then closed again. Zoey took a shallow breath, only then realizing she'd been holding it, and waited.

Not long after that, she heard more shots ring out. They sounded further away, like they were coming from somewhere further away down the hall. Relief washed over her like a warm, comforting wave. Followed by shame for feeling so relieved while others were, at that very moment, being terrorized and possibly even gunned down.

Zoey stayed there for what seemed like forever. Even when she heard the door swing open again a few minutes later, she remained where she was, silent and hidden.

Unless she heard sirens and knew it was a cop, she wasn't giving up her hiding spot.

Murphy High's main floor was the heart of the school. The classrooms, gym, pool, cafeteria, and teacher's lounge were all on the main floor. The second floor was more like an afterthought and much smaller than the rest. It was as if the architect got bored by his own design and had to add the second floor glass enclosed seating area just to make it a little different from the carbon copy school layout, which was T, U or H shaped or some variation thereof. The only purpose the second floor had was to allow access to the upper seating sections facing the pool and gym. Therefore, it only ever got used during tournaments or swim events. As a design feature, it failed miserably. As an emergency access point into the building after a psycho had locked and chained all the doors, it did the job.

A gunshot rang out clear as a bell. Time was up.

Sam was still on the ground after hauling herself in through the small opening. Desperate for something, anything to create a distraction, her eyes darted around the hall before settling on the small red box on the wall with

FIRE ALARM engraved on it. Sam got up, jogged to the wall, and pulled the alarm.

Nothing happened.

After a moment of colorful expletives, Sam stopped. Her mind spun. All she could come up with was he'd somehow disabled the alarm system without bringing the full force of the Fire Department down on them. Frustration and fear were a terrible combination and Sam was doing her best not to give in to the panic she felt rising within like high tide.

A couple of minutes later, another gunshot rang out, but it sounded further away now. Another chased it and another and another until Sam stopped counting. Shots intermingled with screams and she felt sick. Maybe if they'd been able to leave her father's house earlier or if they'd taken a different route to the school, they would have avoided the accident and she could have made it here in time to stop Charlie before the school got locked down.

Enough time had passed that if Mr. Redna had made the call, she should have heard the sirens by now. She needed to find something else to bring emergency services to them. Considering the collision she'd just witnessed and the number of emergency personnel on scene, whatever would bring the police here in the immediate future had to be more than a precautionary check-up. Desperate, Sam looked around for something, anything, but there was nothing of use.

Then she heard it. A vehicle in the parking lot. It looked like a Canada Post cube van cutting through the school parking lot. Sam pulled the gun from her pocket, laid down on the floor, and took aim through the open window she'd just crawled in through. She wasn't sure why the postie had taken a shortcut through the school parking lot, but their poor judgement was her gain. Sam knew there'd be consequences for shooting at a public service vehicle, but at this point she didn't give a damn as long as it brought someone to the school. She aimed for the fender. Taking out a tire might cause the driver to lose control and cause an accident. The back fender looked like the safer option.

First shot hit the fender dead on. The postal truck swerved and almost hit a parked Buick before coming to a shuddering halt. To Sam's surprise, the driver got out of the truck to look around. *Wow, this guy had lousy survival instincts.* Too far away to shout at, and even if she tried it would probably just draw him towards the school. Crazy-With-The-Gun would pick the postal worker off the moment he or she saw him. Shaking her head, she took aim a few feet to his left, hitting the truck square in the middle of the back half. To her amazement, the postie whirled back around to face the school as if trying to locate the source. Despite that, he didn't take off. *Wow! Do I really have to shoot him just to get the guy moving?* Sam took aim a third time. The bullet ricocheted off the ground a foot away in front of him. Now terrified, the postal worker dove into the driver's side and slammed down on the accelerator. He was off in a whirl of dust; the van careening dangerously on two wheels in his haste to leave. Luckily, the two tires in the air came back down to meet the pavement again and continued carrying the cube van away from the school parking lot.

Satisfied now that the cops would eventually come to the school, Sam rose from the floor, ready to face the chaos downstairs. It sounded like the shooter was using a hunting rifle. Hunting rifles were commonplace in most towns, especially in Murphy where the population of hunters outnumbered the population of actual voters two to one. However, considering her father's rifles were just stolen, it was a good

277

possibility that one of his rifles was the one being used. That made her feel even more sick.

Gripping the gun with both hands, Sam descended the stairwell as quickly as she dared to the main level. The halls were empty. After the gunshots, she expected them to be swarming with panicked students as they tried, unsuccessfully, to open the chained doors. That would have been bad, but this quiet eeriness seemed worse somehow. She walked down the deserted hall, looking in classroom windows as she went. The fourth classroom she came to appeared as empty as the rest. She was about to move on when she noticed the tip of a shoe poking out around the corner on the left. Someone was hiding. She tried the door handle again, but it didn't budge. Only the school custodian would have keys, so either the keys were stolen or the custodian had locked it. But why would he lock the students in the classroom?

Then she remembered Tim mentioning there was a new janitor at the school he wanted to check out.

Sam skipped the fifth classroom and went to the classroom door where she'd encountered Mr. Redna and slid into the room as quietly as she could. It was a science lab and, except for the standard lab desks and bar stools, the room looked empty. Sam rushed the length of the room only to stop short when she saw a still figure lying on the floor. He was lying on his back. Even from this distance she could see he was dead, but headed towards her old physics teacher, anyway. Blood darkened the front of his beige sweater vest, his right arm was flung above his head while his left still lay at his side, and his legs stuck straight out in front of him. One of his shoes sat a good five feet in front of his body, suggesting someone had literally blown him off his feet. Sam went through the motions and checked his throat for a pulse that didn't exist.

Then she stood up, slipped the gun in her right pocket, went over to the nearest sink, and retched for a solid minute. Though there was nothing left to be brought up, that didn't seem to matter to her stomach. Once done, she washed off her hands, splashed cool water on her face, drank from the tap and turned back to the room. She took a deep breath through her nose but switched to breathing through her mouth when the salty scent of blood and something more organic hit her nostrils, making her gag again.

Sam now knew where one shell had ended up, which didn't bode well for the students and teachers that remained. Threatening to kill and actually killing were two different things. The shooter just graduated from disturbed to psychopath.

Was she surprised? Not really. Not after what she'd experienced over the last five years.

Was she afraid? Very.

Not trusting her stomach, she was careful to avoid the blood spreading on the floor as she searched for Mr. Redna's mobile. It wasn't on him. She'd about given up when she noticed the reflection of the sun off a glass surface peaking around the corner of the desk a few feet above the outstretched left hand. Sam stepped around the blood spatter to retrieve the phone. It didn't look damaged. Feeling a spark of hope, Sam dialed nine-one-one. Nothing happened. She tried again and again, but to no avail. No dial tone, just a call failure. It showed one bar, so though the signal strength was weak, there should have been service.

What the heck? Sam stared stupidly at the phone for a few seconds. Except for remote locations where cell towers were too far away to pick up a signal, she'd only ever lost cell service in underground structures like parkades. Murphy High was aboveground and had too many windows to credit the signal loss to that. Sam looked through the recent outgoing calls and saw there were nine failed attempts to call nine-one-one, five twenty minutes ago and the four just made by Sam a minute ago. Cursing, Sam grabbed her gun from the right pocket as she slipped the phone into her left. Although useless now, perhaps she'd get lucky and be able to catch a signal later.

The possibility that it might still be a while before the cops came to their rescue meant sitting here wasn't an option. Waiting would only get more people killed, but she had to figure out where the shooter was in the school before she could be of any help.

Sam left the science lab and ran to the classroom down the hall. Just like the other two, the door was locked. She looked in the door window, her breath hitching in her throat at what she saw. Bodies strewn across the room. Some across desks, most on the floor, one sitting up against the far wall. All of them were still and silent and bloody. Just like shooting fish in a barrel.

Irrational as it was, all she wanted to do was scream threats to high heaven and hunt down the bastard bent on massacring the entire student body, but knew the only advantage she had right now was the element of surprise.

In her dream, she hadn't actually set eyes on Charlie. He grabbed Zoey from behind, catching her unaware and throwing her into the classroom the Peter kid was terrorizing. It wouldn't surprise her if Charlie had posed as a teacher or even as the janitor. He was a chameleon, blending into his environment as it suited him.

The cold tendrils of fear brushed down the back of her neck. Knowing she couldn't afford the luxury of allowing fear or panic to cloud her reasoning, Sam forced herself to stop thinking about Charlie. She needed to find Zoey and incapacitate the shooter. *Think, Sam*, she chided herself, *think!*

Before she fully realized what she was doing, her feet took her to the next classroom door. She zigzagged down the hallway, checking each door, searching for the shooter. She'd already gone past two more sets of doors when she heard a shout from a classroom further down the hall. Picking up her pace, she ran towards the sound, finding the source halfway down the hall. A blond kid's face was pressed hard against the small glass window of the door.

"Please, let me out of here!" the blond teenager shouted as he pounded ineffectually at the door.

Sam ran to the kid's door and tugged at the handle, but just like the others, it didn't budge. No one could get out without using a key.

"Open the door!" the kid shouted as he pulled, then banged at it again.

With no clue how to help him, Sam stared back at the panic-stricken kid helplessly. Eyes wide with terror, he redoubled his efforts and started throwing himself at the door with increasing violence. His actions were like those of a drowning man caught under ice. He kept struggling to break through the surface, but the door showed no mercy, his cheek and nose pressed hard against the window.

The only weapon she had was a gun, and Sam knew shooting at the lock wouldn't do much good. The school was built half a century ago. All the classroom doors were solid oak with professionally made deadbolts. It would take more than a couple of bullets to get through it. Every classroom had two entrances, though. Leaving might throw the kid into hysterics, but there was little else she could do. She'd

281

only taken a couple of steps away from the door when a loud bang whipped her head back around.

She ran back to the window and touched the glass the opposite side of which was now splattered with blood. Sam felt helpless, frustrated, angry and, as ashamed as she was to admit it, afraid. She was eight again, terrified to look under her bed after a kid in her grade school told her the bogeyman lived under it and would snatch her away if she grew bold enough to peek. But unlike the imaginary monster she'd had nightmares about as a child, this was a very real monster staring back at her. Sam's breath hitched in her throat.

She expected to see someone much younger terrorizing the students. Instead, she found a middle-aged man standing at the front of the room waving around a handgun. She thought for sure he'd seen her when she saw him staring back at her through the blood spattered window, but he must have been appreciating his handiwork because he turned his attention back to his hostages without a second glance in her direction. Either that or he felt she was no threat.

A quick scan of the room showed most of the students were still in their seats. A few desks sat empty, the bodies littering the floor likely accounted for some of those vacancies. The middle-aged shooter addressing the class had every eye trained on him like their lives depended on it. It sounded like he was teaching a class about plate tectonics at gunpoint. She would have given Crazy-With-The-Gun points for his effective teaching method, but doubted his unwilling students would retain anything if they made it out of this alive. Then, as if he'd heard her thoughts, he threw a question out to his captive audience, testing their retention of his lecture material.

It was the familiarity of his voice that made her stare more intently at his profile until it came to her. It was the geology teacher from her dream, Mr. Morris. She remembered he'd been pretty miffed when Zoey'd walked out on him in the middle of class. However, this wasn't the teenage shooter in her dream. Then again, she wasn't herself in the dream, either. She'd been a teenager named Zoey William. She did another quick sweep of the students present and felt immense relief when she didn't see a blue head in the lot, breathing or not.

If something wasn't done soon, the remaining students would be picked off like the poor bastard at the window. She had her revolver, but shooting through glass would affect her aim, and by how much she wasn't certain. She guessed he was only about six to seven yards away from the other door at the front of the classroom. If she tried shooting him through there, she would have a better chance of hitting him.

Raised voices coming from inside made her pick up her pace. Once at the other door parallel to Mr. Morris, she forced herself to take deep breaths. For accuracy's sake, she had to slow her breathing. She'd never taken a life before, so monster or not, this would be hard.

Sam was a decent shot, but it had been years since she'd done any target practice. There would be only one chance to get it right before he'd duck and hide.

A whimper from the classroom spurred her into action and she took position so her head and gun were now visible through the window. Too busy tormenting his next victim, he didn't notice the threat standing less than twenty feet away. Sam set the teacher in her sights and breathed out as she steadied her hand. She felt like a teenager again only this was no target practice. It was on her exhale when he somehow sensed her presence, because he turned and looked right at her. It made her wonder if he felt the brush of death like she had five years ago when Charlie had her in his sights. She had the satisfaction of seeing his satisfied smile turn into surprise as she pulled the trigger. Sam aimed for between his eyes and although the glass changed the trajectory of the bullet ever so slightly, her target's movements changed the shot the most. It hit him close to the ear. He went down, disappearing from view behind the desk.

Believing Mr. Morris was dead and knowing were two different things. Sam waited, focused, gun cocked.

High on adrenaline, the blood pumping through her veins sounded like thunder in her ears. It wasn't until a minute or two went by and she saw no further movement from behind the desk that she relaxed her grip and lowered her weapon. That's when she picked up the other noises in the classroom. Whimpering, weeping, a voice babbling to the left, someone struggling with the other door. Good luck with that, she thought. A student close to the door where she stood started shouting. Instinctively, her hand tightened on the gun, but Mr. Morris was still out of sight. She refocused her attention on the kid that shouted and noticed him pointing at her.

No, not at her. He was gesturing at something behind her.

"Behind y—!" was all she heard as the realization hit her far too late this time. An iron grip seized her by the hair, and before she had any chance to struggle or bring her gun around, her head met with the solid wood of the door. The door won.

* * *

Sam woke to a swinging sensation, intense pressure on her stomach causing her already sensitive gut grief, and a wicked headache. The first thing she saw was the blue material of a shirt. Looking further down, she made out the person's legs, also clad in the same shade of blue, black loafers and a smooth tile floor. They'd just passed a classroom door on the right. Someone was carrying her down a school hallway. She'd been tossed over this person's shoulders like a sack of potatoes. Her instincts screamed to fight and try to beat the crap out of her abductor, but her precarious position allowed little access to sensitive body parts. If she pounded on his butt, he'd probably just laugh at her.

However, he had hair. She shifted and swung her left hand up to grab a hold of her captor's locks, but her fingers caught only air. Her brain could not catch up to what was happening. No longer suspended over the shoulder, she felt herself falling before being unceremoniously slammed back into a hard, unyielding object, and a steel band cinched painfully across her throat. Now back in familiar territory, Sam already knew who her abductor was.

"You just can't resist meddling in my business, can you, Sam? You know, if I didn't know better, I'd swear you have a little crush on me," Charlie whispered in her ear. Their embrace would have looked intimate if he hadn't had a chokehold on her as he forced her forward down the hall. Anytime she resisted, he'd tighten his arm and choke her off. Twice her vision blurred and darkened around the edges.

"Wanting to crush you and having a crush on you are two totally different things, Charlie. You... should... get a clue," Sam wheezed. She knew it was stupid to provoke him when she was in such a prone position, but she couldn't seem to help herself. However, instead of upsetting him, it only made him laugh.

That's when the unmistakable sounds of crying and a male voice shouting caught her attention. The noises coming from a classroom on their right.

"I'm enjoying our interludes, Sam. It's almost too bad this will be the last. Did you know your name, being a short form of Samuel, means God has heard—"

The sounds coming from the classroom they approached scared the hell out of her.

"—it's just too bad God isn't listening." Charlie whispered in her ear before he swung the door wide and shoved her in by her hair.

Chapter 20

Boots On The Ground

Chief Julie Kabowski arrived at the corner of Highway Eight and Elizabeth Street at 2:04 pm.

This morning she'd gotten up earlier than usual and headed straight for her office to make some headway through the mountain of paperwork piling up on her desk, but made little progress. She knew taking over the Murphy Police Station from Chief Turner, a man who had run it for well over twenty-five years, would be a little painful. Change is always uncomfortable, especially when it's a stranger coming in to take over command. Also, the fact she was a female chief taking over a male-dominated office didn't help either, but she took it all in stride. This wasn't her first foray in to the good old boys' club, nor would it be her last.

However, the multiple murder at Timothy's Auto, involving the outgoing Police Chief's daughter of all people, had thrown a wrench in the possibility of a smooth transition. Not only were these officers not used to dealing with a major crime scene such as this one, but their divided loyalties between the outgoing Chief and herself added more edge to an already strained situation. That and the fact she'd had to call in OPP officers from the surrounding areas to help only increased the tension on already frayed nerves. The OPP was used to running their own show, so a few of her officers' toes got stepped on, forcing her to take on the role of mediator as well. Smoothing ruffled feathers was not something she enjoyed doing. Now with a half a dozen cups of coffee already under her belt, she had more edge than usual, but that was good considering what lay before her.

As lead at a multi-car collision, the scene she walked into illustrated what happens when cars and semis going at high speed played chicken. Too hard to take in at once, she slowed down her sweep of the landscape to absorb everything.

Cars were crushed into each other like soda cans. A Fiat had merged with a hydro pole, sandwiched by the cab of a semi. What was once its occupants, now resembling something akin to ground beef, were crushed between the windshield and the seats which had come up to meet the dash area, accordion style. Black skid marks crisscrossed the road, showing the two semis had tried braking, but the combination of excessive speed and heavy loads made it an impossible feat. One trailer, the dump truck style, had flipped onto its side and lay diagonally across two lanes with the other trailer propped up against it. It had to have had a substantial load of scrap metal because the length of the street was now littered with it. Upon impact, the semi stopped, but its momentum would have launched the scrap metal down the street, hundreds of various-sized metal knives slicing through whatever they encountered. Metal pipes, rusty sheets of steel and thick ropes of rusty wire pierced vehicles here and there, and it looked like pieces even hit some surrounding houses. Kabowski suspected due to their trajectory, they'd also find pieces of metal in the field across the way.

And then there was the aftermath of what happens when crude metal blades traveling at highway speeds meet a wall of soft tissue. That was the real devastation. Bodies and what looked like body parts were scattered here and there throughout the scene. Two fire trucks and three police units had arrived on scene before her, and more sirens sounded off in the distance. She'd ordered dispatch to request all available OPP and any extra paramedic units the surrounding communities could spare. Kabowski started shouting orders before her shoes even hit the asphalt.

Fifteen minutes later, Kabowski was up to her elbows trying to keep tragedies to a minimum and the scene as clean as possible while still getting the job done. Planned police routes had already been taped off and a confirmation that two more police cars and one paramedic unit were on their way, but it still wouldn't be enough. Kabowski was in the middle of talking to dispatch again to ask them to press the urgency of the situation to the other counties when snatches of a heated discussion reached her ears.

A Constable she knew to be fairly new to the Murphy force was talking to Constable Douglas, and heard her name mentioned at one point. She finished up the call, certain the dispatch understood the urgency and turned to face the officers. Attention focussed now, she got the gist of the conversation.

"I need to talk to Chief Kabowski. There's an injured man who kept insisting we check out the high school. He said that something really bad might be going down."

"Like what? And how does he know?" Douglas asked, blocking his path, but when Timmins didn't respond, he continued. "Tell me he at least gave a reason why he thinks something *bad* is about to go down?"

"Let me pass," Timmins said, color rising in his cheeks. Whether it was because of anger or embarrassment, she wasn't sure, but if she had to guess, she'd say it was anger. These two got along like oil and water. Douglas was stubborn and confrontational at the best of times, but to his credit, Timmins wasn't backing down.

"You greenies, I swear—" Douglas said, shaking his head. "Did you at least check to see if this guy had sustained a head injury? Or lost so much blood he could be delusional? This is a huge fucking accident newbie and if you hadn't noticed, we don't even have enough men to deal with this emergency. And now you want to ask Kabowski to send men we don't have on a wild goose ch—"

"We're supposed to take all requests for help seriously, Douglas. I should at least inform Kabowski about the guy's request—"

She'd heard enough.

"Douglas, let Timmins pass," Kabowski barked, stepping in to put an end to the cockfight. She could hear more calls coming in on her radio, so didn't have the time to deal with this right now, but deal she would. "So, where is this guy now?"

"His injuries were pretty serious, so they already took him away by ambulance. I guess he refused to go until the firefighters promised they'd relay the message to us."

"Fine. Go to the high school and check it out after the OPP reinforcements show up."

Shortly after sending Timmins away, Kabowski headed over to the collision experts. They'd figured out it all started when the Fiat drove across two lanes, cutting off a car and a semi, before plowing into the hydro pole. It created a tragic domino effect and was the reason the semi's cab sandwiched the Fiat between itself and the pole.

She got a call from dispatch around 2:38 pm.

"I said no calls unless it was an emergency," Kabowski snapped into the receiver. She couldn't handle anymore surprises today.

"Sorry, Chief, but it is. Will Kotts called us from the post office. He said his new guy cut across the high school parking lot when someone from within the school opened fire on his truck."

"What the h... when?"

"Not long. He said about five minutes or so ago."

Kabowski hung up the mouthpiece without saying another word and scanned the area for Timmins. Seeing only Douglas, she started towards him to find out where Timmins disappeared to, but didn't have to look far. Douglas stood beside a classic blue Ford truck talking to a firefighter. The driver's door was missing, as were the occupants. An officer, momentarily hidden from view behind the truck, stood up. Timmins.

"What now?" Kabowski ground out as she approached the three men. She didn't like surprises and Murphy seemed to be chock full of them. Timmins was the first to talk.

"Firefighter Penning wanted to let us know the passenger had a head injury but refused help. He thought they should inform us because she was acting strange and took off running in that direction." Timmins pointed westward.

"Where's the driver?"

"En route to the hospital. He was the one that insisted we tell the cops they needed to send someone to the high school." Firefighter Penning said, shaking his head. "I just finished hauling out the semi driver and thought I should take a minute to let you guys know about the passenger too."

Kabowski looked inside the blue Ford and, upon spying the handbag, went around to the passenger side. It didn't take her long to find the wallet, although part of her already knew who the bag belonged to. As soon as she saw the driver's license, she cursed a blue streak.

"What direction is the high school?" Kabowski shouted. All three men pointed in the same general direction the passenger had fled. Westward.

Not one who believed in coincidences, this was all the confirmation Kabowski needed. Yet again the chief's daughter was smack dab in the middle of another tragedy, the second within three months, the third if she counted today's horrific crash site. Murphy was going to hell in a handbasket, and now she had someone to point the blame at. Once was unlucky. Twice was suspicious. Three times was a confession in her books.

Kabowski was already shouting orders to her men to go to the high school and as soon as the current scene was under a modicum of control, she'd be joining them. One way or another, she'd put a stop to Sam Turner.

Chapter 21

After School Special

Constable Timmins was the first to arrive at the high school. He tried the front entrance into the school, only to find it chained from the inside. He was on his mike calling in the situation as Constable Douglas's cruiser rolled in. They began circling the school, trying every door as they went, and found each chained from the inside. Someone had locked the school down tighter than a clam at high tide, leaving them no choice but to call for assistance to open an access point for them.

Timmins was already on the radio talking to dispatch when the sound of gunshots coming from somewhere inside the school broke the neighborhood's silence. The waiting was the worst part. Minutes ticked by like hours as each gunshot dropped like a rock in the pit of the men's stomachs.

Firefighter Penning's squad showed up first. After Timmins updated them on the situation, they had to decide on their best point of entry. They chose the east wing entrance because it was the one set of older doors the school had never replaced and where removing the door's hinges would be easier. It was also on the opposite side of the school from where they'd heard shots being fired. If their assumptions were correct, it should allow first responders lead time to evacuate the rooms not under immediate threat.

They finished removing the third and final hinge from the right-hand side. Timmins and Douglas positioned them-selves on either side of the door as two beefy firefighters, who could have been brothers they looked so similar, lifted and pulled the thick oak door away. They'd just moved it out of the entranceway when a flash of white fur slipped past them and disappeared into the school.

Startled, Timmins shouted after the dog, but his cry got cut off by a sharp jab to his ribcage. Any further protest on Timmin's part was quelled by Douglas's icy stare. It looked like the mutt was on its own.

* * *

The power behind Charlie's shove sent Sam reeling. Off balance, she weaved her arms around to regain her footing and avoid falling flat on her face, but her movements didn't compensate for her momentum. She fell forwards anyway. To her surprise, she landed on something much softer and wetter than the tile floor. It took only a second to realize it was a someone, not a something, that had cushioned her fall. She scrambled to get off the unfortunate person, all the while hoping the reason they hadn't made a peep when she'd landed on them was because they were too scared to make a sound.

Now on her knees beside the unfortunate who'd tempered her fall, Sam looked down into the lifeless eyes of a blond girl. By the look of the material at the top of her shoulders, she'd worn a white top to school today, but it was hard to tell that now. The material across her chest and torso glistened crimson. Her stomach, where the blood-soaked material no longer covered it, was a patchwork of lighter and darker regions, and Sam quickly looked away. She didn't want to know what happened to the poor girl, but had a bad feeling she'd find out soon enough.

It triggered a memory of last night's dream when Zoey had landed next to a blond girl named Lizzie, but this couldn't be her. Sam wondered if her denial was based more on her fear of what might happen next, or an objective assessment of this victim compared to her memory of the dream. This girl had dark roots and brown eyes. She remembered the Lizzie in the dream as having natural ash blond hair and startling blue eyes.

A quick glance down revealed the front of her own shirt, and she suspected part of her face, were now stained red with the dead girl's blood. She knew she should look up and assess the room for strategies out of her current situation, but she didn't want to because what lay beyond would likely be far worse. She lifted a hand towards her cheek but stopped inches away from her face when she saw the blood on her palm. Sam's reflexes slowed and her breathing was way too fast. Recognizing it as anxiety, she took deep breaths to calm herself down. That's when the noises coming from all sides of the room began to filter through.

Cries of pain and terror from the center of the room drew her reluctant gaze there first. Four kids in various stages of pain and blood loss stood or sat in the middle of the room while a dirty blond kid with a rifle walked around them. The kid had Dockers on. Zoey called him Peter in her dream. He was smiling. At her. Sam did a quick scan of the room as she rose from her kneeling position. Twenty students were scattered in clusters around the room and at least another half a dozen lay unmoving on the floor. Considering the amount of blood pooled around the bodies, she'd be surprised if any of them were still alive.

"Hello Sam."

The use of her name drew her attention to the one responsible for the senseless slaughter now standing directly in front of her. Odd that she hadn't seen him approach, which told her she must be in shock as well. Peter grinned, looking pleased with himself.

"It is Sam, right?" When Sam said nothing after a minute, he continued. "Yeah, I know about you. You're the one everyone in town believes is as *crazy as a loon.*"

Look who's calling the kettle black, Sam thought, but kept it to herself. Instinct told her not to piss off Crazy-With-The-Gun number two. This kid wouldn't be as receptive to her insults as Charlie had been, who, for whatever reason, seemed to enjoy her talkback.

She had to hand it to Charlie. He'd covered his bases this time with two shooters. Before she thought too hard on that, the boom of the rifle going off jerked her back to her present dilemma. Peter had picked off another one of his unfortunate classmates, a kid who'd tried to make a run for the door but only got three quarters of the way there before being shot down. Sam looked away. The runner was definitely dead. Sam had long passed her lifetime quota for blood and gore.

"Guess Charlie doesn't like you much considering he just fed you to the sharks." Peter bobbed his head back and forth as if in the middle of an animated conversation with a friend. "Yep. You must have really pissed him off." Peter paused as he regarded her for a minute, curiosity clear in his expression. Except for the overly bright eyes, Peter almost looked normal as he contemplated her. Then the look disappeared to be replaced by his weird half-grin again.

The sound of crying reached her ears. She felt immense compassion for the student weeping over his newly deceased friend. But she also felt something else welling up within, dark and angry.

Peter continued on as if what he'd just done was routine. Considering the number of bodies littered around the room, she guessed for him it had become the new norm in the short period he'd terrorized the class.

"So the game is truth or die. As you can tell by the human pincushion you landed on, whom I like to call juicy Lucy, there are consequences to lying."

Sam's gut tightened when someone cried out at the use of the unfortunate girl's name. Luckily, Peter ignored the outcry.

"Rules are simple Sam. If you lie, you die. And I think that makes you contestant number five!" His bright feverish eyes fixed on her, his expression expectant. The only thing that came to mind was that this sadistic, teenage sociopath had already killed and maimed so many people that hell would be too lenient an end for him. She knew Charlie was behind all the carnage today. Still, it didn't make her hatred for this kid any less intense.

Mere seconds before she was about to do something stupid enough to get herself killed, a miracle happened. Movement out of the corner of her eye caught her attention and before she had the chance to make sense of it, it was already jumping towards Peter. No growl or sound preceded it as an all too familiar fluffy flash of white fur jumped into her line of sight. Relief at seeing her faithful friend come to her aid washed through her at the same time as fear of losing him forced her into action. Taking Buddy's lead, Sam snatched the meter stick off the blackboard holder to her right and ran full tilt for Peter. The swiftness with which she grabbed the makeshift weapon and propelled herself towards her adversary astonished even her.

The appearance of a golden retriever in the middle of a locked down school surprised Peter enough he made a critical error. He paused, which was the opening Sam needed. Even as he swung his gun towards Buddy, he was already too late. Sam screamed in outrage as she brought the measuring stick down on the rifle. The impact broke the measuring stick in two and knocked the weapon down. The rifle went off, putting a slug harmlessly into the tile floor.

Adrenaline pumping, she lunged at the teenager, putting him off balance. Peter's eyes widened with shock at the new turn of events. The rifle dropped to the ground as he raised his arms to ward off the attack, but he was already too late. Her hands were around his throat and squeezing with everything she had as they fell backwards over one of his victims. So focussed on choking him out, she barely felt the impact as they landed on the hard tile floor together. Her hands locked around his throat in a death grip.

He tugged and scratched at her clenched hands, but after making no headway, he went after her face. He got a few good scratches in, but she held on. At one point he went for her eyes, but she shook him off and clamped her teeth down on the closest finger. Ignoring his screams, she released it only once he dropped his hands away from her face. It wasn't until he stopped struggling and passed out that she let go of the kid's neck.

Sam shuddered as she looked down at Peter, awestruck by how innocent he looked unconscious. The kid's dirty blond locks and fresh face, although not classically handsome, still held the promise of breaking many girls' hearts once he'd grown into his looks. Sam couldn't help but think of the irony here considering how many hearts he'd broken today with all the death and carnage he'd inflicted.

* * *

At one point, Sam tried to stand, but stopped when the room tilted under her. She wanted to get up and search for the blue-haired girl named Zoey, but her brain wasn't sending that message to the rest of her body. Or perhaps her body had stopped listening. Cold and disoriented, she remained where she was.

Sam didn't know how long she stayed kneeled over Peter's inert form when someone grasped her arms from behind to pull her up and off him. She automatically resisted but stopped struggling once she glimpsed a police uniform with brown hair, confirming it wasn't Charlie. The poor cop's pallor revealed how close he was to losing his cookies, and she couldn't blame him. What happened here was reminiscent of a B-rated horror flick, only it wasn't fiction.

Shouting drew her attention back towards the center of the room. Paramedics came through the door in twos and threes and beelined it for the more critical students as several nervous police officers patrolled the outer edges, their guns raised and ready. She forced herself to relax and called for Buddy. Within seconds, he materialized by her side and sat down. The last thing she needed was a young, nervous cop taking out her best friend.

Feeling a little calmer, she turned her head to direct her question to the young officer restraining her. "I need to find a student. She's a blue-haired girl named Zoey."

When she got no response or even acknowledgement after she'd said anything, Sam raised her voice a few decibels. This time, the young officer acknowledged her with an icy stare. She dubbed him Constable Closemouthed. She wasn't that surprised when he cuffed her hands before leading her out. Buddy followed close behind. Sam scanned the halls and open doorways as they passed each room looking for anyone fitting Zoey's description, but she saw only cops, a few paramedics, and the bodies of the unfortunate students in the rooms they passed. Everyone that still had a heartbeat must have been evacuated from the school already.

They'd cleared the school and were now heading outside. Sam was about to restate her question a third time when she heard a shout. Constable Douglas appeared by their side.

"Hey Timmins," Douglas nodded to the young Constable Closemouthed. "Chief Kabowski wants to talk to this one."

Though the title was accurate, hearing someone call Ka-Bitch "Chief" sounded very odd to Sam's ears.

The young officer shook his head and said, "The chief's coming back, and he told me to look after her until he arrives." Sam already knew how the battle of wills would end, but she had to hand it to the one called Timmins. His greenish pallor betrayed the fact he was close to hurling, but still he stood his ground.

"Nice try, but the former chief's no longer in charge. *Chief* Kabowski has all the authority here." And with that, Douglas took a hold of Sam's upper arm and led her towards an empty black SUV. It had the black reflective paint stating Murphy Police. Douglas surprised her by removing the handcuffs, then held open the back door and waited. Sam made sure Buddy jumped in first, then followed suit.

"Chief Kabowski will be here soon." But before he had the chance to dismiss her by closing the SUV's door, Sam stuck her foot against it to stop it mid-motion.

"Wait. What happened to all the students? It looks like a lot of the classes were cleared already."

Douglas looked a little annoyed, but replied, anyway. "We sent the students home. Either their parents picked them up or teachers volunteered to drive them. Officers escorted the rest home."

"I'm looking for a student. She's got blue hair, so she's hard to miss. Around fifteen to sixteen years old and average height. I think she might still be in danger."

"I don't remember a blue-haired girl," Douglas said and turned away again.

"Please Douglas. Can you ask around? Her name is Zoey William."

Douglas regarded her for a minute, perhaps hoping she'd back down, but she didn't budge from blocking the door. Her father being the former chief, intimidation didn't work on Sam. Seconds nudged by as their standoff continued. He narrowed his gaze before finally caving with a heartfelt sigh and a nod. Satisfied that he'd at least ask around, Sam drew her foot back inside the SUV. Douglas shut the door and strode back towards the school.

Sam looked over at her furry best friend and her heart expanded with love and pride as she thought about what he did to rescue her. Putting her hands on either side of his muzzle, she tilted his head up and said, "Buddy, I don't know how you got out of Tim's house and then somehow found me, but you did it. Thank you so much. You are amazing. You saved my life and the lives of many of the students in that classroom. You're my hero, pup."

Buddy barked twice, then chuffed when Sam hugged him.

After a few more of Buddy's favorite chin scratches, she leaned towards the window and watched the entrance of the school, but kept scratching Buddy's ears. A whine told her Buddy still wanted comfort, and Sam leaned back to allow him better access to her lap so she could rub his belly. Like her, Buddy was still upset. Today was a tragedy beyond any Murphy had seen before, and no one would be feeling better for a long time.

She expected the scene to be chaotic, and it was, but there was also an order to it. Kabowski was speaking to a half a dozen cops before sending them back into the school. Sam had to hand it to her. Kabowski seemed to take it all in stride and was doing a decent job, too.

After what seemed like hours, she saw Douglas emerge from the school and stop to talk to Kabowski. After a heated conversation, Kabowski turned and headed in her direction while Douglas pulled out his police radio to talk to dispatch. Sam's stomach knotted painfully. She already suspected what their conversation had been about and why the new Chief was now striding with such grim determination towards her. Kabowski did everything with purpose because that's the personality she had. Get the job done regardless of what that entailed.

Kabowski swung the back door open, placed both hands on her hips and stared at Sam. A full thirty seconds passed before she reached into her coat pocket, drew out a small pad and flipped it open, all the while keeping her eyes trained on her. Sam held her gaze, staring right back with one overriding thought. *Bring it on Ka-Bitch!*

"Again, I find you at another one of my crime scenes, Turner. And not just any crime scene, but a massacre at the local high school. Not only were you not a simple bystander, but yet again, I find you smack dab in the thick of it. From what I gathered from the surviving witnesses in that classroom—" Kabowski then read from her notes, "the janitor threw you into the classroom where Peter Vance was holding everyone hostage at gunpoint."

Kabowski paused and looked up as if waiting for confirmation. Sam nodded, and Kabowski continued. "After which you lost your footing and landed on a victim lying on the ground." Kabowski raised her eyebrows as she looked Sam over, taking in the bloodstains on her face, shirt and pants, and read aloud. "He forced you to be a contestant in a game called Truth or Die, along with four others." Kabowski didn't bother looking up to see Sam's face, but went on, "Before you played this Truth or Die, another student made a run for the door, at which point Peter Vance shot him in the back."

Sam nodded, trying hard not to think about the kid with the tears on his cheeks again.

"And shortly after that, your dog came bounding into the classroom and jumped at Peter at which point you grabbed a meter stick and struck the gun out of his hands. Then you took him down, nearly strangling him to death in the process. Is that about right?"

There was another pregnant pause as Kabowski watched her for a few more minutes, trying to make her squirm and perhaps looking for a tell to show Sam might be lying to her, but she didn't. Sam merely nodded and returned her stare. "So what about this Charlie fellow that you keep claiming to see? I don't suppose he was there as well?"

"Charlie was the janitor," Sam replied calmly, all the while thinking, *I'm going to be put away after all this.* Kabowski's jawline tightened, but she merely nodded.

"And how did you come to know this would happen?"

When Sam didn't reply, Kabowski narrowed her gaze and said, "There was a pile-up on Highway Eight today. I don't suppose you know anything about that?" Kabowski paused again and Sam said nothing. "There was an abandoned blue Ford registered to a Tim Cox. We also found a purse that belongs to one Miss Samantha Turner on the passenger side, but lo-and-behold, no Samantha Turner. And then I come to find out from a first responder at the scene that a female with a head wound matching your description refused medical help and disappeared in the direction of the high school. And to top it off, I found an extra clip for a thirty-eight snub hand gun in said purse, the same type of gun we recovered in the high school." Kabowski practically spat out the last sentence.

The dull throb in Sam's temple sharpened.

"That gun was fired recently and I bet once we get the results back from running the prints on the gun they will match a Miss Samantha Turner."

Kabowski paused for effect again and Sam couldn't help but think this woman would have made a fine actress.

"Care to explain? Or should I throw you in jail and charge you with accessory to multiple counts of murder now?"

Sam sighed and rubbed her head, hoping it would ease the pain building up behind her eyes. It didn't help. She dropped her hand and told Kabowski what she could of the truth, knowing if she revealed it in its entirety she'd land in jail or the nuthouse, or both.

"Someone broke into my dad's home and stole some

rifles. It looked like a teenager, so we checked out the high school." Sam paused as she regarded her, and then said, "Ask Douglas. He's the officer that showed up after I called it in to report the theft."

Kabowski was already shaking her head before she'd even finished her explanation. "Nope, not good enough. You don't take a gun with you when all you intend to do is alert school officials that there could be a threat at some point in the future because the thief looked like a teenager. Besides, according to your statement to Douglas, no cartridges were stolen, so why the urgency? And why did you have a gun on you?"

Sam remained silent and although she didn't think it possible, Kabowski became even more pissed off.

"I have over forty dead kids and a half a dozen dead teachers in there, and you are the one person in this whole scenario that shouldn't have been in that school. Why did you feel it was urgent enough that you had to run here right after the accident?" Kabowski shouted, inches away from her face.

Knowing she couldn't tell her the truth, that she'd known what was going to happen because of a dream, Sam could only watch as Kabowski's face darkened. Just when it looked like the new chief might haul back and hit her, Kabowski instead took a step back and read Sam her rights. Certain hers was the swiftest arrest in history, Sam sat and waited for it to be over. Then Kabowski slammed the back door of the SUV, got in the driver's seat and started the engine. Although Sam wasn't exactly surprised by this turn of events, she was taken aback by the speed at which it transpired.

Chapter 22

The Big Bad Wolf

"Zoey William, the blue-haired teenager. She made it home safe and sound then?" Sam pressed. She saw the annoyance on Kabowski's face in the rearview mirror, but Sam wasn't about to let it go. She'd already lost too much to stop now. "I asked Constable Douglas to find out what happened to her, and he promised he'd find out. I thought that's what you two were talking about before you came to the SUV."

"She got a ride with one of her teachers," Kabowski stated.

Sam waited, but the seconds ticked by and nothing more was said.

"Which teacher?" Sam pressed. When silence met her question, the fear uncurled and expanded in the pit of her stomach again. "Chief Kabowski, which teacher did you send Zoey William home with?" Although she meant it as a question, the urgency and forced tone said something different. Again, silence. Just when Sam thought she might have to resort to shouting, she heard Kabowski sigh.

"I think Douglas said she got a ride with her geography

teacher or something," Kabowski replied. Sam's breath hitched in her throat.

"Do you mean Mr. Morris, the geology teacher?" She waited for a response, all the while thinking *Fuck, Fuck, Fuck!*

"Yes. Mr. Morris was the one," Kabowski replied, nodding her head, clueless to the terror taking shape in Sam's features.

"Turn the vehicle around." Sam's tone of voice made Kabowski glance at her in the rearview mirror. The mixture of fear, dread, and something akin to anger in Sam's expression must have been convincing, because Kabowski kept glancing back at her, but she didn't slow down.

"Kabowski, you have to listen to me. We don't have time to go through the entire story; however, I promise I'll tell you as soon as we find Zoey. What I will say is this: I had the gun because I suspected something like this was about to go down. I just didn't know who. I shot Mr. Morris today because I saw him picking off his students in his classroom. I thought I'd shot him in the head, but obviously I missed because now he has Zoey." Sam paused. But when Kabowski continued to drive onward, she pressed on. "What about the students in his classroom?" When Kabowski looked at her again. "Room 117?"

Kabowski stared back in the rearview mirror and shook her head. "No, Morris came out of room 113, an empty lab or something."

Sam shook her head and said, "That's the chemistry lab. His home room is number 117."

"Why do you know the layout of the school—"

"I attended Murphy High ten years ago. It hasn't changed much."

"And Morris had a head wound. He said the gunman

shot at him but he got away by ducking into a classroom." Although slow to the party, Kabowski's expression was mirroring Sam's. "Room 117 had no survivors. All the victims were students. No teacher."

Sam cursed. She could still see the students' faces and their relief after she'd shot Mr. Morris. And it had been for nothing.

Kabowski pulled over and picked up the police radio, asking for the home address of a local teacher going under the name Mr. Morris. Kabowski asked her for a first name, but Sam had no clue. Precious minutes ticked by as Kabowski went back and forth with dispatch, but finally they came back with an address. 1035 Willow Avenue, on the other side of town. After asking for another cruiser to meet them there, Kabowski flicked on the SUV's emergency lights, pulled a U-turn and sped back the way they'd come.

"Why Zoey?" Kabowski asked, keeping her eyes trained on the road as cars pulled off to the side.

A gray Chevy in front of them hadn't pulled over yet, wasting more precious seconds. Kabowski gave them a rude awakening by throwing on the siren. The noise startled the driver, who over-steered the Chevy to the side of the road, bringing its right front and back wheels up on to the boulevard's grass. Kabowski muttered something about horrible small town drivers under her breath.

"I don't know. He seems to target the weak and downtrodden, but other than that, I'm not sure why Charlie targets certain people."

"J-E-S-U-S. You said Morris had her, and now you're talking about Charlie again! Just when I start to believe the bullshit you're peddling, you bring up this person who, conveniently enough, no one but you have ever seen." Kabowski was mad and Sam was frustrated, but she couldn't blame her. At least she kept driving towards the Morris house.

There was only one person still breathing that had ever seen Charlie other than herself, Danny from the pizzeria. But mentioning him wouldn't help matters. Her father was the only one who knew Charlie had something to do with Jess's death to which Danny was the only witness to. It was all pretty far-fetched.

Buddy whined, and Sam put her hand on his head to reassure him.

"You don't have to believe me, but I ask that you at least hear me out. It sounds insane, and perhaps it is. As far as I know, I'm the only one that's seen him that knows what he's done." She waited until she caught Kabowski's eye in the mirror. "I'd like to tell someone what I know in case my luck runs out. Will you at least listen?"

Sam didn't wait for a response, but filled Kabowski in as quickly as she could on the details of each time she'd seen Charlie. The first time he'd tried to come through the screen to kill her, the second time outside Timothy's Auto, the third time at physiotherapy impersonating a therapist, and now at the high school impersonating a janitor. She did her best to be as honest as possible while editing out the most unbelievable stuff, like his impersonating a cop, her suspicion that Charlie could read people's thoughts, or the reason she'd been hell bent on getting to the high school was because she'd dreamed about the massacre the night before. Sam couldn't blame Kabowski for not trusting her. Even she had trouble believing it and she was the one experiencing all of it.

"Fine. Let's say for argument's sake that what you say is true. That this guy showed up in all these places and impersonated these people. It's not consistent. He's attempted murder once on a twenty-something, talked to a thirty-something mechanic before said mechanic tried to kill his coworkers, counseled a suicidal teenage gymnast who offed herself, and was a janitor at the high school where a student and a teacher went on a psychotic rampage. Huge coincidence, yes, but there is no consistency," Kabowski said, slowing the SUV.

Sam shook her head and said, "I don't know what it is. With me, he tried to kill me, but most of the time he seems to... instigate it. I know he gets off on the killing, but I think it's more than that. On the night he attacked me, I remember he referred to himself as my *facilitator*. I was pretty depressed the night he approached me and once he had me restrained, mentally he beat the crap out of me. He poked at every weakness, ripped at every wound I had until I was in such pain that I just wanted it all to end. The gymnast was depressed, so I guarantee she wanted to die. Mike the mechanic had an out-of-control gambling addiction. And Peter looked haunted, maybe even beaten down. When I had him by the throat, he didn't put up much of a fight. It was almost as if he wanted me to take him out—"

"What about Mr. Morris?" Kabowski asked.

"I never had a face to face with Mr. Morris. Obviously, he's fucked up because I saw him picking off his students, but other than that, I don't know."

"And Mike the mechanic?" Kabowski asked.

"Mike was angry and seemed to revel in the violence. He fought hard and would have killed both of us if he'd had the chance; however, once confined to the waiting room, he ended up killing himself." Sam dropped her head to rub her forehead harder, hoping it might ease the sharp pain there.

When she looked up again, she saw they were now parked in front of the Morris house. All was quiet.

Kabowski got on the radio for an e.t.a. on the squad car, joining them. Sam watched the house, but she couldn't see anything. Two cars sat in the driveway, but the house was dark. She heard dispatch respond, followed by the click of the mouthpiece as she reattached it to the radio.

"Now what?"

"Now we wait for backup," Kabowski replied.

"We should go in," Sam argued, putting her hand on the divider. She suspected her jailer wasn't as much of a hard ass as she liked to portray and cared more than she let on. Although she figured Kabowski would eventually relent and go in if backup didn't show soon, her gut told her they didn't have much time, if it wasn't already too late.

"We have to get in there *now*. Considering what he did at the school, his entire family and Zoey are in danger here," Sam persisted, voice rising. Her agitation mounted as the seconds ticked by. A bead of sweat trailed down the back of her neck even though the air inside the SUV bordered on frigid.

Kabowski got on the radio again and asked where her backup was. Dispatch said five minutes. Sighing, she put the receiver back.

Sam felt another bead of sweat run down her back as the same overwhelming feeling of panic punched her. She had to get out of this SUV. Desperate, Sam slammed her palms on the divider then raised her voice, "If you want to wait here then fine. I'll go. You can say I overpowered you or something. I'll testify to whatever you want. I don't care. Let me out of this goddamned car so I can help those kids!"

"That's enough—" was all Kabowski got out before gunshots rang out from somewhere inside the house.

Kabowski had the door open and was out of the vehicle in an instant. Gun drawn, she raced for the house. Sam cursed, shouted and banged on the backseat window, but to no avail. Kabowski didn't look back or even slow her pace. Sam watched helplessly as she disappeared around the left side of the house. She then scanned the backseat for anything, but of course there was nothing that could help her out of the SUV. Not knowing what else to do, she wove her fingers through the backseat security divider and shook it in frustration. It rattled in protest, and Buddy whined in response. Frustrated, Sam leaned her head against the side door window and watched the house. Buddy whined again, and Sam reached over and put a hand on his head.

Dusk deepened the shadows on either side of the residence. Soon the house would be engulfed in darkness and then it would be hard to see anything. Sometimes when the night was clear and the moon was bright enough it lit everything like a giant nightlight, but this wasn't one of those nights. Not even a sliver in the sky. It looked like even the moon was afraid to appear in Murphy tonight. The silence seemed to stretch on forever.

The crack of another gunshot, followed by another couple of rounds from a handheld gun. Sam prayed Kabowski got the bastard.

Movement on the left side of the house where Kabowski had disappeared a few minutes earlier caught her attention. Someone was walking. No. Limping towards the SUV, while a smaller individual supported them. As they got close, the one limping turned out to be a blonde teenage girl and her shorter companion was a boy with the same ash blond hair. The girl had on white jeans, so the blood seeping from the wound on her right thigh was a stark contrast against the white fabric. It needed to be tourniquet'd off as soon as possible. She noticed the car key in the girl's hand and prayed she'd open the police cruiser's doors.

To her relief she did and surprised Sam by unlocking all the car doors, including the back seat.

Not needing to be asked twice, Sam swung open the back door and hopped out, with Buddy following close on her heels.

The girl sat in the driver's seat, her legs hanging out the door, while her brother huddled by her side, leaning up against the open door. He looked terrified. Tear tracks stained his cheeks. The girl looked like she was in shock, which wasn't a surprise considering the amount of blood she'd lost. A small, dark puddle had already formed under her right foot.

Must be the Morris kids, Sam thought as she took off her long-sleeved overshirt. Luckily she'd decided on a tank top, button up combination today otherwise this might have been awkward. Sam murmured reassurances as she stepped up to the girl and tied the shirt off tight above what looked like a gunshot wound. The teenager gasped in pain and the boy began crying again.

"Ok, can you tell me what happened?" Sam asked. The teenager's expression changed from dull nothingness to stricken. It took all her effort not to look away from the pain Sam saw in the teenager's haunted eyes. The girl struggled with what to say, but finally found her words.

"Our Dad. He shot mom. She's dead," the teenager replied, the last two words barely a whisper. Sam nodded. She knew Kabowski must have given the kids her keys and could only assume she wanted them to stay in the police SUV.

Sam reached for the kid, but stopped when he cringed and backed into the door. Like she'd do for an injured animal, Sam murmured reassurances again and put her hand out. Though he cringed, he let her touch his arm this time. Explaining what she wanted him to do, she guided him around the SUV and into the passenger side before shutting his door. By the time she returned to the girl, the kid had already scooted up as close as he could to his sister. Sam had the girl swing her legs around until she faced forward. Then, reaching over her, she grabbed the police radio's handset.

"The woman that gave you the keys. Was she hurt?" Sam asked, but she didn't get a reply from either of them. The teenager looked close to passing out and was shivering fiercely. Sam had been in her dad's cruiser so many times she didn't have to think about what to say. "Dispatch, please send an ambulance to 1035 Willow Ave. There's a teenage girl here who's been shot in the right thigh and a boy in shock. There may also be an injured officer on scene. Several shots were fired within the residence, so please use caution." She hung up the mouthpiece without waiting for a response.

Sam then took the keys from the teenager and went around to the back to open the trunk, hoping there'd be some blankets and was rewarded for her efforts. Not only were there a couple of blankets, but there was also a shotgun strapped down in the back. She unhooked the shotgun, grabbed a handful of shells, loaded the gun before swinging it over her shoulder, and stuffed the rest in her pocket. Blankets in hand, she shut the trunk and returned to the kids. She passed the boy one blanket and told him to wrap it around himself tight, which he did without being asked twice. She then wrapped the girl with the other blanket as tightly as she could. There wasn't much more she could do for the kids.

"Keep the doors locked until the police or the ambulance get here. Don't let anyone else in, ok?" She waited until she got a weak nod from the teenager and a shaky "ok" from the boy. And with that, Sam left the keys with them, shut the driver's door and waited until she heard the click of the automatic locks. Cop cars had bulletproof windows, so this SUV was the safest place they could be at the moment.

Buddy followed, but Sam stopped him. "No, Buddy stay." When all she got was a single bark. "Buddy, stay and protect these kids. Ok, boy?" Buddy chuffed in disagreement but sat back down.

Sirens sounded off in the distance as Sam jogged towards the side of the house where Kabowski had disappeared. She was already swinging the shotgun around to hold in front of her as she crossed the grass. Darkness falling reduced visibility considerably in the few minutes it took to take care of the kids, so she had to proceed slower than she wanted to. Sam was familiar with the gun she held in her hands because her dad had had a similar one in his cruiser. It was a special police issue and had a flashlight at the top over the receiver. She left it off, hoping the element of surprise would give her some edge.

Sam stayed close to the house as she headed towards the back. The gate to the backyard was wide open. Within seconds, she crossed the silent yard and opened the screen door. Although it didn't squeak, the noise it made sounded like nails on a chalkboard in the eerily quiet house. It seemed to take forever to shut on its own. She heard the click of the door handle catch and listened for any noise showing where either Mr. Morris or Kabowski might be.

Upon hearing nothing but the light drip of a faucet somewhere close by, she stepped into the kitchen on her left. Spying the knife block, she grabbed one, stuck it in her back pocket and crept around the counter, all the while sweeping her eyes between the two entrances to the kitchen in front of her. The house looked enormous from the outside, but it was hard to tell that now. In the dark, the rooms looked smaller than expected and with so many walls and nooks, it would be easy for someone to hide away in here. It meant she had to proceed at a slower pace than she would have liked. She cleared the kitchen and went left next. Hearing a shout from above, Sam picked up her pace.

She cleared the living room and stood to the side of the stairs leading up to the second floor before she noticed a dark figure sitting on the white steps. Breath catching in her throat, Sam raised the rifle but lowered it again upon recognizing who it was.

About eight stairs up sat Chief Kabowski, legs stuck out in front of her with her back against the wall and her revolver pointed directly at Sam. Her gut told her Kabowski wouldn't shoot, just like she knew Kabowski knew she was innocent. The Chief's hostility was because she didn't understand the threat that had come to Murphy. She'd never come across perps like this before, and with Sam in the middle of it each time, it was hard for her not to be suspicious and hostile. It was all unfamiliar territory, and it was driving Kabowski nuts.

"Where did you get that?" Kabowski hissed, gun still raised. Sam knew it would piss Kabowski off, but right now she couldn't care less.

"SUV trunk. You're hurt," Sam whispered back. Kabowski wore black so she couldn't see where the wound was, but assumed it must be serious since she wasn't up and moving around. "Where's Zoey?"

Kabowski pointed up with her gun while her other hand remained pressed against her side, a good indicator of where she'd been shot. As Sam came parallel to where she sat, Kabowski whispered, "He's got more than one gun and must have a bulletproof vest on. I shot him twice in the torso at close range, but he's still walking and talking."

Sam nodded and stepped over Kabowski. *So a head shot then and this time I won't miss.* Once she cleared the top step, she pressed her body close to the left wall, but stopped when she heard voices again.

"Let me in Zooo-eeeey." A familiar voice said in a sing-song tone. "Or I will huff and I will puff and I will blow this door down!"

"Fuck you, asshole!" A muffled voice shouted through the door, sounding strained and emotional. It sounded like the kid had been crying. And who could blame Zoey with a madman stalking her?

Sam peered around the corner. Mr. Morris was facing a door on the opposite side of the hall, about twenty feet away from her. He had a rifle slung over his shoulder, but held a handgun in his right hand. Sam had a clear shot of his back and right side.

"Tsk, tsk, tsk. Such language and disrespect. That unauthorized exit of yours from my class made me pretty angry, but it did get the ball rolling. You missed an excellent class today. Kids these days are just so disrespectful and none of you ever listen. However, once I made an example out of a few of them, the rest fell in line and every one of those students listened to me. It was a great day in the world of academia, not to mention incredibly enlightening. It's just too bad I had to get rid of my witnesses in the end. But I couldn't let my worst student go unpunished. You with your blue hair and poor attitude. I think it's about time you met your maker Zoey—" Mr. Morris didn't sound angry. He sounded crazy.

"You fucking psycho. You murdered your students. And

I just saw you kill your wife and shoot your daughter. Let me repeat, YOU SHOT YOUR OWN DAUGHTER!"

Mr. Morris continued on as if he hadn't heard her. "C'mon, Zoey, this isn't your first rodeo. I know you've been in this situation before with your own dad. If you open the door now, I'll even give you a running start—" Again Mr. Morris's voice lilted in sing-song fashion.

Sam couldn't help herself and shivered. She didn't know what it was about Charlie, but he seemed to be able to bring out the worst in his targets. Mr. Morris was certifiable and Zoey had no intention of letting him in. Smart girl. To her, it probably seemed like everyone had suddenly gone mad, and who could blame her? First a kid she knows at school goes crazy killing his fellow students, and then one of her own teachers, who she knows and trusts, turns on her. Over a matter of months, Murphy had gone from a sweet bedroom community to a town riddled with psychopaths.

Sam stepped into the hall to get an unobstructed view of Mr. Morris. If he turned his head to the right another forty-five degrees, he'd see her, but he was so focussed on terrorizing Zoey that he wasn't paying attention to anything but her. Sam had the perfect shot. Or would have if she hadn't heard the creak of a floorboard behind her.

Without thinking, she brought her right elbow down and swung the end of the rifle back as hard as she could and was rewarded with a pained "Oomph" as it connected. A glance behind her revealed it wasn't Charlie. She'd taken down an actual cop and by the look of him in his doubled over posture, he wouldn't be much help for a few minutes. He also looked familiar. And then it struck her... it was the young green cop who had refused to listen to her. Timmins. He seemed to be the only one on the landing.

"Well, at least your dislike for me will remain consistent. It's always good to know where you stand with people," Sam whispered low enough only she and perhaps Timmins heard.

The report of a gun going off down the hall startled her, and she turned back to see the bastard just shot the door and was now looking through the hole he'd created in it. Sam heard Zoey shout a string of expletives, which made him laugh. Sounds were coming from below, likely more cops, but she knew they'd never get up here in time to help her.

"The big bad wolf is here, little girl!"

That's my cue. Sam raised her rifle again just as Mr. Morris raised his gun to take aim at his intended target through the hole in the door. Sam found the sweet spot on the back of his head and fired. Mr. Morris careened sideways before sliding to the ground. *There'd be no coming back this time.*

Shouting erupted behind her. Someone dragged her backwards and wrenched the rifle from her grip. Knowing what was coming next, she forced herself to slacken and not fight the hands restraining her. Within seconds she found herself facedown with her head pushed into the carpeted hall floor, her arms grasped firmly behind her, and a knee wedged painfully in the middle of her back.

Yet again, I am on the ground with a jackass cop leaning on my back. How about thanking me for doing your job? She kept the thought to herself, knowing it was best not to irritate the cranky police officer she'd cold cocked moments ago. Sam's shoulder was already throbbing from all the abuse it took today, but she didn't make a sound. At least not until he wrenched her right wrist back to cuff her, straining her shoulder. Sam couldn't hold back a shout of pain.

"Easy Timmins! She just saved that girl's life, so cut her

a little slack. And she has an injured shoulder, so cuff her hands in the front. Turner will go with you willingly," came a tired voice from behind her. Sam had trouble believing what she'd just heard. Of all the cops she knew, her savior was Chief Ka-Bitch. Timmins protested, but was cut off. "Constable Timmins, are you really going to make me repeat myself after I've just been SHOT IN THE GUT?"

Without another word, Sam felt the grip on her wrists ease. She couldn't help but think maybe Kabowski wasn't so bad after all. The knee in her back remained, but after what seemed like an eternity had passed, she was finally lifted off the ground and her hands cuffed in front.

Zoey had long ago been escorted outside to safety. The remaining officers were busy sweeping rooms. A couple of paramedics disappeared into a bedroom at the end of the hall. She recalled hearing six gun shots in total when she was outside, so if the first found its way into Kabowski who returned fire with two rounds into Morris, the fourth into Lizzie, then that still left two unaccounted for. She suspected the paramedics in the bedroom found where the other two gunshots landed.

Constable Timmins escorted Sam down the stairs and out the front door. Flashing lights from at least a half dozen emergency vehicles lit up the dark front yard. More sirens sounded off in the distance and panicked shouts echoed in the street's vicinity. Two officers were sweeping the area. It looked like someone with light blond hair was lying on the road. She could see a cop leaning over them and immediately thought of the Morris kids. She stared, horrified at the thought that the kids locked in the SUV may have been hurt because she'd left them to go play hero.

Sam must have caught Timmins by surprise because she successfully wrenched her left arm free of his hold and ran towards the road. Unfortunately, the officer was young and fast, so even her runner's legs couldn't outpace him and she was brought up short.

"Wait! Can you tell me if that's the girl who was in the SUV? Her name is Liz—" Sam pleaded as she whipped around to face the officer. The officer with the Cerulean blue eyes. Sam didn't have the chance to say a word before pain erupted in her chest and traveled the length of her body and back. Sam felt herself convulsing as she slid to the ground. Then everything went black.

Chapter 23

End Of The Line

Motion rocking her back and forth lulled her back to her early childhood when she'd go fishing with her grandad. She'd never been a fan of fishing, but the rare memories of hanging out with her mild-mannered grandfather, a man who always seemed to have a smile on his face, made her happy. Only the pressure under her knees and across the middle of her back contradicted the memory. Still, the gentle movement was a welcome reprieve from the harsh realities shouting on the periphery of her thoughts, trying to crowd out her current calm. The rocking changed to a floating sensation and for a split second it made her wonder if she wasn't dreaming.

The surreal floating sensation ended the moment her back collided with a hard cushioned surface, dragging her back to her current dilemma and kicking the shit out of any inner calm she'd had a moment ago. She laid there for a few minutes, trying to get her eyes to cooperate and open. Her surroundings finally coming into focus, she found herself lying in the back of a car. No, not a car. An SUV. Her wrists jangled, bringing her focus down to her hands. Handcuffs.

And her chest hurt. A lot. She felt the raised skin on her breastbone and clued in.

She'd been arrested. Again. And tasered. But this wasn't a police vehicle because the safety divider separating the front from the back was missing.

A glimpse of blue hair in the driver's seat made her suck in a breath. With effort, Sam shifted into a sitting position and Zoey's profile came into view.

"Zoey," Sam murmured. Zoey glanced back at the mention of her name, but confusion was the only expression to cross her features. The girl had no clue who she was, but Sam knew the teenager from her dream.

The passenger side door opened, then closed. Her heart dropped. A cop with unmistakable platinum blond locks slid into the passenger seat.

"Leave her alone, Charlie," Sam murmured.

"Tsk, tsk, tsk Sam. Oh, ye of little faith. I'm just here to enjoy the ride. This is Zoey's show."

"What are you talking about?" Sam asked, to which Charlie smiled back at her.

Turning towards the blue-haired girl, she asked, "Zoey, what is Charlie talking about?"

Instead of responding, Zoey turned the key in the ignition, put the SUV in drive and pulled away from the curb. Zoey would be fifteen, maybe sixteen, so she wouldn't have a license yet, but that wasn't deterring her. She seemed to be a girl on a mission, and that scared the hell out of Sam.

"I was enlightening Zoey, or should I say Chelsea, about a few fun facts. For instance, Murphy's former chief of police graduated from the same police academy at the same time as Chelsea's dad. Chief Turner knew Chief Deroras. So well, in fact, they called each other friends."

Zoey turned her head in the direction she was piloting

the SUV, her profile revealing a stain of tear tracks on her right cheek and neck. She wanted to comfort the distraught teenager, but didn't know how. That's when she caught the flash of metal off Zoey's left wrist. *A handcuff? Why would he handcuff her to the steering wheel if this was Zoey's show?* She had no clue where Charlie was going with this. But knowing he'd brag about his latest twisted game, she waited for him to continue.

"So good that Chief Deroras, who suffered from an acute case of PTSD, had a meltdown a little over five years ago. Desperate, he called his good friend Chief Turner for help. Only he hung up on him. Your twin brothers were rowdy that night Chelsea, so after putting the handset back in the receiver, a distraught Chief Deroras decided he needed a little peace to clear his head. He went into the basement, grabbed his baseball bat and taught your brothers a lesson in silence."

"You should be proud of your dad, Chelsea. He got them to stay quiet and cleared his head before you and your mother returned from shopping. I think Travis was still alive at that point, although you'd know better than me."

"Tylor," came the whispered sob from the driver's seat.

Shocked into silence by the horrifying details, Sam searched for something to say, but no words came to her. Sam dug her fingers into her palms to help her focus and remain calm, but the pain didn't help. Her entire body shook. With what, she wasn't quite certain. Shock. Anger. Disgust. Frustration. Rage. A combination of all the above.

"Stop it, Charlie!" Sam shouted, finding her voice again. She knew nothing she said mattered. Not to him. Charlie would do and say what he had to to twist the knife in as deep as possible, because... because he wanted something from Zoey.

"Ah yes. My mistake. T-Y-L-O-R was alive when Chelsea and her mother walked in and found the twins' towheaded skulls caved in. It's too bad Mrs. Deroras overreacted the way she did. Running at him, screaming." Charlie shook his head in mock sympathy. "Chief Deroras neutralized that threat pretty quickly." Charlie chuckled a little, as if recalling a wonderful memory. "Chelsea had no clue what to do. She just stood there and watched it. Didn't you, Chels?" Charlie practically writhed with pleasure at the pain he was re-inflicting.

"I said stop it you fucking psycho!" Sam shouted again, voice rising as she looked at Zoey's profile again. The blue-haired girl's face twisted into a mask of agony, but still she didn't say a word.

"Tylor reached for her as she left her dying brother behind and ran to the safety of a neighbor's house."

"Charlie, you malevolent piece of shit. Leave her alone... she's just a kid!" Sam roared, then she directed her next comment at Zoey. "Zoey, he'll say anything to break you. This is all just a game to him!"

"Oh no. Sam, you misunderstand. This isn't for Chelsea's benefit. It's for yours. And I can't believe our good luck at finding you, the chief's daughter, outside all trussed up for us like a Thanksgiving turkey. Chelsea and I already had a nice, long chat and have come to an understanding of how to right this past wrong." Charlie turned around to face her. Sam was leaning against the front seat of the SUV, but what she saw in his eyes produced an involuntary reaction. Gasping, she drew herself back as far away from him as the seat allowed. Something in Charlie's irises moved. If she had to define it, it resembled little black worms twisting and shifting along a circular skyline of Cerulean blue.

"WHAT are you?" Sam whispered in horror. This, too,

seemed to amuse Charlie, who continued his dialogue as if she'd said nothing.

"We have to get you caught up here, Sam. What you don't know is that your father, Chief Turner, was too busy five years ago to help his good friend when he needed him most. Rude. So in the end, Sam, it was your dad's fault. Chelsea's father went off the rails and slaughtered his family because Chief Turner didn't bother helping his friend during his crisis," Charlie stated a little too cheerily.

The pieces fell into place. What happened to her five years ago wasn't random at all. He'd targeted her and chose that night to produce maximum damage. Charlie hunted Sam down the same night he pushed Chelsea's father into a psychological break. So busy with the attempted murder of his own daughter, Chief Turner wasn't available to help a friend from going over the brink.

"Poor Sam. And here you thought it was all about you that night, huh?" Charlie's chuckling sounded like fingernails on a chalkboard. "Now we can have a family reunion. Chelsea was kind enough to volunteer to drive us to the train station to meet your dad."

She could already see the train station coming into view. There wasn't much time left to find a way out of this.

"Zoey, listen to me. Charlie planned this whole thing from the beginning. He used me and now he's using you. He's trying to break you, so you'll do what he wants and hurt innocent people."

"My name is C-H-E-L-S-E-A," Zoey ground out. Sam's heart dropped with her words. Like so many before her, Zoey sounded like she'd skidded past the point of caring and into the fuck 'em all realm.

The passengers were disembarking from the train. It looked like one of them had a Team Canada Hockey jacket on, similar to the one her dad always wore. It could be a coincidence or it could be her father in line to step down onto the platform. He normally flew back from Kirkland Lake to Sudbury and took the train home from there.

She felt the SUV speed up. If Zoey kept her current course, he'd never be able to get out of the way in time. Sam's stomach twisted. She felt sick knowing Zoey was about to plow them into the inbound train full of people.

Sam stared at Zoey in the rearview mirror, willing her to stop the SUV, but getting ready to lunge at the wheel at the last minute. Then Zoey glanced back. Their eyes met, and that one look spoke volumes. The fear, the anger, the hatred she saw when they made eye contact was unsettling, but the deliberate shift of her pupils in Charlie's direction told Sam it was directed where it should be, at the thing sitting beside her. Although not a hundred percent certain, her gut told her to trust Zoey, so trust her she would. She just prayed her instincts were dead on otherwise many people, present company included, were about to die.

"Tsk, tsk, Chelsea. I thought I'd groomed you better than that."

Fuck. Charlie knew Zoey didn't plan on hitting the train. Before either of them could react, Sam glimpsed the glint of silver slice through the air towards Zoey, and then the teenager screamed.

With little thought to consequences, Sam launched herself off the back seat and threw her cuffed wrists over Charlie's head so the metal chain between the shackles cinched against his windpipe. Using the back of the seat as leverage, she braced her knees against it and wrenched back with everything she had.

The glint of silver caught her eye as the knife flew back at her face. Sam jerked her head to the right and felt the breeze as it passed by her cheek. The knife stabbed the back of the seat to the left, missing her by a mere inch. She felt resistance as Zoey applied the brakes and the SUV careened precariously to the left, away from the train, and towards a brick building that housed the now-closed ticket booth. Sam tried to brace herself, but her body swung to the right because of the momentum brought on by the speed and tight angle of the swerve. She lost the tension she had on Charlie's throat as her legs slid down to the matted floor. As a result, Charlie must have freed himself from her chokehold, because her cuffed hands were empty. Sam attempted to brace herself for the impact, but had little chance at this speed. They hit the building head on. The SUV exploded through the brick wall, which was exactly how it felt. Like they'd hit a brick wall. The SUV came to a grinding halt once most of it was in the building, with only its rear tires still on the outside.

It felt like she'd been bashed by a hammer everywhere. There was a ringing in her ears. Her head hurt and different parts of her body protested painfully as she tried to reposition herself. Sam's saving grace was her position in the back. Although strained, bumped, and bruised all over, she wasn't seriously harmed because her body hugged the back of the seat and held her in place on impact. Zoey was still in the driver's seat, so she must have had the foresight to put her seatbelt on. Charlie, however, was nowhere to be seen.

Bending her arms back to grab the door handle, Sam groaned as her bruised shoulder and forearms protested. She fell out of the backseat of the SUV on to her back, hitting the concrete ground hard. Upon impact, she felt every shard of glass and piece of brick that embedded itself along her back. She could hear shouting, but it was impossible to see anything beyond a few feet ahead because of the dust and smoke. Sam turned onto her side and raised her torso off the ground using her elbow and forearm, then struggled to her knees, gritting her teeth as the glass and bits of brick cut into her exposed flesh and the thin material covering her skin.

Once she felt steady enough, Sam got to her feet and stumbled towards the front of the SUV, leaning heavily on the hood as she went.

That's when she saw the outline of shoes twenty feet in front of her. Although covered in a fine layer of dust, they were the standard issue black police shoes. The rest of the dark form came into view as she advanced towards it. The man was lying face down, head turned to the left. She made out the police uniform and Charlie's trademark platinum blond locks.

Sam bent and, with her still cuffed hands, picked up the largest shard of glass she saw and stumbled over to him. Stepping over his body so she had a leg on either side of him, she kneeled down on to his back. Breathing out, she steadied herself, raised the glass knife above her head, and shoved the piece of glass downwards into the back of his neck. It met with resistance and became slippery making it hard to keep a grip on the sharp edges of the glass. The makeshift weapon was slicing into her hands, but determined to finish the job, she didn't let up and felt it slowly inching in deeper. It was Charlie's day to die.

Above the sounds of the broken building settling and her own overloud breathing, a loud commotion and shouting could be heard outside.

Sam froze when a shiver of movement rippled under her. And then the ground shifted beneath, throwing her off balance. Her grip slipped and her hands slid off the shard of glass as she fell sideways on to her back, slamming her head on the concrete floor. Her back and head were on fire with pinpoints of pain. Their roles now reversed, Charlie hovered over her. A dark substance dripped from his neck.

Charlie had lost his charming boy-next-door good looks. His dust covered platinum blond locks were about the only thing that hadn't changed. His face, upper torso and forearms were shredded from going through the windshield and skidding along the floor. A sizeable chunk of his right ear was missing. His once straight nose, now swollen and lumpy, looked broken in multiple locations and oozed black liquid. A deep cut running down the upper right side of his face revealed the white of a cheekbone. His once pinkish lips looked flayed and almost entirely black now. His eyes had eclipsed into solid black orbs. And his mouth yawned wide, emitting a terrifying sound unlike anything she'd ever heard before.

She tried to sink further into the ground away from him, but the concrete at her back held firm. One of his hands lashed out and wrapped around her throat. Sam was simultaneously terrified, disgusted, and horrified, but more than that, she felt enraged. Luckily, the rage won out over her fear. Sam did the only thing she could think to do. She screamed back and grabbed at the hand holding her by the throat, but the skin was too slick to gain purchase. The yawning black mouth opened impossibly wide. She couldn't see teeth or a tongue, just a black hole.

In desperation, Sam turned her head to the right, straining her arms to feel along the floor in search of anything to use as a weapon. Her eyes lit on Zoey as they flickered over the SUV. She was still in the driver's seat, but conscious now and staring out at them. It looked like she was screaming, and Sam couldn't blame her. The Charlie thing scared the hell out of Sam, too.

Her fingers brushed up against a piece of glass, and she grabbed it. This one was much smaller than the one she'd thrust through Charlie's neck, but beggars couldn't be choosers. With as much force as she could muster with her cuffed wrists and awkward position, Sam shoved her hands up and into its approaching face, jamming the glass into the Charlie thing's right eye. Meeting resistance once it hit the orbital plate, the glass became lodged in her palm as well. That's when its screeching reached a whole new decibel.

It whipped itself backwards, dislodging the glass from her palm, but then rebounded back towards her so fast Sam barely blocked the attack. She intercepted the lunge with the only thing available, her arms. Although she stopped it from reaching her throat and face, it tore chunks of flesh away with teeth she couldn't even see, and Sam's screams crescendoed. A warm dark liquid sprayed over her, but she couldn't tell whose blood it was, Charlie's or hers. Her vision blurred, then cleared, then blurred again as her irritated eyes watered to rid themselves of whatever was raining down on her. Too soon, Sam felt herself weakening, having more and more difficulty fending off the sharp teeth. She wasn't screaming anymore and although the pain in her arms as it tore into her was still present, the sharp edge of it dulled. She knew she had to stay awake and fight, but her arms felt so heavy.

The percussive boom of gunshots and shouting sounded like they were coming from right beside her. The Charlie thing thrashed violently above her with each gunshot until she felt the hold on her throat loosen as its screeching intensified. And then it stopped. Sam's vision swam, but her survival instinct forced her to refocus on the thing still hanging above her. Its mouth slackened and, although it didn't look quite human, it resembled Charlie once again. It shuddered before slumping over to lie on top of her; wet and warm, giving off an overwhelmingly foul stench of rotting rosemary and some sort of metallic tang, making her gag.

It wasn't long before its weight was lifted off her and hands clasped her under the arms to slide her out from beneath it. As soon as she was clear, Sam pulled away from the grip to curl into a fetal position and retch, expelling any liquid that had made its way into her mouth. Having trouble opening them, her eyes burned like someone had sprayed vinegar in them. She thought she heard familiar voices, but there was so much noise she couldn't be sure. She had trouble concentrating on much of anything. Every part of her body hurt like she'd been tossed in the middle of a mosh pit at the height of a Metallica concert, but her eyes and forearms burned like they were on fire. Her mouth felt like she'd been given a mouthful of anesthetic. She tried to roll onto her knees but didn't get very far before collapsing on her side again.

The thought came to her that she must have lost too much blood. She heard talking, but couldn't understand what was being said. Every moment seemed detached from the next. Nothing made sense. It was like trying to solve a giant jigsaw puzzle with most of the pieces missing.

Her pained watery gaze refocussed on the SUV. Zoey was still in the driver's seat, but a uniformed officer was also with her. The digital wall clock next to the giant hole in the wall displayed October 5, 9:39pm. Everything blurred again.

Various voices were raised, their discussion rose in volume until they were nearly shouting. Her name came up. The tone sounded accusatory. More shouting. *Typical.*

* * *

Oct 5, 9:47pm

Sam heard a familiar voice telling her it would be all right. That Charlie was dead. That he couldn't hurt her again. Even in her semiconscious state, she didn't believe that.

Monsters were real. No one could protect anyone from them if they truly wanted to hurt you.

* * *

Oct 5, 10:08pm

Her eyes burned and she couldn't see, but it was the pain in her arms that was near unbearable. Something was holding her down so she couldn't defend herself against the thing, still tearing into her forearms again and again. Sam struggled to free herself, but whatever had a hold of her was too strong and the thing attacking her had so many teeth. People were shouting all around her.

Why wouldn't they help her?

Incessant beeping sounds close by. The Charlie thing switched tactics and started choking her again, but this time it felt like it was pushing its entire hand down her throat. She couldn't breathe. She struggled and writhed to get away from it, but to no avail. Sam gagged and fought to breathe until there was nothing more to give.

* * *

Oct 20, 4:04pm

Sam was vaguely aware of a familiar male voice. Tim's. Talking about Brandy and that Toni was well enough to work now, tempting her with Angelo's coffee and apples with peanut butter. *So tempting.*

* * *

Oct 23, 12:07pm

Her dad's voice. Telling her to come back. They had a lot to catch up on. That Kabowski had asked after her. *That's weird.*

* * *

Oct 25, 9:42am

Buddy's bad breath on her face and husky woof, telling her it was time to get up.

So Sam woke up.

The first thing she was aware of was pain. Everywhere. So much pain, and an overall sick feeling.

The second thing was the light. It was so bright it hurt to open her eyes.

Third thing was the thirst and how sore her throat was. Even strep had never hurt this much.

Fourth thing was fur face licking her hand.

Sam forced her eyes open, even though the light hurt them. Her vision remained blurry no matter how many times she blinked, so she gave up trying to clear them. Even with the blurred vision, she could tell she was in a hospital room. The white walls and antiseptic smell were dead give-aways, as was the bed she was lying on. It had guardrails. She hadn't had a bed with guardrails since she was four. A whine told her Buddy was still beside her, waiting. She lifted a hand to rub his head, but pain shot through her forearm. She could feel bandages on her arms, hands, and many of her fingers.

Taking a deep breath, Sam gritted her teeth through the pain as her hands felt around the bed for a control pad. Her efforts were finally rewarded when her fingers found what felt like a small remote and experimented with the buttons until it raised her into a sitting position. She felt a brief respite once she was sitting up, but it didn't last, and she laid her head back as a wave of nausea washed over her. Lying still, she hoped it would go away, but it didn't. When it became apparent she would not win this battle, she grabbed what looked like a kidney-shaped pan from the tray by her bedside to catch the dark liquid she brought up.

As luck would have it, someone appeared at her side mid-retch, but she was in too much pain to care she had a witness. Her savior held her hair back, then took the pan from her numb fingers when she finished. The person had a noticeable limp. She accepted the warm cloth that was placed in her hand to wipe her face, lay back again and closed her eyes hoping that might ease the pain in her eyes and head.

"It's good to see you're finally awake, Turner."

Sam groaned aloud at the familiar voice. *Of course, it had to be Tim.*

"Not—" Sam croaked. Clearing her sore throat, she tried again. "Not... one of my finer moments... Cox. Thanks... for holding my hair. Remind me... not to party so hard next time," Sam rasped, allowing her eyes to open again. The light was killing her.

After a long pause, Tim said, "You remember you were in a car crash, right?"

Sam nodded, clearing her throat again. "Charlie decided Zoey... should take us to meet my dear old dad.

335

Luckily, she had other ideas and instead... plowed us into the old ticket station... rather than a train full of passengers." Sam's speech was still gravelly, but getting better. Another pause before she added. "So... how's the building?"

"Faring better than you, I'm afraid. There are three contusions, one of which is serious. You fell into a coma a couple of weeks ago. You're lucky Turner."

"Jeez... how long have I been here?"

"Almost three weeks. It's only been over the last few days that you improved. You had us all pretty worried." Tim pulled up a chair to sit beside her and held her hand. She felt strange, like her body wasn't her own. Although everything in her hurt, her arms and eyes continued to burn, so she closed them again. She didn't have to look at him to listen.

"Do you remember what happened after the SUV crashed?"

Sam nodded. "I tried to kill Charlie."

Silence followed her statement. She opened her eyes again to look at him, but her vision was still too blurry to read his expression.

"Wow. I'm both impressed and a little scared of you right now, Turner," Tim said, his voice sounding a little bemused. He went silent again. There was something he wasn't telling her. While her dad babbled when he needed to tell her something he didn't want to, she suspected Tim was the opposite. The more difficult the topic, the quieter he got.

"What aren't you telling me?" Sam asked, pulling her hand away. But when Tim still said nothing after a few seconds, she started getting irritated. "Jesus, Cox. Just spill it already..."

When he continued, his voice took on a serious tone.

"Sam, they found some sort of foreign liquid in your bloodstream."

Sam was silent as she waited for the ball to drop.

"When you were first admitted, there was so much damage done to your eyes that you couldn't see. You don't remember that?"

"No." Sam whispered, looking confused and more than a little disturbed. She tried to think back to her last memories. She recalled trying to kill Charlie with a piece of glass. He threw her off and then leaned over her. Only he didn't look like Charlie anymore. Sam suddenly had a splitting headache. Tim seemed to wait for more, but she had nothing more to say, so shook her head.

"The scariest part was you were in serious condition and your injuries just weren't healing. You had a serious concussion and your eyes and forearms were big open wounds. It was only once your body started expelling what they suspect is some sort of toxin from your system that your wounds began to heal..."

"Toxin?"

"You had large quantities of an unknown substance in your system. It was on your clothes, so they sent it out to have it identified, but so far they're stumped. Because of the amount of tissue damage they found in your eyes, face, throat and forearms, they think it was sprayed on you."

Sam closed her eyes at the memory of warm liquid falling over her arms, splashing across her face and getting in her eyes, irritating them. Burning them. She thought it was blood. Hers or Charlie's, or both. *What the hell had he done to her?* Sam felt simultaneously hot and cold. Though it hurt, she curled her hands into fists to stop their telltale shaking.

"Is there more?" Sam asked. Part of her wanted to know, and part of her didn't.

"Well, the good news is that now you're healing at an accelerated rate. The speed of your recovery has astonished the doctors."

"And the bad news—"

"Sam, the doctors told us there's evidence of rapid cell regeneration, especially in your arms. Usually large open wounds like what you have on your forearms are impossible to heal on their own so they'd planned on removing skin from your thighs to graft it to your forearms, but at this rate it looks like they won't have to. Your tissue is growing back of its own accord."

"Ok. That sounds like good news to me."

"Y-e-s... the bad news is this is all unfamiliar territory. They've never seen this type of tissue regeneration before, so they're concerned... they're concerned it might not stop." Tim paused, letting it sink in. It didn't take long for Sam to get it.

"You're talking about cancer. They're worried the cells will keep regenerating past the point of repair." Sam didn't have to open her eyes again to know Tim nodded.

"You can see me, right?"

To which Sam opened her eyes again and nodded. She heard Tim sigh with relief. Sam blinked and tried opening her eyes wider, but stopped because the more light she let in, the more it hurt.

"Not well, though. Everything is fuzzy, and the light hurts my eyes."

"At first they told us the damage done to your eyes would be permanent, that you'd be blind. But it looks like you have new cell growth in your retinas as well."

Sam took a minute to process that. Most of her pain was

in her arms, eyes, throat, and head, which made sense considering what he'd said. Sam looked down at her bandaged arms again. It looked like Charlie had given her a parting gift. Perhaps it was best she couldn't see the damage he'd inflicted on her yet.

"How's Zoey?" she asked, dreading the answer. She remembered Charlie had stabbed her before they crashed.

"Physically, she's recovering. Mentally, I don't know. When they extracted her from the car, she was hysterical, screaming her head off about Charlie being a monster. Paramedics had to sedate her at the scene. Ever since, she won't talk about what happened, not even with her parents. She asked after you, though." The anger and guilt must have been written on her face because she felt a squeeze on the back of her hand as he said. "You did everything you could, Sam."

"And Charlie? He's dead, right?"

"Oh yeah, he's definitely dead. Timmins and Douglas shot him six times at point blank range, so dead was the only option for him. They took Charlie's body to the coroner, but it decomposed so fast that they had little to look at other than a pile of goop. I guess the coroner thought someone had played a practical joke on him at first by sending him black sludge in a body bag." Tim paused before continuing. "We have a lot more to talk about, but you're tired. Maybe when you're feeling up to it, you can tell me what happened out there."

Exhausted, she nodded, and put her head back down and closed her burning eyes again. "Can you do me a favor and take Buddy with you? I'm sure he'd love to see Brandy again." Only silence met her request and for a moment she thought he'd left, but then she felt his hand again. Squinting her eyes open, she found him still standing by her bed, waiting.

"I'm so sorry, Sam. Buddy's... dead."

Thinking she must have misheard him, Sam squawked, "What?"

"Buddy's gone Sam."

"What are you talking about? He was just here nuzzling my hand," Sam said, looking around for his furry white head, but he was nowhere in sight. Even though her vision was blurry, she'd still be able to see him if he was in the room. Sam could feel her throat tightening already.

Tim cursed, not wanting to tell her, but had little choice. "Buddy was shot that night when he attacked a police officer that was trying to recover the Morris kids from the SUV."

Sam's heart broke. Hot tears streamed down her face. Sam already knew without further explanation what had happened. It was her fault her best friend was dead. She shook her head, furious. "Attacked a cop... No, he'd never do that. He'd only attack someone if they were a genuine threat. I told Buddy to protect those kids, and that's what he did. That cop must have been Charlie."

Tim waited for Sam to settle, then said, "Sam, the Morris kids are both alive and well today, so if what you're saying is true, then that means they survived that night because of Buddy. He's a hero."

Doing his best to avoid her forearms, Tim sat on the side of the hospital bed and gently hugged her. There was nothing more he could say to comfort her, so he just held on and let Sam cry.

* * *

A few weeks later, it became obvious as Brandy's stomach grew that she had received a parting gift from Buddy, which would be a gift for them all. A couple of weeks after that, Brandy gave birth to a litter of four golden mountain pups. Sam had the pick of the litter and took the one that reminded her most of Buddy. He had the Bernese pattern but with a mostly white and tan coloration. She named him Frodo after one of her favorite fictional characters. Like Buddy, Frodo was a natural to train and even had some of Buddy's mannerisms, like his gentleness with toys and drinking too much water when he was nervous. At only four months old, he'd already started bringing her his leash when he wanted to go for a walk. Buddy hadn't started doing this until well into his first year.

Sam and Tim gave a puppy to her dad because he seemed to need a hand easing into retirement. His furry companion accompanied him everywhere, including on his fishing trips.

They gave Zoey the third pup to help her heal the hidden wounds Charlie had reopened. Over time, Zoey came out of her shell more and even accepted doggy play dates with Tim and Brandy, Sam and Frodo, and when he wasn't traveling, her father and his pup, Kahuna.

In a surprising turn of events, they gave the fourth and darkest of the litter to the Murphy police department upon their request.

Chief Kabowski had a closed door meeting with the first two responders, Timmins and Douglas, who shot Charlie at the train station. And then later with former Chief Turner. She also requested a closed door meeting with Sam, to which Sam would only agree as long as everything she said was off the record. Kabowski agreed and for the first time in over five years, Sam answered every question honestly. By

341

the end of the interview, Kabowski had a headache and looked noticeably tired. A few days later, they got a call. Kabowski, having decided they could use the additional canine help, requested a pup. What they weren't told but would later find out was that Timmins and Douglas had been assigned to a special unit that would handle the more unusual cases that landed in their jurisdiction. Their new canine addition, the runt and the only mostly black pup in the litter, would be a part of this team.

Later, when Sam was officially interviewed, she kept her answers short and sweet and lied through her teeth about the things people wouldn't be able to or want to understand. To Tim, she told the truth, but waited for him to ask direct questions. The one thing she'd learned in her first twenty-seven years was that most people didn't want the truth and would more likely end up resenting the person who popped their reality bubble.

A part of her still wished she could go back to blissful ignorance and not know about the thing that went bump in the night and chased her down five years ago.

Tim was right. Sam's wounds healed fast. This last attack left her with more scars to add to her collection, but they were minimal, considering she should have died from the damage the thing called Charlie caused. Her doctors called it a miracle. Sam called it survival. Her sight came back, but it was different now. Objects and colors looked the same, but everyone she saw now had a fog clinging to them. Some were white, others were various shades of gray. Her doctors ran eye tests and brain scans, but they all came back normal.

A few weeks later, she saw someone who, clear as day, was missing the persistent fog that surrounded everyone else. On one of their daily walks, Frodo's hackles went up. It was the first time she'd heard him growl or snap. Shushing Frodo, her gaze flew to where he lunged to pinpoint the object of his anxiety.

It was a beautiful day, and it looked like half the town had come out to enjoy the warm spring weather. Couples strolled along hand-in-hand. A few parents pushed baby carriages. One man pushing a bright blue carriage talked animatedly into his hands-free headset as he weaved in and out of lolly gaggers. A gaggle of giggling women walked past, expanding and contracting like a swimming jellyfish along the sidewalk as they whispered conspiratorially to one another. And many others veered in and out as they overtook the slower walkers.

While everyone else had a persistent haze surrounding them, one person without the fog stood out clear as day. A guy halfway down the block wearing a dark ball cap, dark shirt, and jeans.

Rattled, Sam stared after the man. A part of her hoped he'd turn around, but mostly she hoped he'd just go away. Attention elsewhere, she wasn't prepared for the sudden drag on the lead. She felt her arm jerk forward, pulling her entire body along with it. Just as fast as it started, the forward pull disappeared almost sending her back onto her ass. Stunned, she watched as the leash flew down the sidewalk, bumping, soaring and dragging along the pavement after Frodo's running form.

"Frodo! Come back here!" Sam shouted as she gained her feet and took off after her wayward pup. To her horror, she could see Frodo was heading directly for the dark man. Sam picked up speed until she was flat out running. Shouts of alarm and dismay went up as Frodo weaved in and out of the crowds, almost taking down a couple of people in his haste to reach his target. Sam easily avoided colliding with

343

anyone until she reached the gaggle of women who'd expanded to take over the entire sidewalk. Instead of trying to break through them as Frodo had, Sam dove for the road and went around the sidewalk hoggers. She could still hear people swearing behind them, but she didn't have time to stroke their ruffled feathers.

Frodo was almost on top of the man now. Terrified her pup might actually bite the man, Sam used the last reserve of adrenaline induced speed and lunged for his tether. Though she successfully got a hold of the leash, bringing Frodo to a stop, her feet became entangled when her foot caught an edge in the concrete sidewalk. Unable to regain her balance, Sam braced herself for the fall as she skidded to a painful halt on her knees and left forearm. Without releasing the death grip on his leash, Sam painfully leaned back on her now bloodied knees and pulled the still strug-gling Frodo to her side. She'd opened her mouth to scold him when a shadow fell across them, blocking out the bright midday sun.

Looking up, Sam's eyes widened in alarm as she took in the pale skin, dark eyes, and bits of platinum hair poking out from under the ball cap. The apology on her lips now forgotten, Sam stared into the man's strangely animated pupils. Though she recognized the person looming over her wasn't Charlie, it didn't make her feel any better. Her brain screamed she should fight or flee now, but her body had stopped listening. Instead, she just sat there, the petrified prey frozen in fear, waiting to be picked off by the predator.

Sam watched as the stranger slowly kneeled into a crouch in front of her, just out of reach of Frodo's snapping jaws. His facial expression revealed his fascination. And perhaps curiosity? Without warning, she saw a blur of movement resulting in one hand clamped firmly around

Frodo's muzzle, while the other hovered dangerously close to her right eye. Though Frodo growled and tried to shake his head free of the man's iron grip, her pup's efforts at freedom were in vain.

To onlookers, it must have looked like he was giving her a helping hand after her spectacular fall. Most people barely glanced their way as they walked around them. No one asked if she was okay even though she was sitting there, clearly terrified and bleeding.

"The punishment for staring is an eye, Sam. If it were anyone else, yours would be in my hand right now,"

She sucked in a breath at the threat, understanding a simple flick of his wrist was all it would take to snatch her eye away.

And then the man crouching in front of her was gone.

Sam drew in a deep, shaky breath and closed her eyes for a second. Hearing Frodo whine, she reached over to reassure him. Calmer now, she opened her eyes and, relieved to see the sidewalk in front of her was still empty, allowed her gaze to hunt for the dark stranger. Not seeing him, Sam carefully rose to her feet, all the while allowing her eyes to roam. After another minute of scouring the area, Sam forced herself to turn her attention to the now quiet Frodo staring up at her.

"Ok, boy. Ready to head back?" Frodo's chuff of agreement and tug on his leash was all the confirmation she needed. After another nervous backward glance, a very sore and tired Sam turned and slowly led Frodo towards home.

Afterword

Like most of my stories, *Once upon A Predator* was based on a reoccurring dream that only stopped once the story was written.

It started with a pleasant conversation with a stranger and ended with an irrational act of violence so out of character for that person that it had to be explored.

How could something as harmless as small talk scare someone so badly that it triggered their fight-or-flight response, compelling them to lash out irrationally?

About the Author

Alex Loch is an emerging author of thrillers. *Once Upon A Predator* is Alex's debut book in the psychological thriller series called Dark Amusements.

Alex is currently working on the next book in the Dark Amusements Series, as well as an entirely new thriller/fantasy series tentatively called The Duir.

Also by Alex Loch

This is from Dark Amusements Book #2 coming out in the summer of 2023

Cold. The only sensation cutting through the grogginess threatening to tug them back into unconsciousness. They fought against the heaviness dragging them down as the cold seeped into every crack and crevice.

Floating. Body adrift. Arms and legs suspended. Gravity no longer had them in its grip. Hair loose, tangling around a shoulder, tickling the nose, brushing against a cheek to sweep against the eyelashes, making them flicker.

Disconnected. Thoughts unmoored as much as the body as it drifted. Flashes of memory filtered through semi-consciousness, making the limbs jerk and twitch. An involuntary dance only the unconscious understood the rhythm of.

A distant memory, from another time and place. Of heat, so hot even the top sheet felt like it was burning the skin where it lie across arms and legs. Of panting, like a black dog lying in the hot midday sun trying to cool itself down. And finally, the sudden shock of cold, followed by the excruciating pain of being forcefully submerged in a bath of ice water, which felt very much like now.

Every bone, every joint, every muscle ached in the freezing water. The pain verged on unbearable in the extremities. Hands. Fingers. Feet. Toes. Ears. A spasm caught hold and wouldn't let go. Fingers and toes clutched and clawed as muscles contracted with a will of their own.

No air. Fighting against the rising panic. Lungs trying to expand, to take in air, followed by the irrational fear that they might explode with the force of it. Chest burned. Back bent in pain. Arms and legs flailed out, spine bowed with the strength of the next spasm. Torso jerked and tried to twist away, but the cold cocoon wouldn't let go. Arms reaching out, fighting for life, struggling against the cold bonds holding them in place as the last few licks of life flickered. Reaching for help. For comfort. For hope. For escape. The darkness was the only one that embraced back.

The agony was unbearable.

Mouth opened on a scream, a last refusal to yield to the cold, watery serial killer's embrace. But the frigid water took it as an invitation and flooded the opening. Unable to hold back the flow, the liquid surged through the mouth, the throat, and filled the lungs forcing the chest to expand. Cold. Hard. Agonizingly painful.

The body, now much more like its surroundings than a few minutes ago, was rapidly cooling down. Soon, the two would be indistinguishable. Even a heat signature wouldn't detect the difference between the mass of tissue, bone, and muscle and its watery surroundings.

Eventually the pain began to ease, replaced by a feeling of warmth that spread from the lungs outwards until even the extremities tingled with feeling.

After a few minutes, the eyes flickered open and looked around, but every direction reflected back the same image. Darkness.

There was no break, not even a sliver of light anywhere. Eyes squeezed shut for a count of ten, then wide open again, but there was no difference. It was the kind of dark only found on a moonless, starless night far from any human settlement. Or in a windowless room. Or at the bottom of the deepest lake.

It was the kind of dark that snuffed out any hope of ever being rescued from this cold coffin.

They'd all lied... hell was fucking cold.